ALL OUR YESTERDAYS

OTHER BOOKS BY
ROBERT B. PARKER

WALKING SHADOW

PAPER DOLL

DOUBLE DEUCE

PASTIME

PERCHANCE TO DREAM *(a Philip Marlowe novel)*

STARDUST

POODLE SPRINGS *(with Raymond Chandler)*

PLAYMATES

CRIMSON JOY

PALE KINGS AND PRINCES

TAMING A SEA-HORSE

A CATSKILL EAGLE

VALEDICTION

LOVE AND GLORY

THE WIDENING GYRE

CEREMONY

A SAVAGE PLACE

EARLY AUTUMN

LOOKING FOR RACHEL WALLACE

WILDERNESS

THE JUDAS GOAT

THREE WEEKS IN SPRING *(with Joan Parker)*

PROMISED LAND

MORTAL STAKES

GOD SAVE THE CHILD

THE GODWULF MANUSCRIPT

ROBERT B. PARKER

ALL OUR YESTERDAYS

Delacorte Press

Published by
Delacorte Press
Bantam Doubleday Dell Publishing Group, Inc.
1540 Broadway
New York, New York 10036

Library of Congress Cataloging in Publication Data

Parker, Robert B., 1932–
    All our yesterdays / Robert B. Parker.
        p.   cm.
    ISBN 0-385-30437-4
    ISBN 0-385-31374-8 (large-print ed.)
    I. Title.
    PS3566.A686A79   1994
    813'.54—dc20   94-2583
                                                             CIP

Manufactured in the United States of America
Published simultaneously in Canada

Book design by Susan Maksuta

November 1994

10   9   8   7   6   5   4   3   2   1

BVG

*"And all our yesterdays have lighted fools
The way to dusty death."*

Macbeth

Since this book is about fathers and
sons, and since I am a father particularly
fortunate in his sons, this book is for them, and
for their mother.

Acknowledgments

I have been strongly influenced in this work of fiction by three works of nonfiction. R. F. Foster's gracefully told *Modern Ireland: 1600–1972* gave me a broad perspective on a heritage which belongs not only to the Sheridans but to me through my mother. Ernie O'Malley's impressionistic recollection of the troubles, *On Another Man's Wound,* provided me not only incident, but, when it seemed better than any I could invent, actual language. And from Alan Lupo, in *Liberty's Chosen Home,* I learned more about Boston than I wish to admit. Until I read it, I thought I knew enough.

Robert B. Parker
Cambridge, Massachusetts, 1993

1994
Voice-Over

It was sullen and gusty and snowing like hell when I went to see Grace. There was lightning, and thunder, and heavy wet snow collecting on the roadways. The radio weathermen were hysterical about the possibilities. It wasn't supposed to be snowing, it was almost April, and it was supposed to be a thunderstorm.

It was about five in the evening when I parked in the lot behind Grace's condo and got out and turned up my collar and walked to her door and rang her bell. I could feel the tension radiate from my solar plexus and jangle along the nerve circuitry. It had nothing to do with the weather.

She opened the door.

"Long time," she said.

"Six months," I said.

She stepped away from the door and I went in. The room was opulent, like Grace. Two storied, with a huge lamp hanging down over the oval glass dinner table. Red tile in the kitchen, a spiral staircase in the far left corner leading to a sleeping loft.

"You want a drink or something?"

"Yeah, I'll take a beer."

She got me one.

"Trouble driving here?"

"No."

She nodded at the couch and we went and sat on it. The snow slanted by the wind splatted against the window and melted on contact, making lucid ropes of water as it washed down the dark surface of the glass.

1

"Where'd you go?" Grace said.

She sat with her legs tucked under her. She was wearing blue jeans and a white sweater. Her hair was neat. She had on makeup, but not too much. Don't want to excite Chris.

"Dublin."

"Really?"

"Yeah. After what happened last fall I knew we couldn't just go on as if it hadn't happened. It was too much, too large, too awful. It was going to take more than goodwill to save us. I had to get some distance."

"From me?"

"From me, I think, more than anything else."

Outside, in the dark, the storm energy increased. I could hear the wind. And the snow, pelting at the window, came thicker. I was where she lived, alone with her. She slept here, made supper here, entertained here, made love, maybe, but not with me, here. There was her bathroom, where she stood naked every day under the shower. Where she put on clean lingerie and slipped into her dress. The counter where she had her coffee and left a lipstick crescent on the cup before she went to work. While I'd been gone she'd laughed here with people, told her stories, smiled her brilliant smile, held court, said smart and funny things, in the dramatic, yet somehow offhand without being less dramatic, way she had. I could smell her perfume, her shampoo, her self. My senses, so long deprived of her, were seismographic. I could almost hear her heart beat.

"So what did you do in Dublin?" Grace said.

"Studied in the old library at Trinity College, had tea at the Shelbourne, looked at the GPO, walked up O'Connell Street, drank some Guinness, had dinner at Patrick Gilbaud's, took a tour of Kilmainham Jail, wandered around Dublin Castle, read Joyce, walked along the Liffey."

"And what did you learn, Chris?"

"Everything," I said.

"That's quite a lot."

"It's everything, three quarters of a century bearing down on us. Too much. Too much for us."

"And you're going to tell me about it?"

"If you'll listen."

"And you think it will save us?"

"It might get us free enough to save ourselves."

Grace got up and went to the window and looked out at the dense snow swirled by wind, and shimmered by lightning. Behind the lightning, like ancestral voices, the sound of thunder came. Grace turned back from the window toward me.

"My friends were worried you might try to kill me."

Grace's gaze was very steady on me. She seemed in gyroscopic balance.

"I would never hurt you," I said.

"I know."

She came back again to the couch and sat at the other end of it. No hint of huggy-snuggy. In proximity, we were still separate and Grace was making sure I knew it.

"But you've got a lot of rage."

"I didn't say I wouldn't hurt anyone."

"Do you have a plan for hurting someone?"

"A weak attempt at lightness," I said. "I yearn for the death of anyone you date, but I would never hurt someone you cared about."

"You already have."

"I'm not sure I'm the one that did it, but whoever did it, it had to be done. We'd have had no chance if it hadn't happened."

"And you think we have one now?"

"You tell me," I said. "You tell me there's no chance and it's over. I'll get up, and go, and get on with my life."

She looked at me for a long time in the dead-quiet room, made to seem more still by the storm roiling outside just beyond the lamplight.

"No, I won't tell you that. We've been together a long time."

I didn't say anything. She wasn't talking to me, really, she was thinking out loud.

"But I can't live like we did. It's odd, isn't it? My connection with the man you were, makes me hope that there's a chance for me with the man you may become. But I cannot live with the man you were."

"God save me, I understand that," I said.

She smiled carefully, and only a little.

"So maybe I love you, and maybe you love me, and maybe you can help me understand the awful thing that happened last fall. I'm prepared to listen. Do you want another beer?"

"No," I said.

She nodded faintly, as if she were keeping score somewhere, and settled back a little in her corner of the couch with her legs beneath her and the gulf between us as unbridgeable as the void. I looked past her out the window at the darkness made brilliant by the momentary lightning, at the winter storm penetrating the spring night, and took in a deep breath.

"My grandfather's name was Conn Sheridan," I said. "He was born with the century, in Dublin, and in 1916 he got hold of a Lee-Enfield rifle, and he and another kid sniped, apparently to no significant effect, at British troops during the Easter Monday uprising. By twenty he was a captain in the IRA, maybe for the hell of it, maybe for patriotism, though it's hard to imagine a full-feathered patriot perched up there in the Sheridan family tree. In the four years his aim improved."

1920
Conn

In mid Tipperary, in a pass through the hills, at the village of Hollyford, there was a long, two-storied, whitewashed police barracks with a slate roof. The windows of the barracks were protected by steel shutters, and there were narrow firing slits cut into the walls.

Conn Sheridan stood at the top of the pass, looking down. He was writing in his notebook. Below him a stream had cut its way through the hill, and a road ran along beside it. The village straggled along the road on the downslope. Thatched roofs and zinc outhouses.

Beside Conn was a tall, narrow, high-shouldered Australian Irishman named Seamus O'Gorman. He'd been a sharpshooter in the World War and was the commander of the Hollyford battalion.

"There's a stone wall across the road," Conn said.

"May give you cover, won't help you much getting in there."

"We could fire from behind it, to keep their heads down," Conn said.

"And what?"

"And blow in the gable end."

"The floor of them barracks is six feet higher than the outside ground, bucko. You might as well try to shift the fucking Rock of Cashel."

"You never know," Conn said. "How many rifles in the battalion?"

"Six, plus yours if you'll be using it."

"That's what I brought it for," Conn said.

"Fine."

"Another thing," Conn said. "I am, at least for this operation, your battalion commander. There'll be no need for being too formal, but it'll go better if you don't call me bucko!"

O'Gorman met Conn's eyes. He was a leathery man, nearly Conn's height, older than Conn, and full of a veteran's arrogance for new officers. He held Conn's eyes for a moment. And felt the near physical force of them, and looked away.

"That'll be fine with me, Conn."

Conn smiled. He was wind reddened and sun darkened and his smile was a bright contrast.

"Good," he said.

They walked back down the hill toward the village, rifles slung over their shoulders, khaki ammunition slings slanting across their chests. In the countryside the rebellion was no longer covert. Beyond the village the hills were bright green, rolling toward Glenough under a high, hard sky where white clouds ran raggedly before strong winds.

That night Conn sat with O'Gorman, and the battalion lieutenant, in a slate-roofed little house about a mile from the village. In a kitchen dense with the peat fire, under fat bacon hanging from the smoke-blackened rafters, they studied a map, and ate potato cakes and drank strong tea. The police and military barracks were marked in colored ink.

"There are four barracks within nine miles," Conn said. "Within fourteen miles there are barracks at Shevry, Kilcommon, Annacarty, Cappagh White, Doon, Dundrum, and Rearcross."

"There's a big one at Pallas," the lieutenant said. "Twenty miles. And Goolds Cross, and Tipperary, twenty, and Newport twenty-seven. Soldiers as well as peelers in Tipperary and Newport."

"We'll block the soldiers," Conn said. "Here, at the crossroads," he marked on the map. "And here. How much gelignite is there?"

"Close to half a hundred," O'Gorman said. "A little blasting powder, three pounds and a little of gunpowder, plenty of fuse, and two boxes of detonators."

Conn went to the shed with him to examine the gelignite. It was frozen. They put pots of water on to thaw it. The steam from the bubbling water added to the atmosphere as the three men huddled over the map. O'Gorman's gray wife moved silently about the kitchen, stoking the fire, pouring more tea. No one paid her heed. The tea had been taking heat from the fire all day. It had long since ceased to draw, and begun to stew. Conn swallowed some and shook his head.

"A bleeding mouse could trot across that tea," he said. The other men laughed. They were much older than Conn, especially the lieutenant, a short, plump man who'd been a cook with the British army in India.

" 'Tis a darling thing, Cap'n, sir," he said, "to see a fancy fucking Dublin boy drink proper country tea."

Outside it had begun to rain. A cold rain, barely above freezing.

"How much ammunition?" Conn said.

"Twenty rounds a rifle," O'Gorman said. "Some shotguns, and four hand grenades. There are ten or twelve policemen in the Hollyford Barracks."

"With all the ammunition they'll ever need," Conn said.

They were silent. The rain sounded on the roof, the squares of slate, carefully lapped from peak to eaves, resting on close-spaced rafter poles.

"It makes no sense to rush it."

"None at all, at all."

"We'll burn them out," Conn said.

"How?"

"From the roof," Conn said. "The gable end has only one window. We can keep people away from it by rifle fire, and go up to the roof there."

"Man, dear, It's forty feet. We don't have a forty-foot ladder in the county."

"We'll splice two twenty-footers," Conn said. "We'll make some bursting charges to blow off the slate, and we'll burn them out from above."

"Might work," O'Gorman said. "Who goes to the roof?"

"I will," Conn said. "If I can swallow this tea, I can climb that roof." He smiled his brilliant smile in the smoky room. "With one heroic volunteer."

"I'll go with you, I guess," O'Gorman said.

Conn

They spent the rest of the evening waiting and getting ready. Conn disassembled and oiled the big Webley .45 he carried under his coat. He cleaned and oiled it nearly every day. But he had nothing else to do while he waited. He took the German automatic, 9-mm parabellum, from its holster under his other arm. He oiled the pistol and the magazine spring, tucked bullets into the magazine, put a round in the chamber, and put it back with the hammer cocked and the safety set. The men in the kitchen improvised hand grenades by packing scrap iron in tin cans around a stick of gelignite. Other men arrived, gathering quietly, in the front room, some in the shed; cleaning and oiling rifles, and shotguns, practicing with the spliced ladder against the side of the barn. They didn't talk very much. The rain pattered on the roof. Mrs. O'Gorman and her daughters stayed quiet in the corner of the kitchen, murmuring the rosary.

It was an hour till midnight when a thin little man in a tweed cap and a black raincoat arrived on his bicycle to say that the Volunteers had begun to fell trees and pile stone barricades across the roads. His name was Feeney.

"In the pass," he said, "there are no trees handy, and not enough rocks."

"Can you find a way to block it?" Conn asked.

Feeney grinned.

"I'll have them throw the road over the ditch, Cap'n."

Conn nodded. The fire made a dim reflection on Feeney's wet rubberized coat. Feeney's cap was sodden and shapeless.

"And the wires?" Conn said.

"We'll cut them at midnight, telephone and telegraph both, sir."

At five after midnight they set out. Conn, O'Gorman, five

shotguns, and seven rifles. Because he would be climbing the roof, Conn donated his rifle to Dennis Tracy, who would be in charge of the ground party.

"Musha," Conn said with a wide smile, as they moved out. "I feel like a tinker."

He and O'Gorman each carried two handguns, grenades, hammers and bursting charges, and on their backs each a tin of petrol. Oil soaked squares of sod hung from ropes around their necks. Oil soaked into their clothes. Four men carried the ladder. Others carried paraffin oil in zinc buckets.

The rain wasn't heavy but it came without surcease as they walked silently toward the police barracks. In the slippery darkness one of the men carrying the ladder stumbled.

Some one said, "Jesus Christ, man."

Conn's voice was soft and sharp as he spoke to them.

"Quiet now, lads. The less the peelers hear us, the less they'll know what's happening. A silent assault is a frightening thing."

In the back one of the men murmured, "Cap'n's a stone killer, where'd he come from?"

"They sent him down from Dublin."

Again Conn's voice cut the darkness.

"Quiet."

They went forward in silence. Close to the barracks the laddermen took off their boots. The rifles and shotguns took the places they'd been assigned, three to lay down fire on the gable-end window, the rest to cover doors and windows. The men with the paraffin oil put the buckets down at the base of the gable end and retreated to cover. The laddermen raised the ladder.

Conn and O'Gorman went up, heavy with firearms, burdened with ammunition, laden with explosives, and dripping oil.

There was a chimney near the gable end, and another at the opposite gable. Conn slithered his way across the wet slate roof, straddling the ridgepole, trying to be silent, forty feet up in the murky darkness. When he reached the far end he turned, braced his back against the chimney, and sat on the ridgepole as if he were straddling a horse. He couldn't see O'Gorman at the other end of the roof. He took the hammer from the loop on his belt. It was a long-handled hammer, the kind used for framing, with a twenty-ounce head. He waited a moment, took in a long breath, let it out slowly, and brought the hammer down on the slate. The crack of the roofing slab sounded like an explosion in the still night. He smashed another tile, and poured gasoline into the opening. He unlimbered one of the sods of turf from his neck and lit it and dropped it into the hole. He lit another one as fast as he could and dropped it in, and the flames came up with a yellow roar. He could see O'Gorman now in the blaze they'd started, and they crawled toward each other, breaking through the slate roof, pouring in gasoline, dropping in the blazing oil-soaked sods. His can was empty. He tossed the can aside and it skittered down the roof and off.

From inside the barracks rifle and pistol fire began. Flames flaunted up through the broken roof now, no longer yellow, but red as they began to feed on the wooden interior of the building. Conn dropped one of the grenades and hunched back as its explosion sent flames and smoke up toward him. He threw the other one and missed the opening. The grenade rolled down the roof and lodged in the gutter. Conn lay flat and the grenade went off too close. The concussion deafened him for a moment and it was minutes before the ringing in his ears subsided. He scrambled back toward the chimney. The remaining slate was hot to the touch. He reached the chimney and climbed up on it, and to himself grinned in the flaming darkness. *Praise-be-to-God the peelers don't fire up the flue.* The wind turned the smoke and flames now toward him, now away. His hands were burnt. His face felt singed. He pulled out the parabellum and emptied the clip through the roof into the burning barracks. Then he emptied the Webley and sat with his legs dangling over the inferno while he reloaded. It occurred to him as he did so that his clothing was soaked in oil. *One spark and I go down in history as a fiery leader.* He grinned at his own joke, and fired again into the flames below. From the shed that angled off from the main barracks, police were firing up at him through openings in the roof. He returned fire from the chimney. From inside the barracks a Very light went up through the shattered roof, then another, visible for miles against the black sky.

Below him he could hear his men shouting at the police, taunting them. *Goddamn them.* He screamed down at them.

"Shut up, you fucking gossips."

But the gunfire was too insistent and the roar of the fire too loud for anyone to hear him. A bullet wanged off the edge of the chimney, sending a fragment of brick to slash across his cheek. Conn laughed out loud. A second bullet hit him. He swayed briefly with the bruise of it as it tore into his shoulder.

"Shit," he said.

Then he felt numbness. He could see the blood soaking through his coat around the entry hole. There was a medical kit in his coat pocket. He got a gauze out, folded it, and held it against the wound with his chin. He tied a bandage around it using one hand and his teeth. The bleeding slowed. He loaded, fired, loaded, fired. Then he began to work his way across the ridgepole. His hair was afire; he put it out by running his hands through it. Little leaves of flame leapt up from his oily coat and he beat them out with his hands. The flames exploded up through the roof, blocking his way, preventing him from the ladder. Soaked with oil and gasoline, he would burst into flame if he tried to go through it. He would die here on the roof if he didn't. It was thick fire. The gusting wind made it dance. He thought of that line, was it from Virgil, he used to know it in Latin. Something about it being fitting and beautiful for a man to die for his country.

"Good-bye, James," he shouted.

"Slan leat," O'Gorman shouted back.

The wind gusted in a different direction. The flames leaned away, and Conn scuttled past them to the ladder. *I'll have to look up that line.*

O'Gorman went down the ladder first while the men on the ground fired at the windows and gunports to keep the police down. They gathered behind the stone wall. Across the hills, near the pass, the sky was pale gray. It was almost morning. Out of the near darkness behind the wall Feeney appeared on his bicycle.

"Cavalry," he said, "from Dundrum."

"How soon?" Conn said.

"Ten, fifteen minutes behind. They're having slow going picking through the barriers, Cap'n."

"Pull back and disperse," Conn said softly. "We didn't capture the bugger, but we surely caved it in some."

Dead silent now, the men faded into the thinning darkness, away from the blazing barracks, into the cool, fine rain that fell steadily on the slow dawning countryside.

Conn

Conn lay flat in the ferns, trying for warmth. His shoulder was pounding steadily now. The rain had stopped, but the ground was still wet, and the dew came as he lay there, settling onto his back. His face was blistered, his eyebrows gone, his hair singed short. He could smell the burnt-hair smell of himself. The dawn seemed slow in coming. As it came it brought a low, cold wind that made the ferns rustle. The cavalry went by, column of twos, the chestnut coats of the horses gleaming in the first sun. In the ferns to his left something stirred. Conn turned toward it, fumbling his Webley from its holster with his fire-reddened hands. The sound was a hare, rising for a look around. Its ears were stiff and canted forward, a slight shiver ran along its flanks. Its nose quivered, then its white scut flashed, and it was down, back among the ferns, and gone. Conn put the Webley back under his arm.

The hoofbeats of the cavalry squad dwindled and then were gone. Conn got to his feet. He was light headed and he felt sick. He moved across the fields, away from the road. As day came on it warmed, and the earth began to dry out beneath his feet. There were robins about and larks, that lifted suddenly in front of him, startled by his step. Now and then orange blackthorn berries colored the landscape. As he moved, the heat pulsed insistently in his shoulder. He needed water badly, but there were only the dark amber puddles in the bog, and he knew he shouldn't drink from them.

It was nearly noon when he came upon a small thatch-roofed house among outbuildings. A thick, gray-haired woman in a black dress, with a plaid man's jacket over it, was feeding some hens in the yard. Conn's head was swimming now, and the heat of his shoulder had nearly enveloped him, and the throb of it pulsated through him. He had dwindled inside himself until most of him was expended in simply staying on his feet. He had no thought of what he must have looked like to the woman as he approached.

"A fine morning to you, ma'am," he said as clearly as he could. "I need a drink of water."

"It's considerable more than that you'll be needing," she said, and took his arm, and tried to hold him upright as he pitched forward among her chickens. After that was without chronology. He was carried. His clothes were gone. He was in a bed. The linen smelled of fresh air. Needle. Bandage . . . *Dublin. We can't do it here* . . . truck . . . smell of livestock . . . tarpaulin . . . hay . . . British voices . . . *Lie quiet, lad* . . . jouncing . . . some pain . . . hospital clatter . . . smell of antiseptic . . . white coats . . . ether . . . whirling . . . faster . . . down . . . vortex . . . bottomless.

The first thing Conn saw when he came slowly up out of the ether was a slim blond woman with big eyes, and pale smooth skin. The blond hair was pulled back tight into a twist. He didn't know her, but he knew she was more than just some Cumann na mBan girl set to mind him after surgery. She wore a very fine wool dress, he could see that, and an expensive diamond clip at her throat.

She said, "I think he's waking up," to someone he couldn't see.

"You're American," he said, "or Canadian."

"He's trying to talk," she said.

"He's still drunk from the ether," another woman said. The other woman was Irish.

"Are you American?" Conn said.

"Does he think he's saying something?" she said.

"Yes," the Irishwoman said. "It probably makes sense to him."

"How long before it will make sense to me?"

"It'll be a half hour anyway 'fore he's coherent," the Irishwoman said. "As for making sense, most men never do."

She smiled. Her mouth was wide, and her teeth were very even. Her eyes were wide apart. She dipped a towel in cold water and wrung it out, and wiped his face. He put his hand up toward hers, and missed widely and then forgot what he had put it up for. She laughed and took his hand and put it carefully back on top of the blanket. When she bent forward he could smell her perfume.

"Do you know how he was shot?" she said.

"Shot by a bloody peeler, probably, miss. They shoot our boys as if they were stray rats."

"Will he be safe here?"

"Dublin's not a safe place, miss, for Irish lads that won't crap under to the peelers."

"But they don't know he's here."

"Not for now they don't. We'll move him soon."

He studied the curve of her breast as she leaned over and put the cool cloth on his forehead again. The room was quiet. The canted rectangle of sunlight that came through the high, narrow windows moved infinitely into the corner of the room and became more angular.

"When they do, will you visit me?" he said.

"When they do?" she said. "When they do what?"

"When they move me?"

"Of course I will. How do you feel?"

He smiled and closed his eyes and felt the coolness of the cloth and smelled her perfume. She changed the cloth again.

"Fine," he said.

She laughed.

"Do you know how long ago I asked you that?"

"A bit laggard, am I? Coming out?"

"A bit."

"You wouldn't be able to put your hands on a dram of whiskey, would you?"

"You've been shot," she said. "I don't think you should be drinking whiskey."

"What better time?" he said.

She shook her head.

"What's your name?"

"Conn Sheridan," he said. "What's yours?"

"Hadley. Are you a Volunteer?"

He smiled.

"Brotherhood?"

He held the smile.

"I guess I shouldn't ask," she said.

"These are times for secrets, Hadley."

"I know. Well, I'm for a free and independent Ireland. I want you to know that."

He was beginning to feel the pain of his wound. It wasn't awful, just a low, persistent jabbing sensation. Whiskey would help it.

"It's a fine thing to be for," he said. "You're not Irish."

"No. I'm American. Boston, Massachusetts. But I'm for the cause and I volunteer every day at the hospitals."

"Did you mean what you said?"

"About being for Ireland?"

"No, about going with me when they move me."

"I'll certainly come and visit you."

"Maybe we can have some secrets of our own," Conn said, and smiled at her. He had curly black hair, and the kind of smooth Irish skin that would have shown a high color if he were well.

"I am a married woman, Conn, Mrs. Thomas Winslow."

His smile widened.

"I'll not hold that against you, Hadley."

1994
Voice-Over

The wind out of the northeast pelted the wet snow against Grace's window. Motionless at her end of the couch, Grace waited.

"When I was in Dublin," I said, "I walked along the Liffey and thought about Joyce. You ever read *Finnegans Wake*?"

"Not all the way through."

"Christ, Joyce probably didn't read it all the way through. I was thinking about the way it starts, 'rivverrun,' no capital letters or anything, like in midsentence, and then at the end, you know the ending?"

Grace shook her head.

" 'A way a lone a last a loved a long the,' " I said. "No period."

"Is this how we do it?" Grace said. "You make obscure literary references and I try to figure them out?"

"I never understood the damn book, but I always liked the circular trick, the way the end is the beginning. It's like us, it's all connected backwards and forwards, past and present, 'Along the rivverrun, past Eve and Adam's.' "

"You may have spent too much time reading, Chris."

"Yeah, I know, you're very concrete. But I'm not. I see things and I think of other things. I'm very—what?—associative, emblematic. You look out the window and see a stormy night. I look out and think, *Blow, winds, and crack your cheeks.* It's one of the ways we're different. But it's not a way that should keep us apart."

"It's not what keeps us apart, Chris."

I stood and walked to the window and looked out at the inappropriate lightning flashes in the anachronistic blizzard.

"It wasn't so much different then," I said. "The rifles were mostly bolt action instead of clip fed, and they still had cavalry units, but there were automatic pistols, and Thompson submachine guns. Stuff like that. I've seen some of the weapons in a museum in Dublin. The Webley .45 is a big, ugly-looking brute of a thing, but it's not much different than any revolver that caliber you'd see today."

I could see Grace reflected in the dark window. She radiated patience. *He'll get to it if I just remain calm.* Easy for her to say. I didn't even know what *it* quite was.

"I'm sorry. I guess I ramble."

She smiled.

"A long way past Eve and Adam's," she said. "But that's all right. We'll get there. It's about the rest of our lives; it's okay if it takes time."

I came back and sat down on the couch again, carefully at my end. I felt as if everything needed to be done carefully, as if it could all too easily spill if we weren't careful, and ruin everything.

"It's probably hard for us, late twentieth century, post-Vietnam, to have any real sense of the kind of passion the Anglo-Irish war was fought with. You can still see some of it in Northern Ireland, I guess, but mostly that's sunk into some kind of ingrown religious economic war that has long since started to feed on itself. For Conn Sheridan, a year and a half after the end of the World War, fighting for freedom, everything must have been heightened, enlarged, elongated by the times. Free Ireland, throw off the yoke of tyranny, rid our land after—what?—ten centuries or so of what he must have thought of as foreign oppression. Boys could go through the blood rituals of manhood and never leave the neighborhood. No pushing up poppies in Flanders field to prove yourself. You could do it in Dublin, or

Cork, or Kerry. It was certainly awful in many of its moments, but it must have been fun as hell too."

"You sound wistful," Grace said.

"I am wistful. I've spent my life not doing anything."

"That's a little harsh," Grace said.

I shook my head.

"Always read about it, always studied it, always observed it, even taught it. Never fucking *did* it."

"Did what?"

"Anything. My grandfather fought a war, my father fought a war, I went to grad school."

"That's doing something."

"Sure, but it ain't high deeds in Hungary, is it?"

"Does it have to involve guns?" Grace said.

"At least it ought to involve courage," I said. "Enough courage to at least act, and not just be a poor weak fool seeing both sides of every issue."

"Last fall involved courage," Grace said.

"What the hell did I do?"

"Enough."

I shrugged.

It was hard to concentrate. Grace's eyes were very large, and dark blue. She had a lot of thick auburn hair, and smooth skin and a wide mouth. She was five feet nine inches tall and strong looking, like the California beach girls that play volleyball on ESPN. I had met her in law school and loved her neither wisely nor well ever since. In the years we had lived together I had seen her naked a thousand times. I knew every hint and nuance of her naked body. I could remember exactly how she looked. And now, sitting four feet from her on the couch, I could hardly breathe with wanting to see her naked again. It was barely about sex. It was about possession. I wanted to be the one to see her naked. Not another guy. Me. The insubstantial room around us seemed to coalesce. The momentary couch on which we sat seemed random and kinetic. I could hear my heart. I could feel my breath going in and out. Reality seemed to heel beneath me the way a plane often does at takeoff. I centered on her eyes as she looked at me; held on them as the phenomenological world scattered and regrouped around her, and slowly settled and steadied and became again a small room in a nice condo inside while an odd early spring snowstorm raged and huffed outside, and the girl of my dreams sat quietly at the other end of the couch.

Conn

Under an empty blue sky, half a block from Merrion Square, Conn sat wrapped in a blanket, on a chaise, in the high-walled garden of a house on Clare Street. Against the back wall of the house, snaking up one of the porch pillars, was a thick trumpet vine, leafless yet at the earliest edge of a raw Irish Sea spring. Conn's wound had healed and he was almost well. Hadley was reading aloud to him, some poetry by Yeats. She had kept her word, she had come to see him as he healed.

"Why," she read, saying it right, understanding it, *"what could she have done, being what she is?"* And he joined her, reciting from memory. They spoke the last line in unison. *"Was there another Troy for her to burn?"*

"That's a good one," Conn said.

"Yes," she said.

"Does your husband know you come here?"

"Oh, my God no," she said.

"He's not for a free and independent Ireland?"

"Oh, I think he is," she said, "in his way. But he wouldn't want me venturing among the rebellious ruffians."

"What's his way?" Conn said.

"His way?"

"You said he's for a free and independent Ireland in his way. This is your way. What's his?"

"Oh, well, he's older. He's stable. He believes in good business practices, and a calm homelife."

"He's in business?"

"Yes. He has a factory. Mulroney's Heather Scented Irish bath soap. Mostly for export to America."

"Not Winslow's."

She laughed, the volume of poetry closed in her lap, a forefinger holding the place.

"Now, what would that sound like," she said, "—Winslow's Irish soap?"

"It would sound like an oxymoron," Conn said.

"You're educated, aren't you?" Hadley said.

"Self, mostly," Conn said. "I like to read, my father was a schoolmaster."

She had brought them lunch in a hamper. Cheese and bread and fruit and a bottle of wine.

"I had Cook pack this for us," she said. She handed him an apple.

"Are you well enough to uncork the wine?"

"Yes," he said around a bite of apple.

"Then please," she said, handing him the wine and the corkscrew.

They sat together in the garden and drank the wine and ate the cheese and fruit and bread in the still-weak sunlight of early spring. The wine was a Grave, its flintiness refreshing against the richness of the country cheese, and the sweetness of the fruit. The wine added color to her face, a touch of red along the perfect cheekbones, and her eyes brightened. They finished the bottle.

"Wine's gone too quickly," he said.

"Remember when I met you the first day in the hospital?" she said. "And you asked for a bit of whiskey?"

"And you, being nursie-nursie, said I was too sick."

She smiled and drew a bottle of whiskey from the hamper.

"Now you're well," she said. "It is time to celebrate."

She poured whiskey into his empty wineglass, and some into hers.

"Just like that?" he said. "Neat? Like a man?"

"*Just* like that," she said. And drank.

He sipped from his glass, feeling, for the first time in what seemed too long, the warmth of the whiskey enriching him.

"No pretty little faces?" he said to her. "No delicate wrinkle of the nose, no ladylike heckle to suggest that whiskey is too strong a drink for fragile high church ladies?"

"I'm not fragile," she said. "I like whiskey. I like many things that high church ladies aren't supposed to like."

"Do you, now? Well, that's encouraging."

"It was meant to be," she said.

They sipped their whiskey.

"And Mr. Winslow?"

"I like him too."

"Do you love him?"

She leaned back in her chair, and the pale sunlight rested on her face. She was wearing a mannish tweed suit and a high-necked gray wool sweater.

"Do I love him?" She swallowed more whiskey. "How utterly Irish of you."

"To ask if you love your husband?"

"It's in your nature," she said. "The romance of lost causes."

"Is loving your husband a lost cause?"

"A husband who sees to all your needs, and is proud to have a young and beautiful wife—that is not a lost cause."

"And love is?"

"It certainly should not take precedence," she said.

Her eyes were very bright and the flush on her face was deeper. She poured whiskey into each glass, and leaned back again, her eyes closed, her face to the lukewarm sun. Motionless in the wicker chair, there was about her a kinesis to which his own body vibrated like a tuning fork.

"Practical," Conn said.

"Yes!"

"But pleasure loving," Conn said.

"One does not preclude the other," she said.

As he healed, Conn's strength had come back, and he could

feel it now in the bunching of muscle between his shoulder blades, in the resilience of his neck.

"Good to know," Conn said. His voice seemed disconnected from the burgeoning center of him.

"Good to know both things," Hadley said, her face flushed, her eyes shining. He could see her breasts move as she breathed. He hadn't noticed that before. Was she breathing more, or was he seeing better?

"Are you well?" she said.

"Well enough."

"Well enough for what?" she said, and her bright eyes were full of laughter now.

"Anything," he said.

And she slid forward onto her knees beside him and he put his arms around her. Her mouth pressed on his and opened. He fumbled at her clothing. She helped him. And helped with his and they were naked on the cold grass, tangled in his blanket. He put his hands on her and felt a quiver ripple through her body. She arched against him, her mouth hard against his. His front teeth cut her lip. He tasted her blood for a moment, and hesitated; but she pressed even harder, and moaned softly, and the center of himself seemed to escape him and envelop them both.

"Don't say," she gasped, her mouth still pressed against his, "that you weren't warned."

Then there was only the inarticulate sounds of their lovemaking, and the twitter of finches in the trumpet vine.

Conn

Detectives from G section of the Metropolitan Police were being shot by the IRA on the street in Dublin. Curfew was now midnight to five A.M. Sitting in a café on Grafton Street in the late afternoon, with the high weather clouds scudding fast toward England, Conn drank tea and watched as the city became every day more warlike. The Dublin police were always on the street. And the Royal Irish Constabulary, the Peelers, founded by Sir Robert Peel, responsible only to Dublin Castle. British troops moved about in lorries. Aloof from everyone else, brutal, scornful, and many, the mercenaries swaggered through Conn's city like conquerors. Ex-British enlisted men wore the black-and-tan uniforms for which they were named. Auxiliaries, former British officers, wore dull bottle-green. The men of both forces were combat veterans, blooded in Britain's colonial wars, hardened in the trenches of Europe. Both forces existed exclusively to suppress the Irish rebellion. The detectives and the Secret Service moved about in civilian clothes, but their weapons too were apparent, deadly angular shapes under tight coats.

Conn sipped his tea and whistled "The Peeler and the Goat" softly to himself, the lyrics playing silently in his head.

> *Your hoary locks will not prevail,*
> *Nor your sublime oration O*
> *And Peeler's Act will you transport*
> *On your own information O.*

A young medical student named Kevin Barry was hanged one gray morning in Mountjoy Prison. Crowds gathered early on the damp streets outside the prison, before the sun had dried the dew. British soldiers in tin hats stood with fixed bayonets, shivering in the early day. Armored cars moved over the slick streets, forcing passage through the crowd. A woman began to cry. "The poor boy. The poor boy. God help us all!" She swayed as if she would fall and people on either side held her up. Airplanes circled overhead, flying low, unexpected and alien, watching the crowd, like pterodactyls over prey. The mourning of the crowd rose toward them. "Mother of Perpetual Succor help us," the women cried. "Mother of Perpetual Succor help us." The Tommies stood motionless, bayonets fixed, eyes straight ahead. Most of them were very young. Conn moved among the people, shoulders hunched against the early chill, hands deep in his pockets. *Bad morning for Kevin Barry. Good morning for the cause,* he thought. *Whenever things looked grim for a free Ireland, the British would pitch in and supply another martyr.*

There was a warrant out for Conn. The RIC had captured one of the men from Hollyford, and beaten information from him. So Conn was assigned to IRA headquarters to recuperate. He had few duties as he got well. He attended planning meetings, acrimonious night-long discussions of revolutionary theory. The arguments made him restless. Revolution for Conn was a night on the barracks roof at Hollyford, not extended analysis of Foch's principles. During most of the planning he thought about Hadley. He lived from house to house, never more than two or three nights. Everywhere he went he carried two guns, the big Webley and a Browning automatic. Everywhere he went he was watchful and thought about Hadley. Days he sat in St. Stephen's Green, among the orderly flower beds, where nursemaids pushed prams, and shabby undersized men with narrow faces sat on benches and looked at nothing. He watched the people, and kept an eye out for peelers, and mused on Hadley's thighs and the smooth small slope of her stomach. Sometimes he went to the National Gallery and stared at the paintings hung on high white walls above polished floors in echoing rooms under distant ceilings. He thought of the sounds she made during lovemaking. Sometimes he read in the National Library. Always he was careful. Always he thought about Hadley. He saw her as often as she could get away.

On a soft evening when the spring had flowered into summer, they ate together in the dining room at the Shelbourne Hotel. They sat by one of the high windows that looked out across the traffic at St. Stephen's Green. Lorries rumbled past with British troops standing on the sides. Armored cars with mobile turrets moved along the north side of the Green. Occasionally one would swerve in toward the sidewalk. People would scatter, and the car would resume course. The Auxies walked in groups. People gave way to them. They were professional fighters, tough and arrogant in their dull bottle-green tunics, tam-o'-shanter caps at an angle. Some Auxies paused to look in at the diners. Conn looked back at them. One of the Auxies, a thick-bodied man with an eye patch, saw Conn looking and stared back at him. They held each other's stare and then the Auxie tossed his head contemptuously, and they moved on. Conn laughed.

"Stared him down, did you?" Hadley said.

Around them carefully dressed older people were eating dinner. The waiters, in black coats and white aprons, moved humbly among them, never making eye contact, bowing and murmuring and backing away. *The Irish make terrible subjects,* Conn thought, *but they might make grand slaves.*

"Yes," Conn said. "But I had more eyes than he did."

He laughed again and Hadley laughed with him.

"Ah, Conn," Hadley said in a stage Irish accent, "you darling boy. Look at you, with your curly black hair and your big smile and a strapping lad you be."

"A credit to me race," Conn said.

"And carrying two guns and stare down any Auxie," she said. "You're like a poster Irishman."

"Faith and begorrah," Conn said, and put his hand on top of hers.

The Shelbourne was dangerous for both of them. Hadley's husband was well known among the Ascendancy Irish who often dined there, and Conn, were he recognized, would be shot on sight by any of the British officers billeted in the hotel.

"Where shall we go after dinner?" Conn said.

"It's pleasant," Hadley said. "Perhaps we can find a quiet place in the Green."

Conn took a bite of muttonchop and drank some claret. He knew how dangerous it was here, and he knew that the danger was one reason they came. It excited her. For himself Conn knew that it was foolish to take such risks, but he knew also that Dublin was his city, and he was goddamned if he would let a bunch of foreigners decide where he could eat. And he too enjoyed the danger.

"Be nice sometime if we were to do it in a proper bed," Conn said. He paused and drank some more claret, and patted his lips with the starchy white linen napkin. "With clean sheets, and big pillows. And a door that locked."

"I rather like the excitement," Hadley said. "Doing it where someone might come upon us."

"It's exciting," Conn said. "But it lacks a bit in the area of postcoital languor."

She cut a neat small portion of her salmon and popped it into her mouth, switching the fork from her left hand to her right, the way Americans did. She chewed carefully while he looked at her face, how her big eyes held the light of the candles on the table. The light reflected in the windows now, as the evening came down. He could see them both in the dark window, younger than any of the other diners, sitting close together.

She finished chewing, and swallowed, and said, "I can get languor at home, thank you."

"And love?"

She smiled.

"So Irish," she said, and shook her head. "So Irish."

He wanted to reach across the table and take her and bend her to him and force her to love him as he loved her. He felt his strength, felt the biceps engorge, swollen against the sleeves of his jacket. It was as if, for that moment, he might force her or

kill her. He would make her yield. . . . And then it passed.
. . . He felt the engorgement drain away. . . . And he felt diminished, as if he himself might drain away too. . . . The faith defended, he put his hand on top of hers again, and patted it contritely. He felt the glassy stare of the stag's head mounted high on the far wall of the dining room.

Later, in the Green, among some bushes, squirming beneath him in the darkness, moaning in his arms, she bit his shoulder and drew blood. And when it was over they stayed where they were, in silence, catching their breath, smelling the crushed grass beneath them and the damp smell of the Irish earth, and listening to the sound of the heavy lorries as they rolled by.

Conn

They met on a cold night, in a high-ceilinged room, on the first floor of a four-story pinkish brick town house, in back of Trinity College, just up Westland Row from the train station. Mulcahy himself was there, the chief of staff, and Mick Collins, "the Big Fella," head of intelligence, seated behind a long table with maps and papers on it. The high windows were shuttered from the inside, and the doors were locked. The radiators were full on in the crowded room, and Ginger O'Connell, the training officer, portly and red faced, behind the table, was sweating in the heat. Rory O'Connor and Arthur Griffith made five command staff members behind the long table. Conn sat against the back wall on a straight chair that had been moved in from the kitchen. *If the peelers came fishing today they'd get a lot of big ones,* Conn thought.

"Let us be straight about this," Collins said. "Their Secret Service has been better than ours."

He spoke firmly, as he did everything. He wasn't in fact such a big fella. Conn was taller. But he was blocky and athletic, and the certainty with which he said things made him seem bigger than he was.

"We need to slow it down until we can catch up. No one outside this room knows of our plans. There are few of us, each of you will have to act alone. It is the best way to keep it secret."

Besides the command staff there were twenty men in the reeking hot room. Collins looked around slowly, making eye contact with each of them. Conn felt the force in the Big Fella's gaze when his turn came.

"We've all fought, we all know that it's harder alone. Harder to act with resolve. It is why each of you was asked to volunteer. You are the best we have."

Conn knew this was so and he was proud to be there. Still, it was one thing to fire at an anonymous enemy in the midst of a firefight. It was another to assassinate a man with a name, in his home, perhaps in his bed, sleeping with his wife. . . . He wondered if Hadley slept with her husband. He had seen him once, on the street with Hadley, walking on the west side of Merrion Square near Leinster House. A solid man, in his forties, with dark brown hair and a short thick beard like Grant, the American Civil War general. Hadley had made no sign as they passed, her hand resting lightly on her husband's crooked arm. He had a pleasant face with a look of intelligence about it. There was about him what Conn thought of as the American look, as if he always slept soundly and dined well, and spent time out of doors. Conn felt something nearly like camaraderie with this man who did not know him. They had shared the same woman, felt the secrets of her body. He imagined bursting in upon them, revolver drawn, and Hadley's husband startled sitting up in the bed beside her. . . . Of course they slept together.

"It is important that it all happen at the same time," Mulcahy said. "I want everyone in Ireland to be talking about it on the way to Mass tomorrow. Not only will we cripple their intelligence with this single simultaneous stroke, but it will be a statement, also, of how seriously a free Ireland must be taken."

Mulcahy's thick blond moustache was in odd juxtaposition, Conn thought, to his dark hair. It made him look a bit silly. But he wasn't silly. Dickie was a good man. So was Mick. All of them were in this dark inherited brotherhood of idealism and savagery. All of them loved Ireland and hated England and loved each other. And he among them hated and loved as they did, though he loved Hadley Winslow more.

The wallpaper in the room had a design of Doric columns in pink and white. The ceiling molding was thickly ornamental. The radiators hissed and pinged with heat. There was no sound from the street. *It is an emblem*, Conn thought, *of the essential Irish soul: hot, secretive, and dangerous, sealed up with history.* Conn smiled to himself. *And about to do some damage.*

Collins took out a big gold pocket watch and studied it for a theatrical moment.

"Eleven o'clock. Time—if you're going to reach your target before the curfew," he said. "Wait till it's after midnight, Sunday morning. And then be quick. It needs to be finished by sunrise."

The men stirred. Each of them had a handgun, most had two. There were perhaps a dozen hand grenades in the room as well. Some of the men carried knives. Conn didn't carry one. Sticking a knife into a man was a bit much, he thought.

Outside, the cold darkness was a brief refreshment from the steam ridden meeting room. But soon the chill became unpleasant and Conn buttoned his overcoat around his neck and turned up the collar. His target was a British Secret Service man named John Cooper, who lived on Haddington Road near the Beggar's Bush army barracks. Collins's intelligence report said he lived in one side of a two-story house with his wife. There were no children. There was no dog. Cooper would be the only man in the house. He was described as thirty-five, balding, medium height, medium weight. Nothing unusual to identify him. A nondescript government functionary who had gone to bed peacefully and would die before morning.

In the still darkness Conn walked along Mount Street, among the endlessly similar four-story eighteenth-century brick buildings. The sky was clear black and the stars were bright. The moon was only a sliver above him and the stillness of the low city with its orderly streets and symmetrical green parks seemed penetrating. The streets were empty, and his footfall was loud and rhythmic as he walked. He liked the sound. The weight of his guns was comfortable under his coat. When he first began to wear them they seemed heavy, but now they were part of him, no more uncomfortable than his shirt. A steel-plated Lancia went by with a guttural purr. It slowed as it passed Conn, but it did not stop, and soon it picked up speed and drove on, ugly and implacable like an ancient nocturnal carnivore. If they stopped him he'd make a fight of it. He might be able to lose them in the back gardens of the neighborhood, and even if he couldn't he would rather go down like a soldier of the IRA, which he was, with his guns in his hands. He smiled as he walked, liking the image of himself, two-gun Sheridan, and smiling at his own boyish heroism, though he was proud of it too, and he knew it to be real.

At Haddington Road he stopped half a block east of Beggar's Bush before the two-story row house with a red door. He was on his own. There had been no instructions. How he killed this man was up to him. He didn't like it much, but he'd do it. He'd sworn an oath to a free Ireland, and this balding youngish man he was about to kill had chosen to be a Secret Service officer, had chosen to repress the Irish people, had chosen to run the risk that he was about to incur. Certainly this man had sent over many a good-hearted Irish lad.

Conn took the big Webley out, and cocked it, and held it by his side. He walked briskly across the street and up the front steps and rapped loudly on the front door. After a moment he rapped again. There was movement inside the house. The front door opened a crack and a voice said, "Who is it?"

"From the Castle."

The door opened wider.

"What the hell are you doing at this hour?"

"John Cooper?" Conn said.

"Aye."

Conn raised the gun and shot him point blank in the middle of the chest, and again. Cooper's mouth opened but he was dead before the sound got there and he fell backwards into his front hall. Conn put the gun back and turned briskly and walked back down the stairs. Behind him he heard a woman scream, "John, dear God, they've killed you." And then he was around the corner and onto Shelbourne Road walking fast in the still night.

John Cooper.

Conn

"They are going to send me to Cork," Conn said.

They were walking on Wilton Terrace. The sun was bright and magpies made shrill noise along the banks of the canal.

"Must you go?" Hadley said.

"Of course."

"Because they say you must?"

"Yes."

"Don't go," Hadley said.

"I have to. I'm a soldier. I go where I'm sent."

"But it's not like a real army," Hadley said. He was watching the glisten of her lips as she spoke.

"Real enough," he said. "Will you come with me?"

He could smell the lavender scent of her cologne, close and immediate against a faint background of water scent from the canal.

"To Cork?"

"Yes."

"I can't do that."

"Why not?"

"Why, I'm married. I live here. I have a house."

"But you love me," Conn said.

She was wearing a green silk dress under a light coat. Her hair gleamed in the sunshine. White ducks drifted on the surface of the canal.

"Of course I do, but I can't go traipsing off to Cork with you. Where will we sleep? In a hayloft?"

"We can stay with people in their homes."

"And while you fight with the Black and Tans, I stay home by the peat fire and do what?"

"Hadley, it's a war. It's the best we can do. I can't leave you."

"I don't want you to."

Conn held both her upper arms with his hands.

"Come with me. It's the only way."

She raised her hands and pushed at him.

"Conn, you're squeezing too hard. It hurts."

He dropped his hands.

"It'll be an adventure, girl. It'll be us, always together, in the countryside, making love every night in a different place."

Hadley shook her head.

"Stay here, darling, with me, in Dublin."

"I can't stay in Dublin, Hadley. I'm too hot. I was one of the gunmen Bloody Sunday. I killed a Secret Service officer named John Cooper."

Across the canal an old woman had come to feed stale bread to the ducks. They glided toward her rapidly, making a ripple of V's in their wake.

"You were one of them?"

"Yes."

"And now you have to run."

"I'm transferred, to Cork. To fight there."

They sat together on one of the green wooden benches along the canal. Several ducks banked in toward them hopefully, and, ignored, cruised back toward the center of the canal.

"I can't go with you, Conn. Accept that. I can't. I have a husband, a home. I am the spoiled daughter of rich Bostonians. I can't traipse around the bogs of Ireland, like a camp follower, while my lover fights a guerrilla war."

Conn felt as if the air around them had no oxygen. He heard his own voice, as if it were someone else's, remote from him in time and space, filtered by distance.

"Then I'll desert," the voice said.

Hadley's eyes widened and she seemed to rock backwards slightly, as if to catch her balance.

"Desert? And do what?"

"Doesn't matter," Conn said. "We'll go somewhere, any-where you wish. We'll stay here or go to America, we'll be to-gether."

"Hiding?" she said.

"Not in America," Conn said. She was appalled by the wild-ness of his eyes, and the frantic intensity of it. She felt as if soon it would wash over her and she would disappear. "We could live anywhere in America, or France, or Australia. Wherever you'd like, and I'd work."

"What would you do, Conn? What do you know how to do? You're a gunman."

"I'd do something and we'd be together."

"And the cause? The oath you took?" Hadley was searching with a feeling of increasing desperation for something to stop him with. His need was luminous and tangible. It frightened her. She had lost control of this adventure.

"Fuck the cause," Conn said. "Fuck the oath. Fuck the world. Only you matter, Hadley. Only you. I would give up everything for you. . . . I will. . . . I have."

She stood. She could taste something very much like panic in the back of her throat.

"No," she said. "No. No. No."

"Yes," Conn said and the word hissed out like venting steam. "Yes. I love you, and, Goddammit, Hadley, you love me."

He stood facing her, barely inches between them, not touch-ing her. She backed away a step. She seemed exhausted.

"Not enough," she said in a small flat voice. And backed up another step, and then another, and then turned, and began to run along the canal toward the pleasantly arched little bridge where Baggot Street crossed.

He didn't chase her. But he called after her without regard for who might hear.

"You can't run from me, Hadley. I'll make you love me enough."

She continued running clumsily in her high-heeled shoes, holding her skirts clear, crying as she ran.

"I'll make you, Hadley. I will not give you up."

And then she had scrambled up the little rise to Baggot Street and across, and he couldn't see her anymore.

Conn

She lived in a four-story red-brick town house with a bright blue door on the north side of Merrion Square. The bricks were the color of cheap rouge, put on early and worn too long. There was a damp chill in the air, and the sky was low and gray. Thin rain fell lightly, and the smell of coal fires drifted fragilely among the wet leaves in the square.

He stood against the low iron fence that ringed the square and watched her door. He paid no attention to the rain, or the cold. If he felt it at all it didn't register. He saw the curtains move once in one of the front windows, as if someone were peeping out. He stayed where he was, his guns holstered and dry under his mackintosh, his gaze nearly hypnotic on the house. There was no wind to drive the rain. It fell straight down, without force. The streets gleamed with it. The bright blue door opened and Hadley came out wearing a dark blue woolen coat, with a stand-up collar. The coat was buttoned up to the throat. On the top step she opened a black umbrella, and got under it, and walked across the street to where he was standing.

"I can't have you standing out here like some milk calf in the rain," she said to him. "One of the servants has already mentioned it. My husband will notice, or someone will tell him. What in hell are you doing?"

"Waiting for you."

"Waiting for me to do what?"

"If I stood here, I knew you'd come out."

"All right, I'm out. What do you want?"

"I want you," Conn said. His voice was very soft, and nearly uninflected. He was saying things he'd imagined and rehearsed. It was as if he were talking to himself.

"Goddamn you, Conn Sheridan. You can't have me. You did

have me. It was exciting. You are good at sex and fun to be with. You were a lark that got out of hand. Now you don't have me. It's over. Let it go. Get back to killing people, again, for the Republic."

"I love you," Conn said.

"You'll get over it," Hadley said. "I'll get over it."

She kept the umbrella sheltered close to her head, so that as they talked they were faceless. She looked at his chest. He stared down at the unyielding fabric of the black umbrella.

"I will never get over it," Conn said, spacing the words carefully.

"You'll have to," she said.

"I won't."

They were silent then in the hushed sound of the rain. A bicycle hissed by, its rider pedaling carefully on the slick street.

"I won't," Conn said again.

"Well, I will," Hadley said, and turned away under her dark umbrella and walked back across the street to her house.

He didn't move. She didn't look back. The rain was very fine, he noticed. It made everything gleam. The blue door seemed a brighter blue. *And the small rain down does fall,* he thought, and wondered where he'd read that. He felt solid in his stillness, like a frozen boulder across the street from her blue door. There was not even panic in him anymore, only resolve, which grew as time passed, and seemed to fill him like ballast.

And he was still motionless when they came for him. A RIC car came up the north side of the square and a lorry full of Auxies came down from the other direction. They were around him before he could move. If he had wanted to move. Which he didn't. He made no effort to draw either of his handguns. He made no attempt to run. He stayed rock silent, deep inside himself, ballasted with resolve, nearly impervious to anything other than his romantic resolution.

They took his weapons and handcuffed him. A RIC officer went to the house and brought Hadley to the door. He pointed at Conn, she nodded. He looked implacably across the street at her. Their eyes met. She held his gaze for a moment, nodding as the officer spoke. Then she turned and went back into her house and closed the bright blue door.

1994
Voice-Over

" 'He knew when he kissed this girl, and forever wed his unutterable visions to her perishable breath, his mind would never romp again like the mind of God.' "

"You talking about your grandfather or about yourself?" Grace said.

"I'm talking about Jay Gatsby," I said.

"Sure."

"And Conn Sheridan."

"Un-huh."

"And me."

Grace didn't say anything for a while. We sat in the bright room surrounded by the dark storm with the careful space between us on the couch and thought about our situation.

"Tell me a little more about you and me and the perishable breath business," Grace said.

"You know the story," I said.

"The Great Gatsby? Yes."

"It's about a lot of things," I said. "But certainly it's about obsession."

Grace nodded. I could hear the wind outside the condo. It was an odd juxtaposition of forces. The strong wind driving snowflakes so saturated that they flattened softly against the window, making no sound.

"And you're obsessed?" Grace said finally.

"With you," I said. "Or I have been. It runs in the family."

"Not love?"

"Sure, love too, that's what makes it tricky. To separate out the obsession and the love. And keep one, and deep-six the other."

"And you've been able to do that?"

"Yes." I smiled at her. "It's my turn. One Sheridan a century."

"Could you describe the obsession a little for me?"

"I was in love with love," I said.

"Rather than with me."

"Yes."

"Which is to say you used me to fulfill yourself."

"Yes."

Grace thought about it, her face serious and beautiful, with the first hints of maturation showing in the laugh lines around her mouth. The white sweater was wide at the neck and I could see the definition of her trapezius muscles. Most women had none, and their necks and shoulders always looked a little angular to me. I knew she'd be even better looking when she was older.

"That seems a better deal for you than for me."

"Yeah, it was, in the sense that I had to have it. But it was also like the myth about the guy up to his neck in water who was dying of thirst but couldn't drink because when he did the water dipped out of reach."

"Meaning?"

"Meaning I couldn't get you to love . . . no, not love . . . I couldn't get you to enter the obsession."

"I'd have disappeared," Grace said.

"Yeah, but the obsession would have been complete," I said. She smiled.

"How nice for you," she said. "And you're not obsessed anymore."

"No. Now I love you."

"How can you be so sure?"

I took in some air slowly, and let it out, and felt all right.

"Because I can leave you," I said.

"Do you plan to?"

"No. I plan to let you see me and where I come from and who I've become and ask you to marry me. If you can't, then I'll be sorry, and I'll say good-bye and find someone who can marry me."

"Would you really?" she said. Her eyes seemed bigger than they had been and there was a sense of kinesis behind her calm face.

"I love you. I'd miss you for a while. But, yes, I will."

"And you can live with that?" Grace said.

"After last fall, I can live with anything," I said. "Happily and well."

Conn

The gray granite walls of Kilmainham jail were six feet thick. The windows narrowed like gunports and were placed so high that at six feet two inches, Conn could just reach the window ledge with his fingertips. Gas jets sputtered feebly, flaring occasionally and falling back so that the flame was barely a blue glimmer above the nozzle. The door to his cell was iron, with a small peephole in it. Through the peephole Conn could see the length of cells on the other side of the corridor. A stench came from the rarely flushed jacks, out of his vision, at the far end. Men who had to use it were escorted by a military policeman from a Welsh regiment. He carried his revolver in his hand as he walked them there and back. The stone chill of the jail was penetrating, and Conn was cold all the time. There were some dirty army blankets in a pile on the floor, but they were inadequate. Everything was inadequate to the impersonal weight of the British Empire. Beneath this vast pile of disinterested stone, Conn was a buried fleck of rubble in the blank cell where Hadley had put him.

His first night Conn slept badly, shivering on the floor among the blankets. In the morning a prison orderly came down the corridor yelling, "Burgoo up, Burgoo." Conn got a cup of thick soupish tea and a chunk of bread. Later he was taken to the yard. It was narrow, with high walls, broken by very small barred windows where occasionally featureless faces looked out from cells indistinguishable from Conn's. The underfooting was gravel with occasional patches of weedy grass breaking through.

The other prisoners walked with him, single file back and forth across the small space in a half circle. No talking was allowed, but some took place anyway. The older prisoners had learned to speak without moving their lips.

"Where you from?"

"What have they got you for?"

Conn didn't answer. They often put informers among the prisoners. Silence came easily to him anyway, for he was still deep inside himself.

There was no organization in the prison population. The British kept them as separate from one another as possible. Occasionally they were put in an identity lineup, brought to the yard, and paraded before anonymous witnesses inside a closed zinc box with a viewing slit in it. A cardboard sign with a number on it was hung by a string around each prisoner's neck.

They would try Conn and hang him. He knew that. But first they would attempt to pry the names of others from him. They had not as yet. They were letting him soak in the despair of the jail.

A priest brought him an egg and showed him how to beat it first and pour his tea over it. It made the tea taste as if there were cream in it.

To protect themselves from bombs, the British took hostages from the jail. A prisoner rode in each truck with his hands tied to a steel bar above him. In one truck a sign that said, BOMB NOW, was hung around a prisoner's neck.

Down the corridor from Conn a prisoner named Kenneally sang loud songs of Irish heroism. Someone next to Conn would chime in with alternate verses. The guards screamed at him, "Shut your fucking hole."

When the singing continued, the guards charged down the corridor to Kenneally's cell. When they got there it was silent. But behind them in another cell the song picked up. And a voice from still another cell called, "I'm here, Mary Ann, I'm here."

He was given some books, but he didn't read them. A newspaper was slipped under his door one day but he let it lie, and when the guards saw it they took it away.

Each morning they washed in groups of four from rusty enamel basins. The men around Conn talked with each other as they splashed water on themselves in the numbing cold. The guards warning to stop talking was continuous and useless. Only Conn was silent.

Sometimes it would rain and Conn would hear it pelting against the vast walls. It seemed a sound of unimaginable distance, an outside sound in an inside world. The sound of rain would make some of the prisoners weep.

The men scrubbed the flagged floors of their cells, dipping dirty rags in cold water until their hands and wrists were blue.

Most of the prisoners around Conn had killed someone or were thought to have killed someone. The wing was called Murderer's Wing and the guards were cautious. Just before lights-out an orderly came around and tumbled a slop bucket into Conn's cell. He wouldn't be allowed out until morning.

There was neither time nor distance in the jail. Sometimes the walls seemed to shrink in on Conn, and sometimes they expanded airily, as if there were no limit and one could walk forever. He didn't know how long he'd been there.

A British officer came to his cell, with a narrow-faced Cockney guard. The officer was round faced and pop eyed with high color.

"You've one chance, Sheridan," he said. "You'll tell us the names of the others, or you'll hang."

Conn was sitting against the wall with his knees up and his forearms resting on them. He paid no heed.

"Stand at attention for the officer," the guard said.

Conn didn't move. The guard kicked him. Slowly Conn turned his head and stared at the guard.

"You want to die, boy?" the officer said. "Is that it?"

Conn felt a small jag of excitement trill along the ganglia. It was the first thing he'd felt since the blue door closed. He felt himself smile suddenly. He looked up at the officer.

"Captain, dear," he said, "I don't give a shit."

The guard started to kick him again, and the officer put out his hand. He stood staring down at Conn for a moment and then shook his head.

"Fucking Irish," he said as if to himself, and jerked his head at the guard. The big iron cell door groaned shut behind them and the bolt clanked home.

Conn stayed where he was. His ribs hurt where the guard had kicked him, but he ignored it. He was fascinated instead with the flicker of feeling he'd experienced. It was as if the first hint of regeneration had stirred under the snow. What was it? The prospect of dying? Did he seek it so avidly that its promise brought him hope? He stood and walked to the door and turned and walked back to the wall. It was only a few steps. He leaned on the wall with his palms flat against it and his cheek pressing the chill stone. He felt the roughness of the granite. No, it wasn't death that thrilled him. It was that it didn't matter. He didn't care if he died or didn't die. Nothing mattered and the thrill he felt was the thrill of freedom. No constraints. No restrictions. *If God is dead all things are possible.* He rolled along the wall until his back was against it and he said aloud,

"Fuck it."

And his voice sounded so alien and odd in the cell that he said it again louder and laughed and the laugh echoed even more oddly under the oppression of stone and iron.

"And fuck the English."

He drummed the flat of both hands in manic counterpoint against the wall.

"And fuck the rebellion."

A guard appeared at the peephole for a moment.

"And fuck you too, Hadley."

The guard's eye disappeared from the peephole and Conn leaned against the wall and flexed his back and bounced against it. And laughed to himself.

"Nuns fret not," he said aloud. And laughed again, and rubbed his hands softly together. If you didn't care, then it didn't matter. Nothing mattered. And fear and need mattered no more than comfort and love. They could kill him but they couldn't scare him. They could keep him but they couldn't crush him. It didn't matter. She didn't matter. She couldn't kill him. And perhaps, someday, he might kill her.

"Fuck her," he said aloud. And then smiled again, and said, "That too, maybe."

1921
Conn

Spring developed slowly outside Kilmainham jail. Inside, as if responding to it, prison discipline began to ease. The guards in Murderer's Wing who had seen their prisoners filtered through the image of the skulking gunman, began to relax as they saw the men banter with each other, ragging and laughing. The prisoners laughed at the jail rules, much as their keepers did. And an enlisted man's camaraderie began to develop, which realigned guards and prisoners against their mutual enemy, the officers. The guards left the cell doors unbolted when the officers weren't around, and the prisoners moved freely about their cellblock.

A short, thick soldier from a Welsh regiment leaned in Conn's open doorway smoking.

"So you plugged one of the bloody ferrets did you?" he said.

Conn grinned at him.

"Of course not."

"Did you shoot him outright or did you put a bomb through his window?"

"You must be thinking of someone else," Conn said. "But if I had done it, I'd have shot him, face to face."

"Face to face is the way," the soldier said. "I don't like the bloody bombing. Seems a coward's way."

"You fight a war against a foreign invader," Conn said. "You do what you have to do."

The soldier offered him a cigarette, Conn took it, and a light. They smoked in silence for a moment.

"You think we're invaders?"

"Are you Irish?"

"Of course not."

"Are you in Ireland?"

The soldier nodded slowly.

"In armed force?"

The soldier grinned.

"Foreign invaders," he said.

They smoked again in silence. A prisoner who called himself the Old Gunner went by on the way to the jacks.

"Jail regulations do not permit fraternization with the prisoners," the Old Gunner said in his best impression of an upperclass accent.

"Bugger the jail regulations," the soldier said.

The Old Gunner continued down the hallway laughing.

"Hard to see why you're on the outside and I'm on the inside."

"I was in Belgium," the soldier said, "slaughtering Huns. If I'd been born in Saxony I'd have been in Belgium slaughtering Tommies."

He shrugged.

"Handy-dandy," Conn said. "Which is the justice, which the thief?"

"What the hell does that mean?" the soldier said.

"Shakespeare."

"You a bloody schoolmaster?"

"I read a lot," Conn said.

"So how'd they catch you?" the soldier said.

"Somebody turned me in."

"A traitor?"

"A woman."

"By God, that's hard, isn't it?"

Conn nodded.

"You fucking her?"

Conn grinned.

"Seemed like the right thing to do at the time," he said.

"Always does at the time, don't it?"

"Always," Conn said.

He took a pack of cigarettes from his pocket.

"I'm off duty in ten minutes, you may as well keep these."

Conn took the cigarettes, and slipped them inside his shirt.

"They're going to hang you," the soldier said.

"They're going to try," Conn said.

The soldier nodded slowly and kept nodding as he thought about it.

"Sure," he said. "If they can."

Conn

Conn's soldier came for him one morning when, outside Kilmainham jail, April had begun to warm.

"They want you in the major's office."

Conn stood up.

"You may be in for a knocking around," the soldier said.

"Doesn't matter," Conn said.

"Would matter to me," the soldier said.

Conn shrugged.

There were two men in the room. One the officer who had questioned him before. The other was a captain. Conn had never seen him. He was as big as Conn, with black leather gloves on his thick hands.

"Your name is Conn Sheridan," the major said.

"Yes."

"Say sir."

". . . sir."

"Where did you get the gun, that you killed John Cooper with?"

"I didn't kill John Cooper."

The captain hit him in the chest with his heavy right fist. Conn rocked back, steadied himself, and smiled.

". . . sir," he said.

The captain hit him a left hook on the cheek and Conn fell. He stayed down for a minute, his head hanging, trying to get it clear.

"Get up," the major said. "Who gave you the gun?"

Conn got slowly to his feet. He didn't speak.

"Are you going to answer?"

"No."

The captain hit him, and his nose began to bleed. Blood dropped to the floor.

"So you are ready to suffer?"

"Sure."

The captain began to batter him with lefts and rights. He must have been a boxer once. The punches were short, with the full drive of his legs and shoulders behind them. Conn rocked with the punches, trying to slip as many as he could.

"Turn around," the major said.

Conn did so.

"See those photographs? Some of those men refused to speak and they are dead."

"Fuck 'em," Conn said, and looked at the big captain and grinned with the blood streaming down his face. "And fuck you too, bucko."

The captain knocked him against the wall.

"Will you fight me?" he said to Conn.

"Another time," Conn said. "When it's just you and me."

"You're afraid."

Conn's lips were badly puffed and one eye was swollen shut. He laughed.

The major went to his desk and took a Webley .45 service revolver from the drawer. He brought it over to Conn, broke it open, and showed him the full cylinder.

"You know what this is?" the major said.

Conn didn't speak. He saw the major through a kind of shimmering haze, as if at a distance through heat. He focused through the haze on the round brass center-fire backs of the bullets. His teeth felt loose and thick. The warm taste of his own blood filled his throat.

"You don't know, I'm not going to help you," Conn said.

"Stand against the wall, you swine," the major said. He seemed nearly hysterical with anger. "I'm going to give you a count of three to name some names."

The major raised the revolver and Conn stared at the dark mouth of it, and along the bluish barrel. His vision blurred again. There was sweat in his eyes, and maybe blood, and around his eyes the flesh was beginning to puff. One eye was nearly closed.

"One," the major said.

Conn began to sing. The sound of the song seemed to come from no place. He could hear the words he was singing but they seemed unconnected to him.

I know my love by his way of walking,

"Two." The major cocked the hammer back with his thumb.

I know my love by his way of talking,

Conn took in as much air as he could, as if storing it for a long voyage. He pressed his back against the wall. He thought of John Cooper for a moment.

"Three."

The major fired. Conn saw the muzzle flash, heard the sound, and felt nothing. It was a blank. The smell of it was strong in the room.

I know my love by his eyes of blue.

"Well," the major said. "You'll hang anyway."

He turned away from Conn, put the revolver back in the desk drawer, and left the room. The big captain lingered for a moment while Conn's soldier and another guard came in. He nodded at Conn with some sort of approval.

"I've seen people behave worse," the captain said. Then he jerked his head at the guards and left the room as well. The soldiers took Conn back to his cell.

Conn

The Old Gunner came into Conn's cell.

"Where'd you get that sweet face?" he said.

"From the noble hearts in the Intelligence room."

"Keep cold water on it," the Old Gunner said. "It'll heal, but you'll not look as pretty again."

"Pretty enough," Conn mumbled. His lip was still swollen tight and it was hard to speak.

"We're going to get you out," the Old Gunner said. "There's a gate at the far end of the yard, locked with an iron crossbar, secured with a big padlock. Are you game?"

"Sure."

"There'll be a package come in tonight," the Old Gunner said. "Bolt cutters. Maybe a gun."

Conn splashed cold water on his face from the dirty basin. The water that fell back was pink.

"Grand," he said.

"We're not going to let them hang the only man they've arrested for Bloody Sunday," the Old Gunner said. He took the enamel basin and went for more water.

At teatime Conn's soldier came into Conn's cell and closed the door. He unbuttoned his tunic and took out a package, and gave it to Conn. It was heavy and Conn knew it was the bolt cutters.

"Here's something else you'll like," the soldier said.

He took a revolver from his pocket. It was a Smith & Wesson .38, blue steel, with walnut grip and a three-inch barrel. It was loaded. Conn put the revolver in his belt under his shirt. The bolt cutters had two detachable three-foot handles, for leverage. He wrapped them in a shirt and tumbled two other shirts over it in a corner.

"Your sister brought it," the soldier said.

Conn had no sister. It must have been one of the Cumann na mBan girls.

"She's a good girl," Conn said.

The soldier pushed his cap back on his head and wiped his forehead with the back of his hand.

"I don't hold with boxing a man around when he's got no chance."

"Don't care much for it myself," Conn mumbled.

"Don't like to see a man hanged either," the soldier said.

"Specially me."

The soldier nodded.

"You ought to try boracic acid on that face," he said.

"I'll go right to the chemist," Conn said with difficulty, "and buy some."

The soldier nodded at the package hidden under the pile of shirts.

"Maybe soon," he said.

During the day, at exercise time, Conn hung the bolt cutters over his shoulder under his shirt when he went to the yard. He padded the cutters with torn strips of underclothing so that they wouldn't rattle. He carried the .38 in his pocket. Cells were often searched when they were empty and the safest place to hide his tools was on himself. In the yard Conn and the Old Gunner scouted the gate, studying the bar-and-padlock setup, locating the likely places where a night guard might be. They paid as much attention as possible to the patterns of night-guard behavior—when the guards slept, when they went to the jacks, how often they patrolled. There were two sets of night guards: a group of five in the cell next to Conn, and four more around the corner in the corridor next to the Old Gunner's. They slept restlessly, their weapons beside them. But they rarely stirred from the cell they slept in after lights out.

Alone in his cell Conn rehearsed with the Smith & Wesson. He practiced quick draws from his belt under his shirt. He got his hand used to the grip. He sighted along the barrel, and felt the weight of the gun and six bullets. Everything still hurt when he moved. And he still couldn't breathe through his nose. Conn had tea with the Old Gunner in his cell, and their soldier came in. He had his tunic unbuttoned, and his cap pushed back.

"Mick Collins said your name will go down in Irish history," he said to Conn.

" 'Specially if I'm hanged," Conn said. "Causes love martyrs."

"You're a cynical bastard, Conn," the Old Gunner said. "They won't hang you. We'll get you out of here."

"If the bolt cutters work," Conn said.

"They'll go through that bar like it was butter," the soldier said.

"And if they don't we can fight," the Old Gunner said. "You've got the revolver, Conn. We can disarm the guards, and rush the main gate, bayonets fixed."

"Two of us?"

"Three," the soldier said.

"What three?" Conn said. "We can't trust the others. You never know who's going to be a pigeon."

"I'm your third, Ga blimey," the soldier said.

The Old Gunner put out a hand and the soldier shook it. Nobody spoke for a moment.

"Good soldiers make bad jailers," the soldier said. "Nobody'll try that damned bloody hard to stop you."

"And when we get out," the Old Gunner said, "there'll be lads from the Fourth Brigade to support us."

"So when do we go?" Conn said, speaking thickly, his mouth still swollen from the beating.

"Soon as you've healed enough," the Old Gunner said. "And we'll let Lloyd George explain to Parliament why they couldn't hold the one man they'd caught for Bloody Sunday."

In a week, the swelling around his eyes had receded enough so that he could see normally. His lip was still puffed, but less so, and his speech was nearly normal. A week and three days after the bolt cutters came in, they were ready to try.

That afternoon Conn said to the soldier, "Lend me sixpence for the tram."

"I can give you five shillings," the soldier said.

"No, sixpence will do. I'm tired of this place."

The soldier laughed and handed him the silver.

"If it only cost sixpence all of us would go," he said.

The soldier would leave the Old Gunner's door open—the padlock closed but not locked, so that it looked secure. The Old Gunner could reach through the peephole and unlock it. Conn's door had no padlock, but the lock could be opened from the outside by pressing against the jamb with the handle of a spoon.

An hour after lights out, the Old Gunner walked in stocking feet past the soldiers sleeping near him and came to Conn's cell. His boots were slung by the laces around his neck. He struggled silently to pop the bolt on Conn's cell door. In the silence Conn could hear the soldiers in the nearby cell. One of them muttered in his sleep. Several of them snored. He was listening so intensely in the darkness that Conn could hear the sound of the running water that never fully shut itself off in the toilet down the hall.

The bolt clicked back. They edged the door open, slowly, so that it wouldn't squeak. Conn too had his boots around his neck. He gave the cutters to the Old Gunner, and held the .38 in his hand. They moved silently down the corridor past the guardroom, up the iron stairs. The iron door at the top was not locked. They went through it to the exercise yard. The ground was damp and the exterior walls were clammy in the night. The gravel was thunderous as they crunched across it in stocking feet. And the moon glared down like a spotlight.

At the gate the Old Gunner worked with the cutters while Conn stood pressed into as dark a corner as possible with his .38 drawn. He heard the Old Gunner laugh.

"Like butter," the Old Gunner said.

They pushed half the gate open slowly. It groaned as they did so. Then they were out in the bright night. They pushed the gate slowly closed behind them. In the darkness to their left they heard movement and Conn saw the outline of a soldier's peaked cap. Conn put his left hand out to stop the Old Gunner, and crouched a little and brought the .38 up. Had they been tipped? Were they waiting? A shot would wake up the garrison. Another figure stirred beside the soldier and Conn realized it was a woman. He could smell her perfume in the soft, damp Dublin night. Conn edged closer. The soldier and the woman were locked in an embrace. The soldier was fumbling beneath her blouse. Conn smiled. It might be a trap, but it wasn't a trap for him. He edged back to the Old Gunner.

"Love," Conn said.

A different figure appeared, wearing a tweed scally cap.

"Liam Sullivan," the figure whispered. "Fourth Brigade. Catch the tram on the South Circular Road. We'll keep the soldiers busy."

"Are the girls yours?" the Old Gunner said.

"Hired for the event," Sullivan said.

"Fucking for Free Ireland," Conn said. "How sweet."

"Actually it's your freedom they're fucking for," Sullivan said. "But it's still a good cause."

As they moved silently along the outside of the jail wall they passed other soldiers and women, in various degrees of intimacy, and then they were away from the jail. Sullivan vanished into the darkness. They boarded a tram on South Circular Road and mingled with other people. Around them Dublin spread out as if it had no limit. The dun brick looked bright, there were people with colored scarfs and laundered clothes. The signs on stores and taverns seemed sprightly and amusing, and the air seemed to breathe very easily. They listened to the talk around them, and laughter. With senses sharpened by deprivation, they smelled food, and the pleasant yeastiness of the Guinness Brewery, and the fertile wet scent of the river.

Conn

"You were born to be shot, Conn," Michael Collins said. "They'll never hang you."

"I'm through with it, Mick," Conn said. "I've no heart for it anymore."

"You swore an oath, Conn. Just like I did. We'd not rest until Ireland was free."

Conn shrugged.

"I'm not the same man," he said.

Collins looked at him thoughtfully. His round, smooth face showed nothing.

"It wasn't the jail," Collins said after a moment.

Conn shrugged.

"It's the woman," Collins said.

"You know about her?"

"It's my profession."

"Doesn't matter what it is, Mick. I'm through. I have no more heart for causes."

Collins nodded.

"Amazing," Collins said. "You are one of the hardest men I ever knew. In a fight. Facing death."

Facing death. Conn smiled to himself. Collins's rhetorical flourishes would have seemed laboriously stilted in most men. In Collins it was so much a part of who he was that it seemed normal speech.

"You'd go up against anyone," Collins went on. "One man or ten. But one woman"—Collins shook his head—"she broke you."

"She betrayed me."

They were silent.

"Thanks for getting me out," Conn said.

"I like you, Conn. Or I used to. But we got you out because it was good for Ireland that you escape. The only person arrested for Bloody Sunday. In their strongest jail. It weakens them, Conn. That's the point."

"There'll be reprisal," Conn said. "Somebody'll hang for my freedom."

"And we'll have another martyr. It's not an adventure, Conn. It's a war."

"Well, it's neither one for me, Mick. I'm out of it."

"Then go away, Conn. Go far. South Africa, Australia, America. It won't help us if they catch you. It'll help us if you disappear."

"I don't want to stay here," Conn said.

"Good. A lot of our boys don't like quitters much."

"Doesn't matter," Conn said.

"Nothing matters, does it?"

"No."

"I'll arrange it," Collins said. "Where do you want to go?"

Conn had never thought of where to go. He'd only thought of leaving.

"The United States," Conn said. "I'll go to Boston."

Collins grinned suddenly.

"Fancy that," Collins said.

1994
Voice-Over

"You walk along the River Liffey," I said, "which cuts right through the middle of the city, and there's a bunch of barrel-arched bridges. And the arches reflect in the water and make a circle. You walk along the river, past Guinness Brewery, and veer up past Heuston Station and go up a hill and there's Kilmainham Jail, this—Christ, I don't know—Stonehengeian pile of granite block, right in the middle of a bunch of neat small houses with neat small yards. So I went in. You can't go except on a tour, so I tagged along. And, Jesus . . . abandon all hope ye who enter here."

Grace waited, her gaze resting on me, calm and guarded so that it felt heavy. Though it seemed a little less guarded to me than it had. Always when she listened, she gave you her full attention and you felt as if you were saying things of absolute grace and significance.

"It felt like you'd think a prison would feel: ponderous, un-yielding, and hopeless. There was a light rain the day I was there. Actually there's a light rain most days in Dublin, I think. And the rain didn't make it more cheerful, but even in the present day, you know, now, when I was walking around in there, and now it's just a museum, I felt"—I looked for the right word—"like despair. I felt buried underneath this atrocious heap. It wasn't a cold day, maybe fifty-five, sixty, but inside the walls it was freezing. You knew what it must have been like to be caught in the gears of the British Empire. They were entirely indifferent, and they must have ground exceeding fucking fine."

"And yet he escaped," Grace said.

"He was an indomitable bastard," I said.

The thick snow had begun to pile up along the bottom of the window, its whiteness making the night storm blacker.

"Except that it sounds like he didn't care about anything."

"There's freedom in that."

"There's freedom and there's freedom," Grace said.

"True."

She looked at me again for a time.

"There's indomitable and indomitable too," she said.

"What the hell does that mean?" I said.

Grace shrugged.

"We'll see."

I waited but she didn't say anything else. Lightning startled outside the window, and thunder rolled in after it. The space between the light and the sound had narrowed as the heart of the storm moved toward us.

"A little after Conn left Ireland, they had stopped fighting England and started fighting each other. Michael Collins was killed by some other Irishmen, on the other side of the treaty issue.

"But Conn cared no more about that. He was over here. He arrived late in 1921 and joined the cops. The police strike was only two years before, and the force was pretty much starting over, and so was Conn. It was a match made in heaven. He was a charmer. I've seen pictures of him. Tall, strong looking, black curly hair, bright eyes, with a kind of go-to-hell look in them, you know? Like Errol Flynn. In fact much like myself."

Grace smiled.

"And one of his missions in life was to score every woman in Boston. Sort of a fuck-you to Hadley, I suppose."

"I thought Irishmen were sexually inhibited," Grace said. "Hung up on their mother and the Blessed Virgin, whom they quite often confused with each other."

"You shouldn't generalize," I said. "Anyway, he started out walking a beat in the West End with a guy named Knocko

Kiernan. I've actually met Knocko. I was a little kid, and he was a fat old guy drinking beer in his undershirt, when my father took me to see him once. But he still had funny eyes—like Robert Benchley, you know? eyes that know life's secret, and it's funny? Lot of Irishmen like him, about half of them, the other half thinks life's secret is tragic. I'm not sure yet which kind I am."

"Maybe a complete one," Grace said. "Maybe you're both."

"So he's walking a beat in the West End, which isn't even there anymore. Nice high rise condos—if you lived here you'd be home now. And they bust some bootleggers, and roust some loan sharks, and one day they caught a guy trying to murder an old lady. It wasn't great sleuthing, they just came across him in the act. But they saved the old lady and collared the guy and it made the papers. Martin Lomasney wrote a letter to the *Post* about it, and the mayor, James Michael Curley, had his picture taken with them, and in a while they were both detectives. And in another while they were both, still partners, working homicide out of Headquarters. Is this a great country? Or what."

"Land of opportunity," Grace said.

1931
Conn

They went to Boylan's, next to City Hall, which meant that Knocko Kiernan's wife, Faith, who had arranged the blind date, considered it important. Conn had a pint of whiskey with him in his coat pocket and he and Knocko were already aglow with it when they met Faith and Mellen Murphy in the restaurant.

"Mellen's a very pretty name," Conn said.

"Thank you," she said. "It's Mary Ellen, actually. I think my father invented the contraction when he was mad at me and couldn't get 'Mary Ellen' out without sputtering."

Her hair was the color of honey, and her eyes were very large and blue. She was slim, and wore a green dress with a lace collar. Her only makeup appeared to be lipstick, and she wore a small crucifix on a gold chain round her neck. Conn smiled to himself when he saw the crucifix.

We'll see about that.

"Hard to imagine getting mad at you," Conn said.

The waiter came with menus.

"Well have some glasses and ice," Knocko said. "And a siphon of seltzer."

"It is not permitted to drink here," the waiter said. He was a small dark man. "It's the law. Prohibition."

Knocko was bald, and jowly. He looked like the caricatured Irish policeman who appeared occasionally in *The Evening Transcript*. His face reddened.

"Maybe you'd like to have the place shut fucking down for a couple weeks," Knocko said.

"Francis," his wife said. "Your language."

"I'm sorry sir," the waiter said. "Management—"

"Fuck management," Knocko said.

"Francis!"

Conn stood up. He rested a hand on Knocko's shoulder, for a moment, as if calming a restive horse. Then he said, "Excuse me," to the table, put an arm over the waiter's shoulder, and, smiling, steered him a few steps away. With his back turned so that only the waiter could see it, he took out his badge and showed it to him. He smiled broadly.

"Just bring us the setups, guinea-wop. And shut the fuck up," Conn said in a pleasant voice. He nodded his head encouragingly. "You unnerstand?"

It wasn't the badge, as much as it was what the waiter saw in Conn's eyes.

"Yes, sir," he said. "Sorry."

Conn gave him a little pat on the back. And came back to the table.

"See that, Francis?" Faith said. "That's how a gentleman handles things. No need for rampaging round like a great sow."

Knocko winked at Mary Ellen.

"A sow is a female pig, Faith, if you'll be insulting me, for Crissake, at least get it right."

The waiter returned with glasses and ice and seltzer. Conn took the bottle from his inside pocket and mixed them all a drink.

"Make mine very weak," Mary Ellen said. "I really don't know how to drink very much."

"Plenty of time to learn," Conn said. They drank and looked at the menus. Mary Ellen drank in very small sips, and Conn could see that she didn't like the taste. He looked at himself in the mirror behind the bar. He was wearing a blue suit and vest and a red-and-blue tie with a collar pin. His white shirt fresh laundered by the Chinaman. His face had a healthy, windburned look and the blue suit set off his eyes and made them look even more piercing than they were.

"What did you say," Mary Ellen asked, "to make the waiter change his mind?"

"Sweet reason," Conn said. "I explained to him that while Prohibition was the law of the land, Knocko and I were the law of the city."

Mary Ellen smiled and took another tiny sip of her drink and tried to keep from wrinkling her nose at the taste.

"It's lovely, the way you speak, you're born in Ireland."

"In Dublin," Conn said. "Left ten years ago."

"Was it the troubles?"

Conn smiled at her.

"I was hoping to meet you," he said.

"You're very gallant," Mary Ellen said.

"Just ask the waiter," Knocko said. He had drunk two whiskies since the waiter brought the glasses, and his face was bright.

"Oh, Francis," Faith said.

"You live at home?" Conn said.

"Yes, and I work for Judge Canavan."

"Secretary?"

"Yes. He's a friend of my father's."

"Judge Murphy?"

Mary Ellen nodded.

"You know my father?"

"Just by reputation," Conn said. "He's a defendant's judge."

"My father is very softhearted," Mary Ellen said.

Knocko mixed up another whiskey and soda. His tie was loosened, his collar open, and his vest gapped above his belt. He gestured the waiter to them.

"We'll have oysters," he said.

"For four, sir?"

"Yeah, bring them for the table."

"Would you care to order anything else, sir?"

"Just bring the freakin' oysters," Knocko said. "We'll let you know what we want next."

Faith leaned forward across the table toward her husband. She spoke softly with her lips barely moving.

"Francis, you straighten out."

Knocko smiled and drank his drink. But he seemed uneasy. *Pussy whipped*, Conn thought. He swallowed some whiskey, felt it cold at first, then warm. He smiled to himself. *Aren't they all?*

The oysters came, on a silver platter served on a bed of ice. Mary Ellen eyed them uncertainly.

"Was a brave man, first ate an oyster," Conn said. He put one on Mary Ellen's plate, and a tiny dab of horseradish, then he offered her the meat on the small fork provided. She closed her eyes and opened her mouth and Conn popped it in. She swallowed without chewing.

"Like communion," Conn said.

Mary Ellen drank some from her whiskey and soda to wash it down.

"Wasn't so bad, was it?" Conn said.

Mary Ellen smiled. "No," she said. "It wasn't."

"Next time you might chew it," Conn said. "In time you might like it."

"I'm learning," Mary Ellen said.

"You certainly are," Conn said.

"You're a good teacher," she said.

"Yes," Conn said. "I am, in fact."

Conn

Conn sat quietly beside Mellen at Mass on a warm June morning. He enjoyed the scent of her: the soap she'd used in her morning bath, the floral shampoo with which she'd washed her hair, the perfume she'd sprayed lightly in the hollow of her throat. He liked the seriousness in her face as the Latin Mass rolled sonorously on. He liked the clear polish that made nails gleam as she fingered her rosary, and, when she knelt, Conn remained seated and studied the contour of her buttocks under the white summer dress. *Kneeling enhances a woman's ass.*

The parish was Irish. The sermon was about the Blessed Virgin and her Beloved Son. He could hear the reverential capital letters in the priest's smug voice. Mother love and virginity. Echoes of his childhood. He could have been in Dublin. *It's not whiskey,* Conn thought, *keeps the Irish from ruling the world.* The smell of incense, and the ringing of the bells, the impenetrable rhythmic Latin, the cassocks, and organ music, the dreadful martyrdom, the resurrection and the life, prayer, confession, contrition, the collection baskets passed by men in ill-fitting black suits that smelled of camphor, the flat wafer on the tongue, ohmygodIamheartilysorry. Conn smiled to himself. *Foolish bastards.*

They walked afterwards through the red-brick-and-wrought-iron South End in the fresh June sunshine. He put his hand down beside hers and she took it.

"Do you like going to Mass, Conn?" Mellen said.

"Yes," he said, and smiled down at her. He was nearly a foot taller. "You?"

"Yes. It's very comforting. I always feel closer to God when I've been."

"Yes," Conn said. "And I like the sense of connectedness.

People heard that Mass in Ireland when Hugh O'Neill was a boy."

"Who's he?" Mellen said.

"First earl of Tyrone," Conn said. "The last great leader of Gaelic Ireland."

"I don't know much about history," Mellen said.

" 'Tis a pity," Conn said, "that you were brought up here, darlin'. Had you been brought up a proper Irish girl, you'd know more than you wanted to about Hugh O'Neill and Cuchulainn and the dear Battle of the Boyne."

Conn could go in and out of stage Irish dialect at will. When he wished he could conceal his brogue almost entirely, though he could never say *Massachusetts* quite right.

"I know about Parnell," Mellen said. "But the nuns told us he was an adulterer."

"He was that," Conn said.

"And Mr. De Valera."

"I knew him."

"Did you, now?"

"Him and Michael Collins, Mulcahy, the whole bunch."

"Oh, my," Mellen said. "I think I'm with a hero."

"I think you are," Conn said.

They took a subway together to Park Street and walked past Brimstone Corner, along Tremont Street to the Parker House. Breakfast at the Parker House was something they had done for several Sundays after Mass.

"Would you like to talk about the troubles?" she said to him over shirred eggs and broiled tomato.

He smiled at her and shook his head.

"I'd rather talk about you," he said, "and maybe me."

"Why, Mister Sheridan," she said, and cocked her head, like a proper virgin, the way her mother had no doubt taught her. When she smiled her cheeks dimpled.

Conn's face became suddenly solemn.

"I know," he said. "We've been so, sort of, you know, *carefree,* up to now, I guess it seems a little odd to suddenly start talking about, ah, *us.*"

"Oh, no, Conn, dear. It's not odd. I think about *us* too."

"Ah, Mellen, that's good to hear."

"Have you doubted that I like you, Conn?"

"I knew you liked me . . . as a friend. I guess what I have wondered is, if I was"—Conn shrugged and dropped his eyes slightly—"more."

She blushed. Conn's face remained solemn. She put her hand across the table and rested it on his. She was quite red now.

"Of course . . . you are more than a . . . friend," she said. "I like you very much."

He raised his eyes slowly and met hers. They looked at each other for a moment.

"Good," Conn said. "I'm glad."

Their eyes held. Conn waited. He'd learned patience in Kilmainham Jail. The lesson had been valuable. He drank some coffee. She turned her attention to the eggs, eating properly, taking small bites, her back straight, bending forward slightly from the waist, her left hand in her lap. *Proper upbringing.* Conn drank some more coffee. Mellen took a tiny bite off the corner of a piece of toast and chewed and swallowed and patted her lips carefully with her napkin.

"How could you not know that I care about you, Conn?"

Conn put the coffee cup down. He nodded gently.

"I know. It's my own foolishness. But you're so attractive, and I'm just an immigrant Paddy copper."

"Oh, Conn, don't be silly. You're the handsomest man I know, and you're very learned. And my father says you are the best detective in Boston."

Conn shrugged a little. And smiled, letting the glint of laughter show in his eyes.

"Well, maybe in Boston," he said. And they both laughed. "I'm a bachelor, I know, with little experience, and it makes me foolish; but I guess that it scares me when you don't show your feelings."

She was silent as she thought about this. He waited calmly. She frowned, and he admired how the little cleft appeared between her eyebrows.

"We do kiss," she said.

"Like sister and brother," Conn said.

"Mother of mercy, Conn. I've not known you more than a month. I try to be proper."

"Of course you do," Conn said. "And you should. But my heart isn't as wise as my head, and you're very beautiful."

She smiled then, and blushed again, and put her hand once more on top of his.

"I do like you, Conn, very much. And I have strong feelings too, God help me. But I don't wish to give in to them. I don't wish to be sinful."

Conn put his other hand on top of hers, and stroked it gently.

"Of course not," Conn said. His smile was affectionate. "I'm just a foolish, fearful bachelor. Don't be paying me any mind."

"You're not foolish, Conn. You're very dear," Mellen said.

And Conn smiled at her some more.

Conn

They went to Braves Field on a Saturday afternoon. They rode the streetcar out Commonwealth Avenue to Gaffney Street and walked down to the field with its very un-Boston stucco façade and serial archways. Fenway Park, where the Red Sox played, was appropriately New England with an ornamented brick front on Jersey Street. From the outside, Braves Field looked Californian to Conn, though he'd never been to California.

The Dodgers were in town and the crowd on a bright, hot August afternoon was large. Mellen held Conn's arm as they pushed through the jam around the entry gates to the press entrance. A uniformed usher winked at Conn, tipped his hat to Mellen, and waved them on through.

"You don't have to pay?" Mellen said.

Conn shook his head.

"Is it because you are a policeman?"

"I did a favor," Conn said as they walked to their seats.

"Well, you must have done a lot of them, because everyone seems to know you."

"I try to be kind," Conn said.

"You're softhearted like my father," Mellen said.

"Not a bad fault," Conn said gently.

"Not a fault at all," Mellen said.

They had box seats along the first-base line. They had peanuts and scorecards. Conn tilted his straw boater forward to shield his eyes. Mellen wore a white visor, to keep the sun off her face.

"This is not a tennis match," Conn said with a smile.

Mellen laughed.

"I burn so easily," she said. "And I get all freckly even if I don't burn."

"That's not freckles," Conn said. "That's an Irish tan." He patted her knee gently.

Conn had never played baseball, and had never fully come to like it in nine years, but he wanted to distance his Irish past and few things were more American. He knew all the teams and players, and who hit well and how the game was played. Mellen had never been to a game.

"Are these good teams, Conn?"

"Dodgers are so-so," Conn said. "The Braves are bad."

"Who's that little player, there?" Mellen said.

"Rabbit Maranville," Conn said. "He's playing shortstop."

"He looks like a little boy."

The pitchers were Socks Seibold for the Braves and Dazzy Vance for the Dodgers. There were no runs until the sixth inning, when Babe Herman hit a home run into the jury box in right field and the Dodgers won, one to nothing.

They rode the streetcar back through Kenmore Square where it dipped underground and rumbled under Commonwealth Avenue and parts of the Boston Common. It stopped at Park Street station, and they got off.

They came out of the underground into the glaring late afternoon sun, and walked, holding hands, down across the Common toward the Public Garden. To their right the golden dome of the State House gleamed hotly in the August heat.

"When's the last time you rode a swan boat?" Conn said.

"I don't think I ever have," Mellen said. There was a fine sheen of sweat on her forehead, and her face was red. Conn too felt the sweat under his shirt, and his gun, worn back of his right hip, under his seersucker coat, felt heavy.

"Well, we'll do it," Conn said. "And then maybe we'll stop at Bailey's for a soda."

They glided slowly around the small lagoon on the pontooned pedal boats with a realistic oversized swan concealing the pedal apparatus. The young man pedaling the boats looked as if he were riding the swan. There were several other passengers, mostly children. Everyone fed the ducks who followed the swan boats around the lagoon like tugs escorting a transatlantic liner.

The children tried to fool the ducks with peanut shells, but the ducks paid no attention.

"How do they know the difference?" Mellen said.

"Ducks are smarter than they look," Conn said.

"That's good," Mellen said, and leaned her head against Conn's shoulder.

The sun was still bright but had moved farther west and the shadow of Beacon Hill began to move shade across the Beacon Street side of the Public Garden. When they left the swan boats they walked to a bench in the shade and sat. Conn put his arm around Mellen's shoulder.

"What is it you'll be wanting to do now, my fair colleen?" Conn said.

"You did promise me a soda at Bailey's."

"I did."

"Well, we could go up there and do that, and then we could go to my house."

"And sit on the piazza with your parents?" Conn said. "And rock, and say, 'Bejaysus it's hot'?"

"My father would never let you use the Lord's name like that in his house."

"Not even on the piazza, when, bejaysus, it *is* hot?"

Mellen rubbed her cheek against Conn's shoulder.

"Not even then," she said. "But it's all right. They're not home. They went up to Nahant for the weekend."

"And left you home alone?"

"My sister and her husband live downstairs. Besides, I wouldn't go."

"Why not?"

"You know why not," Mellen said. "I wanted to see you."

"Well, you got your wish," Conn said. "And what'll we do at your house? Just you and I alone? With your sister downstairs?"

"We'll sit on the piazza," Mellen said, "and rock and say, 'Bejaysus it's hot.' "

Mellen began to giggle, and Conn laughed.

"Well," Conn said. "Let's start with the soda."

And they stood and walked hand in hand back up across the Common toward Tremont Street.

Conn

Mellen lived upstairs in a three decker on K Street in South Boston which her father owned. It had gray clapboard siding, and an open porch off the back of each of the first two floors. Mellen's sister lived with her husband and small child on the first floor. Mellen, her mother, and her father lived on the second floor. The third floor was unfinished, except for Mellen's bedroom.

It was a narrow house, two rooms wide and three rooms deep. There was a small den. The dining room was to the right. Off the dining room was a front parlor with an upright piano in it. The parlor was never used. The French doors connecting it to the dining room were always closed, and in the winter it was left unheated.

The kitchen, with its big cast-iron stove, was the heart of the house. All the rooms connected to it except the parlor. Mellen's parents slept in a bedroom off the back corner of the kitchen. There was a pantry with an icebox and a soapstone sink and next to it the bathroom. There was a huge table in the kitchen covered in oilcloth, surrounded by chairs. There was a big leather rocker, a daybed, and a broad expanse of linoleum-covered floor. The walls were half wainscoted in narrow pine boards, installed vertically, and stained a dark walnut. Above the daybed was a picture of Jesus holding his robe open to reveal his bright red heart. The room smelled of kerosene, and when the stove was in use there would be a periodic burp from the kerosene bottle as it fed fuel to the stove.

Under the overhead light an easel was set up. On it was an unfinished oil painting of an idealized mountain scene, a small lake in a declivity among uniform mountains. The smell of the oil paints mixed with the kerosene; and the scent of cigar smoke insisted through both smells.

The windows had been closed all day, and the house reeked with heat. Mellen hurried about opening windows.

"You wouldn't have a drink in the house, would you?" Conn said.

"Yes. My father keeps some," she said. "My mother doesn't like it, but Pop likes his jar of whiskey."

She went to a broom closet on the wall near the dining room and rummaged behind some mops and brought out a bottle of Jameson's Irish whiskey.

"We don't have any soda," she said.

"Water'll be fine," he said. He went to the stained oak icebox and chipped ice off the big block in the top with an icepick. He put the ice in a water glass, added whiskey, and cold water from the water bottle in the icebox.

"Would you care for a dram?" he said.

Mellen shook her head hurriedly.

"Oh, no, no. I really shouldn't."

Conn looked at her with his head tilted and his eyes smiling.

"Shouldn't you, now, Goodie Two Shoes? And should I be drinking alone?"

"I sometimes wonder, Conn, if you don't do everything alone," she said. "But . . ." She sighed a little and got herself a glass and held it out while he put a splash of whiskey in the bottom. He added ice for her, and water.

They took their drinks out onto the back piazza and sat on the spare kitchen chairs that furnished it. Below them was a small patch of board-fenced backyard. There was a little brown grass and a lot of bare spots. To the left at the end of a narrow drive-way was a cinder-block garage. Across from them were the piaz-zas on the back of the three-decker on the next street.

Pigeons who roosted under the eaves above them were still busy and the noise they made was comforting. The summer evening was coming on. It wasn't dark yet, but there was a blue-ness to the light that softened the ugly houses and gentled the heat. They sat quietly. Conn put his hand out and she took it and held it in her lap. Conn raised his glass to her and she touched it with hers and they drank.

The blue air darkened, and the sun went down, the sound of pigeons quieted. Conn refreshed their glasses. When they drank, the soft sound of the ice in the glasses seemed lyrical in the blue evening.

"You date other men, Mellen?"

"Of course, lots. But none since I've met you."

"I figured you were popular."

"Actually, what I said is not quite true," Mellen said. "I dated lots of boys. You are the first man."

Conn smiled in the darkness.

"There must be many women in your life, Conn."

"Not lately," Conn said. He allowed a tinge of sadness to show in his voice. "There was a woman once, but . . ." His voice trailed off.

"Did she hurt you?"

"Yes."

"Oh, Conn."

She squeezed his hand.

"Was it a long time ago?"

"Yes."

"In Ireland?"

"Yes."

"Oh, Conn, you can forget her. I'll help you forget her."

"Yes," Conn said, his hand lying still in her lap. "Yes, you will."

He drank, and turned toward her.

"You have."

She brought his hand up to her face and rubbed it against her cheek and kissed the back of it.

"I'm glad, Conn. I want to make you happy."

She finished the small remnant of her drink.

"I do make you happy, don't I?"

"Yes," Conn said softly.

He took both their glasses and went to the kitchen and mixed fresh drinks. As he chipped ice in the pantry he could see his face in the darkened window. He grinned at himself. He started back through the hot kitchen with a glass in each hand, and she met him there, near the unfinished oil painting. She put both her arms wordlessly around him and tilted her head back. Holding the glasses carefully he bent his head forward and kissed her softly. She pressed her lips hard against his kiss and held it and slowly opened her mouth. Behind her back he shifted the two drinks into his right hand, holding the glasses by the rim, and squeezed her tight against him with his left arm. Her tongue touched his and withdrew and then touched his again and then thrust fully into his mouth. He bent her slightly backwards and reached out and put the two glasses on the table. Then he put both arms around her, and they kissed fiercely. Her mouth widened as they kissed and she arched her back a little and thrust her hips against him. She was gasping for breath, rubbing her hands up and down his back. He maneuvered her gently to the daybed and eased both of them down onto it.

"Conn," she said hoarsely, "we mustn't." She was rubbing her cheek against his as she said it, and her hands still moved up and down his back.

"Shhh."

Conn stroked her shoulder and arm. He moved to her breast. She stiffened momentarily, and then put her hand on top of his and pressed it harder against her. With his free hand Conn carefully unbuttoned her blouse. He slid his hand inside her blouse and then inside her brassiere.

"No," she whispered, "Conn, darling, we can't."

Conn kissed her and held the kiss. He could feel her heart pounding behind her breasts. She held his head with both her hands, kissing him harder. He put his hand under her skirt. She groaned and arched her pelvis.

"Conn," she gasped. "Oh, God, Conn. Darling. No."

He moved his hand gently, she moaned and then put both hands flat against him and pushed, wrenching herself away, and lay with her back half turned to him, her blouse unbuttoned, her breasts exposed, her skirt tangled around her hips.

"We can't," she said. "We can't. . . . We can't."

She spoke in choking gasps. Her shoulders heaved. She was shivering in the hot darkness as if it were cold. Conn sat up on the edge of the daybed without touching her. He was silent. She began to cry.

"I'm sorry," she said between sobs. "I'm sorry, Conn."

"Sure," he said.

"If we were married," Mellen said, tears tracing down her face. "We have to wait until we're married."

Conn didn't say anything. He stood and began to straighten out his clothes.

"This is too hard on a man," he said. "I'll have to go."

"No," Mellen said. She turned from her side onto her back. She seemed unaware of her undress. "Please, Conn."

"It's too much," Conn said. "You want to, I want to. You respond. I respond. You pull back. It's too much for me."

Mellen was crying hard, full body crying that exhausted her.

"Conn, please. I can't. We're both Catholic. You must understand. I promised God."

He stared down at her in the half-light. Her breasts spilled out of her brassiere. He had pulled her underpants down. She was naked to him. Her pale thighs entirely vulnerable.

"A man can't go through this," Conn said softly. "You'll have to choose. Me or God."

He waited for a moment. She was crying too hard to speak. Then he shrugged and turned and picked up his straw hat and walked toward the front door. He was in the den when she called after him in a strangled voice.

"Conn."

He had his hat on and his hand on the doorknob when she called after him again, her voice shaking.

"I will, Conn. I will."

In the dark hot den, Conn smiled to himself. He took the

straw hat off and set it carefully on the deal coffee table and turned and walked slowly back into the kitchen.

"So it's me?" Conn said.

She lay as he had left her, on the couch.

"God forgive me," she said.

He helped her strip naked on the daybed and then looked at her nakedness as he slowly took off his own clothes and lay down beside her. He explored her thoughtfully. He taught her what he knew, and helped her as she needed it. While they coupled she made so much noise, he wondered if the police would appear. And when it was over and they lay on the narrow daybed, their bodies slippery with sweat, beneath the sacred heart, she pressed her face against his neck and cried, and murmured over and over, "I love you." Conn lay quietly beside her and rubbed her back softly and smiled and imagined Hadley Winslow.

Conn

Knocko picked Conn up in front of the Brighton Avenue apartment house at quarter to eleven on a bright September morning.

"When I called in, Captain wanted to talk with you. I said you were taking a leak."

"You're a fine Irishman, Knocko."

"Who you fucking this morning?" Knocko said.

"Lovely little Protestant girl," Conn said. "Named Sheila Hinkley. Husband's a school principal."

Knocko put the car in gear, let the clutch out, and eased the car out into traffic.

"Don't think I ever fucked a Protestant," he said. "Imagine it's about the same."

"Funny, isn't it," Conn said. "It's always about the same, but you always want to try another."

"So tell me about it," Knocko said. "For Crissake, I drop you off, pick you up, and cover for you while you're fucking. At least I should get to hear about it."

Conn grinned.

"You should get out more, Knocko. Be good for you."

"Not if Faith caught me," Knocko said. "Sheila go down on you?"

Conn told him.

Knocko was full of admiration.

"And you're still fucking Mellen?"

"Sure," Conn said.

"Man, I was betting against you on that one," Knocko said. "I told Faith, she wouldn't believe me."

"All it takes is patience," Conn said.

"Well, Conn, darlin', it's a tireless worker you are."

"Every man needs a hobby," Conn said.

Knocko tapped the siren and drove through a red light at the merge of Brighton and Commonwealth avenues.

"Where we headed?" Conn said.

"Chinatown."

"The killing in the mah-jongg parlor?"

"Un-huh."

"Shit," Conn said. "I hate Chinatown."

"Good noodles," Knocko said.

"Yeah, and you can get your shirts done nice. But the fucking Chinamen won't talk to you and if you chase one he's into one of those buildings and it's like chasing a rat through a maze."

"So, we just let them shoot each other?"

Conn shrugged.

"Might as well," he said. "We never catch anybody anyway."

"Hey, put in the eight-hour day, draw the eight-hour pay," Knocko said. "At least we're fucking working."

"I've already put in two hard hours," Conn said.

Knocko grinned.

"It may have been hard, Conn-boy, but I wouldn't call it working."

"You would if you did as much of it as I do," Conn said.

"Nobody does as much of it as you do," Knocko said.

And he and Conn were both laughing as Knocko pulled in beside a hydrant on Tyler Street, and they got out.

Conn

There were two Chinatowns. There was the one that fronted on the streets, where tourists strolled; and the real one, where the Chinese lived close together. The real one existed in alleys, and passageways behind the restaurants bright with garish dragons, and the export-import businesses with fronts made to look like Asian temples. The Boston police supervised tourist Chinatown. The tongs ran the rest.

The mah-jongg parlor was a narrow building behind the Shanghai Dragon restaurant. It was little more than a shed with unpainted clapboard siding, and no windows. It was lit by a big industrial ceiling fixture. The room was nearly empty at midday when Knocko and Conn walked in. Knocko palmed his badge at the narrow, middle-aged Chinese man sitting on a stool near the door smoking a cigarette.

"You the head Chink?" Knocko said.

The Chinese man wore black pajamas, and a black skullcap over a pigtail. He looked at the two men with eyes as expressionless and flat as two ovals of black jade. Smoke drifted slowly from his nostrils as he exhaled. He said nothing.

"Listen, Moo Goo, a guy got murdered here the other night. What can you tell me about that?" Knocko said.

"No speak," the Chinese man said.

Conn was looking idly around the room. It was full of unmatched tables and chairs. At two of the tables there were mah-jongg pieces. At one of them a cigarette smoldered in an ashtray as if it had been hastily stubbed out.

"Yeah, sure," Knocko said comfortably, "none of you fucking speak. Unless of course somebody got some money, wants to buy your fucking sister, huh, Chop Chop? Then you speak like the fucking queen of England."

The Chinese man showed nothing. He didn't move except to smoke his cigarette. Conn put his hand under the edge of one of the mah-jongg tables and tipped it over, scattering the game on the floor.

"Oops," he said. And smiled at the Chinese man.

Knocko took a small shabby notebook from his shirt pocket and opened it and leafed through it, periodically moistening his huge thumb, until he found what he was looking for.

"Victim was guy named Pieng Wong, alias Joe Wong, alias Jo Jo Wood, male, Chinese, age twenty-three, alleged tong enforcer."

Conn walked aimlessly about the room, tipped over another table. The Chinese man smoked his cigarette.

"What we hear is his tong sent him around to talk to you 'cause you weren't paying the regular fee. And you weren't paying the regular fee because your tong said you didn't have to. And Jo Jo said you did have to pay and somebody from your tong settled the issue by putting a couple of slugs into Jo Jo's belly. We'd kind of like to know who that was. Whadda you hear, Ching-a-ling?"

"No speak."

Knocko shook his head and put the notebook back in his shirt pocket. The Chinese man put a fresh cigarette in his mouth and lit it with a kitchen match. He shook the match out, dropped it on the floor, and inhaled a long drag on the cigarette. He was letting the smoke out slowly when Knocko hit him backhanded across the face, and slapped the cigarette out of his mouth. The Chinese man's expression didn't change. He reached into his pocket and took out another cigarette.

From a door in the back of the mah-jongg parlor four other Chinese men appeared. They were young, and slim. Three wore the black pajamas and skullcap and pigtail. One of them wore a double-breasted blue pinstripe suit, gleaming black shoes, and a diamond stickpin in his red silk tie.

"Aha," Conn said. His face brightened as he saw them.

The one in the blue suit said, "My uncle doesn't speak English."

"And you do," Knocko said.

The four men spread out in a loose semicircle.

"I speak your language," the Blue Suit said. "The language you just spoke to my uncle."

"You threatening a police officer?" Knocko said.

The Blue Suit smiled. His three companions were expressionless. The uncle had a new cigarette lighted and was smoking, though his lip had begun to puff.

"Perhaps I am," the Blue Suit said.

"Then let's see," Conn said. His eyes were open wide and he smiled. "Let's get right to the threatening and see if you're any good, Chinaboy."

All four men looked at him silently. He walked several steps toward them, holding his coat open. The handle of his holstered service revolver showed, butt forward on the left side of his belt. His voice was pleasant.

"See, the gun's still in the holster. See how many shots you get off before I get it out."

"Conn," Knocko said.

"Fuck 'em, Knocko," Conn said. "Let's see which of us is afraid to die." He spoke again to the Blue Suit. "You crazy, Chinaboy? You as crazy as I am? You want to see? Let's see. We'll shoot. I been shooting since you were eating goo goo berries in Shanghai."

The Blue Suit spoke to Knocko.

"Your friend is not afraid to die?"

There was strain in Knocko's voice.

"No," Knocko said. "He ain't. He don't give a shit."

The Blue Suit nodded slowly.

"Fact is," Knocko said hoarsely, "he don't give a shit about anything, that I know about."

The Blue Suit nodded again and glanced at his companions.

"Hard to do business with someone not afraid to die," the Blue Suit said.

Conn held his coat back with his left hand. He held his right hand, fingers wide and slightly flexed, at waist level. His knees were relaxed, his feet comfortably balanced. He was smiling.

The Old Man, smoking his cigarette, said something in Chinese to the Blue Suit. The Blue Suit replied in Chinese, and the Old Man spoke again. The Blue Suit nodded. Conn shrugged his shoulders once to loosen them, and waited.

"My uncle says there may be another way."

"Like what?" Knocko said. His voice was tight.

The Blue Suit made a wait gesture with his hand. The Old Man spoke again. The Blue Suit nodded.

"My uncle says that Jo Jo's tong was trying to extort us. We cannot, of course, allow that."

"*We* meaning your tong," Knocko said. His voice was still gravelly with tension.

The Blue Suit shook his head.

"We are a social club," he said. "We play mah-jongg."

"Sure," Conn said with a grin, "and keep four shooters on the payroll in case somebody cheats."

"Our young men band together down here," the Blue Suit said. "The Boston Police Department rarely visits. We try to protect ourselves."

"So what's your deal?" Knocko said.

"We could pay you to come by once in a while and look in on us," the Blue Suit said. "To protect us from Jo Jo's tong."

Knocko relaxed visibly. His face widened into a friendly smile.

"Now, by Jesus Christ," Knocko said. "There's a thoughtful offer. Conn, don't you think that's thoughtful?"

"A darlin' offer," Conn said and smiled. He was still looking steadily at the Blue Suit. He still held his coat open, his right hand poised. "Though on the whole, Knocko, I'd just as soon shoot the little yellow bastards."

"Conn, it's a good offer, boy. We'll take it," Knocko said.

Conn shrugged.

"We'll take half what Jo Jo wanted. You have any more trouble from his tong, you give me a call. My partner and I will stop in now and then."

"And the case is closed on the unfortunate passing of Jo Jo?" the Blue Suit said.

"Absolutely," Knocko said. "Person or persons unknown. No evidence against anyone here."

"And your partner? Does he have any objection?"

"Conn? No, course not. I told you he don't give a shit, about anything. Am I right, Conn?"

"Sure," Conn said.

The Old Man got off his stool and went around behind the counter. He bent over out of sight and after a moment reappeared with a handful of currency. He counted it out in two equal piles onto the countertop.

Knocko counted with him, his lips moving silently. When it was done, Knocko picked up one pile and folded it in half and slid it into his pants pocket. He took the other pile and walked to Conn, and folded it in two and tucked it into Conn's shirt pocket. Then Knocko backed toward the door. Conn let his coat drop and turned his back on the four Chinese men and walked toward the door after Knocko. As he passed the Old Man, he said, "I thought you 'no speak.'"

There was no expression on the Old Man's face.

"I listen," he said.

Conn grinned as he left the mah-jongg parlor.

Conn

They were walking on the beach at the foot of K Street. He was still on shift, but she had called him in tears and said she had to see him. Her face was still tear streaked and her voice was shaky as they walked on the sand.

"You haven't called me in a week," she said.

"I know, Melly, I'm sorry. I have a heavy caseload right now, and"—he spread his hands—"what can I say, the time got away from me."

He leaned over to kiss her and she turned her head.

"It's not been the same since the first time, at my house, when we did it," she said.

"It's never the same twice, Mel, but it's elegant, every time."

She shook her head.

"It's like, once you got me," she said, "you could cross another one off the list, and start looking for the next virgin."

Conn gazed calmly out at the ocean that moved brightly in the early fall sunlight, the waves coming rhythmically in onto the beach without surcease. They walked well above the linear detritus of seaweed and driftwood that marked the high tide line in the sand. He never had understood why people liked to walk on the beach. The sand made for hard walking as it shifted beneath his footfall. Some of it got in his shoes. When she was through he'd have to take his shoes off and empty them out.

She had begun to cry again as they walked. She made no effort to stop the tears, or to cover her face. The beach was empty. There was no one to see her.

Conn was courteous.

"Should we stop seeing each other, Mel?"

She stopped and turned to him, her face wet, her eyes puffy.

"I missed my period," she said. Her voice was thick with crying.

Conn nodded gravely. He waited. She didn't say anything else.

"Have you seen a doctor?"

"Yes."

Conn waited another moment. Again she didn't speak.

"Ah," Conn said finally.

"I couldn't go to our doctor. I put on my mother's wedding ring, she never wears it, and went up to Lynn. They said I was pregnant."

"Yes," Conn said.

"You have to marry me."

"Have you thought about an alternative?"

She shook her head violently, her eyes squeezed nearly shut. She wasn't looking at him now. She was looking down, at the indifferent beach.

"No," Conn said. "Of course not. Does the judge know?"

She shook her head.

"You have to marry me right away," she said.

Conn nodded slowly, as if to himself, and shrugged.

"Sure," he said. "Why not?"

Conn

It was midafternoon, at a speakeasy on Chandler Street where the cops went. Conn and Knocko were drunk at the bar. There were pool tables and a detective from vice was playing pool by himself, stopping occasionally to drink beer from the bottle. The soft click of the balls made most of the noise in the almost empty room.

"I know you almost since you got here," Knocko was saying. "I been your partner five years now."

"Seems longer," Conn said.

Knocko ignored him.

"And I don't fucking understand you any better than I did when you got off the fucking boat with a brogue like a Kerry fishmonger."

The vice detective tried to put the seven ball in the corner pocket and missed and swore to himself as if it mattered.

"Nothing to understand," Conn said.

"You don't think so," Knocko said. He drank some whiskey. "You don't think so. Take the time in Chinatown, in the mah-jongg parlor. You remem'er that."

Conn nodded.

"We got five chinks want to give us money to go away, tough chinks, with guns, and you don't want the money. You want to shoot it out. You wanna help me unnerstan' that?"

Conn shrugged.

"I got a wife, and about two hundred kids," Knocko said. "And you want me to shoot it out with five chop-chops in some fucking mah-jongg parlor. For what? That's what I don't get. For fucking what?"

"For nothing."

"For nothing. Isn't that darlin', for nothing. Instead of pocketing couple hundred bucks a week, I can take five in the belly and bleed to death in a fucking mah-jongg parlor. What's wrong with you, Conn? I'm serious. I wouldn't prob'ly ask if I wasn't drunk. But what the hell is wrong with you?"

"Unlucky in love, Knocko."

"You mean Mellen? For Crissake, you just got married."

"It's not Mellen."

The vice detective kissed the nine ball into a side pocket and set himself up for the ten ball in the corner. He laughed, and took a pull from an unlabeled brown beer bottle.

"Conn, Goddammit, if I'm gonna get shot because of you I want to know why."

Knocko pointed a thick forefinger at Conn's chest.

"Is there anything in there? Is there anything scares you, or makes you happy, or does anything?"

Conn took a deep swallow of whiskey. He felt it move inside him, spreading through him the way it did. He listened to the click of the balls on the pool table.

"No, there isn't," Conn said softly.

There was a sound in Conn's voice that Knocko had never heard. Suddenly, Knocko didn't know what to say. The two men sat silently. The vice detective finished his solitary pool game. He put his cue stick away, drank the rest of his beer, racked the balls, and left. The bartender was at the other end of the bar reading a newspaper. Conn and Knocko were alone.

"I was in love," Conn said. "She turned me in to the English."

"During the troubles."

Conn nodded. He was looking at his reflection in the mirror behind the bar.

"And that's it? That's why you don't care about anything? I mean, I ain't trying to tell you it was nothing, but, Conn, people get over things."

"I'm over it," Conn said. "I stopped caring about it a long time ago. But it was so hard to stop caring about her that I had to stop caring about everything. You understand that?"

Knocko shrugged. "So what's that got to do with wanting to shoot the Chinamen?"

Conn stared into his whiskey glass, turning it slowly in his hands.

"I won't let anybody threaten me," he said. "One of the rules. You got no feelings, rules get to be important. You know?"

"You ever have any fun?" Knocko said.

"Sure I have fun. I fuck, I drink, I like a good meal."

"Nothing else?"

"That's about it."

"How about Mellen?" Knocko said.

Conn shrugged.

"You knock her up?" Knocko said.

Conn nodded.

"Christ," Knocko said. "I coulda sent her someplace. You didn't have to fucking marry her."

Conn shrugged again.

"I know," he said.

"So why did you?"

"Why not?" Conn said.

Knocko was silent. Conn was silent, staring at his drink.

"That woman," Knocko said finally. He didn't look at Conn. He looked instead at the mirror. "The one in Ireland . . . That woman killed you, Conn."

"I know."

Conn raised his head slowly. Two tears ran silently down his face. They both saw the tears in the bar mirror.

"Oh, shit," Knocko said.

1994
Voice-Over

"Knocko said Conn wasn't really on the take," I said. "Knocko was, and proud of it; but he says Conn didn't really care about taking money or not taking money. When Knocko worked up some graft, Conn would take some, the way you might share some popcorn if it was offered. But he never seemed interested.

"Marrying Mellen didn't change him any."

"No," Grace said. "I imagine not."

"Mellen became somebody he serviced as necessary, and other women was where he put his money. I guess he didn't solicit graft, that was Knocko's deal, but stylish womanizing was expensive. This was during the Depression, remember, and a guy with a little money could buy a lot of things. He could take them to the air-conditioned movie theater. He could take them to eat at Locke-Ober's. He could give some stumblebum a dollar for an apple. He could afford a room in a good hotel for seductions. There were about five million people unemployed the year my father was conceived, but Conn Sheridan was not one of them. He had steady work."

"My father was born, a little, ah, premature on the seventeenth of September, 1932. Conn took Mellen to the hospital about four o'clock in the morning and then sat and read stories in *Black Mask* magazine, which he probably found pretty funny, being an actual cop. Nothing happened, so he left and went down on Canal Street to an all-night movie and watched Paul Muni in *Scarface*, which he probably found pretty funny too and came out and had some eggs and bacon in a diner under the elevated and went back to the hospital where Mellen was lying in bed crying and feeding his son, Augustus Sheridan, my father, who at the time weighed just under seven pounds, as befits a kid slightly premature. . . . I like to think Conn felt something, that he saw his son and felt something for the first time since Hadley turned him in. . . . But I don't know if he did or not. Gus says he thinks Conn tried. But . . . what I know is that Mellen could never really see Gus the way new mothers are supposed to see new babies. He was an emblem of her sin. And from the day of his birth he never looked at her face and saw joy."

1935
Conn

Conn lay quietly on his back on his side of the bed, his hands behind his head.

"We haven't done it, since before Gus was born," Conn said.

Mellen was in the bed beside him. It was a big bed. There was space between them.

"I know."

"Kid's three years old," Conn said.

"I'm sorry," Mellen said.

The ornamental tops of the bedposts always reminded Conn of asparagus tips. The posts themselves were shaped like fluted baseball bats. Conn used to think what fine bludgeons they would make, if you sawed them off.

"Sure you are," Conn said. "So's my pecker."

"I wish you wouldn't talk like that," Mellen said.

"Or think like that," Conn said without anger. "Or be like that."

Mellen lay quite stiffly on her side of the bed, her face turned away from Conn. Her rosary beads lay in a neat gather on her bedside table.

"What we did before we were married was sinful," she said. Her voice was flat.

"A couple of Our Fathers should take care of it," Conn said, "a nice act of contrition."

"Please," Mellen said, "don't mock the Church."

"Hard not to," Conn said. "All the pantywaist priests looking to diddle the altar boys."

Mellen turned onto her side, away from Conn, and put her hands over her ears.

"May God forgive you," she said. Her voice seemed frozen.

"He might," Conn said quietly. "You won't. You'll never forgive me. Hell, you'll never forgive yourself."

"Our marriage is founded on mortal sin, Conn. Our son is the product of mortal sin."

"And you won't forgive him either, will you?"

With her back to him and her knees drawn up, Mellen was gracelessly angular under the covers. She clutched the bedspread about her shoulders, as if she were cold, though the June night outside their bedroom was very mild.

"What you can't stand," Conn said thoughtfully, as if he were talking to himself, "is that you liked it."

She made no sound.

"That's the dirty little secret," Conn said musingly, "and I found it out. You like to fuck, saints-preserve-us. And I'm the guy knows it. And I'm the guy proved it to you. You're married to me because you like to fuck."

Mellen stayed rigidly on her side with her back to him, the spread held tightly around her.

"And Gus, the poor little bastard, reminds you every day that he's here because you like to fuck."

Mellen began to pray to herself in a soft flat voice.

"Hail Mary, full of grace . . ."

"You can never fuck again, but it won't go away," Conn said.

"The Lord is with thee . . ."

"The feeling will always be there."

"Blessed art thou amongst women . . ."

"The hot feeling down at the bottom of your stomach when you think about it."

"And blessed is the fruit of thy womb, Jesus."

Conn had nothing else to say. He lay still on his back in the warm night and listened to his wife saying Hail Marys repetitively, and remembered his time with Hadley Winslow.

1942
Gus

Conn bought some sea worms and rented a rowboat and took Gus fishing in Pleasure Bay. The water was a hard, clear gray, as Conn rowed out from the dock. Occasionally there would be a thin iridescent oil slick, remote evidence of a tanker sunk in the North Atlantic. Gus was always excited by an oil slick. It was not bloodthirstiness, Conn knew, so much as the sense of connectedness Gus felt to the large events of the world. It was the same sense that the sixteen-year-old Conn had felt outside the GPO, Easter week, sniping at British soldiers. It had been a long time since Conn felt connected to anything.

Conn shipped his oars, dropped the anchor, felt it catch. He watched Gus thread the squirming sea worm onto his hook, carefully. Gus was a little scared about the pincers. But he didn't say anything. Conn made no offer to help. Hooks baited, they fed the lines out over the gunwales of the rowboat. They were after flounder. Each had a lead sinker on the end of the line, and several baited hooks about ten inches above the sinker. When the sinker hit, each of them jigged the line to make sure that the sinker was just touching, and kept it that way, just bumping the bottom, the line held in gentle tension over the crooked forefinger.

Conn was home no more than he had to be. Fishing was one of the few things they did together. Until Gus made his first communion they used to fish every Sunday morning while Mellen was at Mass. Now that Gus went with her, the fishing happened at odd moments.

A harbor patrol boat chugged past them. One of the crewmen studied them as he went by.

"Why are they looking at us?" Gus said.

"Make sure we're not German saboteurs," Conn said, "sneaking in to blow up the L Street Bathhouse."

"Honest to God?"

Conn shrugged. "Sort of."

Gus watched the patrol boat ease out of sight past Castle Island.

"I wish I was in the war," Gus said. "You?"

"It can be fun," Conn said.

"Were you in a war?"

Conn smiled and didn't say anything.

"Well, were you?" Gus said.

Conn's face hardened in a look Gus had come to recognize. Conn shook his head. There was a tug on Gus's line. He jerked it upward to set the hook, and began to haul it in, hand over hand, feeling the fish struggle at the other end. Gus was careful to hold it clear as he brought it into the boat, the way Conn had shown him, so as not to knock it loose on the gunwales. He unhooked it, and put it flopping in the bucket, rebaited the hook, and dropped the line in again, letting it uncoil from the floorboards where it had fallen. The line tangled. Conn watched silently while Gus struggled with the snarl. The boy made no progress and finally looked at his father.

"Can you do it?" he said.

Conn shook his head.

"I can't get it undone," Gus said.

"Then you can't fish," Conn said.

Tears began to form in Gus's eyes.

"How come you won't help me?" he said.

Conn was silent for a moment. The sun was behind Gus and Conn had to squint into it to look at him. Seagulls rode the low waves around the boat, waiting for the discarded bait, or fish guts, or sandwich crusts that they had learned to expect from fishermen. The birds seemed entirely comfortable on the ocean surface, moving on it as easily as the ocean itself moved. On it, in it, yet free to fly away.

"You might as well learn it now, on stuff that doesn't matter much," Conn said finally. "You got to untangle your own stuff. You get snarled up with other people and . . ." Conn didn't finish. He seemed to be looking past Gus into the sun, his eyes nearly shut.

Gus felt a little scared and a little excited because he realized his father was talking to him about real things as if he were an adult.

"What do you mean?" Gus said.

"You're on your own, kid. Sooner you know that, the sooner you get used to it."

"Ma says God will take care of me," Gus said.

He didn't care so much what the answer was, he didn't want the conversation to end. It was rare when his father talked about much of anything.

"Your mother thinks God's a lot more interested than I've found him to be," Conn said.

"Ma says I should be a priest," Gus said.

Conn was silent for a moment, squinting at the boy. Then he laughed.

"You won't be no priest," Conn said.

As they talked Gus worked at the tangled line.

"I don't know what I'm going to be," Gus said.

"That'll sort of take care of itself," Conn said.

"Ma prays for stuff," Gus said. "She says if you pray hard and you're good, God gives you what you pray for."

"Sure," Conn said.

"You believe that, Dad?"

"No," Conn said. "But maybe I was just never good enough."

1946
Conn

When Conn arrived at the church there were two patrol units from the City Square Station, and an assistant medical examiner. The victim was a little girl.

"I'd guess about twelve years old," the ME said to Conn. "Where's Knocko?"

Conn didn't know any of the patrol cops. He put his badge on his lapel where it would show.

"In court," Conn said. "Be there all week."

They were standing in the drab cellar of the church. One of the patrol cops was talking to the priest. Conn looked down at the little girl on the floor under the table. The skirt of her plaid school uniform was bunched around the waist. Except for her brown strap shoes and white ankle socks she was naked below the waist. There was blood in her hair and pooled under her head. There was a trace of blood on her right thigh. A brown teddy bear wearing a plaid bow tie nestled in the crook of her left arm.

"What's your name?" Conn said to the patrol cop next to him.

"Shaughnessy, Sergeant," the young cop said. He avoided looking at the girl.

"Conn Sheridan. You find her here?"

"Yeah. Under the table. The tablecloth was hanging down. Looks like somebody tried half-assed to hide her."

"Who discovered the body?"

The young cop nodded at the priest.

"Father was down here getting ready for some kind of meeting."

Conn glanced around the room.

"She been raped?" Conn said.

"Some sort of penetration," the ME said. "There's some blood."

"Usually is, kids her age," Conn said. "What killed her?"

"Gunshot, I assume," the ME said. "We'll know more once we get her on a table."

"Recent?" Conn said.

"Not today," the ME said, "more likely yesterday. Something special, though. There's tooth marks on her right buttock."

"He bit her on the ass?" Conn said.

"That would be the technical description," the ME said.

Conn nodded and looked at the young cop.

"Do we know who she is?"

The young cop shook his head.

"Father says she may be in his parish. Says he doesn't recognize her, but it's a big parish."

"And he's probably a busy man. Call the station, see if she's been reported missing. Anyone seen her underpants?" Conn said.

The young cop shook his head and headed for a phone. Conn asked the other cops. They hadn't seen her underpants.

"Look for them," Conn said.

One of the cops said, "Maybe she didn't have any, Sergeant."

"Sure she didn't. A ten-year-old Irish Catholic girl from Charlestown, in her school uniform, going to a meeting in the church. Sure she wouldn't be wearing underwear."

"How come you know she's Irish Catholic?" the cop said.

"Because I'm a fucking detective sergeant," Conn said. "Find the underwear."

The assistant medical examiner straightened. "You finished with her, Conn?"

"Not yet," Conn said. "Tell the wagon to stand by."

The assistant medical examiner started for the door.

He said, "Give them a shout when you're ready."

Conn turned to the priest.

"What do you know, Father?"

The priest shook his head. He was round shouldered and dark haired with a permanent shadow of a beard. His cheeks bore a fine filigree of broken blood vessels, and his dark eyebrows were very heavy. When he was close to him Conn realized that the priest was not even middle aged yet.

"You can't identify the victim."

The priest shook his head again.

"When's the last time the room was used?"

"This afternoon. CCD meeting here ended at four-forty."

"So she arrived here after that," Conn said. He was talking to himself, but the priest answered him anyway.

"Yes, she would have had to."

"What was the meeting you were preparing for?"

"The meeting? . . . oh, the meeting . . . we called it VASE —Volunteer After School Enrichment. College students would come in to tutor poor children. I've canceled tonight's meeting, of course."

"How often did it meet?"

"Every weekday."

"Same personnel?"

"Excuse me?"

"Same college kids teach the same poor kids every day?"

"No. It's a popular program. We have different teachers and different students every day."

"Anybody else use the space?"

"No, not really. It's quite small. Mostly we use the Knights Hall on Rutherford Ave."

"How old were the kids?"

"Grammar school, ages six to twelve."

"You got a list?"

"A list? Of what? The students?"

"Students and tutors."

"Yes. I'm sure we do. I have an enrollment book in the church office."

"Go get it."

"Now?"

"Right now."

"Of course," the priest said. He went across the small basement and up the stairs toward the church above.

Conn stood silently looking at the crime scene. The room was low ceilinged. The stone walls had been painted yellow. There were folding chairs stacked against the far wall, and several tables with the legs folded leaning against the near wall. Small windows near the ceiling let in a little light, but most of it came from the two fixtures with green metal shades that hung from the ceiling on short cords.

The young cop came back into the room.

"Girl fits her description reported missing last night, about eleven o'clock," the young cop said. "Parents last saw her yesterday morning when she left for school."

"Name?"

"Maureen Burns," the young cop said.

Conn continued to look silently at the crime scene. One of the patrol cops came back. Nobody could find the girl's underpants.

"Must have taken them," Conn said. "Souvenir."

The priest came down the stairs with a brown-covered spiral-bound notebook in his hand. He gave it to Conn. Conn opened it and glanced down the names. One of them was Maureen Burns.

"Do you think it's one of the students?" the priest said. He seemed less vague than he had been. Conn smelled the whiskey on his breath.

"Yeah."

"Is that why you want to see the list?"

"The cellar of the local church is not the first place you think of if you're planning to molest a ten-year-old girl, you know?"

"God have mercy," the priest said softly.

Conn smiled faintly.

"Hasn't shown much so far, has he, Father?"

"No."

Conn had expected a cliché about the Lord's mysterious ways. The priest was better than he'd expected.

"Go talk to the parents," Conn said to the young cop.

"I gotta tell them?" the young cop said.

"Take the priest," Conn said.

Gus

Gus always liked how high the ceilings were in church. Though the Mass bored him, he liked the feeling of elevated space in the room, and the vague participatory sense of tunneling back through time. The feeling was strongest at Christmas, when Gus could feel an almost tangible connection between himself and the manger in Bethlehem.

His mother kneeling beside him seemed the exact opposite. Hunched ecstatically over her rosary, she appeared to shrink in upon her spirit, hugging the sacred mysteries into her imploded self. Tight, narrow, impacted, her faith intensified by reduction, she fumbled her beads throughout the Mass like an amulet, even as she listened to the sermon, nodding her head in rapt assent.

Gus liked the jeweled colors of the stained glass too, although the bright windows always seemed to him like a painting of a painting, the figures in them rendered from statues. *On the other hand, where you going to get a real saint to pose?*

He noticed when he was quite young that no one in the church art appeared happy, not the statues, nor the stained glass, nor the carvings, nor the bas-relief stations of the cross. As a small boy he simply noticed this, as he got older he wondered about it. Shouldn't they be happy? What about eternal bliss? He wanted to ask his mother about it, but he didn't. He knew intuitively that the answers would not make sense to him, and that the question itself would be condemned.

Gus's father never came to Mass. Not even Gus's first communion. Gus avoided the subject with his father because Conn always seemed scornful of it, and it made Gus feel disloyal to his mother. He looked at her now, kneeling beside

111

him, her eyes shut, her hands fondling the rosary, her lips moving. *At least she's got something to do,* Gus thought. The Latin Mass was largely meaningless to him. He hadn't been to parochial school. On the other hand he'd gone regularly to catechism on Saturday mornings, while the Protestants slept, without learning to understand the Mass. And most of his friends who had been to parochial school didn't know what was going on in church either.

Sometimes he stared at Deirdre Mulvoy's frolicsome bottom, kneeling in front of him. Usually she wore her school uniform, but on Sundays she dressed up for church, and the dress, which Gus thought was silk, hugged her backside. Looking at her made Gus feel hot. He feared he would go to hell. He looked away, at the windows, at the stations of the cross, at the languishing Jesus crucified above the altar. But still he felt the hotness, and inevitably he would look back at Deirdre's bottom, as she knelt in prayer.

His mother received communion every Sunday, and insisted that Gus receive with her. Which meant that every Saturday he had to go to confession. Usually Gus had only the same venial sins to confess, that he had confessed to last week. He would enter the darkened booth to speak to the priest sitting invisibly beyond the partition, the curtained window between them. Gus would kneel, and say the words.

"Bless me, Father, for I have sinned. My last confession was a week ago, and these are my sins. I have impure thoughts, sometimes. I swear. I disobey my parents, sometimes."

"Say three Our Fathers, and three Hail Marys, and make a good Act of Contrition," the priest would say from the dark.

And Gus would begin, "Oh, my God, I am heartily sorry for having offended thee . . ."

And the priest would say it along with him in Latin. When he finished he would leave the confessional, walk to the front of the church, kneel at the altar rail, and say three Our Fathers and three Hail Marys as carefully as he could, trying not to run the words together, smelling the permanent church smell of incense and empty space.

He always left the church feeling safe in the knowledge that if a truck were to run him down now, he would avoid the flames of hell.

Conn

Maureen Burns's father was a longshoreman. Her mother was a waitress. They identified the remains of their daughter, age ten years and seven months. The priest was unable to comfort them. Maureen's father said to the priest, "You pray, Father, all you fucking want to. But if I can find the son of a bitch I am going to kill him."

The priest glanced at Conn.

Conn said, "I got no problem with that."

The priest nodded slowly.

"God forgive me," the priest said. "I don't either."

Conn nodded a slight acknowledging nod at the priest, and turned and walked away, out of the morgue, along the drab corridor, out of City Hospital, into a bright April day. On Harrison Avenue, he sat in his parked car, with the window down, reading the coroner's preliminary report. The full autopsy would come now that the parents had ID'd the body.

The blood was the same blood type as the victim's. Evidence of penetration but, so far, no trace of semen. Cause of death was apparently the gunshot wound in her head. The progress of rigor indicated that she had probably been dead at least eight hours when she was discovered. If this was in fact the case, it meant she had been killed elsewhere and brought to the church basement. Conn put the report aside.

He took a folded sheet from his inside pocket and opened it. It was the names of the tutors that the priest had given him. It could have been someone else. It could have been a random killing. But it was hard to imagine the killer riding around with the corpse in the car until he found an open door in a strange church. It was pretty surely someone who knew the church. Could be the priest. But, the tutors were a good bet. There were fifteen college students on the list. Thirteen of them were girls. That figured—most boys didn't teach grammar-school kids. Except maybe child molesters. He didn't completely eliminate the girls. He'd heard of cases where the molester was a woman, but not often. Conn didn't take the idea very seriously. He licked the tip of his pencil and drew a line under the names of the two males: Alden E. Hunt, and Thomas J. Winslow, Jr.

Conn stopped breathing. The shock of the name jagged through him as if some interior fabric were ripping. Thomas J. Winslow, Jr., Harvard University, Cambridge, Mass. Conn took some air in slowly through his mouth, and let it out, and took in some more. Thomas J. Winslow, Jr. He knew it might not be Hadley's son. He knew there were many Thomas J. Winslows in the world who might send their children to Harvard. He'd seen the name in the papers now and then, though he never knew if it was the same Winslow or another Winslow, and he never wanted to. But he didn't know it wasn't Hadley's son. And if it were? This time it was thrust upon him. This time there was no way not to know. He felt his throat tighten. He felt his solar plexus clench. For a moment he felt disoriented, as if this Boston spring day were taking place in some alternative state of being, and he was a confused observer. The street blurred and he realized his eyes were tearing. He took in more air, and wiped his eyes, and wrote the number 1 beside Alden Hunt's name. No need to rush. Maybe Hunt was the guy. Beside Thomas J. Winslow, Jr., he wrote the number 2.

Conn

It was a Thursday morning. Knocko was back from court, and he and Conn were drinking coffee in a diner on Kneeland Street.

"I'm in court for a week," Knocko said. "The jury convicts him. The judge suspends the sentence. And the asshole strolls without any time to do."

He took a bite of his doughnut.

"Shoulda shot the bastard when we grabbed him," Knocko said.

Conn nodded.

"Let's think about that," Knocko said. "We find the perp in that Charlestown killing."

Conn stared down at his coffee. It was in a thick white mug that was showing signs of age.

"I'm on that alone, Knocko," Conn said.

Knocko ate the rest of his doughnut. He drank some coffee and wiped his mouth with a paper napkin.

"Something I should know, Conn?"

Conn shook his head. Knocko drank the rest of his coffee, put the mug down, and stood. Conn stood with him. Knocko said, "Thanks, Vinnie," to the counterman and they left without paying.

From his desk, Conn made some phone calls. He learned that Alden Hunt was a member of the Tufts Glee Club and had been singing close harmony in Brunswick, Maine, during the time that Maureen Burns must have been killed. With his pencil stub, Conn drew a line through Hunt's name.

Conn talked with Thomas J. Winslow, Jr., in his room on the second floor of a Harvard dormitory on Memorial Drive.

"Conn Sheridan," he said when the boy opened the door. He

showed his badge. "Boston Police Department." He smiled. "Nothing to be nervous about, just a routine investigation."

The boy asked him in. He was an ordinary-looking boy. Pale blue eyes, round head, pale blond hair, pink face. Medium weight, medium height. Sturdy build.

Conn sat down on the edge of the bed. He took out a small notepad and opened it. He took out his stubby pencil. He didn't need the notebook. He never forgot anything. He rarely wrote anything down. But it disarmed the people he talked to, and he always took it out. He looked down at it as if to refresh his memory.

"Thomas J. Winslow, Jr., right?"

"Yes, sir."

Conn wrote it down just as if it were one name in many and he'd forget it if he didn't.

"Parents' names?"

Conn felt the phenomenon he had always felt when the stakes were mortal. He seemed to relax in upon himself. Like a hibernating animal whose metabolism slows to get it through the winter. His breath came easily and deeply. His shoulders and arms seemed supple, his spine relaxed. It was as if he were suddenly sensitized to the pull of gravity. The cop part of him seemed to be operating independently.

"My father is Thomas J. Winslow, Sr.," the boy said. "My mother's name is Hadley Winslow."

Through the front window Conn could see the river moving pleasantly eastward, flowing toward Boston Harbor where it would mingle with the Atlantic Ocean, into which, three thousand miles away, the River Liffey emptied.

"How old are you, Tom?"

"Eighteen."

Four years older than Gus. Conn scribbled the age in his notebook, as if it were important.

"Both your parents alive?"

"Oh, yes."

"Where do they live?"

The boy gave Conn an address on Beacon Hill.

"How come you don't live at home?"

"I wanted the campus experience. My parents thought I should have it."

Conn nodded.

"Brothers and sisters?"

"No, sir."

"Only child."

"Yes, sir."

Conn smiled at him.

"Me too," Conn said.

The boy seemed encouraged.

"What is this about, sir?"

Conn continued to smile.

"There was a murder, couple days ago. Found a girl dead in Charlestown, church basement."

The pinkness in the boy's face seemed to become blotchy. He started to speak and stopped and cleared his throat and tried again.

"Why are you asking *me* questions, sir?"

"Just routine background information," he said kindly.

The boy nodded jerkily. He seemed nearly paralyzed. The cop part of Conn thought, *Un-huh!*

"Routine stuff," Conn said nicely. "Things I need to know."

Conn leaned forward slightly and his voice became suddenly hard.

"Like did you shoot her before or after you bit her on the ass?"

The boy's face was very pale. His mouth opened wider and Conn could hear him gasping as if he weren't getting enough air. Then the boy stood up, took a step toward the door, and fainted.

Un-huh!

Conn

Conn put his notebook away in his inside pocket, and squatted beside the boy. He felt the boy's pulse. The pulse was strong. He checked to see if he'd swallowed his tongue. He hadn't. Conn stood and looked thoughtfully around the room. His calm was so deep, it was almost lassitude. Methodically he began to search the room.

As Conn searched, the boy on the floor stirred and opened his eyes. Conn continued. The boy looked blankly at him. Conn was neat in his search. He picked things up and put them back, carefully. The boy edged himself toward the wall, and wormed into a sitting position with his back against the wall. He stared around the room for a moment, then focused on Conn.

Conn's search technique was not linear. He had found over the years that most people hid things where you'd expect them to, so that it was more efficient to search a room in order of decreasing likelihood.

"What are you doing?" the boy said.

Conn didn't answer him or look at him.

"What are you looking for?"

Conn lifted the mattress off the iron bed frame. There was a pair of small white cotton underpants on the spring. Conn picked them up and let the mattress drop. He folded them carefully and slipped them into his coat pocket, and turned and looked at the boy.

"How did you get into Harvard?" Conn said.

The boy stared at him. The pallor was gone. He looked feverish. Conn smiled.

"I been a cop now twenty-four years," Conn said. "And you are the stupidest fucking pervert I've ever met."

"What do you mean? I don't know what you mean."

Conn shook his head sadly.

"You kill someone, and you stash her in a place where you'd be an automatic prime suspect. And then you keep the one piece of evidence that will sizzle your ass. Did you want to get caught?"

The boy climbed to his feet, his back still against the wall. His movements were slow. Conn knew how he felt. He remembered the claustrophobic weakness in his legs when they took him to Kilmainham Jail.

"I don't know what you mean."

Conn sat on the boy's desk, one foot on the floor, one foot on the desk chair. His coat was open and the butt of his service revolver showed. Conn nodded toward the bed.

"Sit down," he said. The boy hesitated against the wall. Conn saw his eyes move toward the door. It was too far. He'd have to go right past Conn. Conn knew he had no strength for it. He nodded toward the bed.

"Sit," Conn said.

The boy sat on the edge of the bed.

"You need a glass of water or anything?"

The boy shook his head.

"Tell me about it," Conn said softly. Looking at Hadley's son, the stillness seemed to fill him up, to spread through every capillary. He felt quiet, and very steady.

"What?" the boy said. His eyes were red, and he couldn't hold Conn's gaze.

"About Maureen Burns," Conn said softly. "About how you pulled down her pants and bit her on the ass and fucked her."

The boy began to cry. Conn continued to speak softly. His voice sounded kind.

"And killed her," Conn went on. "And where you did it. And why you dumped her in the church."

The boy's crying intensified.

"And what the teddy bear was for."

Conn smiled encouragingly.

"Stuff like that," he said.

The boy made no attempt to stifle the tears. He sat on the bed with his arms clutched in on himself, crying hard.

"You probably feel like you couldn't help it," Conn said. "Like you couldn't stop and when it got under way and she was weak and struggling you probably didn't want to stop because the feeling was there. Like a big surge, and then you bit her and that hurt and you fucked her and that hurt, and she was probably crying and then you were through and you didn't want to hear her crying. That's about how it went, isn't it? Everybody always assumes that guys like you kill the victim to cover it up. But that's not why, is it?"

The boy was sobbing, shoulders hunched, head down. Conn seemed not to hear him.

"You didn't want to listen to what she'd say about what you did," Conn said gently.

Then he was quiet and there was no sound in the room but the boy's hard crying. Conn waited, sitting perfectly still on the desk. The boy cried.

"I feel bad for you," Conn said after a while. "You go along and everything is fine and then something happens. You didn't plan it. You didn't mean it. You didn't really want it to happen. But it happens. Homicide in the commission of a felony. Murder one. Eighteen years old, and you'll be put to death before you're nineteen."

The boy was rocking now. Hunched and crying, hands still locked between his knees, he bent far forward and back, and forward and back.

"Wasn't what you had planned," Conn said. "Was it?"

"I didn't mean to," the boy gasped.

"I know you didn't," Conn said. "None of us mean to. But it happens, and we're stuck with it. How many little girls you molested?"

The boy shook his head.

Conn was patient. "Now don't bullshit me, Tom. I can't help you if you bullshit me."

The boy, still rocking, nodded his head.

"So how many?" Conn said.

"There were three others," the boy said. His voice was clogged and he spoke very fast. "That's all. Just three. I never hurt them."

"Good," Conn said. "You know their names?"

The boy shook his head.

"They know you?" Conn said.

"No."

Conn clasped his hands behind his head, and smiled.

"How nice," he said.

There was something in Conn's voice that the boy heard. He raised his head and looked at him.

"You got a place?" Conn said.

The boy nodded.

"Where?"

"Weston."

"You kill her there?"

"Yes." The boy's voice was thick with crying, and barely audible.

"Let's go take a look," Conn said.

"Now?"

"Yeah, now. You're in the machine now, kid, and the machine doesn't care about you."

"Yes, sir."

"You got one chance, Tom," Conn said.

The boy stared at him.

"Maybe I can fix it."

The boy waited.

"We'll need to talk with your mother."

"No."

"You've forfeited the right to say yes or no, Tom. Get used to it."

"You can fix it?"

Conn smiled at him. *A light in the darkness.*

"You can?"

"Maybe," Conn said. "First we'll look at your place. Then I'll talk with your mother."

Conn

In the center of Weston, invisible from the street, accessible through a locked gate, at the end of a narrow dirt driveway hidden by foliage, balanced beneath overarching trees, on the edge of a thin brook that ran on down through town and emptied into the Charles River, the ornate little house was as singular and alone as if it had been clapped together in the wilderness. Wisteria coiled unchecked over much of the house. There was a cupola on the roof, and a tiny siege tower at the southeast corner. The windows were bright with colored glass, and the wooden bridge over the brook was elaborately scrolled.

Conn parked in front of the overgrown porch.

"Who's this belong to?" Conn said.

"My dad," the boy said. On the ride from Boston, the boy had begun to attach. He had stopped crying. Conn was his only hope, his savior. He put all his confidence in Conn.

"He never uses it?" Conn said.

"No. He foreclosed it during the Depression and couldn't sell it, so he kept it. Then, when I got my license, my mom suggested I could use it as kind of a clubhouse. Place to keep my stuff."

The boy unlocked the front door, and they went in. The big living room was dominated at the far end by a floor-to-ceiling fieldstone fireplace. There was an overstuffed chair and a huge sofa, organized around the fireplace. There were half a dozen huge stuffed animals posed around the room. The floor was littered with fashion magazines and comic books. There was a half-empty bag of potato chips on the coffee table. On the fireplace mantel were two empty Coke bottles, and a half-wrapped Sky Bar. A Daisy Red Ryder model air rifle stood in a corner, near the fireplace. In a bookshelf built in beneath the front window were a collection of boys' books by Joseph Altsheler and Albert Payson Terhune and John Tunis.

"You kill her here?" Conn said.

The boy nodded earnestly.

"Where'd you get the gun?"

"It's my father's."

"What did you do with it afterwards?"

"I put it back."

"Clean it?"

"I don't know how."

"If you don't clean it after you use it you'll eventually pit the barrel."

"I didn't know that."

Conn didn't say anything. The room was quiet. It had a closed-up, unoccupied smell, made thicker by the dampness of the stream that ran close to the foundation.

"You know why you killed her?"

"No."

Conn nodded slowly, his eyes ranging over the silly room, a child's idea of a hunting lodge.

"What was the teddy bear for?"

"I don't know."

"Why'd you take her underpants?"

"I don't know." The boy was beginning to resent all these questions.

"Why'd you take her to the church?"

"I couldn't leave her here," the boy said with a faint hint of exasperation. *These things are self-evident,* his tone said.

"Why didn't you just dump her on the side of the road?" Conn said.

"I don't know."

Conn put his hands into his back pockets and stood looking at the smallish blond boy. He had barely any beard.

"No. Of course you don't," Conn said.

Conn

The Winslows lived in a big brick town house behind a black wrought-iron fence on Beacon Hill, set back from Mt. Vernon Street by a brick courtyard. Conn took a business card from his pocket.

"Give this to your mother, and tell her I'll see her alone," Conn said.

"What if she's not home?" her son said. His voice was thin and full of tremolo.

"I'll wait," Conn said.

A black maid let them in and showed Conn into the front room. It had floor-to-ceiling windows that looked out over the courtyard to the street. There was a green marble fireplace with an ornate walnut mantel. There were books on the shelves and leather chairs. A walnut inlaid radio and record console stood against the far wall.

While he waited, Conn stood with his hands in his pockets looking out the window. The house seemed to hum with silence. Outside the window a middle-aged couple walked ordinarily by on Mt. Vernon Street. When he had first come to Boston he had looked up Thomas Winslow in the phone book. There were seven of them. He didn't know the middle initial. And he had closed the phone book and put it away, the way a recovering alcoholic might put the unopened bottle back in the drawer. Now, standing in her front room, he felt as if the bottom had fallen out of his soul and all of him was in danger of draining away. The magnolia trees in the courtyard had begun to bud up, but it was much too early in April for them to do more than that. They wouldn't be showy until summer. By August they'd be nondescript. She would take a little while. She would have to deal with the shock of his name. He doubted the kid would tell her what he'd done, but here was a cop wanted to talk to her about him and that would distract her.

Conn knew he looked much the same as he had twenty-six years ago in Merrion Square. He hadn't gained weight. His hair was graying, but his face was unlined. He knew she wouldn't appear until she had arranged herself. He waited. He wondered how he would feel if someone brought Gus home to him this way. He shook his head in the empty room. He knew that he would feel very little. He was a good kid, too bad he couldn't matter more. Too bad anything couldn't matter more. Too bad the possibility of anything mattering had been harrowed from his soul by Hadley Winslow.

He heard the door open behind him.

He took in a long breath as if to fill his descending emptiness with air.

He turned.

Beautiful.

She was in white. Her hair was blonder than he remembered, almost platinum, and pulled back from her face. Her eyes were very big, her mouth was wide. Time had marked her, without diminishing her. There were tiny crow's-feet at the corners of her eyes, and a barely visible hint of amusement around the corners of her mouth. She closed the door behind her and stood where she had entered. She held his card in her hand.

They stared at each other.

She said, "Hello."

"Hello."

"It is you," she said.

"Yes," he said. "That Conn Sheridan."

"It's a long time."

"Twenty-six years."

"I don't know how I feel," Hadley said.

Conn waited.

"You're a policeman now," she said.

Conn nodded.

"You're here about my son."

"Yes."

She walked across the room as if it were about to buckle. She sat on the arm of one of the big leather chairs. She gestured toward the leather couch.

"Will you sit down?" she said.

"No," Conn said.

"Why are you here?" she said.

"What did your son tell you?"

"He said there was a policeman who wanted to talk to me alone."

Her lower lip was still soft looking. Her breasts seemed as firm as they had been before he went to prison. The line of her thigh, as she sat on the arm of the chair, was as graceful and firm as it had been before he expunged it from his memory in Kilmainham Jail.

"He's killed a little girl," Conn said quietly.

Hadley shook her head.

Conn waited, his hands still in his pockets.

"No," she said.

Conn was still.

"He could not," Hadley said. "He didn't. No. He would not do that."

Conn waited.

Hadley stood suddenly, and seemed for a moment to lose her balance. She put a hand on the chair back to steady herself; then she walked to the fireplace and put both hands on the high mantel and leaned her forehead against it and stared into the cold opening.

Conn took Maureen Burns's underpants from his coat pocket and unfolded them and put them on the coffee table in front of the couch.

"She had been sexually assaulted. Her underpants were missing. I found them under the mattress in your son's room at the college."

"That proves nothing," Hadley said. Her gaze still fixed on the clean, empty firebox.

"He confessed," Conn said.

"No," she said. She turned from the mantel to stare at Conn. "I will not let you do this. I swear to God I will not let you."

She put a hand on the mantel and steadied herself. Then suddenly her legs seemed to give out and she sank to her knees on the thick Persian rug. She made no sound. But tears formed in her eyes and rolled down her cheeks.

Conn waited. She cried silently. Then she looked at him.

"Will you help me?" she said.

Conn walked across the room and helped her to stand. He took her arm as they walked to a chair. He helped her to sit. Then, with his foot, he hooked a green leather hassock over in front of the chair and sat on it facing her.

"Probably," he said.

Conn

"This can't be a complete surprise," Conn said.

"How can you possibly say that?"

"I been a cop most of the time since I saw you last," Conn said. "Guy does something like this, he's been off center for a long time."

"My son is a fine young man," Hadley said.

"Except that he shot a female child after he fucked her."

Hadley leaned back a little and pressed her arms down firmly on the arms of the chair. Her face was pale and she was breathing audibly through her nose.

"Is this your revenge?" she said. "After twenty-six years to get your revenge on me through my son?"

Conn didn't speak. He sat silently on the hassock, his forearms on his thighs, his hands clasped loosely in front of him. He looked steadily at Hadley. He felt as if everything were unspooling very slowly, as if he and Hadley were suspended somehow in a viscous crystalline fluid. Tears came slowly to Hadley's eyes and began again to move quietly down her face. She leaned forward and put her hand on both of his.

"Conn," she said, "you have to help me."

He nodded.

"You're right, of course," she said. She seemed to have wrenched herself back into control. "Even as a boy he had an unhealthy interest in little girls. His father caught him playing doctor once, and was livid. I think if I hadn't intervened he might have beaten him severely."

Conn nodded, his eyes on her face.

"That why you got him the clubhouse in Weston?"

"Anything," Hadley said. "Anything to distract him. It was a constant fear. He didn't like other little boys. He liked to play with little girls and we never dared leave them alone."

"When was the first one?" Conn said.

"He was ten," Hadley said. "With a three-year-old girl."

"Parents know?"

Hadley shook her head.

"I don't know if she ever told them anything. We never heard from them. She was the daughter of a Charles Street shopkeeper. I don't think she even knew Tommy's name."

"How'd your husband feel about that?" Conn said.

"I never told him," Hadley said. "There were other times. I always managed to cover up."

"Ever talk to a doctor?"

"I couldn't tell anyone," Hadley said.

Conn felt the weight of her hand on his, felt the force of her eyes, smelled her perfume, looked at the curve of her thigh beneath the sheer white dress. Hadley's voice dropped slightly. It was husky, almost hoarse.

"I've lived with this alone," she said. "Until now."

"So your husband doesn't know?"

"No."

"So nobody knows but you, me, and the kid?"

"I had to protect him," Hadley said.

"From his father?"

"From everyone," Hadley said.

"And how will you protect him from me?"

Hadley didn't speak for a moment. Her eyes were on Conn's face, moving, examining him as if looking for an opening. She took her hand from on top of his and leaned back in her chair and folded her hands in her lap.

"I will find a way," she said.

Conn stood and walked to the window and stood looking out with his hands in his hip pockets.

"So how come you turned me in?" he said.

"I beg your pardon?"

"Twenty-six years ago," Conn said, looking out the window at the placid life moving by on Mt. Vernon Street. "How come you turned me in to the British?"

"Oh, God."

Conn kept his face to the window.

"I was twenty," she said. "I had done what I was supposed to do two years earlier. I married the man I was supposed to marry. Older than I was, solid, stable, successful. Old money, good family. I was a virgin."

"So was Maureen Burns," Conn said.

"Who . . . oh . . . the little girl?"

"Un-huh."

Hadley steadied herself in her chair. Conn's back was very straight as he stared out the window.

"My wedding night," Hadley said, "was not the stuff of dreams. Thomas is a forceful man, but not"—she paused, looking for words—"Thomas is not a passionate man."

"And he didn't grow more passionate with time," Conn said.

"No."

"So you rounded up a few passionate Irishmen to fill the void."

"Not a few," Hadley said. "You."

The sun had moved westward as the afternoon progressed, and now, as Hadley looked at him, he was a dark outline against the bright window. He turned slowly and faced her. His hands in his hip pockets caused his coat to pull back. His revolver showed at his belt.

"But it got out of hand," he said.

"Yes."

"You were after a little poon tang, I was after forever."

"There's no need to be coarse, Conn. You meant a great deal to me. I would have been your mistress all our lives had you let me."

"But you wouldn't leave your husband."

"I couldn't. I wasn't bred to dash round the world with a—a gunman. Look at you, you're still a gunman."

"So you couldn't tell me that instead of calling the peelers?"

"I did tell you that, Conn. I told you that in the park, by the canal. You wouldn't hear me."

Conn nodded slowly. He had no need to think back. He had lived that time in the continuing present since it happened.

"And you wouldn't go away. When I looked out and saw you there, in front of my home, in Merrion Square, my heart nearly stopped. If my husband had ever seen you . . ."

"Thomas is a dangerous man, is he?"

"Rigid, Conn. And harsh. He thinks things are all certain. It would have ruined everything if he'd seen you. You were so fierce. I had to make you leave. I was never prepared for the intensity. You wouldn't leave. I didn't know what else to do."

"Did you know they were going to hang me?"

"I didn't know what would happen. I couldn't think about it. Conn, I was twenty."

"And your kid's eighteen and a pervert," Conn said.

Hadley put her face in her hands.

"You better think about it," Conn said.

Conn

"So who was my replacement?" Conn said.

"Replacement? I"—She shook her head. The declining sun had now edged into the room and it made her hair seem bright —"I couldn't. Not after you. There's never been anyone after you."

"Un-huh."

"You think I'm a whore. I've been a good wife and mother, Conn. I have been loyal to my husband. I love my son."

Conn, silhouetted darkly against the window, took his hands from his pockets and clapped silently. She looked away, into the cold fireplace. Her voice seemed to be coming from somewhere else. It was almost as if she were alone.

"Are you married, Conn?"

"Yes."

"Do you love your wife?"

"No."

"Did you ever?"

"No."

"Why did *you* marry?"

"I knocked her up."

"So you have children?"

"Yes."

"Are you a good father?"

"Probably not. I try."

"How many children?"

"One son."

"Tommy's age?"

"Four years younger."

"You love him."

Conn was silent for a moment and the question lingered in the sunny room.

"As best I can," Conn said.

He could feel her in the room. She pulsed out energy that only he could feel, *like a dog with a silent whistle*. It surprised him. He thought he had gone far enough inside. But here it was, the shock of her energy pulsing in him. *April is the cruelest month.* He felt something almost like amusement that he was remembering scraps of poetry. *Maybe I should buy a mandolin.* He moved away from the window and stood by the fireplace with his arms folded. The bright sunlight was on her face as she leaned forward. He was motionless by the fireplace, his soul clenched like a fist against the surge of feeling.

"There has not been a day," Hadley said softly, "that I have not thought of you, Conn."

Conn remained intensely motionless.

"You have thought of me," Hadley said. It was not a question.

Conn nodded.

"With anger," Hadley said, "certainly."

Conn nodded again.

"But perhaps with something else?"

"Perhaps."

Conn's voice was raspy.

"Things come around, don't they?" Hadley said. "I betrayed you long ago, and now, years later, and in another country, you may have your revenge."

"I can't leave that kid walking around loose," Conn said. "He'll do it again."

"There are doctors," Hadley said. "There's a sanitarium in Switzerland."

"Been preparing for the moment," Conn said.

"I've known he's not right," Hadley said.

"What about Maureen Burns?" Conn said.

"I—I'm sorry about the little girl. I truly am. But it is too late to help her. I can't think about her. I have to help my son."

"Actually," Conn said, his voice still hoarse, "you have to get me to help your son."

"If you will let him go, I will send him to the clinic in Switzerland. He will never harm anyone again."

"The cure rate is not good for perverts," Conn said.

"He will be out of harm's way," Hadley said.

"And your husband," Conn said. "What will you tell him?"

"He loves me," Hadley said. "I can get him to do what I want."

Conn didn't speak for a while. The silence explored the room slowly and filled it the way water rises in a bucket.

"It's my case. I could bury it," Conn said. "You swear the kid was here that night. I believe you. I write the report. I don't mention the underpants. Or the confession. Or the gun. Or the playhouse in Weston. The report gets filed. It's done."

"Will you do that?" Hadley said. Her voice was hushed.

Conn didn't answer. Hadley got up from her chair and stood in front of him. She put her hands on his shoulders. Her face was upturned and close to his. Her lips seemed glistening. He could feel the involuntary contraction of his muscles, when she touched him.

"Will you?" she said. Her face was so close to his that her lips brushed his as she spoke.

"Better clean that gun," Conn said. "The old man sees it, he'll know it's been fired."

She nodded.

"You will," she said.

Conn knew he wasn't trembling. He knew he was as still as a boulder. But he felt as if he were trembling violently. He kept his arms folded, not touching her. She moved her hands down along his arms and unfolded them and pressed herself inside them, and pressed her mouth on his and put her arms around his waist. She moved against him so that the whole resilient sleek length of her insisted upon him. And he broke. The passion so silently contained for twenty-six years engulfed him and he held her hard against him and kissed her blindly.

The kiss lasted for a long time. Then she moved her mouth away from his, and put her head back a little, still thrusting her body hard against him, and said, "Maybe it isn't too late, Conn."

He held to her as if to lose her was to drown and said nothing.

"My husband will be home," she said.

Conn didn't move.

"But I could meet you somewhere . . . tomorrow."

She pressed her cheek against his, and rubbed her hands along the long muscles of his back.

"Will you help me with my son?"

She could see herself, her face pressed to his, in the mirror above the fireplace. Her lipstick was smeared, her mouth already puffed a little from the ferocity of his kiss, her eyes were wide open.

Conn spoke finally. His voice was very hoarse.

"Sure," he said. "Why not?"

Over his shoulder, in the mirror, behind him, she watched herself smile.

Conn

Conn walked across Mt. Vernon Street, and down Joy Street. He paused for traffic at Beacon Street and then crossed and went down the stairs into the Common.

Fool me once, he thought, *shame on you. Fool me twice, shame on me.*

He was walking slowly on the long path across the Common, the one that ran the diagonal and ended on Boylston Street near Park Square.

I should send that kid over.

He could still smell her, feel the press of her against him, taste her lipstick. He was barely there, in Boston, on the Common, heading for Boylston Street. There seemed to be no sound around him. The pigeons flocked silently about him and broke like scattered leaves as he walked through them. The life of the park around him seemed phantasmagorical. Others walking the long path seemed as soundless as ghosts. Cars drifted faintly along the borders of the park like memories. The barely budded trees were angular and still in the pale air of the late afternoon, and the squirrels glided translucently from limb to limb.

She was going to let them hang me.

He imagined her naked. Or was he remembering? Imagination and memory mingled like vapors in a bell jar. He was permeated with the image of something he had never seen. Hadley at forty-six, perfumed with affluence, enriched with station, elegant and compliant, silk lingerie, stockings, breasts, thighs, the slope of her belly. The touch of her mouth. Frightened, vulnerable.

Conn reached Boylston Street. He paused. He had walked this way aimlessly. He had no thought on where next to walk. It had been years since he thought of Dublin. Boston was the

world he knew. Dublin was remote. But now, standing on Boylston Street, he looked at the old familiar city as if it had just
been rough-formed of primordial clay. The yet ungreening
grass of the Common looked raw. He had a moment of vertigo,
suffused with feeling he could not contain.

I'll do it again, he thought. *I have to, God help me.* He stood
motionless at the end of the long path, as if he needed to get his
bearings. He smiled at his own near prayer. *He hasn't done a hell
of a job so far.* Silently, the old colonial city wound down around
him like a slow carousel when the music had stopped and the
machinery was coasting to a halt.

Conn arched his back, and stretched his neck, and flexed his
shoulders.

Softly he said, "Once more unto the breach, dear friends,"
and laughed out loud and turned and walked back the way he
had come.

Conn

At ten o'clock in the morning he had already checked into a room at the Parker House, and was waiting for her in the lobby, by the elevators, when she came in wearing a wide-brimmed spring hat and white gloves. Her New-Look suit was dark blue, the skirt to midcalf. Her silk blouse was white. She wore white high-heeled shoes. She carried a white straw purse. Around her neck was a stone marten wrap. She smiled when she reached him and put her arm out. He took it and without a word guided her into the elevator.

"Five," he said to the operator, and they stood in silence as the elevator rose.

Their room had flowered wallpaper, and a double bed with a rose-colored satin spread, and one window that looked out over School Street at King's Chapel. On a small table by the window was a bottle of whiskey and a bucket of ice and a siphon of seltzer.

"Would you like a drink?" he said.

"Yes."

While he made two drinks, she took off her stone marten wrap and draped it over the back of a chair, and removed her big hat and placed it on the dresser. He handed her a drink. They touched glasses. And drank.

"Thomas has agreed that Tommy go away to school in Switzerland," Hadley said.

There was a small armchair next to the table by the window, but neither of them sat in it. Nor did they sit on the bed. They stood, drink in hand, facing each other under the blank beady inspection of the stone martens' artificial gaze.

"Does he know why?" Conn said.

"No. I told him that Tommy was having some trouble at school and the school had recommended it."

"Does he believe you?"

"I don't know. It doesn't matter. He acquiesced. Thomas is remote from his son."

Conn drank some of the whiskey. Only a small drink. He did not want to miss any of this.

"And the school will take him?"

"Yes. I wired them today."

"What if they don't take him?"

"I told you," Hadley said. "I've been preparing for this. I have done all the research. They are already committed to take him. And treat him."

"And contain him?"

"Yes. It's what this school is for."

There was a silence. Hadley drank a substantial swallow of her drink. Her dark lipstick marked the glass.

"Maybe they'll cure him," Conn said. "It happens."

"Maybe."

Hadley drank again.

"Can we make a bargain?" she said.

"I think so," Conn said.

"We can be what we were. We can be lovers. But my son is spared, and my husband doesn't learn of it."

"Your son or us?" Conn said.

Hadley finished her drink and turned and made herself another one.

"Both," Hadley said. She was much calmer today.

Conn nodded. He took a very small sip of his drink. He too was calm. He felt a stillness at the bone, as if his anticipatory physical self were holding its breath.

"Promise?" Hadley said.

He nodded again.

"Say it," Hadley insisted.

"I promise."

She had her glass half raised to her lips and she studied him over the rim for a moment.

"I trust you," she said.

She put the glass on the table by the window and turned back toward him and smiled. Wordlessly she took the rope of pearls from her neck and put them on the bureau. She took off the suit jacket and hung it over the chair, covering the unblinking stone martens. She unbuttoned the cuffs of her blouse and then the blouse itself and took it off and folded it neatly and laid it on the bureau beside her hat. She wore a white bra with small scallops of white lace on it. The skin of her arms was smooth. Her shoulders were firm, and the white straps of the bra made very little indentation. She stepped out of her shoes, and pushed them carefully under the table, one of them standing, the other on its side. Her skirt had a button and a side zipper which she released. She made a small movement with her hips and let the skirt slide to the floor. She was wearing a white half slip with lace at the hem. She bent and picked up the skirt and smoothed it, and laid it over the jacket on the back of the chair. She tucked her thumbs inside the waist of the slip and slid it down, did the same hip movement again, and let it fall around her ankles. She stepped out of it, and left it where it fell.

Conn watched her gravely. He made no move to undress. His face showed nothing.

Under the slip she wore white silk panties, hose, and a white garter belt. The panties had lace at the leg openings.

She paused and picked up her drink and swallowed half of it. Her eyes met his, and she seemed to stand more erect as if she were proud to display herself in her elegant white underclothes. She drank again and put the nearly empty glass back on the table. She reached behind her and unhooked her bra and hunched her shoulders and let the bra slide forward down her arms. It dropped to the floor and she let it lie there next to her slip. She straightened. Her breasts seemed unaffected by motherhood or time. Her breasts looked to Conn as they had when he first saw them in the garden of the house on Clare Street twenty-six years ago. Her lips were wet from the whiskey and soda, and they glistened. Her eyes seemed to have gotten larger and darker, the pupils widening until there was barely any iris. She looked at him and her face was serious. Their eyes held. She slid her underpants down her thighs, bending forward to guide them past her knees. Then she straightened and let them drop and stepped out of them. Except for stockings and garter belt she was naked.

"You look like a French postcard," Conn said. The ice in his drink had melted. He didn't want the drink anyway. He put the glass on the bedside table.

She smiled for the first time.

"You ain't seen nothing yet," she said.

She carefully unsnapped the garters from the tops of her flesh-tone nylons. The stockings began to sag. She reached behind her and unhooked the garter belt and dropped it onto the table. Then, balancing first on one leg, then on the other, she got out of her stockings. He noticed that there was polish on her toenails. At one point she seemed to need help with her balance, putting a hand on the back of the chair.

She stood erect, facing him. Except for her rings, she was stark naked. She seemed blonder than he remembered her in Dublin.

"I'm going to make another drink," she said. "Would you like one?"

"No, thank you," Conn said.

"While I'm mixing it, perhaps you would like to take your clothes off, or have you grown modest in your middle years?"

Conn smiled slowly.

"I have a lot to be modest about," he said, and took his gun off his belt and put it, still holstered, on the bedside table.

They were naked together, facing one another in the quiet hotel room.

"Adam and Eve," he said.

"After the Fall," she said.

She took a long drink of her whiskey and put the glass on the table and stepped to him. She touched his shoulder where the scar of the old bullet wound remained.

"I remember," she said.

He nodded. They were so close that her nipples brushed his chest. He was motionless. She put her arms around his waist and pressed herself against him.

"Conn," she said, "let go."

She spoke with her lips brushing his and then she kissed him hard and opened her mouth and his arms tightened around her. After a time she pulled her mouth away from his.

"Too tight," she gasped. "You'll hurt me."

He knew how strong he was. He knew he could squeeze harder if he wished. He continued to hold her tightly for a moment, then relented, letting his hands rest quietly on her buttocks.

"We should lie down," she said.

"Yes."

On the bed beside her, Conn felt frightened. As if he were about to step off a ledge in the dark. But the feeling was wan compared to the rich insistence of desire.

Her lovemaking was as expert as his. Conn registered this dimly as they explored one another on the bed. His expertise was hard earned. Years of experience. Where had she learned hers? But the question buried itself, as his fear had buried itself, lost in the pulsating realization of a quarter century's containment. She had no inhibitions. Nothing she would not do. Nothing she did not know how to do. She was still the woman who had liked to make love in odd places, thrilled by the danger of discovery. Some of the time she whispered profanely to him, urging him, entirely conscious of his every response. Some of the time she seemed lost in a drama of her own, asking him what he was doing to her, not talking to him, he knew, speaking only to enact a private passion. He didn't care. He had his own private passions and she was first among them.

"I want you to fuck me in the chair," she whispered.

"Anywhere at all."

She made love skillfully in the small armchair, her back arched, her head thrown back moaning as if in labor. The clothes she had so carefully draped across the back of it fell to the floor in a tangle, the stone martens curled like weasels in a tangle of silk and linen. When it was over she got up quickly and went into the bathroom and ran the water in the tub.

Conn

Knocko was putting most of a glazed doughnut into his mouth in front of a doughnut shop on Clarendon Street near Warren Avenue.

"I was with a woman the other day," Conn said. "Claims she's got no sex life. Says she and her husband do it about once a year to celebrate the Fourth."

Knocko grinned at him as he swallowed his doughnut.

"You been shagging my old lady?"

"You must have some kind of sex life," Conn said. "All those children."

Knocko peered into the white paper sack on the car seat between them.

"That's the problem," Knocko said. "Faith's afraid if I fucking sneeze she'll get pregnant."

"You could take precautions."

"Not if you're as Catholic as Faith is."

Conn shrugged.

"Anyway," he said. "This woman I'm with, she knows stuff would make you blush."

"Yeah? Like what?"

Conn shook his head.

"So what I'm wondering," Conn said, "is where she got so good at something she almost never does."

Knocko chewed on his second doughnut.

"Maybe she was stepping out on the old man, before you come along," Knocko said.

Conn drank some coffee and looked out the car window.

"Maybe."

Knocko finished his doughnut and started the car. He let the clutch pedal out and pulled away into the traffic.

"Anything on that kid got killed in Charlestown?"

"Dead end," Conn said. "Only had a couple suspects. They both had alibis. No physical evidence. I got nowhere to go."

"Get him next time," Knocko said. They were driving on Columbus Avenue. "He'll show up again. Fucking perverts never settle for once."

"Yeah."

Knocko turned onto Massachusetts Avenue past the Savoy Ballroom. A light rain had started to fall. Knocko slowed the car. The huddle of black men standing outside the Savoy had retreated from the rain into the doorway. They were careful not to look up as Knocko surveyed them. He fed a little gas, shifted up into second, and drove on. At Huntington Avenue, Knocko turned right toward Copley Square. Conn looked blankly across the intersection at Symphony Hall, red brick, ivory columns. They passed Pierce's in Copley Square, across from the Public Library. Hadley probably shopped there, Conn thought.

"You ever been in S. S. Pierce?" Conn said.

"Do I look like a guy eats fucking snails, for Crissake? No, I never been in there. You?"

"No," Conn said.

They idled at the stoplight by Trinity Church.

"You wanna do me a favor?" Conn said.

"Sure."

"Look into a guy named Thomas J. Winslow," Conn said. "Rich guy. Lives on Beacon Hill. I'd do it but I don't want anyone to connect us."

Knocko's face was expressionless, his eyes automatically cataloging the intersection.

"Whaddya want to know?"

"Whatever there is," Conn said.

"What do I tell people when they ask me why I'm looking?"

"You do it so they don't ask."

Knocko tilted his hat forward and turned up one edge of his collar. He narrowed his eyes and looked at Conn over the upraised collar.

"Knocko Kiernan," he said. "Secret agent."

"This is not what you might call line of duty," Conn said. "Whatever you find out you tell me, then you forget it. This is personal."

"He the husband?" Knocko said.

Conn looked out the rain-streaked side window of the car and didn't answer.

1994
Voice-Over

"Nineteen forty-six," I said. "My father was fourteen."

"And my father was eighteen, and your grandfather arrested him," Grace said.

"Well, actually he didn't exactly arrest him."

"Been better if he had," Grace said.

"Been better if Adam didn't eat the apple," I said. "If he had arrested him there'd never have been you."

"And maybe that wouldn't have been such a great loss either," Grace said.

"To me," I said.

"God," she said, "I hope we can get past this."

"This isn't what's in our way," I said. "We were estranged before last fall."

"It does not help," Grace said.

"It's part of who we are," I said. "Help or hurt."

"I'm going to make some tea," she said. "You want some?"

"Sure," I said, and followed her into the kitchen and sat on the stool across the counter from her while she moved about in her kitchen (not ours). From this angle I could see, through the living room window, one of the streetlights at the far end of the parking lot. It was blurred by the fat snowflakes and haloed the way light sometimes is in snow. Looked pretty, for a streetlight.

"I knew Daddy went to school in Switzerland," Grace said. "I never knew why."

She shivered as if she were cold and hugged herself, rubbing her hands along her upper arms.

"He went with your grandmother," I said, "in late May 1946 in a first-class compartment on board the *Queen Elizabeth*. Hadley stayed with him a week near Zurich and returned without him to Boston in the middle of June."

"And there wasn't a big ruckus about the little girl's death."

"A small ruckus," I said. "But her family wasn't prominent, and there was no money, and the investigating officer couldn't find a suspect."

"Do you think it bothered Conn," Grace said, "to turn loose a man who had murdered a child?"

"His deal included putting the kid where he could do no harm," I said. "He knew the kid wouldn't stay in that school forever. Maybe they'd cure the kid before he left. Maybe the kid would outgrow it. Maybe the kid wouldn't outgrow it. But every Thursday while the kid was in school in Switzerland, Hadley would, ah, rendezvous with my grandfather. And that's what he knew most of all. Everything else he forgot."

"Yes," Grace said. "Of course."

"Conn would make breakfast for Gus while Mellen was at early Mass, which she went to every morning."

"A bride of Christ," Grace said.

I shrugged.

"Bride of somebody . . . and when Gus left for school, Conn would meet Hadley in a hotel. He knew all the house detectives, and a room for a couple of hours was easy to arrange. Hadley liked variety. During the first year, they used the Parker House, the Somerset, the Kenmore, the Lincolnshire, the Manger, the Buckminster, the Copley Plaza, the Ritz, the Lennox, the Statler, the Avery, the Bradford."

"But who counts?" Grace said.

I smiled at her.

"Always alone," she said.

"Yeah."

"Never went out together, never saw friends, never planned to marry, or have children, or build a house, or try a new restaurant."

"No."

"Just fuck for an hour once a week."

"Yeah."

Grace shook her head.

"My God," she said. "What could anyone expect from that, after they'd tried all the new positions?"

"Your grandmother probably expected to save her child."

"Only that?"

"It's a big only."

"Of course it is," Grace said. "But you know what I mean."

"Yeah, I do. . . . I don't know if there was more. Maybe. Maybe she liked coercion. Maybe she hated herself. Maybe she loved Conn in some disfigured way."

"And what did he get?" Grace said.

"Conn? Pussy, revenge, ownership. Sex and anger get sort of tangled up. Especially in men."

"Which Sheridan are we talking about now?" Grace said.

"All of us."

1947
Conn

In March, on the anniversary of her death, there was a memorial Mass for Maureen Burns. Conn attended, stood in the back of the huge, half-empty church, listening to the echoing Latin ritual. He did not genuflect when he entered. He made no move to kneel during the Mass.

Catholic churches always felt the same, and sounded the same, and smelled the same, to Conn. He thought of his childhood. His childhood, before Hadley, seemed foolish to him, and fraudulent. He thought about his son. *Too bad*, he thought. *I could have been a hell of a father.* His life, when it did not discomfort him, seemed more like someone else's. Only the Thursday afternoons with Hadley seemed *his* life, what the rest of him did the rest of the time seemed apart from him. *If I can keep Mellen from fucking him up beyond hope, maybe that would be something.* The priest continued his singsong in a language Conn had never understood. *I probably can't. . . . I can try. . . . I owe him something.* The priest explained in English that the innocent martyrdom of little Maureen Burns was a signification of redemption. Conn didn't listen. *Unfortunately, I owe him more than I've got*, Conn thought.

When the Mass ended he left the church. He did not touch the holy water. He did not bless himself.

Conn

On a clear evening in October, Conn sat with Knocko at a back table in Steuben's Restaurant on Boylston Street, near Tremont, eating bratwurst and drinking German beer.

"Thomas J. Winslow, Sr.," Knocko said.

"Took you long enough."

"You wanted it quiet, right?"

Conn smiled and nodded. He had not mentioned his request for information since he'd asked for it more than a year ago.

"Okay then," Knocko said. "There's a Thomas Winslow, Jr., nineteen years old, goes to school in Switzerland. I figured senior was the one you were interested in."

Conn nodded. The German beer was dark and more bitter than he liked.

"Born in Boston, May 21, 1884, which makes him sixty-three, now. Married Hadley Rogerson in 1918. He was thirty-six, she was eighteen. One child, the aforesaid, Junior."

Knocko picked up a fat white bratwurst in his fingers and wiped it in some brown-flecked yellow mustard and bit off a third of it. He chewed slowly. Then he put down the bratwurst and took a bite of rye bread and chewed it and drank some of the dark heavy beer, and wiped his fingers and mouth carefully with his napkin.

Conn smiled.

"You're so fastidious, Knocko."

"Fucking A," Knocko said. "Winslow comes from old Yankee money. Worked in the family bank in Boston until he got married—Suffolk Savings and Loan. Then in 1920 he was over there with you—Dublin, Ireland, running some kind of soap factory that Suffolk foreclosed on. Went over there with his wife, right after he married her. Some sort of a honeymoon, I guess."

Knocko's face was without expression. "Combine business and pleasure."

Conn sipped the dark beer.

"They come back in 1922. Probably to get away from the troubles. And they been here ever since. He took over the bank in 1941. Bank's very successful. They were conservative before the crash, Winslow's got a bundle."

Knocko ate some more bratwurst.

"What else?" Conn said.

"There's gotta be something else?"

"How long you been a cop, Knocko? There's always something else."

"Well," Knocko said, "those are the facts. The rest is hearsay."

"I got nothing against hearsay."

"The kid has been bothersome, I hear. Can't put a finger on it. Never been arrested. But he went to a series of private schools, the kinds of schools where they send problem kids. Left Harvard after his freshman year."

"Know what his problem is?" Conn said.

Knocko shrugged.

"Dunno," he said. He looked at Conn silently for a moment. His face was empty. "Winslow has problems with his wife."

Conn waited, both hands holding the half-drunk stein of dark beer. His face was as blank as Knocko's.

"Like what?" he said.

"Like she fucks around," Knocko said.

"Yeah?"

"Often."

"Un-huh."

"Know a guy," Knocko said, "used to work with me, got fired for fucking up a homicide case in Allston. Runs a big private agency now, in town. 'Bout twenty times richer than we are."

"Sherman Lane," Conn said.

"Right," Knocko said. "Dumb fucker, but he talks good. Anyway, maybe fifteen years ago, one of Winslow's lawyers comes to Sherm, asks him to keep tabs on the Missus, very confidential."

"And?"

"And"—Knocko shrugged, and spread his hands—"she was sleeping with a lot of guys. Once, twice a week. Different guys."

Knocko emptied his beer stein and waved it at a waiter.

"Hey, Heinie," Knocko said. "I need another beer."

"And?" Conn said.

"And nothing," Knocko said. "Sherm got paid, never heard nothing more. She and Winslow are still together."

"Maybe she stopped," Conn said.

"Maybe," Knocko said. "Or maybe he decided it wasn't worth the publicity or maybe she would have taken him for too much dough. Or maybe he don't give a shit, long as he gets his."

"Or maybe he loved her," Conn said, "and couldn't give her up."

"Sure," Knocko said. "Maybe that."

Conn

That October the Brooklyn Dodgers played the New York Yankees in the World Series. As Conn walked on Boylston Street, there were people gathered in front of a store window watching the game on television. The game was on the radio in the ornate lobby of the Copley Plaza Hotel. The announcer was Red Barber. Bill Bevens, the Yankee pitcher, had a no-hitter in the sixth inning.

Hadley came in wearing a blue-and-white polka-dot dress, and a wide-brimmed blue hat. The dress had a wide white belt. The hat had a wide white hatband. Conn watched her cross the lobby toward him. *She always walks into a place like visiting royalty.*

Their hotel room was in the front, facing St. James Avenue, over looking Copley Square, with Boylston Street beyond, and Trinity Church to the right. As soon as she entered the room, Hadley took off the white belt and began to unbutton her dress.

"Take a minute," Conn said. "Maybe we could have a drink together. Talk a little."

Hadley stopped, with the top two buttons of her dress unbuttoned. She smiled an odd half-smile.

"What would you like to talk about?" Hadley said.

"You, me, the Hit Parade, us, the Russians, romance, the World Series, love."

Her odd half smile became fixed.

"I'm required to talk too?" she said as if to herself.

He moved to the table and made them drinks. She took hers, still standing, and drank some.

"It just seemed to be getting too wham-bam-thank-you-ma'am," Conn said.

"Oh?"

"Come to the hotel, undress, do it, get dressed, go home. Not much of a relationship," Conn said.

"A relationship?"

"Yeah."

"Isn't fucking enough?"

Conn felt again the feeling he'd had the first time, in the Parker House, as if he were about to step blindly off a cliff. He took a breath and stepped.

"Making love might be nice?"

"What's the difference?" Hadley said.

Conn shook his head. She stared at him and drank from her glass.

"You want me to love you?" she said.

"Might be nice," Conn said.

She drank again. They were never together long enough for Conn to be sure, but he always suspected that she drank too much when she got the chance.

"Well, of course, I do," Hadley said. "I always have."

Conn was watching her.

"Even all those years with Thomas Winslow."

"Yes," Hadley said. She moved closer to him. "All those years, I remembered, and I was sorry about Dublin, but . . . I didn't know where you were. You might have been dead."

"Yeah," Conn said. "I might have been."

"Oh, Conn, damn you, we've been all through this. Life has played with us. But we're together again. Why not take what we can?"

"And there was no one else, all that time," Conn said. "Just Hubby and me."

"Yes."

"Faithful to your husband. Loyal to my memory."

She raised her glass to drink. It was empty. She handed it to Conn.

"What's wrong?" Hadley said. "Why are you talking to me like this?"

Conn mixed her a fresh drink.

"There's got to be more than you lie down and I jump on top of you."

"We do a little more than that," Hadley said.

"You know what I mean."

"No, Conn, I don't." Hadley took her glass from him and drank. "What the hell do you mean?"

Conn walked to the window and stared out it. Copley Square was out there, but he didn't see it. He didn't see anything.

"My information is you have regularly cheated on your husband since you've been married."

Behind him was silence. Conn didn't turn around. He waited, his sightless gaze fixed on the bright window. He heard the ice click in her glass, heard her swallow. Finally she spoke.

"Where would you get such information?"

"I'm a cop," Conn said. "I find stuff out."

"And you believe it?"

"It's good information."

He heard the ice click again. He turned slowly.

"It's true, isn't it?" Conn said.

She finished her second drink, and took a big breath.

"Would it have helped anything if I'd told you?"

"It might have."

He mixed her a drink. And one for himself.

"Do you feel better knowing?"

"No."

Hadley smiled faintly and shrugged.

"What happened to 'There could never be anyone after you?'" Conn said.

"It was what you wanted to hear," Hadley said. She drank some of her new drink.

"And that's what you do, tell me what you think I want to hear?"

"I told you something you didn't want to hear," Hadley said, "by the canal, in Dublin, twenty-seven years ago."

"At least it was the truth, Hadley."

"And you wouldn't hear it," Hadley said.

"No," Conn said softly, "I wouldn't."

"I'm not a whole woman, Conn. I love my son. But I don't think I can ever love anyone the way you mean. I came as close as I could get with you in Dublin."

"Not close enough," Conn said.

"I know. But as close as I could. I need security, Conn. Tom provides that."

"But that's all?"

"No. Tom and I have a perfectly normal sex life."

"You lied about that too."

"I thought you'd like to hear it."

"And you need more than a perfectly normal sex life."

"Yes," Hadley said. "Very badly."

"So you sleep around."

"Often."

"And I'm one of the people you sleep around with."

"Yes."

"But not the only one."

"There's something wrong with me, Conn. I can't . . . if I think there's only one man, I—I despair. . . . I can't."

Holding her drink in her left hand she fumbled the rest of the buttons open with her right hand.

"So there's nothing to talk about, after all," Conn said. "Wham-bam-thank-you-ma'am."

"We have a deal," Hadley said. "You protect my son, and I fuck you every week. A deal's a deal."

Conn slapped her. Even in his anger, he pulled it, and it didn't knock her down. But it sent her glass flying across the room, and it made her lip bleed. She took a step back and shrugged out of her dress. Her eyes glittered. She made no effort to wipe the blood that trickled from the corner of her mouth. Conn's voice was hoarse.

"You are a mortally sinful bitch," he said.

She stepped gracefully out of her slip and placed herself

against him. Her eyes were bright and hot and her voice was almost guttural as she looked up at him and spoke.

"And you are my punishment," she said, and jammed her mouth against his.

Gus

Lying on the bed in his room, Gus listened to the sixth game of the World Series, on the brown plastic GE table radio that Conn had just bought him for his fifteenth birthday. When it was over, he came out of his room, excited, and went downstairs to see if Conn were home, and had heard the game. Conn was sitting at the kitchen table with his coat off and his sleeves rolled, drinking whiskey. Gus was surprised. His father rarely drank at home.

"You hear the game?" Gus said.

"Part of it," Conn said.

"Bevens had a no-hitter," Gus said, "going into the ninth. And Lavagetto hit a double off the screen in right and Miksis and Gionfriddo both scored and the Dodgers won. One hit."

"Sonva bitch," Conn said. And Gus realized his father was drunk.

"Where's Ma?" Gus said.

Conn jerked his head toward the den.

"Get a glass," Conn said. "Have a drink with me."

Gus glanced toward the den. His mother was usually in there, with the shades down, rocking, reading her missal. Gus got a water glass from the kitchen cabinet and sat down again. His father took two ice cubes from the half-melted refrigerator tray sitting on the table, and put them in Gus's glass and poured some whiskey in over them. Gus sipped some without flinching. He and his friends drank beer when they could get someone to buy it. But his father had given him whiskey before, and he was used to the taste. His father drank with him. He was solemn.

"You're a good kid, Gus."

Gus nodded. He didn't know what to say.

"Too bad I'm not as good a father as you are a kid," Conn said.

"You're a good father."

"Maybe all a man can hope for," Conn said. His voice was slow, and he was looking past Gus, out the kitchen window at the bright October afternoon that was slowly fading into evening. "Just have a kid comes out all right."

Conn poured some more whiskey for himself. Mellen came from the den and stood in the doorway, her arms folded. She wore a gray housedress and white shoes. A hole was cut in the right shoe to relieve pressure on her small toe. Her gray hair was pulled back tight, and rolled into a small bun at the back. When she spoke her voice was barely inflected.

"It's bad enough you bring your bad habits home, Conn, without you should be inflicting them on your son."

Conn looked at her and Gus was a little scared by the look in his father's eyes.

"Well, Melly, darlin'," Conn said. "Don't you look fetchin' this afternoon."

Mellen's mouth thinned, and her face tightened with disapproval. Gus knew the look.

"You're drunk," she said.

"I certainly hope so," Conn said.

Gus sat very still.

"Go to bed, Conn," Mellen said.

"With you?"

"Conn, not in front of the boy."

"Why not?" Conn said. "He's already shavin'. Probably getting laid too."

"Conn!"

"You getting laid, Gus?"

Gus said, "Jesus Christ, Pa. In front of Ma?"

Mellen said, "Augustus Sheridan, don't you use that kind of language in *my* house."

"*My* house," Conn said, and laughed. There was no amusement in the laugh. "You hear that, Gus? *My* house. I bought it. I pay the fucking mortgage every fucking month, but it's *her* fucking house."

Gus said, "Pa!"

Mellen lunged at him from the doorway, her face pale and tight with anger. She bent from the waist to put her face in front of his.

"Don't you speak that way to me, as if I was one of those cheap women," she said. "Don't you dare speak to me that way."

Conn appeared to ignore her.

"If you're getting laid, kid, don't knock them up. You have to marry one, you're in for a long, ugly life."

Mellen punched him in the chest with both fists. Conn stood in one smooth motion and pushed her away. The force of it staggered her against the wall. She leaned against it for a moment, dazed. Then she began to scream. Conn took a step toward her. Gus stood and pushed in front of his father.

"Leave her alone," he said.

Conn looked down at his son.

"Sonva bitch," he said. "You are a good kid."

"She's my mother," Gus said.

"You can't stop me yet," Conn said. "Someday, but not yet."

"She's my mother," Gus said again.

"Yeah," Conn said. "I know."

Conn stood silently looking past his son at Mellen, who was holding her face in her hands and making low shrieking sounds. Then he looked at Gus.

"You're doing what you should," Conn said.

Then he turned back toward the table and finished his drink. Mellen was still leaning on the wall screaming. Her nose was bleeding.

"Remember," he said to Gus. "Fuck 'em and run. Don't love 'em."

"Pa," Gus said, "get out of here till you're sober."

Conn nodded.

"Fuck 'em and run, kid. Fuck 'em and run."

Conn took his coat off the back of the chair where he'd hung it and walked out of the house.

1952
Conn

At fifty-two, Hadley still looked good, Conn thought, as he watched her undress. The curve of her backside had softened a little, but her stomach was still flat and her breasts were holding up. She hung her clothes up neatly in the closet, and went into the bathroom, and ran the water in the tub. She stood naked in the bathroom door while the tub filled.

"How is your son?" Hadley said, her face softening artfully. "You never speak of him."

"He's in Korea," Conn said flatly. "Twenty-fourth Infantry Division."

"Oh, dear."

"Gives Mellen something to pray about," Conn said.

"I hope he'll be all right."

"Yeah."

"He will be, Conn. I know he will."

Conn didn't speak. Hadley was tanned except where her bathing suit had covered her, and the contrasting whiteness seemed to highlight her sexuality.

"Tommy's coming home," she said.

"Yeah?"

"The doctors say he is cured."

"Sure."

"His father wants him to start in the bank so he'll be ready when Thomas retires."

Conn shrugged.

"Is it all right?" Hadley said. She seemed heedless of her

nudity, as if it were her natural condition. How many Thursdays, in how many hotels, Conn wondered, had he looked at her naked?

Conn shrugged again.

"No problem," he said. *Maybe he is cured.*

She smiled brightly and turned and got into her bath. Conn went to the window to look out at Commonwealth Avenue. It was June. The trees were in full leaf along the mall. The avenue looked orderly and pleasant. Hadley came out of the bathroom drying herself with a towel. When she was dry, she dropped the towel on the floor and lay on her back on the bed. Conn stared down at the trees. Hadley waited quietly. Conn turned and looked at her. The tan body, the white highlights, still slightly damp, her face empty. Slowly he loosened his tie. He didn't want her, really. It was almost as if he were doomed to do this, to pound futilely at the temple door, and never gain admission. *The hell with the temple door*, he thought. *Settle for the pussy.*

1954
Conn

They were on Harrison Avenue. Knocko was driving, as he always did.

"Gus joined the forces of law and order?" Knocko said.

"Yeah. City Square. Gets credit for Korea."

"Good deal for these new kids," Knocko said. "Two years head start on the pension."

Conn had a big paper cup full of black coffee. He took a pint of Irish whiskey from his coat pocket and poured some into the coffee.

"For Crissake," Knocko said. "It's eight in the fucking morning."

"Get my heart going," Conn said. He sipped the coffee. Knocko turned off of Harrison Avenue and parked near Tyler Street.

"Collection day?" Conn said.

"Friday morning, time to make the rounds," Knocko said. He got out of the car and walked down the alley to the mah-jongg parlor. Conn drank coffee and waited for Knocko. When the cup was half empty he added more whiskey. Knocko came back up Tyler Street and got in the car.

"Been collecting money from this place for twenty-five years," Knocko said. "For protection."

"Sure," Conn said. "Protection."

"Well," Knocko said sadly, "now we gotta earn it."

"I thought we did earn it," Conn said. "I thought we were getting paid to protect them from us."

"Last six, seven years," Knocko said, "bunch of new gooks coming in. Deserters, mostly, from Chiang's army after the Commies chased him out."

"Land of opportunity," Conn said.

Knocko jerked his head toward the mah-jongg parlor down the alley. "They're trying to take Chou over," he said.

"So let's tell them not to," Conn said. His coffee cup was empty.

"You all right for this?" Knocko said.

"Sure," Conn said. He took the whiskey from his pocket and had a drink and offered it to Knocko. Knocko shook his head. Conn capped the bottle and put it away. Knocko started the car and they drove two blocks and parked on Beach Street in front of a small variety store with Chinese characters lettered on the window. Knocko looked at Conn again.

"In there," he said. "Guy we want is named Lone."

"Like in Ranger," Conn said.

"Yeah," Knocko said. "Like in Ranger."

They got out of the car.

"You okay for this?" Knocko said again.

"I was born for this," Conn said.

"Yeah, well, I wasn't. So don't be a fucking cowboy."

"Hi yo, Silver," Conn said, and they walked into the store.

It was dim inside, and smelled of odd things. Some smoked duck hung on hooks near the front window, and a variety of peculiar looking roots and unrecognizable vegetables lay on a narrow table across the back. A slender Chinese man stood behind the table counting money. He wore a white shirt open at the neck. A maroon silk scarf filled the opening. His movements were graceful and precise as he transferred bills from a large pile into smaller piles separated by denomination.

Knocko took out his badge.

"You Lone?" Knocko said.

Without looking up the Chinese man nodded. He separated a twenty from the big pile and put it on top of a smaller pile with the other twenties.

"Boston Police Department," Knocko said.

Lone continued to count his money.

"You know a guy named Chou runs a mah-jongg parlor on Tyler Street?"

Lone nodded, concentrating on his counting.

"We got a complaint."

Lone nodded again. He took the pile of twenties and pushed them across the table at Knocko.

"Okay?" he said.

Knocko grinned.

"Good idea," Knocko said, "but we been taking Chou's money for years. We sell him out first chance we get and who else will give us money?"

Conn was leaning against the door frame looking at the smoked ducks.

"No?" Lone said.

"No," Knocko said.

Lone nodded and brought his right hand up from below the table. In it was a .45 automatic, the hammer already back. He must store it cocked, Conn thought idly.

"You go," Lone said.

"Now, Lone, we can't do that," Knocko said. "You hear me say we're policemen? You're threatening two policemen, Lone."

"You go."

Knocko frowned.

"Hey, Lone," Conn said from the doorway.

The muzzle of the gun deflected slightly toward Conn. Conn grinned. He thought of the last time he saw Mick Collins. *You were born to be shot.*

"Fuck you," Conn said, and walked into the gunfire.

Gus

Up front in Holy Cross Cathedral, Mellen in her new black dress prayed audibly along with the priest, kneeling beside her son at the funeral mass that Gus knew Conn would have laughed at. Knocko Kiernan was there with Faith, and most of his children. The police commissioner and the mayor were in attendance, and all the members of the City Council. Afterwards they gave Conn a full killed-in-the-line-of-duty burial. Police from all over the state were in the burial procession. A bugler played taps. A volley of shots was fired.

At graveside Gus stood with Mellen on his arm by the pile of newly turned earth, which had been covered with a tarp. Across the grave, somewhat apart from the crowd of mostly official mourners, Gus saw a middle-aged blond woman wearing a black hat with a veil.

She must have been something when she was young, Gus thought.

After the burial, while Mellen was at the center of a great circle of condolences, the blond woman came to stand beside Gus.

"I'm Hadley Winslow," she said softly. "I knew your father."

"Thanks for coming," Gus said automatically.

"He was a better man than he may have seemed," Hadley said.

Gus turned to stare at her. She smiled at him, patted his upper arm briefly, and walked away. Gus stared after her.

Probably was, he thought.

Gus

"How's your mother?" Knocko Kiernan said to Gus.

"She's in there with the rosary beads. Her and God."

"Better than nothing," Knocko said.

Gus shrugged. They were sitting at the table in Mellen's kitchen. Each with a glass of whiskey. There was a bottle on the table between them.

"It wasn't police business," Knocko said. "We was there to protect a guy was paying us."

Gus nodded.

"I figured that," Gus said.

"Yeah?"

"You hear stuff," Gus said. "I'm glad you killed the gook."

"Me or him," Knocko said. "First guy I ever shot."

They were silent, looking at the whiskey, not drinking it.

"My father never cleared his piece," Gus said.

Knocko shook his head.

"Gus," Knocko said, "I . . . to tell you the truth, Gus, it didn't seem like he tried."

"Just walked into it," Gus said.

Knocko nodded. "He was always like that, never seemed to give a shit."

"I know."

"Conn was a stand-up guy," Knocko said.

"Conn was crazy," Gus said.

"Hell, Gus."

"He was, the old lady too." Gus jerked his head toward the bedroom. "They drove each other fucking crazy all my life."

"I knew him before you was born. Before he met your mother. He was a good man, Gus. It was just . . . he just had, like a part missing, you know?"

"Yeah."

They were silent. Each looking at the whiskey. Neither drinking it.

"He gimme something to give you," Knocko said. From an old brown briefcase, on the floor, between his feet, he took a large manila envelope and put it on the table in front of Gus.

"What is it?"

"I dunno. He never told me what it was. Just said it was your insurance policy. Said give it to you if he died."

"When'd he give it to you?"

"Six, eight years ago," Knocko said. "It was Jackie Robinson's rookie season, I remember that, 'cause we were talking about him when he give it to me."

"Nineteen forty-seven," Gus said.

"Yeah."

"And you never looked?"

"No. Was for me, I'd a looked. Conn said this was for you. Nobody else, not Mellen or nobody."

"Lot of people would have looked," Gus said.

"I ain't one of them," Knocko said.

"No," Gus said. "You're not."

1955
Gus

When Gus came home from work, his mother called to him from her chair in the parlor, "Is that you, dear?"

"Yes," Gus said. He took off his uniform jacket and hung it up in the front closet.

"You going to come in and tell me about your day?"

"In a minute, Ma."

Gus went to the kitchen and opened a can of Ballantine ale. He took a swallow, and then took the can in with him to see his mother.

There were no lights. It was early evening, and there was snow outside, which made everything brighter, so that the room was less dim than it often was. Her Bible was on the table near her, and her rosary. A loosely crocheted lap robe sprawled over the back of the Boston rocker that she sat in. She wore her housedress. She had a number of them and they all looked the same to Gus, though he knew she changed them regularly.

He gave her a kiss on the forehead, and went to sit across from her on the couch.

"I wish you wouldn't drink so much," Mellen said.

Gus sipped his beer.

"You ought to try it," he said. "Loosen you up a little."

"And I hate seeing you with a gun."

Gus nodded patiently. It was a catechism he knew by heart.

"I want to carry a lace hankie," he said, "but they won't let me."

"It was guns killed your poor father."

Whenever she said this, Gus always knew better. The gun might have been the instrument, but it wasn't the cause. But he never commented.

Mellen stared out the window.

"You going to make us something for supper?" she said.

"I'll make you something," Gus said. "I'm going out."

"Again?"

"Ma, I went out two Fridays ago."

"Where are you going?"

"Gonna have dinner with friends at the Bavarian Rathskellar."

"What friends?"

"Guy I know, Butchie O'Brien, owns a tavern in Charlestown. Him and his wife."

"And you?"

"Me and a friend of Butchie's wife."

"Is she your date?"

"Yeah, I guess so, blind date."

Mellen was silent for a while, looking out the window.

"There's a ham in the icebox," Gus said. "You want some ham and potato salad, maybe?"

"Be careful, Gus," Mellen said. "You're a young man, and these women are a great temptation."

"I haven't even met this one, Ma. She's a blind date."

"I know women, Gus. I know them as a woman and as a mother. And I know you, as only a mother can, as someone who carried you in her womb. Single young men are vulnerable to sex. It seems so desirable."

Gus finished his beer. He knew this catechism as well. And he knew there was no way to divert it.

"But no matter how desirable sex seems, if you give in to it you will regret it."

Gus stood. He wanted another beer.

"If there is temptation," Mellen said, "think of the Blessed Virgin. Think of me. Stay pure for me, Gus. Save yourself for marriage. Make me proud."

"Sure, Ma. You want some tea with your supper?"

Gus

Dancing with Peggy Sheehan was more fun than Gus could remember having. She would lean a little back in his arm, so that she could look up at him—the posture would make her thighs press against his—and she would talk. Gus was always quiet and he always felt too quiet when he was with a woman. Peggy didn't seem to mind. In fact she didn't seem to notice. Her eyes were bright and her face was animated, and she would talk about what happened at Jordan Marsh, where she was a stenographer in the credit department, and what happened at home in Lynn with her sisters, and the fun she'd had last year when they all went up to Salem Willows. She used a bright lipstick, Gus noticed, and she enjoyed a drink. The smell of her—perfume, cigarette smoke, liquor—seemed to promise enchantment. And her laughter seemed perpetual and enduring, sounding in Gus's imagination long after they'd said good-night.

They began to kiss good-night on the second date, and by the fourth time he was able to put his hand on her breast, outside her sweater, and that was as far as it went.

"None of that," she would say if Gus tried for more. "Only my husband will get to do any of that, Mister Pushy Pushy."

"I'm sorry," Gus would say, his voice raspy with desire.

And Peggy would say, "Oh, I know, Gussy, men always try. They can't help it."

And Gus would be grateful that she wasn't angry.

"My mother's always warning me about you sex crazed women," Gus said once, as they sat in the Eliot Lounge after work. Peggy was drinking her third Cuba Libre.

"Oh, phooey on your mother," Peggy said. "Your mother

this, your mother that . . ." She drank. "Hell with your mother."

And she laughed. And he laughed.

"Hell with her," Gus said.

1956
Gus

She undressed in the bathroom, and insisted that the lights be off before she came out. Gus was in bed under the covers, when she came to the bed wearing a long nightie with small bows at the neckline. She got into bed beside him and pulled the covers up, and closed her eyes.

"Don't you hurt me," Peggy said. "I'm not very big."

She spoke a little girlish lisp that had seemed cute to Gus when they were dating, and *very* came out *vewy*.

"Me either," Gus said.

As they had the first sexual encounter of their marriage, she lay very still, with her eyes closed. He'd thought about this time a lot, about her trim, sturdy little body naked in his bed. He'd imagined a more erotic consummation. The whores he'd had on R and R in Tokyo had been lively. He knew that much of that had been pretense. But they had been fun. And they seemed, some of them, to enjoy it. Of course Peggy was no whore, and it was her first time.

She's scared, he thought.

Sometimes she seemed to clench as if in pain.

"You okay?" Gus said. "Am I hurting you?"

Eyes closed, she shook her head grimly.

"Go ahead," she said. "Go ahead."

He tried to be careful.

She'll relax in a while, Gus thought, *and it'll be better.*

1960
Gus

"You've got to get me some help," Peggy said. She was on her first bourbon. Gus knew he had maybe ten more minutes before she would be drunk and there was no further talking to her. They were at the kitchen table. Chris was on the floor playing with an assortment of plastic cowboys and Indians Gus had bought him.

"We got no money, Peg."

"Well, damn it, get some. He never lets me alone."

"He's a little kid," Gus said. "You're his mother."

"He never goes out, he never goes three feet away from me. See him, right under the damn table. It's as far as he gets."

She drank her bourbon. *About five more minutes*, Gus thought.

"I think it's better if we talk about this later, Peg."

"So the little darling won't hear?"

"Can't be good stuff for him to listen to."

"Maybe he'll learn something," Peggy said. "Give me some rest. You better do something, Gus. Or I'll be in the hospital."

Gus looked at his son. Chris's nose was running and he had a cough. Gus could tell by the set of his shoulders that he was listening, and Gus knew how smart he was. Chris would understand what they were saying. Gus felt very heavy.

"Peggy," Gus said, "every day about ten thousand women have about ten thousand babies and take care of them without having a damned breakdown. For Crissake, take care of your kid. You're his mother."

She finished the bourbon and poured some more, with a new

ice cube. She was heavy now. She'd never lost the weight she'd put on when she was carrying Chris.

"You're out there every day in your uniform with your shiny badge, and your big gun. You stand around, drink coffee, direct some traffic, flirt with all the girls. And you think you work hard. Well, let me tell you something about work, Mister Big Shot policeman. You should change a few thousand shitty diapers. Maybe you'd know something. Three years old and not even potty trained."

Gus took in some air. He'd changed enough diapers, but he knew there was no point arguing. He felt as if his whole self was in a contraction. He thought of hitting her. Even the thought of it was a kind of release. He looked at Chris, sitting stiffly on the floor, moving the toy figures intensely about.

He said, "I'll get you some money, Peg," and stood and scooped his son up in his arms. "Let's you and me go out to the store and buy a toy or something."

The boy was stiff in his father's arms. As they left the kitchen, Gus could feel Chris staring over his shoulder at his mother.

"Don't hurry back," Peggy said.

1994
Voice-Over

"They didn't know what to do with me," I said. "I wasn't like anything they'd ever expected, if they ever actually thought about what they expected."

"Most people probably don't," Grace said. "They think, *We'll get married and have children*, and have some vague image of the Gerber baby gurgling on their knee."

"Not us," I said.

"No."

"Sicklied o'er with the pale cast of thought."

Grace smiled, though not very much.

"Maybe you are not Prince Hamlet, nor were meant to be?"

She never said things at random, like I did, simply because they popped into her head. Her mind didn't work associatively. She was encouraging me, though not very much.

"I always remember," I said, "when my father would go to work when I was a little kid, I was scared, because I felt like there was no one to take care of us."

"You and Peggy."

"Yeah."

"God," Grace said, "how awful."

"For her too, I suppose. I'm way past liking her. Or forgiving her, for that matter. She was pretty unforgivable. But I can sympathize with her. She was overmatched. Here I was this sickly precocious kid, smarter than she was when I was very young—and I knew it at some scary, not quite conscious level. I entered

181

very early into a conspiracy to pretend that she was not more childlike than her child."

"You probably scared her," Grace said.

"Sure. Because she also knew at some not quite conscious level that she was more childlike than her child, that she herself needed to be taken care of, so how was she supposed to take care of me? She was scared because she didn't know what to do. Scared because she seemed to have no maternal instinct to trust, scared because her husband seemed to know what to do and seemed to have a parental instinct and seemed to trust it and seemed to take better care of me than of her, though she needed it as badly as I did. If she lost him, not his love, and apparently not his lovemaking, but if she had lost his—what—his adultness, it would have been as bad as if I lost him. We'd both have been orphans in the storm."

"And that," Grace said, "made her mad as hell."

"At him, at me. Every day. Every day that he was able to take care of me when she couldn't, every day when he had to take care of her when she couldn't, every day it rammed home her failure, and her helplessness, and every day enraged her."

Grace had made some smoked turkey sandwiches with yellow mustard on whole wheat bread. We were eating them and drinking tea, at her counter. The limb of a tree outside was thrashing in the wind and its movement, alternately shadowing and revealing the snow-blurred streetlamp at the end of the parking lot, made sporadic patterns on the high stark white wall of her living room.

"You seem to understand her plight very well," Grace said.

"Yeah," I said. "Funny you should notice."

Grace had cut the sandwiches diagonally into triangles; she took a significant bite of the pointed end of one.

"So what did he do?" she said.

"Gus? He got me away from her as much as he could. Which was hard, because he had to work. He was our sole financial support. But he'd take me places, and then he got some money."

"Un-huh," Grace said.

"I guess we know where. . . ." I said.

"By blackmailing my father," Grace said.

"Yeah . . . For me, I think. So I could go to a private kinder-garten. I hated the kindergarten and it scared me to be away from my mother. But it calmed her down a little. That way she had mornings free, and only had to deal with me until my father came home, if he was working days. If he was working nights, she didn't have to deal with me at all, because he'd get up when I came home from kindergarten, and play with me. I was too shy to play with other kids, and it must have driven my father crazy, because I wasn't interested in anything he knew anything about. I didn't like baseball, or fishing, stuff like that."

"So what did he do with you?"

"He read to me a lot, and we went to museums and historical restorations and places: Plymouth Plantation, *Old Ironsides*, the Museum of Fine Arts."

"Gus doesn't seem like a Fine Arts kind of person," Grace said.

"But I was," Chris said. "It was less the exhibits than the place. Museums are a controlled environment. I liked that. I felt safer there."

"Was your mother better?"

"At least different. Gus had hung it up, really. He never ar-gued with her. They didn't talk much or go out much. They slept in twin beds, and I'm sure that's all they did. I think she was probably relieved that she didn't have to . . . ah . . ." I looked for a word.

"Service him," Grace said.

"Yeah."

"So it was better."

"It was quieter, but they still had their battle, and I was the place they fought it. My father had no one else to love. My mother was jealous of it and wanted me for herself. Not as a child, but as a playmate, or maybe plaything, I don't know. To her I think I was more like an anatomically correct doll. And once I reached a point where I was less dependent, didn't require her to be a grown-up, then we sort of got on better. There was a period, a kind of stasis, after I had become less needy, and before I became too smart, when she could sort of relate to me like a plaything, or a pet."

"But you had your father, you knew he loved you."

"Yeah. I knew that, but sometimes I would think he loved her. In retrospect he didn't, he was just trying to find a way to make her a mother for me. But the stakes were too high when I was little. I couldn't afford any uncertainty."

"Poor Gus," Grace said.

"Yeah, he's a pretty straight-ahead guy, not stupid, but I think probably not so complicated then as he's become, and he was faced at home with this dysfunctional wife and this odd little kid that he loved. And he couldn't make it work."

"And he had a mother too," Grace said.

"Yeah, and she was no day at the beach either."

"But he did love you and he does."

"Oh, God, yes," I said. "Too much probably."

"Sort of a variation on the Sheridan tradition," Grace said.

"We are an obsessive lot," I said.

1970
Chris

He went with his father to Fenway Park. He was fourteen and disinterested. He was agile enough and, like the grandfather he'd never met, he was tall and naturally strong, but he didn't like sports. He never had. He'd rather have gone to the movies. He felt sullen as they went in, got peanuts and a program, and walked up through the stairwells. His father paused at the top of the stairs and looked at the bright green space, for a moment. Chris found the gesture really assy.

They were behind the first base dugout in some box seats that someone had given Gus. The Red Sox were playing Detroit. Chris didn't even know what the Detroit team was called, and he didn't want to know.

"See this guy," Gus said, pointing, "the guy in right for the Tigers?"

That's what they were called. Big deal.

"That's Al Kaline."

Like it matters.

"I know you don't know him, but just remember him. Someday you'll be proud to tell people you saw him."

In the box next to them was a man, his wife, and four boys. All of them had baseball gloves. The older two had scorecards, as did the man. The mother was still attractive. Her hair was blond. Her eyes were shaded by a big straw hat. She held the smallest boy on her lap, and pointed things out to him softly. The father and mother brushed against each other often in the box and when they did they usually looked at each other and

185

grinned. They looked at each other often when one of the boys said something they liked. And they grinned when they did that too.

"They gonna pitch Lolich today?" one of the kids asked in that annoying know-it-all way kids had when they talked sports.

"Bad news for Yaz," his brother said.

"Look at the arms on Willie Horton," his father said.

"Which one's he?"

"Black guy down there by the batting cage."

Chris looked at the thickly muscled black man standing next to what must have been the batting cage. He couldn't think of anything to say.

"You like this okay?" Gus said. "You don't like it we don't have to stay, you know? Tickets were free, don't cost us anything either way."

"I don't want to leave," Chris said.

The game started, and Chris watched it as hard as he could, but nothing much seemed to happen and when something did happen it didn't look very interesting. And he was never sure when he should cheer. The four boys in the next box were raucous and excited. Chris found them irritating. He looked at his father and saw him glance at the boys and their mother and father. And a surge of recognition went through him. Suddenly and clearly he experienced his father's loss. He would later think of it as an epiphany. The people in the box next to them were what Gus had hoped to be. The woman in the next booth holding the small boy on her lap leaned over and whispered in her husband's ear, he whispered something back, and she reddened a little and they both laughed, and Chris saw before him the unutterable gulf which loomed beneath his father, and experienced it as if it were his gulf, and knew for a moment what his father had lost and never spoken of, as if he had lost it.

He looked at the big man beside him, thick bodied as a tree stump, as unyielding as adamantine. His father looked at him and smiled and put one of his thick arms around Chris's shoulders and patted his upper arm.

"It's nice of you to come with me, Chris," he said. "I know it's not your favorite thing to do."

And Chris nodded without speaking and looked away toward the game in progress so that his father wouldn't see the tears which filled his eyes and blurred the bright green field before him.

1974
Gus

When Gus dropped him off at college, it was the first time Chris had been away from home. They drove up alone. The car was packed with things Peggy had decided Chris would need at college, but Peggy's back hurt her, she said, and the long ride would aggravate it, and then she'd have to stay in a motel, and she could never sleep in a strange bed.

"How'd Ma hurt her back?" Chris said as they drove west on Route 2, through the still summer landscape.

"I don't know," Gus said. "Hard to remember when she didn't have a bad back."

"She ever see a doctor?"

"Once. He told her she'd had a muscle spasm, suggested she do some sit-ups to strengthen her stomach."

"Sit-ups?" Chris said. "Ma?"

Gus smiled.

"I never saw her do any sit-ups," Chris said.

"No," Gus said. "I don't think she'd want to give up her bad back."

They were quiet. Chris's face was tight, the way it always was when he was scared. When he swallowed, Gus could hear him. Gus felt much the same way, but he'd learned to bury it deeper. At Chris's dorm there were a lot of station wagons with the make-believe wood on the sides, a lot of mothers in cashmere sweaters and plaid skirts, a lot of fathers in Brooks Brothers sportswear. *Very few Paddies*, Gus thought. *Very few coppers*. The incoming freshmen all seemed tanned and blond, wearing standard-issue tennis sweaters. Chris looked at Gus for a moment and both of them felt the abyss beneath them. Then they took the luggage and trudged into the dorm.

"I won't hang around," Gus said.

Chris shook his head in agreement.

"You'll be fine," Gus said.

Chris nodded.

"Sure," he said.

Gus didn't know how to do this. He felt clumsy, he put his arms awkwardly around his son and hugged him. Chris felt awkward too.

"Call," Gus said.

"Sure."

"And remember the Sheridan family motto," Gus said. "If they don't like it, fuck 'em."

Chris smiled a little, and Gus saw him swallow, and felt his own throat close. He made a small punching gesture with his closed right fist and turned and left.

That night he ate dinner alone at a Holiday Inn. At a table across the dining room a young man and woman had a baby in a portable bed. The woman took the child out of the bed, and held him in her lap as they ate dinner. Gus watched them, and felt his eyes fill. He thought he would cry. But he didn't. *Probably don't know how*, Gus thought.

1994
Voice-Over

The insistent snow fell heavily in the spring night. There was no steady gentle fall, nor drift of fine whiteness, rather the heavy plop of thick flakes designed to be rain.

"And," Grace said, "of all people for you to run into, little Grace Winslow, of Beverly Farms. Tom Winslow's only daughter."

"All the colleges, in all the world," I said. "You had to walk into that one."

"It is a little eerie," Grace said, "given the connection between our families that I'm the one you ask to dance."

"I thought you looked like you'd come across," I said.

"And you were right," Grace said.

"Eventually."

"I suppose you could say that the meeting may have been accidental," Grace said. "But then, when we found out that our families knew each other, it helped us select each other out."

"Thank you, Ms. Darwin," I said.

"You'd rather believe in destiny?"

"If I knew exactly what I'd rather believe in," I said, "we'd probably be married, raising children."

Grace nodded.

"You were so smart. I'd never known anyone as smart, and yet you didn't talk like all the boys I knew that went to Deerfield Academy and the Middlesex School. And you were such a wiseguy."

"It was my disguise," I said.

"It was more than that," Grace said.

"Yeah. Maybe it was. I'd started noticing very early in life that things are not as they are alleged to be."

"Yes," Grace said. "And you knew that sooner than most of us."

"Hell of a lot of good it did me," I said.

"It's the basis of knowledge," Grace said.

"For me it was the basis for paralysis. You know? Like the guy, whatsis name, in *The Iceman Cometh*, a poor weak fool seeing both sides of every question?"

"Your father and grandfather were men of action," Grace said.

"Don't I know it."

"What did it do for them?"

"I rest my case."

We were back in her den sitting on her couch, still a space between us, but Grace wasn't pressed quite so far into her corner, I thought. *Always the optimist.* My voice was getting hoarse from talking. I sipped some tea. Grace served the tea with honey and lemon, in big crimson mugs.

"My father used to take me to the station with him sometimes. All men. Everyone so sure of themselves, or seemed so, with their guns and nightsticks. They respected toughness, and courage, and action, and certainty. And everyone respected Gus. He was a stand-up guy. And what I hated every time I went there was the fear that I wasn't."

"But you wanted to be like him."

"I thought I did," I said. "But I couldn't be a cop. Jesus, I just couldn't."

Grace nodded. *Of course*, the nod said. Her eyes seemed bigger to me, and maybe kinder than they had been when I arrived.

"So I become a lawyer. I thought I'd be a criminal lawyer, but when it came down to it, and I had the law degree and had passed the bar and was ready to practice, it seemed too . . ." I searched vainly for the word I wanted.

"Participatory," Grace said.

"Yeah. That's good," I said. "Participatory. So instead, I went back and got a degree in criminology. Then I didn't have to catch criminals, or defend them. I had only to study them. And not even criminals, I got farther away than that. I could study the abstraction—crime!"

"Perfect," Grace said.

I nodded slowly, looking through the dark window at the thick white storm.

"Just perfect," I said.

1979
Tommy

It was not easy for him. Never free. Never able to shake loose. Two generations of Sheridans, knowing his secret. Using it. It was too much. Too much pressure. He thought all the time about the girls now. The pressure. He hadn't been with anyone since that girl in Charlestown, before he got sent away. But he'd thought about them every day. He'd wanted them every day. And now the pressure. Gus Sheridan. The gangsters. His own daughter, dating Gus Sheridan's son. It was too much. He had to have relief. He felt as if he'd been overinflated. As if the surface tension of his very self would burst and scatter. He needed a girl. Smooth body. Innocent legs. Pale skin, unwrinkled, unblemished, still smooth. Compliant. Respectful. Not mean. Not someone who had breasts. Not someone hairy. Not someone who had children. Not someone who wanted things. Who wanted you to do things. Not scary.

After thirty-three years. He had to have a girl. He stood and put on his coat and left his office.

"I've got some meetings," Tom told his secretary. "I'll be gone the rest of the day."

1993
Gus

Peggy was on her first bourbon. She was dressed up in a bright red polyester jacket and skirt, with a rhinestone rabbit on her lapel and a blue rayon scarf at her neck. Her short gray-brown hair was tightly permed. Her chunky cheerleader's body had fattened over the years, and there was a roll of flesh that showed above the constriction of a corset. Her neck was short and fleshy and her head sat very nearly on her shoulders. Gus sat beside her. Across the table was their son, Chris, and his girlfriend, Grace Winslow. They had a table by the window, where you could look out at the slick black water of the harbor. His son was monochromatic in dark jacket, shirt, and tie. Chris was taller than his father, and his clean-shaven jaw was shadowed with a heavy beard kept barely in check by the razor. Gus could never get used to seeing whiskers on his son's face. He could never see him except in the timeless compression of their thirty-six years. The infant in the hospital nursery, wrapped, and tilted head-down to allow things to drain. The five-year-old, swallowing nervously and yawning with anxiety while he watched *Tom Terrific* on television and waited for the school bus. Time past and time present crowded in every time on Gus when he looked at the boy, now a man, and the density of memory and emotion pressed inarticulately against his intrinsic containment. *My son.*

"How's Harvard, Christopher?" Peggy said.

"Fine, Ma. I'm teaching a graduate seminar this semester."

"May Brennan's son is teaching at Bishop Fenwick, she says. He's doing wonderful."

195

Chris nodded.

"Bishop Fenwick is a very good high school," Peggy said. Her glass was empty. The waiter came by and asked if she'd like another.

"Just a small one. Old bones, you know, need a little lift."

"Chris was offered the chair in his department," Grace said. She was strong looking, with huge blue eyes. Nearly as tall as Chris, with fine laugh lines at the corners of her wide mouth. Her thick auburn hair was pulled back from her face and tied with a black velvet ribbon. Even seated there was about her a kind of robust elegance. Even motionless she seemed somehow kinetic, full of exciting implication.

"What's that mean?" Peggy said. Her tone implied, as it always did, that, if she didn't understand it, there was something wrong with it.

"Head of the Department of Criminology," Chris said.

"That's nice," Peggy said. She was looking for the waiter. "They must like you."

"Probably has more to do with the quality of my work," Chris said. "I hope."

The waiter brought Peggy's second bourbon. She drank some.

"You're not going to get anywhere," she said, "if people don't like you. I'm telling you that right now. You make people mad at you, you'll never get anywhere."

"I turned it down," Chris said.

Gus nodded.

"You are making a mistake," Peggy said. "I'll tell you that here and now. You turn it down and they'll never offer it again."

"I'm not interested in academic administration," Chris said. "I like research."

"Just like your father," Peggy said. She drank some more of her second bourbon. "Two lumps. Two bumps on a log. Lump bump. If it wasn't for me your father would still be a dumb detective somewhere. When they wanted to promote him, I told him then what I'm telling you now. They don't ask twice. If it wasn't for me he'd be a nobody today."

Gus sat perfectly still. His Scotch and soda was barely tasted in front of him. He tried not to get drunk in front of his son.

"So, Peggy," Grace said, "how's your bridge group these days?"

"I played today with May, and Stella, and Catherine Rose, at Stella's house. She had an elegant lunch for us. And I bid three no trump and everyone said I couldn't make it, and I did." Peggy was animated. She drank the rest of her bourbon and clinked the ice around in the empty glass to attract the waiter. "Catherine Rose said to me, 'Peggy, you are a bridge star.' She's a love."

"Good for you," Grace said. She smiled brightly. Gus could feel the amusement and the anger in her. *My son and Tommy's daughter*, he thought. Sometimes it seemed to him that the Winslows and the Sheridans were dancing to the music of infinity, generation by generation, two stepping blindly into hell. Peggy ordered her third bourbon. Chris had another beer.

"Beer'll put the weight right on your belly," Peggy said. "You're at a very vulnerable age. Look at your father."

Chris said, "Dad looks pretty good to me."

"He's got a belly on him," Peggy said. Her words were starting to slur. "You'll have one too if you keep drinking that beer."

The waiter came and took their food order. If you could get her eating, you could keep her from getting too drunk. Peggy ordered baked stuffed shrimp. And another little drink. The waiter went away. At the next table a young woman was having a birthday, and the waiters brought her a cake with a candle and sang "Happy Birthday." Peggy sang along with them.

How could she be his mother? Gus thought. *How could I have permitted my son to be born to her?*

Gus

It was April, early evening, raining, and almost dark when they came across the McArdle Bridge with the siren on. They saw the blue lights first, turning on top of four cruisers pulled up nose-in beside a boatyard on the East Boston side. The cruiser head-lights shone on the boatyard, and the yellow crime-scene tape looked kind of pretty in the light.

The unmarked division car pulled up onto a shoulder behind the cruisers, and Billy Callahan shut the motor off. The siren tailed away weakly. And they got out. It was a hard rain and cold. Gus turned up his coat collar and stuck his hands in his pocket as they walked toward the group of uniforms gathered behind the hull of a dry-docked fishing boat. All of them wore yellow slickers in the rain.

The yard was a jumble of ropes and broken boards, and jerry-built boats sitting off center in their cradles. The partial bright-ness of the headlights distorted them even more than their own-ers had, and they loomed like imperfect animals in the shadows.

A patrol sergeant named Daly spoke to Gus.

"He's down here, Captain. It's Corky O'Brien."

"I know Corky," Gus said.

One of the patrol officers handed Gus a flashlight and he put the beam on the body on the ground. Face up, eyes unblinking in the rain. The blood which had dried around his nose and mouth was washing slowly away in a pinkish trickle.

"He looks like he took a beating, Captain," Daly said.

Gus nodded.

"Wasn't what killed him, though," Daly said.

He nodded again. The patrol people were usually pretty eager at a murder. Wanted you to know they hadn't missed anything.

"Somebody shot him behind the right ear, see?" Daly put the beam of his flashlight on the entry wound. "Looks like a small caliber to me. Maybe a .22, there's no exit wound, means the bullet's still in there."

"That's great," Billy Callahan said. "Why'd you bother calling homicide?" Billy was very protective of Gus.

"Hey, fuck you," Daly said.

Gus walked on past the body and down to the edge of the slip, where two more misshapen fishing boats bobbed on the black water. The ocean smelled brackish, as if it had insinuated among these rotting pilings too long. The rain came steadily. The hair was plastered to Gus's skull. Behind him he heard more sirens as the crime-scene people showed up. Gus hunched his shoulders a little to loosen them, and turned and walked back toward the body.

"Let's get out of the rain," he said to Billy Callahan.

"Sure, Captain. Patrol hotshots got this fucker about wrapped up anyway."

They walked back up toward the car. Billy Callahan had his head tipped a little forward so that the water running off of the brim of his scally cap cleared his chin and splashed onto the chest of his raincoat.

In the car Billy said, "You know the victim, Captain?"

"Hoodlum from Charlestown."

"He connected?"

"Got four brothers," Gus said. "They run their own outfit."

Down the slope, in the headlight glare, the man from the coroner's office was squatting beside the body. He had on a tan raincoat, and a felt hat. A clear plastic cover protected the hat. Nobody wore hats like that anymore. It made Gus think of his father.

"Corky's knuckles were skinned," Gus said.

"You think it was just a fight, Captain?"

Billy had been his driver for ten years, and a cop for twenty. He lived with his sister, went to Mass every Sunday, and spent his free time lifting weights. He was stupid and goodhearted and would walk into the mouth of a cannon as required.

"No," Gus said.

Billy nodded vigorously. He thought so too.

Gus

Town Liquors was in Thompson Square, part of a brick strip mall that developers claimed would help upscale Charlestown. The plate glass window was full of big white tear sheets scrawled with splashy Magic Marker announcements of how cheaply you could buy Canadian Club, or Miller beer. Billy waited in the car while Gus went in.

"Butchie around?" Gus said.

The counter clerk was a thin, pale guy with a potbelly and too little hair combed sadly over too much scalp. He wore sunglasses.

"Sure, Captain, in back. You know the way, I guess. Huh?"

Gus went past the counter and through the back room stacked with beer cases and into another room that had been partitioned off with plywood and left unpainted. The door was green, obviously from another incarnation, and it hung on big strap hinges. There was a padlock hasp, but no padlock. He didn't knock. The geek at the counter would have hit a button.

Butchie O'Brien was sitting in a big green leather swivel chair behind a big gray steel executive desk with two telephones and a loose-leaf calendar on it. A lamp with a big green shade hung from the ceiling over him.

"How you doing, Gus?" Butchie said. "Have a seat."

Butchie nodded at a gray metal chair with a darker gray seat cushion. He was taller than Gus and slender, with a nearly bald head and a good tan, and his movements were graceful and economical. He wore a wide handlebar moustache, which was mostly gray. He had on a colorful sweater, and a diamond ring on his little finger.

"Sorry about Corky," Gus said.

Butchie's tan face didn't change expression. He nodded.

"You see him?" he said.

"Yeah."

"Somebody worked him over pretty bad before they shot him," Butchie said.

Gus nodded.

"You on it?" Butchie said.

"It's a homicide," Gus said.

"And you're the homicide commander," Butchie said. "You got anything?"

"No," Gus said. "You?"

"Family matter, Gus. We got theories. We're exploring."

Gus shrugged. Butchie's eyes were pale blue, and flat, like the surface of a beach pebble.

"I mean it, Gus. Nobody treats one of us that way and walks. You unnerstand?"

"Sure," Gus said.

Butchie looked at his desk calendar, then leaned forward to study it.

"Well, by God," he said. "About that time of the month isn't it?"

Gus didn't say anything. Butchie didn't expect him to. He took out some keys and unlocked one of the desk drawers and took out a metal cash box. He opened it. Took out some bills, closed the cash box, and put it away. He put the bills in an envelope, and tucked the flap in without sealing it.

"Here you go, Gus," Butchie said, and held out the envelope. Gus took it and slid it into his inside pocket without counting the money. Gus never counted it in front of Butchie, and Butchie never shorted him. There are rules for everything.

"I won't be able to come to the wake," Gus said.

"I unnerstand, Gus. It wouldn't look right. You come across anything you'll let us know."

"Sure," Gus said.

"Best to the missus," Butchie said.

Gus

The first drink of the day. Scotch and soda. Tall glass, lot of ice. Enough soda to make the Scotch a translucent garnet. It felt clean and brisk, as if it would purge his system of the day's accumulated toxins. Gus knew better, but it was pleasant to pretend. He put his feet up on the glass-top coffee table, and leaned back on the white couch. Mary Alice came over with a glass of white wine and sat beside him and put her head on his shoulder. With her left hand she rubbed the top of his thigh.

"Getting old, Sheridan?" she said.

"And fatter," Gus said. "Every year."

She moved her head a little on his shoulder, and rubbed her cheek against it sympathetically. Mary Alice worked in the mayor's office. He never had known what it was exactly she did. And she was committed to dressing for success. Just home from work, she had on a tailored black suit, with a little kick pleat, and a white blouse with a little black-and-white polka-dot scarf simulating a necktie. She rubbed his thigh gently.

"I'm going to be sixty-one," Gus said, "in the fall."

"You don't look it," Mary Alice said.

Mary Alice had a penthouse in Longfellow Place, a high-rise warren of stewardesses and young stockbrokers that had jumped from the ruins of the old West End. It had a working fireplace and a big view of the Charles River, and the charm of a Ramada Inn. It cost two thousand dollars a month, which Gus paid.

Gus finished his drink, and Mary Alice made another one, and poured herself some more white wine. She wiggled a little when she brought it to him. It was not conscious, probably. Mary Alice had a little wiggle when she was standing still. She handed over the drink and cocked a hip.

"You seem low, Sheridan. Old lady giving you cramps?"

Gus shrugged. Mary Alice sat beside him again. The fire was working well now, and danced happily in the designer fireplace.

"The kid?"

"No," he said. "Chris's fine. He's doing great."

"Well, he should be, all that education. How old is he?"

"Thirty-seven."

"And working already," Mary Alice said.

"Don't talk about my kid," Gus said.

"He's not a kid, Gus. For Crissake, he's thirty-seven years old. Isn't it time to let go of him?"

And hang on to what? Gus thought.

"Talk about something else," he said.

Something in his voice scared her.

"Sure," she said. "Sure I will."

Gus put his head back against the couch, and closed his eyes, and put his hand over hers on his thigh and patted it.

"I saw in the paper some mobster got killed," Mary Alice said. Very perky. "You working on that?"

"Corky O'Brien. Yeah."

"How's that going?"

"It's going to get worse," Gus said. He kept his eyes closed. Mary Alice was gently rubbing his thigh again.

"You know who did it?"

"I will soon."

"You have a lead?"

Gus smiled with his eyes closed, and shook his head.

"Then why do you think you're going to know soon?"

"He'll turn up dead," Gus said. "Probably killed the same way Corky was."

"You know that?"

"Yeah."

"And you can't stop it?"

Gus shook his head again.

"That's awful," Mary Alice said.

"Corky's no loss," Gus said. "The guy who killed him won't be either."

"I meant for you, awful for you."

Gus shrugged and patted her hand again.

"Doesn't make any difference to me," he said.

"What does, Gus?"

He opened his eyes and looked at her.

"Fucking's nice," he said.

And Mary Alice giggled and said, "You got that right," and put her glass of wine on the table and turned her face up toward his.

Gus

It was almost the same as last time, except this time it was morning and it wasn't raining, and they came in through East Boston and down Meridien Street. But the boatyard was the same, and the body was nearly the same.

"Jackie Malloy," Gus said, looking down at him.

"Beaten up badly and shot behind the ear," one of the detectives said. "Small caliber."

The detective was John Cassidy. He was a thin guy with round gold-rimmed glasses, who looked like he should have been a priest. There was a harsh spring wind coming off the harbor and Cassidy had his hands in his pockets. His overcoat collar was turned up, and his chin sunk into it.

"Even up for Corky."

"Don't know that, Captain," Cassidy said.

Gus didn't say anything. The wind blowing off the harbor smelled of sewage. He turned and let the wind blow against his back.

"Stay on it, Johnny," he said. "Come talk to me when you get through here."

"Sure, Captain."

Gus walked back up toward the unmarked gray Chevy that Billy drove him around in.

"We'll go to the office," Gus said when he was in the car. "Use the siren, I don't want to fuck around in the traffic."

Billy liked that, Gus knew. He liked to use the siren and the blue light and force through traffic as cars squeezed left and right for him. When he could, Gus let him do it. They went through Chelsea and up over the Mystic River Bridge, which was officially the Tobin Bridge, which no one called it. Even with the siren it was heavy going in the morning traffic, but better than the tunnel, where there was no place to squeeze. Gus sat in front, beside Billy, as he always did, and read the paper.

"So, you think it's the O'Briens and the Malloys starting up, Captain?"

"Yes," Gus said without taking his eyes from the newspaper. He had it folded over into a manageable size, the way people do on the subway.

"So it's Butchie O'Brien's turn again," Billy said.

Gus was reading the real estate listings. He thought often about moving. West of the city someplace, Concord maybe, a big place with a lot of land sloping down to the river, fenced so the dogs could run loose. He held the image—a meadow and a river and the dogs running free.

"And they'll buzz somebody, and then the Malloys will have to buzz somebody, and so forth and so on," Billy said.

Gus ignored him. Billy didn't mind. He talked because silence made him uncomfortable. He didn't expect Gus to respond. Gus thought about his meadow. The dogs should be hunters, pointers probably, maybe a retriever in there too, and they'd course the meadow, bounding about with their mouths open, and then push into the river and swim with their heads up and come out and shake themselves dry and look up at him with their tongues lolling.

"And so forth and so on," Billy said again. Sometimes when he found a phrase he liked he said it several times. "And so forth and so on."

Billy parked on Berkeley Street and Gus got out and went in to work.

Chris

"Why doesn't your father tell her to shut up?" Grace said.

Chris shrugged. "Just make it worse. You try and shush her, or argue with her, she gets hysterical."

"Do you think she knows she's a drunk?"

Chris stopped for the light at Leverett Circle.

"Old bones," he said in imitation of his mother's girlish manner, "need a little lift."

The light changed and he moved out onto Storrow Drive. Grace was turned in the front seat beside him, her hands folded in her lap. She always managed to look simultaneously lively and elegant, even when doing simple things, like sitting and listening.

"And," Chris said, "he may love her."

"God," Grace said. "I hope not."

"She was a lot of fun when she was younger. Like a playmate —very bubbly and playful and full of energy. She didn't get fat really till I was grown."

In the darkness to their right the lights from East Cambridge splashed on the thick black river surface. Traffic at this time of a weeknight was desultory on Storrow Drive, and the backs of the riverview brick town houses along Beacon Street to their left were mostly dark.

"I remember when I was a little kid, she came into my room late at night, home from a party, and gave me a big kiss and patted me and laughed. Her breath smelled of booze, and lipstick, which I remember as a very nice smell, very festive. And she was giggly and looked very pretty in the light from the hall, all dressed up. Jesus, did I love her."

"Maybe you still do," Grace said.

"I don't think so. I've thought about it. And I don't find any love in there."

"And yet you let her treat you like a stupid child."

Chris was silent.

"You let her get away with it," Grace said.

"My father has always valued restraint," Chris said.

"He lets her get away with it too."

"Yeah."

"It's not right. You're both grown, accomplished men. Who gives a fuck about Boopsie Poopsie's son teaching in high school, for Crissake? You don't drink a lot of beer. Your father's not fat. She shouldn't be allowed to say things like that to either of you."

"Gracie," Chris said, "feel free. Next time she's abusive, jump right in."

"I can't do that. She's not my mother."

"That's right," Chris said.

"Oh, for Christ sake."

"Don't give me *Oh, for Christ sake*. She isn't your mother. She's not your problem."

"She'll be my goddamned problem if she's my mother-in-law. She'll be a bundle of laughs as a mother-in-law."

"You wouldn't have to marry her," Chris said.

"So what do I do when she's treating my husband like an incompetent child?"

"You let your husband handle it," Chris said wearily.

"What happened to 'jump right in'?"

"You want to not marry me because you don't like my mother?" Chris said.

"Oh, God, Chris, don't be such an asshole."

They were silent. He drove up the ramp at the Anderson Bridge and turned right on red toward Cambridge. Chris felt his eyes stinging as if he would cry. He blinked to clear them, and felt himself going inside, the way he always did when he'd misbehaved and his mother had been sulky. His father had been like that, he knew. Probably his grandfather. *Maybe fucking Adam, for all I know. Gotta go somewhere.* At the duplex house on Walker Street, they got out and went in without speaking. Chris was still silent and deep inside when he fell finally asleep.

Gus

Pat Malloy sat in the front seat of Gus's private car in the parking lot of a Dunkin' Donuts shop in Union Square, Somerville, and drank a large coffee, black with two packets of Sweet'n Low.

"No doughnuts, Gus," he said. "I'm trying to drop some weight. The old lady's on my ass."

Gus nodded. He broke a plain doughnut in half and took a bite from one half.

"How many fifty-year-old guys, she says, my size I see walking around?" Pat said. "And I say you don't see many guys my size walking around any age. I take a size fifty-eight suit, you know? and she says you don't see any that are fifty because they're all dead, she says."

Gus swallowed some doughnut, took a sip of coffee, put the cup back on the dash.

"She's worried about you, is all," he said.

"Shit," Pat said. "Don't smoke, don't eat, don't drink. Pretty soon it'll be no fucking—and then what are we going to do with our spare time, Gus?"

Gus looked through the front window at the people waiting in line to buy doughnuts. He wondered why everyone always looked tired in doughnut shops.

"Patrick," he said, "I don't want this thing with the O'Briens to turn into anything more than it is."

"What thing?"

"You kill Corky, they kill Jackie."

"I didn't kill nobody, Gus."

"Sure," Gus said. "And nobody did Jackie."

"We're taking care of that," Pat said.

"That's what I don't want, Patrick. It's one apiece now. Why not let it lay."

"Fucking bozo kills my cousin, Gus?"

"Even up for Corky," Gus said.

"Corky earned it, Gus. You unnerstand. Corky insisted on it. Jackie was just in the wrong place at the wrong time."

"It's even, Patrick."

"Hey, Gus. Am I a man or fucking what? Some asshole buzzes my cousin, Jackie, that I grew up with. And I say, 'Oh, sure, okay, we're even'? There ain't no fucking even in our world, Gus. There ain't no fucking tie games. You gotta know that much."

"So you cap one of theirs and they cap one of yours and what? It's a war. It spills over into the rest of the city. The press rolls around in it like a hog in shit. I can't sit on that, Patrick."

"You can't, huh? You forget who you are, Gus. You unnerstand? You are thinking like you are a cop. Like you are a homicide fucking dee-tective. You ain't. You are my fucking employee, Gus. I got a record of every dime I've paid you, since you were a beat cop in City Square. I pay for your pussy. I put your fucking kid through fucking Harvard. You take my fucking money and you do what you are fucking told. You don't tell me what you want. I fucking tell you. End of story."

Gus ate the other half of his doughnut in silence. He sipped another swallow of coffee from his cup.

"Go ahead, Patrick," Gus said. "Give it to me straight, how you feel about my suggestion."

Pat shook his head.

"Don't you fuck with me, Gus. You're crazy. We been doing business, what, twenty-five years? You always been crazy. All the time acting like you're better than me and all the time with your fucking hand in my pocket. I'm telling you now, one time only, Gus. Don't go thinking like you're a cop. Don't fuck with me."

Gus nodded.

"Nice talking to you, Patrick," he said.

Pat heaved himself slowly sideways and out of the car. He stood with the door open, bent over, looking in at Gus.

"Don't fuck with me, Gus," he said. His voice was flat. "Remember what I'm saying to you."

"I'll keep it in mind, Patrick," Gus said. They looked at each other for a long, motionless moment. Then Pat shut the car door and Gus put it in reverse and backed out of the parking lot.

Chris

"Chris, we have to talk," Grace said.

"Sure," Chris said. "Let's talk."

"I can't stand the way we are connected," Grace said carefully.

"What the hell does that mean?"

"When I come toward you, you back away. When I pull back you envelop me. I don't know how to be, with you."

"For Crissake, why not just be," Chris said. "Follow your instincts."

As he spoke Grace was shaking her head. There was no anger in her voice, but there was frightening certainty.

"No, that's a rap you've laid on me for a while. It's no good. You won't let me be instinctual. I'm like some kind of Rorschach test for you, where sometimes I look like one thing and sometimes I look like something else. Since we were children I've been the bang board of your family pathologies. I can't stand it. I have to get out of here."

Chris felt the heaviness, the unalterable systemic closing down. He could think of nothing to say as he slowly imploded, his physical self collapsing in on his soul.

"You need to be alone, Chris. You need to be able to get along on your own. . . ."

"Grace, Jesus Christ . . ."

"I'm going to go away for a while," Grace said.

The silence came down upon him like settling dust.

"Just like that?"

"No. I've been thinking about it for a long time. I've gotten a place of my own, and I'm going there for a while."

"Now?"

Grace's face was gentle.

"Yes," she said. "Now. I'll stay in touch. I'll call you in a while."

"Is there someone else?" Chris said.

"I'm not leaving you for someone else. But I have to go now."

"Can we not tell anyone?" Chris said.

Grace stared at him for a moment.

"Please," Chris said.

"Okay," Grace said. "For now."

He stood and watched her go, and after she had gone, he stared out the window after her, so deep inside that he barely existed. This couldn't be. It was supposed to be forever. He was going to be safe, forever.

Gus

It was Friday night, ten after six. Gus was in the mayor's office. Parnell Flaherty stood with his back to Gus, looking through his big picture window down at Quincy Market. Gus had always assumed that Quincy Market was where overweight white suburban couples went if they died in a state of grace. Nonetheless, it was a hugely successful urban renewal project, and Parnell Flaherty was proud of it.

"Centerpiece of this city, Gus," Flaherty said.

He was six feet two inches tall with white hair, a youthful, healthy, ruddy face, and bright blue eyes which seemed never to blink. He played competitive handball every morning before work and his clothes fitted him effortlessly.

"Sure is, Mayor," Gus said.

Gus always addressed the mayor by title, even though he had known Flaherty since Gus was a detective and Flaherty a young prosecutor, newly graduated from BC Law.

"You go there, Gus?"

"Every time I need to buy a life-size porcelain llama," Gus said.

Flaherty turned and grinned at Gus.

"Wasn't designed for you, Gus. Or me either. Pulls a lot of people into the city."

Gus nodded. They weren't enemies. But they weren't friends either. Gus knew he hadn't been invited in to talk about Quincy Market.

Flaherty turned and looked back down at the market complex and the Central Artery beyond it and the waterfront on the other side of the Artery.

"Never should have been built, that Artery. Cuts the city off from the water."

Flaherty stood with his hands in his hip pockets, the soft drape of his suit jacket spilling around his hands. He always said *city* in boldface.

"Be glad when we get it underground," he said.

He turned suddenly and took his hands from his hip pockets. The suit jacket fell perfectly back into line.

"Where's my manners?" Flaherty said. "Sun's set, and I haven't offered you a drink."

He walked to the sideboard at the other end of the big office.

"What'll it be, Gus? Scotch?"

Gus nodded.

"Soda," he said. "Lots of ice."

Flaherty made the drinks expertly. He brought one to Gus, and took his own, Scotch on the rocks in a squat thick low ball glass, around behind his desk, and sat down. He put one foot up on a half-open desk drawer and tilted back in his high-backed red leather swivel chair.

"I been mayor, Gus, for eighteen years," Flaherty said.

He rolled the Scotch whiskey around over the ice cubes in his glass. Gus drank some of his Scotch and felt some of the tension leave him. The first drink of the day, tall glass, plenty of ice, and soda, with the clean bite of the whiskey edging through. There were few things that made him feel so good at so little cost.

"Eighteen years is enough," Flaherty said.

"Be enough for me," Gus said.

Flaherty grinned and swished his whiskey around some more, watching it slide over the ice cubes.

"Sometimes I think it was the fucking busing. We're still fighting with it. Sometimes, Gus, I think it killed this city."

Gus shrugged. His drink was nearly gone. Without asking he stood and went to the sideboard and mixed another. He looked at Flaherty, who had barely touched his drink. Flaherty shook his head, and Gus came back and sat.

"So I'm getting out," Flaherty said. "I'm not going to go for mayor next November. I'm making a run for the Senate."

"Which seat?" Gus said.

He was comfortable now. There was whiskey in his hand and more where it came from. He could sit in this comfortable chair and let Flaherty talk as long as he wanted to.

"Walsh is retiring," Flaherty said. "He's going to announce next week. Ill health."

"What's wrong with him?"

"Probably got the clap," Flaherty said. "Way he spends his free time."

Gus nodded. So Flaherty wouldn't say. Didn't matter. He didn't really care what was wrong with Walsh. He drank some Scotch.

"So I'm going to be the nominee."

"How about the primary, and the convention?" Gus said. Just to be saying something.

Flaherty smiled.

"I'm confident that the electorate will honor me with the nomination," he said.

"So it's bagged," Gus said.

"Yeah."

Gus nodded.

"Congratulations," he said.

"But the election's not bagged. I would if I could, but I can't. I'm going to have to win the election. What's going on between the O'Briens and the Malloys in Charlestown?"

"Somebody killed a head knocker named Corky O'Brien and dumped him in a boatyard in East Boston. Corky was one of Butchie O'Brien's brothers and Butchie runs half the rackets, approximately, in Charlestown. Week or so later somebody killed Jackie Malloy, in the same way, and dumped him in the same boatyard. Jackie is Pat Malloy's cousin. Pat Malloy runs everything in Charlestown that Butchie doesn't. That's what I know."

"And what do you think?" Flaherty said.

"A Malloy killed an O'Brien, and the O'Briens killed a Malloy for revenge."

"Will it stop there?" Flaherty said.

"I doubt it," Gus said.

"That's a problem," Flaherty said.

Gus shrugged.

"You know these people?" Flaherty said.

"Yeah."

Gus got up and made himself a third Scotch. This time Flaherty took a refill.

"You see my problem, Gus," Flaherty said. "So far, no problem. Couple of small-time thugs get dumped. No loss. City's probably a better place for it. But . . ." He swirled the Scotch again in his glass and took a taste.

"If it keeps happening and if a body pops up"—Flaherty pointed with his chin—"in the Market, say . . . then my Republican opponent will be able to suggest that as mayor I was soft on crime."

Gus drank some Scotch. The piercing pleasure of it had passed. Now it was more a matter of maintenance.

"I want you to do something about this, Gus."

"They don't always do what I tell them, Mayor."

"I want you to be on this personally," Flaherty said. "I want you to find a way. Nobody wants a senator that's soft on crime."

"Do what I can," Gus said.

"Do what you must," Flaherty said.

Gus smiled, more to himself than anyone, and sipped his drink.

"You know which dim-witted Wasp the Republicans are going to run against you this time?" Gus said.

Flaherty was silent for a moment. He swirled his Scotch and drank some and put the glass back in his lap, where he held it in both hands. Then he smiled carefully.

"Actually, I think you know him," Flaherty said. "Cabot Winslow."

The good feeling went away. Gus felt suddenly very sober. He sat perfectly still, without speaking.

"Tom Winslow's boy. You know the family, don't you?" Flaherty said.

Gus nodded. He put the half-drunk Scotch and soda on the side table.

"In fact," Flaherty said, "doesn't your boy go with the sister?"

Gus nodded again.

"Kind of," he said.

Flaherty smiled, and shook his head.

"And him a fine Irish bucko," he said. "Times change, Gus."

"I don't want Chris to be a campaign issue," Gus said. He looked steadily at Flaherty. Flaherty returned the stare. Then he shook his head.

"Not my style, Gus."

Gus didn't say anything. The ice melting in Gus's drink made a little clink as one cube slid against another.

"How's a Paddy ever get involved with the Winslows?" Flaherty said.

Gus shrugged. "My father knew Tom's mother and father in Ireland," he said.

Flaherty sipped his drink. Gus left his where it was.

"Cabot'll run the usual Goo Goo campaign. 'The Micks have corrupted the city. Trust me, I went to Harvard.' It won't help my cause any to have an Irish gang war banging away all over the city."

"So far, Mayor, you got two stiffs in a boatyard in East Boston."

"I don't care where they ended up," Flaherty said. "They're from Charlestown. And they're Micks. They get strung out on a point of fucking honor and it'll go on until there's no one left."

"It could," Gus said.

"And it'll spill out," Flaherty said. "And some yokel from Sudbury will get in the way and the talk shows will go crazy."

Flaherty let his chair come forward and leaned over his desk, still holding his drink in both hands.

"I don't want Cabot Winslow coming in and fucking up my city."

"You're sure he'd fuck it up," Gus said.

"Of course he would. The Goo Goos deal in theories. A city is people, Gus. You know Cabot, Gus?"

Gus nodded.

"What do you think?"

"He'd fuck it up," Gus said.

Flaherty nodded his head and kept nodding it.

"So plug that gang war up for me, Gus."

"Sure," Gus said.

Gus

Mary Alice said, "So you've been talking with Hizzoner."

Gus said, "You don't miss much, do you?" and dropped his raincoat over the back of the straight chair in the foyer, the way he always did.

"Us City Hall insiders," Mary Alice said. "See all, know all."

She came over and kissed him on the mouth and leaned against him and let the kiss linger. Then she went to the sideboard and made him a drink.

"He wanted to talk to you about the election," Mary Alice said.

Gus sat in his chair and put his feet up and tipped his head back against the cushions and closed his eyes.

"How'd you know that?" he said.

"That's all he talks to anyone about," Mary Alice said. "Senator Flaherty. The chance to finish out with a little class, national recognition. He wants this worse than I've ever seen him want anything."

"He wants me to prevent a gang war," Gus said.

"Those murders in the boatyard?"

"Yeah."

Mary Alice came over and sat on the footstool beside him. She had on high heels and jeans and a man's blue shirt, with the shirttails tied in front. Pearls showed at her throat. Her nails were manicured and done with a neutral polish. She wore no rings.

"You think there will be a war?" she said.

"Um-hum," Gus said.

He rested the cold glass against his forehead for a moment.

"Like the Hatfields and the McCoys," he said.

"Anything you can do to stop it?"

222

Gus shook his head.

"These guys aren't punks," Gus said. "They are bad guys, and brutal, and the world would be better off without them. But they keep their word. They protect their own. They require respect. They have rules and they're willing to do whatever it takes to keep them intact. This thing will go on until one side is gone."

"Gone?"

"Nobody left."

"You mean dead?"

Gus opened his eyes and smiled at her.

"Yeah," he said. "Dead."

Mary Alice hunched her shoulders as if to ward off the cold.

"You sound like you admire them," she said.

"There's things they stand for," Gus said. "They got rules."

"And that makes them good?"

Gus shrugged.

He held his glass out and Mary Alice took it and made him another drink. She handed it to him and sat on the arm of his chair with white wine in one hand. With her free hand she massaged his neck.

"You got any rules, Gus?" she said.

He shrugged again.

"You know who the Republicans are going to run against Flaherty?" Gus said.

"Un-uh."

"Cabot Winslow."

She continued to rub his neck while she thought about this.

"Your son's girlfriend's brother," she said.

"Yeah."

"Is your son serious about her?"

"I think so," Gus said.

"Will they get married?"

"Don't know," Gus said.

The Scotch wasn't doing much yet. He'd had several with Flaherty and now two with Mary Alice. But the time between had probably ruined it. He felt heavy and slow.

"Well, shit," Mary Alice said. "I don't know what I think about that. It might be kind of complicated, I guess. I mean with you and Flaherty and all. On the other hand it's got nothing much to do with you, really."

"I don't like it for the kid," Gus said. His glass was empty. He heaved himself up, leaving her sitting on the arm of the chair, and went and got the jug wine from the refrigerator and freshened her glass. Then he made himself a big drink, mostly Scotch, a splash of soda, and sat down again. She put her chin gently on top of his head.

"I don't see what harm would come to Chris," she said.

"Hard to figure," Gus said.

The third Scotch began to lift him a little.

"Flaherty mentioned it to me tonight. I don't like it. Flaherty's a mean prick."

"I don't see how Chris could get hurt, Gus. You worry about him too much."

"What else do I have to worry about?" Gus said.

His eyes were closed again. Mary Alice continued to rub his neck, up where the base of the skull sits on the big neck muscles.

"You might worry a little about yourself, now and then."

Gus shook his head.

"You might," Mary Alice said. "You're worth worrying about."

"I'm worth shit," Gus said. "Just like my old man, two generations of fucking bog-trotting Paddies, married to the wrong broad. Hired muscle, rattling doorknobs and busting heads, working for the Yankee dollar."

"Gus!"

"Going nowhere, worth nothing. Married to a hysterical fucking cow. No, he's the one. My son. Break the chain. Be something decent. Have some land. Dogs."

The image was there again. The hunting dogs coursing the meadow, barking excitedly, rolling over each other in play, looking back up the hill at him. And beyond them the dark river with the sun glinting off it.

"Gus, don't say things like that. You're a successful man. You're a police captain. Homicide commander. You make good money."

"Better than you know," Gus said into the black void behind his closed eyes.

Mary Alice stopped rubbing his neck. She sat upright and stared down at his face.

"Are you on the take?" she said softly.

He didn't speak or move. He sat with his eyes closed and his face expressionless.

"Are you, Gus?" she said.

He was still. She didn't ask again. He drank. She sipped her wine. Then she put her hand back down and began to rub his neck again.

"You asked me if I had rules," he said.

She nodded.

"The kid is my rules. He's what I stand for. He's all I believe in. You understand? Him only, nothing else."

"Not even me, Gus?" Mary Alice said. "A little bit?"

He opened his eyes then and stared up at her.

"I like you, Mary Alice," he said, "and I don't lie to you. Settle for that."

She took his glass and put it on the floor and slid onto his lap and kissed him. Her mouth opened. Her tongue moved insistently. He opened his mouth to hers, allowed her tongue in. His arms were around her loosely. She put hers around his neck and twisted herself against him, her back arching, her thighs sprawled openly across him. She took one of his hands and placed it between her thighs.

"Jeans are kind of tough," Gus said softly.

"You could take them off," she said with her mouth against his.

"I may be getting a little long in the tooth for fucking in chairs too," Gus said.

Mary Alice giggled.

"I'm not thinking about the length of your tooth," she said, and stood up in a quick fluid movement. She stepped out of high heels, unzipped her jeans, and slid them down her thighs. She used one foot to step herself out of the jeans. Gus looked at her from the chair as she thought he looked at everything. His face was nearly empty, touched only with a hint of amusement, or contempt, she never knew which, and if it was contempt, she was never sure for whom. His eyes ran slowly over her body, looked at her breasts, which were still good, she knew, and down the slope of her stomach, which had softened a little, but not too much. She put her hands on her hips and stared back at him, and for a moment there was no sound, and no movement in the room, as if the two of them were locked in this fierce tableau.

Then he smiled and said, "You still look good, Mary Alice."

And he stood and put her suddenly on her back on the floor, and made love to her without removing his clothes. As always, she was noisy: moaning, and talking, wildly antic through every experienced ritual of foreplay and culmination. As always, he was silent: focused and skillful until the moment of ejaculation, when he buried his face against her neck and clung to her savagely while the spasms passed. Sometimes when he did that she thought he might be crying, but there were never tears, and when it was over his eyes were always dry.

They lay beside each other on the floor. Her head rested on his arm. She rolled her head toward him.

"Is it like this when you fuck Peggy, Gus?"

He didn't answer for a time, staring up at the smooth white ceiling. *Plasterboard skim coated*, he thought. *You don't see an actual plastered ceiling much anymore.* Then he rolled his head over and met her eyes.

"I don't fuck Peggy," he said.

Gus

"You don't fuck her, Gus?"

He was sitting at her kitchen table while she cooked some eggs. She had put her shirt back on, and buttoned it up. The tails of it hung to her thighs. He drank some Scotch. The pleasure was gone from it. He no longer felt good, but he knew he'd feel worse if he stopped. Now he just had the heavy feeling, and the hard need not to let it go.

"No," Gus said.

"Never?" she said.

Mary Alice tilted the pan and pried the edge of her omelet so that the still-runny center would cook. Gus smiled.

"Hardly ever," he said.

"Jesus, Gus. That's no marriage."

"What the hell do you know about marriage?" he said.

"I had a lousy one," Mary Alice said. She dropped some mushrooms into the center of her omelet and folded it over. "I know one when I see it."

Gus shrugged.

"Do you ever want to?" Mary Alice said.

"Fuck Peggy?" Gus made a brusque laugh. "Why would I want to do that?"

"Lot of husbands and wives like to do it," Mary Alice said. She slid the omelet onto a platter and put the toast in. "You want coffee?"

Gus shook his head. Mary Alice put out some jam and a bottle of ketchup, and served her omelet, cut in two, on two plates. The toast popped. She buttered it and put it on a plate between them. Then she poured herself some more white wine and sat down to eat. Gus drank some Scotch and soda. He was mixing them very dark now.

"She can't cook for shit either," he said.

Mary Alice was quiet. Gus poured some ketchup on his omelet. He took a bite and chewed it silently, and drank some more Scotch.

"She used to have a tight little body," he said. "And she was lively and cute, and chatty. I was kind of proud of her. She never liked sex that I could tell, but she let me because it was, you know, Catholic stuff. Wifely duty, and having a baby. All that shit. And then after Chris was born it was like, well, that's done. And she didn't want to do it anymore. Birth control was sinful and she had a tipped womb and her back hurt. And taking care of Chris made her exhausted. Truth is when I married her she was a cute little girl and she never got to be more than that. Except now she's not cute."

Gus drank the rest of his Scotch and went for more. Mary Alice sat very still. Gus rarely talked to her about anything.

"Bad back was a godsend to her," Gus said. "Now she wedges herself into her fucking corset and straps herself in . . . like body armor . . . fucking chastity belt."

He brought the Scotch back and sat down with it and looked at her hard across the table. There was always that hard edge in Gus, always something a little frightening, a little exciting.

"And she got fat," he said. When he was drunk his speech slowed down, but he never seemed to slur. "A lovely sight in her corset."

He took a drink.

"And when she takes it off you can see the grooves it made in her fat. Course, you don't see her that much with it off, 'cause she dresses and undresses in the closet."

He drank again and stared into the glass while he swallowed.

"We got twin beds now."

He drank again and stared at the wall past her head for a long time. It was an empty wall, no pictures, nothing to decorate it. Mary Alice sipped her wine, and finished her omelet. Gus's omelet cooled on his plate with only a bite gone.

"Why'd you marry her, Gus?"

"Better than daily Mass with my mother. . . . And, I wanted a kid. I was all my old man ever cared about. Which wasn't much."

"Why do you stay with her, Gus?"

"After Chris? I left her, she'd have got the kid," he said. His gaze stayed on the wall.

"Maybe not," Mary Alice said.

"We're Irish," Gus said. "And Catholic. She'd have got the kid."

"What about now?"

Gus shrugged.

"Too late," he said.

And he stared at the blank wall as if it would stay confusion.

Debbie McBride

Girl Scout Troop 3 from Abington was just filing through the gate to see *Old Ironsides* when they heard the firecrackers. A man came running toward them from the direction of the Mystic River Bridge, and then a car came, going too fast, weaving among the orange-striped plastic barrels that marked the construction way, and there were more firecracker sounds and the man fell sprawling forward and they all heard Mrs. Simpson, who was in charge of them, say, "Jesus, Mary, and Joseph." And the car pulled away and the man didn't move where he had fallen and it seemed very quiet. Then someone noticed that Debbie McBride had fallen down too. And she didn't get up either, and Mrs. Simpson ran over to her and looked at her and they all heard her say, "Jesus." And a cop came running from down by the museum and in a while there were ambulances, and police cars, and more policemen than there even were in Abington. And through it all the man in the street and Debbie McBride both lay very still, and didn't move.

Mary Alice

"A fucking Girl Scout," Parnell Flaherty said to Mary Alice Burke. "An Irish Catholic fucking Girl Scout from the suburbs."

He was walking back and forth in his office in front of the window that looked down on Quincy Market.

"I knew it would happen. I knew those assholes would shoot a civilian."

"It could be worse," Mary Alice said.

"Sure," Flaherty said. "It coulda been the pope, from fucking Rome."

"She didn't die," Mary Alice said.

She was leaning her hips against the edge of Flaherty's big conference table behind the couch. She had on a black silk suit with a short skirt, a cardigan jacket, and a man-tailored white shirt, open at the throat. There was a rope of pearls around her neck.

"Isn't that swell?" Flaherty said. "The plucky little dear can tell her story over and over again. And we can see pictures of her in her cute little hospital bed and hear her cute little interviews on the six o'clock news and the eleven o'clock news, and the noon news and the sunrise edition of eye-opener news. They killed her we'd have had to get through the funeral and then it would have been over."

Mary Alice smiled. "Mister Warm," she said.

Flaherty tossed his head.

"Winslow has been killing me on crime in the streets. This is going to feed him for a year."

"Maybe it's done," Mary Alice said.

"The O'Briens and the Malloys?" Flaherty shook his head. "Gus says it's a blood feud."

"So it could happen again."

"And again," Flaherty said. "And again. They don't give a shit."

He turned and stared down at the Marketplace.

"Crime Wave Sweeps Hub," he said. "Fear Grips City."

"Any intelligent voter will know it's not your fault," Mary Alice said.

Flaherty turned from the window and looked at her with his arms folded across his chest.

"Yeah, sure. Both of them," he said.

"So what can you do?" Mary Alice said.

"The electorate doesn't like it when you do nothing," Flaherty said. "Even if nothing is the thing to do. They like action. Even if it's the wrong action."

"Granted."

"So we do something," Flaherty said. He continued to stare at her, arms folded, motionless against the cityscape below his window. Mary Alice assumed he was posing, as he often did. "You got any ideas?"

Mary Alice raised her eyebrows.

"You're a smart broad, Mary Alice," Flaherty said. "I'm interested in what you got to say."

Mary Alice pursed her lips and was silent for a moment while Flaherty kept his pose in front of the window and waited.

"You need a special prosecutor, or investigator, or commissioner, or whatever you decide finally to call it. Somebody appointed by you personally to bring a stop to this deadly gang war that threatens the very fabric of urban civility."

"Urban civility," Flaherty said.

He began to walk again, arms still folded, pacing back and forth in front of his window.

"Urban civility," he said again, as he walked.

Mary Alice waited. Flaherty had his head down as he paced. His eyes were nearly closed.

"So who?" he said.

Mary Alice took in a deep breath and said, "Chris Sheridan."

Flaherty froze in midstride. His eyes slitted, his arms folded, his head down, he stood absolutely still while Mary Alice listened to the tick of the big old Seth Thomas clock on Flaherty's desk. Then he slowly straightened and turned his head toward her, his eyes wide open now.

"Gus Sheridan's kid."

Mary Alice nodded.

"He's a lawyer," she said. "A nationally known criminologist, son of a cop."

"And he goes out with Cabot Winslow's sister," Flaherty said.

Mary Alice smiled.

"Would he do it?" Flaherty said.

"I don't know."

"You been fucking Gus for ten years," Flaherty said. "You must know something."

"I didn't know it was common knowledge," Mary Alice said.

"It's not. I know it. I know a lot of things. Would he do it?"

"I don't know. I've never even met him."

Flaherty nodded.

"What do you think Gus's reaction would be?"

Mary Alice shrugged.

"He loves the kid," she said. "I know that."

Flaherty started to pace again.

"You think Gus cuts any corners?" he said.

"I'm not here to talk about Gus," Mary Alice said.

"Sure," Flaherty said.

Flaherty walked back and forth. The Seth Thomas clock ticked.

"Gus is a handful," Flaherty said. "You understand him?"

"No."

"Don't want him for an enemy."

"He's not likely to be your enemy if his kid's on your side," Mary Alice said.

Flaherty nodded.

"How about you, Mary Alice? You got something going? You got some motive here?"

Mary Alice smiled and shook her head without speaking.

Flaherty tossed his head again and laughed.

"Course you do. Everybody does."

Mary Alice remained quiet. Flaherty slapped his hands against his thighs to some internal rhythm for a moment. Then he smiled.

"Let's get Chris Sheridan in here," he said, "and offer him the job."

Chris

Grace sat across from Chris at a corner table in the bar at the Casablanca. It was an airy room for a barroom, with bright murals of scenes from the movie, and a long half-circular bar along one side of the room. They hunched forward a little as they talked to each other.

"It seems like a good idea to meet like this once a week, and talk," Grace said. "I think it's important to keep talking."

"Yeah."

"Sometimes I'm so worried about you, I can't breathe," Grace said.

"But not quite worried enough about me to come back," Chris said.

She shook her head.

"No. That's not a reason to be together."

Chris nodded.

"Yeah," he said.

With both hands, Grace turned her wineglass slowly in front of her.

"I think you need other relationships," Grace said.

"You mean dating?"

"I mean open your life up. New friends, new relationships, men or women."

"You think I should start dating men?"

Grace smiled.

"No, I don't think that's your style," she said. "But you need to see other people."

The Casablanca served Yuengling on draft and Chris was drinking it. His glass was empty and he looked for a waiter, found one, and gestured for a refill.

"How about you?" Chris said carefully. "You seeing other people?"

Grace smiled brightly and nodded. The waiter brought a new glass of beer and took away the empty.

"I went to New York last weekend with a friend. . . . A guy friend."

Chris could feel himself start to sag. The weight of it settled at the top of his stomach like a stone. It was hard to swallow and he felt as if the air was too thin. Carefully he picked up the glass and carefully sipped some beer, and carefully put the glass down, fitting it exactly back into its ring of moisture on the napkin.

"Must be a fine man if you're with him," he said. "Anyone I know?"

Grace shook her head.

"Where'd you stay?"

"The Pierre."

"Nice," Chris said.

"You all right?" Grace said.

"Sure," Chris said. "You want to go to New York and fuck somebody, your business. We're separated. I don't own you."

"You ought to open out your life, Chris."

"How was it with the guy? Better than what you're used to?"

"Both of us were quite scared. He's married."

"Swell," Chris said. "You can fuck up another relationship too. Way to go, Gracie."

"We can't talk like this, Chris. It doesn't do anyone any good."

"How am I supposed to talk? My girlfriend leaves me and goes to New York and balls some guy friend. I'm supposed to say *bon appétit*? You love this guy?"

"No. Mostly, I'm trying to find out if I love you."

"Jesus," Chris said. "You mean you don't know?"

"Nor if you love me."

"You don't know that?"

"No. I need to find out. You do too."

"By fucking some guy in the Big Apple?"

Grace stood.

"I need to go," she said. "I can't let you beat up on me for too long."

"Maybe we should just say so long and let me get on with my life," Chris said.

"I'd like to keep talking, Chris."

Chris stared down at his beer.

Grace turned to go.

"Next Wednesday," Chris said.

"Yes."

Chris looked up from his beer and stared after her as she walked out of the bar.

Gus

Harvard Stadium was empty and dead silent in the late afternoon. Gus sat with Chris in the first row above the field, with the thin April sun on his face. Beyond the open end of the stadium the Harvard athletic complex sprawled along Soldiers Field Road. And across the river, the new red brick of the Kennedy School was bright through the still leafless trees.

It was one of the ways they kept contact. Gus would come over once a week and work out with his son in the Harvard Gym. Chris did mostly light repetitions on the Nautilus machines, keeping his form. Gus lifted heavy. Usually they had little to say to each other, and the exercise made not talking easier.

"I needed to discuss something," Chris said.

He sprawled beside his father in chinos and Top-Siders and a pale beige cashmere sweater—no shirt. The sleeves were pushed up on his forearms. His dark brown Harris tweed jacket was folded beside him on the stadium seat. Chris was taller than his father, as tall as Conn had been. His dark hair was longish and carefully cut. He was clean shaven, with the shadow of a heavy beard. If he were going out for an evening he shaved a second time. Gus's beard, were he to let it grow, would be reddish, flecked with gray.

He looks like my father, Gus thought.

Chris's eyes ranged over the empty stadium. Gus waited.

"Parnell Flaherty wants me to be a special prosecutor on these gang murders," Chris said.

Gus was quiet. He sat with his forearms resting on his thighs, his hands clasped loosely.

"I know it's a way to pull Cabot's fangs on the crime issue," Chris said. "But it would be a hell of a break for me."

238

"Sure would," Gus said. He looked carefully at his hands.

"National coverage, a chance to deal with some actual crime, you know, instead of writing another fucking paper for *JSPC*."

"Theory and practice are different," Gus said. "Doesn't mean one's more important."

"Yeah, I know. But being an academic criminologist is like being a literary critic. You know all about it but you can't do it. I want to do it."

"Here's your chance," Gus said.

"I know."

"So do it."

"I don't know, I mean I'll be sort of undercutting Grace's family. Her brother wants to be senator, and the old man wants it more than he does."

"Tommy won't object," Gus said.

Chris looked at his father for a moment as if he were going to ask something. Then he let it go.

"I haven't talked with Grace about it yet."

Christ, he's talking to me first.

"But she and her brother aren't close. She thinks he's 'a dumb prig.' "

Gus grinned.

"You're right," he said. "They're not close."

"So I think I'm okay there."

"Even if you aren't," Gus said, "you can't decide based on what she wants. First you decide what you want to do, then you ask her how she feels about it and then . . ." Gus shrugged and turned his palms up.

"Grace is hard to ignore," Chris said. He looked at Gus. "What about you?"

"Am I hard to ignore?"

"Isn't it sort of undercutting the homicide commander if the mayor appoints a special prosecutor to look into some murders?"

Gus shook his head.

"Doesn't matter," he said. "I'm five years from my pension. I'll retire as a captain. There's nothing to undercut."

"Part of the job is to see if the police are doing their job right. That means you."

Gus shrugged.

"I thought you and Flaherty were pals," Chris said. "Why would he put your own son in over you?"

"I know Parnell a long time. Doesn't mean we're pals."

"But your own kid?"

"Maybe Parnell's doing me a favor," Gus said.

"It could be shrewd, I suppose," Chris said.

Gus was looking out the open end of the stadium now, squinting. In the openings among the buildings, across the road, he could see little splashes of the dark river. Chris was thinking out loud.

"He gets me to defuse Cabot and at the same time avoids making you mad because it's a good chance for your son."

"Un-huh. He also thinks he's getting a Harvard Goo Goo that he can lead around by the nose."

"You think he's right?"

"No."

"Hope not."

"Remember," Gus said, "he's got to deal with both of us."

"I don't need you taking care of me," Chris said.

"I was thinking we could take care of each other," Gus said.

They sat quietly for a time. Chris sprawled with his elbows resting on the seat behind him, Gus bent forward, his arms resting on his legs.

"So how does it make you feel?" Chris said.

"Feels okay to me," Gus said.

"No, I mean how do *you* feel? Not how does it feel?"

Gus shrugged.

"It's one of the things you do, you know, shift the question just slightly so you can stay closed."

"Maybe staying closed works for me," Gus said.

Chris looked at the patches of river.

"Maybe," Chris said.

The patches of river continued to move and stayed always the same.

"Always hard for me to talk with you, you know," Chris said. "But it's harder being quiet."

Gus nodded.

"You seem to be okay with quiet," Chris said.

"You get older, being quiet gets easier," Gus said. "How's Grace?"

Chris took in a long breath and let it out slowly through his nose.

"She's a piece of work, isn't she?"

"I like her," Gus said. "She's got juice. How about you. You love her?"

"I don't know," Chris said. "She's, she's got so much, what? . . . voltage, you know . . . it's like living with a cloudburst. . . ."

"There's worse things," Gus said.

Chris nodded.

"You going to marry her?"

"I don't know. My marriage models aren't too good, you know?"

"Yeah," Gus said. "I do know."

There were pigeons circling down onto the stadium floor, maybe a dozen of them. Gus watched them circle and then settle, pecking at whatever they pecked at in the grass, ordered by some sort of internal rules that Gus didn't know. *Like everybody else*, Gus thought.

"How do you stand her?" Chris said. "Why don't you ever confront her? Tell her to shut the fuck up?"

The pigeons flew off suddenly, all together. Gus leaned back and stretched his neck, turning his head slightly back and forth as if to ease a crick. He shrugged.

"She's your mother," he said.

"Yeah, well, don't do me no favors."

"She doesn't know anything," Gus said. "Simple stuff, like

how to write a check, or when to put gas in the car, or how to get to Cambridge. The world's a mystery to her, and all she knows how to be is a bratty, know-it-all little girl."

Chris was sitting upright now, leaning forward with his forearms resting on his thighs.

"Do you have sex?" he said.

Gus smiled a little.

"No."

"So what do you do?"

"For sex?"

"Yes?"

Gus smiled.

"Love is hard," he said, "but sex is easy."

"You have a friend."

"Yes."

"Does Ma know?"

"The things your mother doesn't know," Gus said, "placed end to end would reach Omaha."

"I'm glad I know this," Chris said.

Gus shrugged.

"That's one of my problems, you know? You never stood up to her. You never said, 'Peggy, that's enough.' "

"Wouldn't do much good," Gus said. "She can't act different. She is what she is. Just mean a fight and I always thought it wouldn't be good for you, see your parents fight."

"You could have left her."

"And you? Leave you alone with her?"

Chris shrugged. They were both quiet. The pale sun was gone. Cars along both sides of the river had their lights on.

"Take Flaherty's job," Gus said. "I have no problem with it, and your in-laws won't object."

"You have a lot of influence with Tom Winslow," Chris said. "It's strange."

"Known Tommy a long time," Gus said.

They stood. Chris looked down at his father, shorter and wider than he was, at the flat red Mick face he'd looked at all his life, at the thick neck, and the arms tight in the jacket sleeves, and always the air of distance. He knew his father would walk in front of a train for him. But always still the airspace around him, that even Chris had never quite penetrated.

Four inches taller and thirty pounds lighter, the son patted his father's shoulder for a moment, and then they walked together out of the stadium toward the parking lot.

Gus

At night the Bay Tower Room, sixty stories up, was a public restaurant. But at lunch it was a private club full of bankers and stockbrokers. Gus sat near the window with Tommy Winslow and drank some club soda. To his left the Custom House Tower gave scale to the high setting, and beyond it, across the harbor, Gus could see planes coming and going at Logan Airport. He'd worn a gun every day for nearly forty years, and he usually noticed it no more than his wallet; but he could feel its weight here among the suits. It made him smile.

"Something funny?" Tom asked.

Gus shook his head.

"I don't get up here often," he said.

"It's okay for lunch," Tom said. "At dinner it's full of people from Worcester."

The waiter brought their salads. They ate in silence. Tom ate quickly, putting too much salad per bite into his mouth. He was tall and spare with square shoulders, and a long nose. His receding gray hair was straight and long and combed smoothly back.

"Parnell Flaherty's going to appoint my kid as a special prosecutor on these gang killings," Gus said.

"The hell he is," Tom said.

There was a hint of salad dressing at one corner of his mouth and he dabbed at it with his napkin.

"Parnell's a smart fella," Gus said. "Figure it'll dehorn Cabot on the crime-in-the-streets thing."

"Because of Grace," Tom said.

"Um-hmm."

"I don't want him to take it," Tom said.

Gus shrugged.

"I mean it, Gus. It will fuck up this campaign. Cabot is going to be the best senator money can buy."

Again Gus shrugged.

"For Crissake, Gus, do you ever talk?"

The waiter cleared their salad plates, put down their entree, and retreated.

"Chris's going to take the job," he said.

Tom Winslow's eyes behind the old-fashioned round black-rimmed glasses he wore were small and flat.

"I don't like that, Gus."

Gus put his fork down and folded his hands on the edge of the table. He leaned forward toward Tom.

"Tommy, we've known each other all our lives. You ever remember a time when I gave a fuck what you liked?"

Tom's face had a nice tennis tan. It was hard to tell if it might have flushed a little under the tan. His eyes stayed steady.

"I've never given you trouble, Gus."

"And I've never given you trouble, Tommy."

"All that we've done together. I've been cooperative. I've helped make you . . . very comfortable."

"Chris's going to take this offer and you're going to support him," Gus said.

"My child has a stake in this too," Tom said.

"Not my problem," Gus said.

The sat silently. Neither ate. Across the harbor an American Airlines 767 sloped in over the Fargo Building, lowered gently over the harbor, and landed silently.

"Cabot wants the Senate," Tom said.

"You want it," Gus said.

"Same thing."

"And maybe you can buy it for him," Gus said. "Don't matter to me."

"Chris will be a roadblock," Tom said.

Gus stared at Tom without speaking.

"But it's a free country," Tom said.

Gus stayed quiet, the weight of his gaze on Tom Winslow.

"I won't stand in his way," Tom said.

"In fact you'll urge him on," Gus said.

"I said I won't oppose him."

"He won't do it if he thinks it will cause trouble for Grace's family," Gus said. "You'll have to urge him to do it."

"Sure," Tom said. "I'll urge him."

The waiter came, and asked if they were through. They said yes, and the waiter took away both plates and brought them coffee. Out beyond the harbor, the sky was bright blue, and the water mirrored its color, so that it was hard to tell where the horizon was.

"We're all right, then?" Tom said.

"Us? Sure, Tommy, we're dandy."

"And our, ah, special relationship continues?"

Gus smiled at him over his coffee cup.

"Till death do us part, Tommy."

Gus

At their big house in Beverly Farms, the Winslows had a party for Chris Sheridan, to celebrate his appointment. That was the spin they were going to put on it. Cooperation beyond family, beyond affiliation, to rid the city of its current plague. They even invited Debbie McBride, Gus noticed, still in a wheelchair, but recovering, thanks-be-to-Gawd, cute and plucky in her Girl Scout uniform, wheeled about by her mother. Mrs. McBride was pale, with fat thighs. In her flowered dress with puffy sleeves and a low scooped neck, she looked like a character from *Fantasia*. Parnell Flaherty was not there.

Gus stood near a six-foot black marble fireplace nursing a tall Scotch and soda watching Peggy flounce about among the rich people, screeching with laughter at everything said, clutching her bourbon in both hands. She drank bourbon on the rocks only. Not through a highly developed taste preference, but because it was the only thing she knew the name of. Even with bourbon if someone gave her a brand-name choice she would be puzzled and Gus would have to specify for her. Peggy was wearing a heavy white brocaded dress with a blue scarf over her shoulders and bright blue shoes. She looked, Gus realized, a bit like Debbie's proud mother. Only older, and fatter. She had the mannerisms of a junior high school girl, titillated by a rich swirl of events she didn't understand. She was flirty and provocative, which Gus mused was not easy while crammed into a steel-stayed corset.

A young woman from the caterer, in tight black pants and a white shirt, came by, and offered Gus an endive leaf with sour cream and a dab of salmon roe. Gus shook his head and the young woman passed on. Gus looked thoughtfully at her tight young backside. He drank some Scotch.

Laura Winslow, Tommy's wife, said, "You're not eating, Gus."

Gus smiled at her.

"This isn't Paddy chow, Laura," he said. "I'm waiting for the boiled potatoes."

Gus liked Laura Winslow. She was tall and genuine with short hair, strong forearms, and a good tan. Her eyes were wide apart, and there was always the implication of amusement in them. She was said to be a good tennis player, and she always seemed to him a lot smarter than her husband. Gus could never figure out why she'd married a twerp like Tommy Winslow, though now and then he felt a hint of resignation in her that seemed like his.

"How do you think Chris feels about this party?" Laura said.

Gus shrugged. "We don't always talk about stuff, Laura."

"You value restraint, Gus. So does Chris."

Gus nodded.

"I was a little worried that we were kind of putting him on the spot," Laura said.

"He could have said no."

"I suppose he could have," Laura said. "But that would have put him rather on the spot too."

"The whole deal puts him on the spot," Gus said. "He didn't want to be there, he could have walked."

"He says you supported him."

Gus nodded again.

"Tommy supported him too," Laura said.

"Decent," Gus said.

Laura looked at Gus without comment. Then she said, "Yes."

In front of them, Peggy was dancing. She held her electric-blue scarf stretched out across her chest while she swayed to seductive music that only she heard. She dipped low in front of a tall man in a yellow linen blazer, and dropped the scarf to reveal fat white cleavage. She slowly drew the scarf across the cleavage while she gazed up at the man with her eyes half closed. Then she twirled across the room and danced for a shorter man with a dark tan and white hair.

Gus and Laura watched her.

"Yvonne De Carlo," Gus said without inflection.

Laura smiled and moved off to talk to another guest. Gus took a mushroom cap off a serving tray and ate it. The mushroom cap had been filled with spinach and broiled. He went to the bar and got his drink refilled and stood near the bar. His son came over carrying a bottle of Catamount beer. Chris always drank beer, almost always from the bottle, and always the local beer.

Across the room Peggy had spread the scarf across her shoulders and was looking back over her shoulder at the white-haired man with the tan. She twitched her hips. He said something and she shrieked again with laughter, and twirled away from him.

"Ma's doing the dance of the seven veils again," Chris said.

Gus nodded.

"Doesn't that bother you?" Chris said.

Gus took in some air and let it out.

"She's having a nice time," he said.

"Yeah, but everyone else thinks she's an asshole."

Gus looked around the room.

"What's one more?" Gus said.

"See there you go again, closing off."

Gus shrugged.

"You want me to say your mother's an asshole, Chris?"

"I want you to say what you feel."

Gus stared at the cold fireplace across the room. He took a pull at his drink, carefully, not too much. He didn't want to get drunk at his son's party.

"Chris," he said, "mostly I don't know what I feel. And mostly, I guess, I don't want to."

"It's no way to live," Chris said.

"I know," Gus said.

Tom

As the gate locked automatically behind him, he felt the thickening pressure he always felt when he came to the house, a commingling of surreptitiousness, excitement, desire, safety, and guilt. He parked the car amid the unrestrained bushes and got out.

She greeted him at the door as he'd taught her to. Arms around his neck, kissing him on tiptoe, one foot off the ground, toe pointed backwards. He was very precise about this. She had ribbons in her hair. She wore one of the little flowered pinafores he'd bought her, with white ankle socks and saddle shoes. Her make up was careful and extensive. Lip gloss, blusher, green eye shadow, mascara. She wore a lot of expensive perfume.

When they were through kissing at the door, she took his hand and led him into the living room. It was the same room it had been for forty years, updated with a vast television screen on the wall to the left. There was a frantic music video playing on the screen. He shut it off. Compact discs and videotapes were scattered on the floor. A box of pink tissues sat on the table. But the boy's books were still there in the bookcase, the Daisy air rifle still stood in the corner. He squatted by the big fireplace and lit the fire that was already laid there. She went to the kitchen and made him a martini as he had taught her, and brought it to him, and sat on the arm of the big chair and stroked his hair, the way he insisted, while he drank his martini, and stared into the moving fire. When he finished his martini he began to fondle her, and after that, they went to the bedroom.

Chris

Chris sat across from Cabot Winslow in the dining room of the Harvest Restaurant in Harvard Square. Grace sat between them. It was late in the lunch hour and the dining room was nearly empty.

Chris studied his menu. He felt the wringing tension in his solar plexus when he was with Grace. He wondered if Cabot knew. Cabot was so flat that, if he knew or not would have little effect on his behavior.

"This is complicated for us," Grace said. "I thought we ought to talk, just the three of us, and sort everything out."

"No problem, Grapes," Cabot said. "Chris and I will just each go about our business. I'll run for the Senate. The Chris-man will clean up the city."

Chris hated the way Cabot talked. He hated being called the Chris-man. He hated the way Cabot called his sister Grapes. He hated the bow ties that Cabot always wore. He often thought it would be fun to bust Cabot's nose for him. But then he imagined Cabot down and bleeding, and he felt bad for him, and a little frightened at what he'd imagined, and he promised himself he'd never do it.

"That sounds fine, Cab, and you probably think you mean it," Grace said. "But if he does clean up the city it'll hurt your chances for the Senate."

"I'm not running on Flaherty's failures, Grapes. I offer myself to the voters as I am. I hope to be elected on the issues."

Christ, Chris thought, *even to his own sister he talks like a political speech.*

"And if you're not?" Grace said.

Cabot shrugged gracefully.

"And what about Daddy?" Grace said.

Cabot shrugged again.

Chris swallowed some beer.

"I'm sorry, I've put us all in this position," he said.

Cabot shook his head and made a dismissive gesture.

"Please, Chris. No one is suggesting that."

"I could have said no to Flaherty. I thought about it. I knew it would make things awkward for you"—he looked at his girl-friend—"and for Grace. I thought about it a lot."

Cabot listened attentively. Polite. He was a large young man with a pale square face, and reddish hair. In a few years he'd be portly. But there was about him a gentility that served to make him more graceful than he should have been. *Breeding*, Chris thought. *Six centuries of being upper class.*

"Maybe you could share with Cab some of your thinking," Grace said.

He looked at her. She was twirling her wineglass by the stem. Most of the wine remained untouched. Sometimes he thought he'd like her better if she drank a little . . . or ate too much . . . or tore off her clothes in the kitchen some morning and fucked him on the floor. . . . *Six centuries of being upper class.* . . . He lingered at the thought of taking her on the floor. Of overpowering her and . . . The longer they were apart the more implacably and angrily he wanted her.

"I needed to do something," Chris said.

Cabot raised his eyebrows.

"Emphasis on *do*. I never *do* stuff. I just talk about stuff."

He drank some beer from the bottle.

"You know?" he said.

Cabot looked courteously puzzled. He wasn't, Chris knew, a very bright guy.

"You're too hard on yourself, Chris. You are, after all, a full professor," Cabot said, "at Harvard University. You could have been chairman of your department. Had you chosen."

"Where I could deal with those issues of twin significance—tenure and promotion—until my teeth fell out."

Cabot was drinking bourbon on the rocks. He sipped some. Grace put her hand on Chris's forearm.

"You think of Gus as someone who *does* things," Grace said.

"Sure. My father's a cop. He investigates crime. He arrests bad guys."

"But crime goes on," Grace said. "And there are still as many bad guys."

"Good point, Grapes," Cabot said. He glanced around for the waitress.

"So what?" Chris said. "You Wasps always think it's about results. It's not. It's about what you are."

"Us Wasps?" Grace said. "As opposed to what? you Micks?"

Chris shook his head and shrugged.

"You know what I mean," Chris said.

The waitress came and Cabot ordered another round of drinks, although Grace's glass was nearly full.

"No," Grace said when the waitress left, "I don't know what you mean. I thought you'd outgrown that poor snob affectation: 'we-authentic-Irish-versus-you-effete-Wasps.' "

"I just meant that we come from a different upbringing. You know, 'the rich are very different.' "

Grace smiled and looked down at the still surface of her undrunk wine.

" 'Yes, they have more money,' " she said.

The waitress came with the second round of drinks. When she left, Cabot took a sip of his and looked at Chris.

"So, you took the job, really, because you wanted to be a cop . . . like your father?" Cabot asked.

Chris opened his mouth, and shut it, and stared at Cabot's blank, comfortable face. *Asshole.*

"Well," Chris said, "it's a little more complicated than that."
"Oh?"

"But that's close enough," Chris said.

He looked at his menu.

"New Zealand Venison Medallions," he said. "I think I'll have them."

"Good for you," Cabot said. "Lower in fat and cholesterol than chicken."

Grace was quiet, looking at her two glasses of wine.

"I believe I'll have the salmon," Cabot said.

"Omega oils," Chris said. "How about you, Gracie, what are you eating?"

Grace stared at her full wineglasses and didn't answer until the waitress arrived to take the orders . . . then she said she'd have a salad.

Gus

It was sunny and seventy-two with a small breeze coming off the Mystic River. Gus sat at an outdoor table of a fast-food restaurant near Wellington Circle with Pat Malloy and two of his crew. They were drinking coffee. Malloy had his black, with two packets of Sweet'n Low. The sound of traffic on the Mystic Valley Parkway was steady in the background. Gus sat beside Pat Malloy on one side of the table. One of Malloy's brothers, Kevin, sat across from them beside Chuckie Dugan, who was a cousin.

"Nobody meant to buzz the Girl Scout, Gus," Malloy said. "Besides, she ain't even dead."

"I told you it was going to happen, Patrick," Gus said. "And I told you that when it did the shit would hit the fan."

"So you're a smart guy," Chuckie Dugan said. "So what?"

Gus turned for a moment and looked at Dugan. He was young, maybe twenty-four, a body builder wearing a World Gym tank top and a thick gold chain at his neck. He had a lot of black hair combed straight back. He stared back at Gus.

"You know what Flaherty has done," Gus said to Pat Malloy.

"Yeah. When I saw that I said, hey, this is great. I mean, if Gus can't control his own kid, who can he control? Huh?"

"I don't control him," Gus said.

The tables were on a poured concrete patio outside the fast-food restaurant. A ragged line of crabgrass had forced its way up in along the crack where the concrete of the patio met the hot top of the parking lot.

"Chuckie?" Pat Malloy said.

He nodded his head at the empty paper cups on the table. Chuckie Dugan got up and went to get more coffee.

"Black," Pat Malloy yelled at Chuckie, "couple Sweet'n Low."

"Okay, I hear what you're saying," Pat Malloy said to Gus. "I got kids. I understand. You don't control them, sure. But you divert the suckers, you know. You kind of steer them around trouble, best you can."

"Kid cleans this thing up, mean a lot to him," Gus said. "I'm going to help him."

Chuckie Dugan swaggered back with the coffees. He put one down for Pat Malloy and another for Kevin. He left Gus's in the middle of the table, took his own, and sat down. Gus paid no attention. He was looking at Pat Malloy.

Pat Malloy said, "Are you fucking with me, Gus?"

"I may."

"Or you may not?"

"Or I may not."

"Or you might end up in the ground," Pat Malloy said.

Gus shrugged.

"Everybody does," he said.

Pat Malloy drank some of his coffee. Then he sat back and folded his arms and stared at Gus. A truck hauling tandem trailers went by on Route 28 and the surface of the coffee trembled with the vibration of it.

"That what you got me out here to tell me?" Pat Malloy said. "That you're going to help your kid try to bust me?"

"I didn't say that."

"What exactly did you say, Gus?"

"I want the kid to get credit for saving the city. I didn't say it had to be you."

"Butchie?"

"Maybe."

"Or?"

"Anybody," Gus said. "Long as somebody takes the fall, and the shooting stops. Don't matter to me who goes down."

Gus jerked his head at Chuckie Dugan.

"He'd do."

Chuckie Dugan said, "Hey, asshole."

"Sure he would," Pat Malloy said. "Or my brother Kevin. Huh? Shit, how 'bout my old lady? Gonna dump somebody, might as well get something out of it."

Kevin Malloy grinned. Chuckie Dugan saw him and grinned too.

"You can pick him . . . or her," Gus said.

"Pat, what're we talking about?" Chuckie Dugan said. "I could dump this asshole right here."

Pat Malloy grinned.

"You think so?" Pat Malloy said.

Chuckie Dugan looked puzzled for a minute, but he pushed on.

"Sure, and if we need to we dump his kid later."

Gus turned his head slowly and looked at Chuckie Dugan. His face was blank. Then he reached across the table and took a handful of Chuckie Dugan's hair, stood, and yanked him forward across the table. Gus brought his knee up as Chuckie sprawled toward him and drove it into Chuckie Dugan's face. The blood came at once. Gus slammed him to the ground and let go of his hair and kicked him in the stomach. Gasping, Chuckie rolled away and tried to get up and Gus kicked him again in the face and Chuckie went backwards, still scrambling. He got unsteadily to his feet, the blood streaming from his nose, one eye already closing, his arms up trying to protect himself, backing away as Gus came toward him. Gus put his left hand in his jacket pocket and came out with some brass knuckles. There was no expression on his face. He hit Chuckie with the brass knuckles on his protecting forearms and, when he dropped them in pain, on the right side of his face. Gus's hands were very quick. He hit Chuckie three times with the brass knuckles while Chuckie was going down. On the ground Chuckie curled into a ball, half conscious, only instinctive now, trying to get away from it. Gus kicked him in the kidneys. Chuckie's body jerked every time Gus kicked him. The tank top was soaked with blood.

"Gus," Pat Malloy said.

Gus ignored him. He moved around the balled form on the ground, kicking it methodically, carefully, without hurry. Pat Malloy got up and waddled over and stood carefully in front of Gus.

"Gus," he said again.

Kevin Malloy had a gun out, a Glock 9-mm. He rested it on the table, waiting for his brother to tell him what to do. On the ground Chuckie moaned a little.

"I can't let you kill him, Gus."

Gus's breath was coming in big, steady drafts. He shifted his blank gaze from the body on the ground, and looked at Pat Malloy. The gaze remained blank for a time and the breathing stayed heavy, and then it began to slow, and something returned to his eyes. He put the brass knuckles into his left-hand jacket pocket. When he spoke his voice was quiet.

"Sure, Patrick."

"Kevin," Pat Malloy said, "get him into the car. I'll be along."

"Like that, Pat?"

"Like that," Pat Malloy said.

Kevin shrugged and half dragged, half carried Chuckie toward the car.

"Kid's made a mistake," Pat Malloy said. "Figured you for old and slow."

Gus shrugged.

"Good for him, maybe, to learn something," Pat Malloy said.

Gus's breathing had slowed.

"You lemme think on this situation a little," Pat Malloy said. "I don't want it to get down to where it's you or me, you unnerstand, Gus."

"My kid's gonna come out of this looking good, Patrick. How we do that don't matter none to me."

"I got family too, Gus. But I figure you owe me a lot of years on the cushion, you know?"

"I owe you shit, Patrick. You got what you paid for."

Pat Malloy shrugged.

"Don't be crazy, Gus. I know how crazy you are." He jerked

his head toward the car. "Now Chuckie knows too. Gimme a little time on this."

Gus nodded slowly.

"I'm a little crazy too," Pat Malloy said.

"I know that, Patrick," Gus said. "Why I thought we should have this nice talk."

"You gonna talk with Butchie too?"

Gus didn't say anything.

"Sure you are," Pat Malloy said. "Just don't be crazier than you got to be."

"Sure, Patrick."

"And, Gus," Pat Malloy said. "Above all, do not fuck with me."

He turned and walked heavily toward the car. Gus stood, feeling the wind off the Mystic River, and watched him until he was in the car and the car had driven away.

Gus

The meeting was in Flaherty's office at City Hall. Gus was there, and Chris, and the Suffolk County DA whose name was Kendall Robinson, and the police commissioner, Michael Sullivan, who had been a street cop with Gus nearly forty years before. Robinson had brought his chief prosecutor, a good-looking dark-haired woman named Fiora Gardello, who was rumored to have a butterfly tattooed on her butt. Mary Alice Burke sat near Flaherty's desk, and a blank-faced gray-haired woman in a dark dress sat just out of circle with a steno pad and a Bic pen.

Flaherty's suit jacket was hung over the back of his chair. He sat behind his desk with the sleeves of his white shirt rolled halfway up his forearms, his tie loose and his collar unbuttoned. The morning sun, slanting in past the Custom House Tower, made bright rhomboids on the floor beyond his desk.

"First of all, Chris," Flaherty said, "welcome aboard."

Chris nodded.

"Everyone in this room knows and admires your work, and every one of us is looking for great things from you."

Chris smiled and nodded again.

"I believe you've met everyone. I'm sure you'll be able to work with the homicide commander, here," Flaherty said, and grinned his wide grin.

"Unless he keeps calling me Sonny," Chris said.

Everyone laughed. *He seems comfortable*, Gus thought.

"Mary Alice will take care of you for staff, office, car and a driver, pens and pencils, anything that requires a little horse sense," Flaherty said.

Chris grinned at her. Gus felt very still inside.

"We should talk after this meeting," Mary Alice said.

Chris nodded. "I can use any horse sense I can get."

"Our purpose today is to bring you up to speed, and, hopefully, to establish the working interactives. Gus, you want to give Chris, and the rest of us, an overview of these gang killings and where the investigation stands?"

"That won't take long," Gus said.

Chris grinned at him.

"Here's what we know," Gus said, "and what we can bring to court. We know that the shootings are a vendetta between the Malloys and the O'Briens in Charlestown. Everybody know who they are?"

Gus looked around. Everyone nodded.

"It started when on April third, somebody, probably several somebodies, from Malloy's crew beat hell out of Corky O'Brien, and shot him with a .22 caliber gun behind the right ear, resulting in his death. Eight days later somebody from the O'Brien outfit did the same to Jackie Malloy. Same beating, same caliber bullet behind the ear. Dumped him in the same boatyard between East Boston and Chelsea."

"Not the same gun," Fiora Gardello said.

"No."

"No further identification on the guns involved?"

"No. There were no shell casings around, but that doesn't mean anything. Both of them were probably shot somewhere else, and dumped."

Fiora Gardello nodded as if she'd learned something important.

"Then on Patriot's Day, Allie Flynn, who is Butchie O'Brien's nephew, got shot to death over in front of *Old Ironsides*, and a Girl Scout from Abington got wounded."

Chris sat quietly listening. Gus had told him all this already.

"Same gun?" Fiora said.

Gus shook his head.

"Shotgun, twelve gauge. Girl Scout got hit with some stray pellets."

"No luck tracing any of the guns?" Fiora Gardello said.

Gus looked at her silently for a moment. Then he shook his head without comment.

"Witnesses?" she said.

"None."

"So how do you know that the O'Briens and the Malloys are shooting each other?"

Again Gus paused before he answered. Flaherty was leaning back in his chair, his hands clasped behind his head. Sullivan, the police commissioner, shifted in his chair. Robinson, the district attorney, gazed out the window toward Faneuil Hall. Chris kept his eyes calmly on Gus.

"Informed sources," Gus said.

"And we can't force them to testify?"

Gus knew that Fiora knew better. She was grandstanding for the mayor and the new special investigator, and mostly, probably, for herself. Fiora was a pretty good prosecutor, but she was regularly proving that she wasn't afraid of men, and she took herself very seriously. *Nice line to her thigh, though,* Gus thought.

"No, we can't," Gus said.

"And even if we could," Chris said, "my understanding is that what they could tell us does not constitute evidence, being rather more in the form of knowledgeable speculation."

"Then perhaps Captain Sheridan should present it that way instead of as fact."

"There's truth and there's fact," Chris said. "And Captain Sheridan is presenting the truth. We're simply short of facts at the moment."

Fiora Gardello looked a little startled, but she nodded and stopped talking.

Gus felt excited. *Jesus Christ,* he thought. *He's pretty good. I always see him with his mother.*

"We don't know the button men," Gus said. "But we know" —he smiled at Fiora—"though we can't take it to court, that whoever did the shooting was doing what he'd been told to do by Butchie O'Brien, on the one hand, and Pat Malloy on the other."

"And there'll be more," Flaherty said.

"You can count on that," Gus said.

"Who's on it, Gus?" Sullivan said.

"I'm on it," Gus said. "But day-to-day it's Johnny Cassidy."

"I should talk with him," Chris said.

"I'd like to assign him to you," Gus said, "if there's no objection. And Billy Callahan for your driver."

"Cassidy's a good man," Sullivan said.

Chris nodded. "I'll talk with you and Mary Alice after the meeting," he said.

"Informants?" Fiora Gardello said. "Can we turn someone?"

Again Fiora was talking just to talk. Again Gus was silent for a while, looking at her.

"Tell you what, Fiora," Gus said finally. "You pin a badge on the outside of your jacket, and go over to City Square this afternoon, and ask anybody you run into what time it is, and see if they tell you."

Fiora raised her eyebrows.

"How about surveillance?" Flaherty said.

"What do you think, Chris?" Gus said. "Maybe four-man details, three shifts, round the clock, oh, say, fifty guys total— Malloy and O'Brien? What's that?"

"About six hundred men," Chris said.

"Michael?" Gus said.

The police commissioner smiled and shook his head.

"A little hard to staff," he said. "Less the city wants to give us a budget for it."

Flaherty still sat with his hands behind his head. One foot propped on the edge of the desk. The shoe gleamed with fresh polish. He grinned.

"Just a thought," he said. "How about electronic?"

"Sure," Gus said. He nodded at Robinson. "You got a judge'll give me a court order?"

Robinson in turn looked at Fiora Gardello.

She nodded. "Charlie Murphy's probably our best bet," she said. "I'll get back to you."

Everyone was quiet. Nobody had any real idea what to do. The meeting made them feel like they'd done something. It was like most of the meetings Gus had been to.

"Well," Chris said, "we have two obvious goals. We want to stop the killing. And we want to arrest, try, and convict those responsible. We know who that is, the business is to catch them."

Everyone was quiet. Flaherty and Mary Alice and Fiora Gardello nodded.

"Now a question, for this room only. What's the priority? Stopping the killing? Or arrest and conviction?"

"Arrest and conviction would pretty well stop it," Fiora Gardello said.

"Not necessarily," Chris said. He looked at Gus.

"Depends who you arrested and convicted," Gus said. "You bust the shooters and it'll roll along uninterrupted. You get Patrick and Butchie in jail and it might stop, it might not, or there might be a war of succession."

"The electorate cares more about peace than justice," Flaherty said. "Get the shooting stopped."

"Sure thing," Chris said.

1994
Voice-Over

Grace had shifted on the couch. She had put her feet on the floor and was leaning forward, her hands folded in her lap, leaning toward me.

"That was hard," Grace said, "to take on that kind of a job with so much at stake—not only the public problems, but your family, us . . ."

"I had to," I said. "I was losing you."

"Did you think I required a public figure?"

"No. I know you didn't. Don't. But I knew I had to be a different man than I had been, and here was a thing I'd have never done, before you left me. It was a way to change myself."

"What would you have done before we separated?"

"Stayed home, read some books, published a paper, taken an even-handed view of everything. Stayed safe. Claimed I didn't need anything but you."

Grace smiled.

"Yeah," she said, "that sounds about right to me."

"And I had to do it alone."

"You got to work with your father," Grace said.

"Yeah. But I defined *alone* as being without you."

"You got to do your father's kind of work."

"Yeah."

"And you'll be a man, my son?"

"Oh, hell, Gracie, I don't know. I did it to change myself. I did it to show you I could change myself. I did it to get you back."

"What I've never quite gotten," Grace said, "is that part of it. You'd do anything to get me back, you defined happiness as being with me, but you wouldn't marry me."

"Marriage has not been the road to success in my family."

"Sure, but there's more."

I nodded.

"There was the rage," I said. "It helped keep me separate from everything. Detached, observational, unengaged. Even from you."

"Rage at . . . ?"

"Everyone I ever loved. My mother, for being what she was, my father for failing to protect me from my mother."

"I figured that was my job," Grace said.

"Yeah, and I needed you to do it. But, having learned to feel rage for everything I loved, I transferred some of it onto you. And like everything else, too close an entanglement, too full a commitment—in this case, marriage—ran the risk of kicking off that rage, of letting the genie out of the bottle."

"Yes," Grace said. The word came in a soft rush, almost a hiss, almost like a sigh. "That's it, the attracto-repello quality, I never could figure it out."

"But you felt it," I said, "and backed away, and I experienced it as betrayal, and felt more rage. I needed to keep you. But I couldn't marry you."

"And then I left," Grace said.

"And took up with another guy."

"The final betrayal," Grace said.

I grinned.

"The most recent, at least. I kept working on this thing, and working on this thing—this rage thing—and finally, I had to test it. I had to take Flaherty's job."

"Was it scary?"

"More than the spoken word can tell," I said.

"But you did it," Grace said.

"Yeah. And my dad helped me."

Gus

John Cassidy sat in Gus's office at Berkeley Street. His slim hands were folded in his lap. His eyes behind the gold rims were without expression. He had a white display handkerchief folded into points in the breast pocket of his gray suit. He had unbuttoned his jacket when he sat and the butt of his gun, worn inside the waistband of his trousers, showed against the white broadcloth of his shirt.

"I gave him Billy Callahan," Gus said.

"Billy's a good man."

"Dumber than mud," Gus said.

"You wouldn't want to fight him," Cassidy said.

Gus nodded.

"I want you to work for Chris too," Gus said.

"How about him?"

"He needs an investigator. He wants you."

"Why?"

"Because I told him you were the right one."

"Me and Billy Callahan, huh?"

"One each," Gus said. "Brains and muscle."

"This voluntary?"

"No."

Cassidy smiled. There was no warmth in the smile. It was simply a technical recognition of something amusing.

"I'm proud to accept, Captain."

"I knew you would be," Gus said.

Cassidy raised his folded hands from his lap and examined them for a time, then he placed them back in his lap and looked back at Gus.

"Can we talk a little, Captain?"

"Yes."

"I see why you want Billy Callahan with your son. He's been with you forever. And he's good with trouble."

"And I trust him," Gus said.

Cassidy nodded.

"We never gave each other no grief," Cassidy said. "But we don't really like each other."

"No," Gus said. "We don't."

"I got no complaint about that. People get along; people don't. You always been square with me."

Gus didn't say anything.

"But why me?" Cassidy said. "Why do you want me to work for your son?"

"I trust you," Gus said.

"To do what?"

"To do your job," Gus said.

"Which is?"

"To stop the gang killings."

"And you figure I'm the man for that?"

"You're the best cop in the department," Gus said.

Cassidy sat still while he thought about that. He didn't argue the point. Gus knew he thought so too. He sat with his pale fingers laced in his lap, one leg crossed over the other. Gus could imagine him like that on the other side of the confessional, in a turned-around collar, carefully deciding the appropriate penance.

"We all know who's doing the killings, Captain."

"That's right."

Cassidy was silent again, looking at his hands. After a time he looked back at Gus. His eyes were mild and blank through the round gold-rimmed glasses.

"You want me to push this, Captain?"

"All the way," Gus said.

"You push something like this really hard, Captain, things come out."

"I know," Gus said.

"No secrets, Captain?"

"None."

"We both know these guys are connected, Captain."

"That's right."

"I follow it where it leads," Cassidy said.

"That's right."

"Even if it leads right back into the department."

"That's right."

Again Cassidy paused.

"You'll get what you need," Gus said. "Commissioner's behind this. Mayor's behind this."

"Sure," Cassidy said. "Where do I report?"

"Chris is working out of City Hall," Gus said. "See Mary Alice Burke in the mayor's office. She'll direct you."

"Starting today?"

"Starting right now," Gus said. "I'll take care of reassigning your caseload."

"Yes, sir," Cassidy said.

He stood and turned toward the door, and stopped and looked back at Gus. For a moment he looked awkward. Gus had never seen him look awkward.

"Maybe I was a little wrong about you, Captain."

"Maybe it doesn't matter if you were or not," Gus said.

Cassidy nodded and went out. Gus sat quietly and drummed with the blunt end of a ballpoint pen on his desktop. Then he put the pen down and got up and looked out his window at Stanhope Street.

Gus

In the food court of a shopping mall, on the Cambridge Canal, across the bridge from Thompson Square, Butchie O'Brien sat at a pedestal table with Gus, eating a green pepper pizza and drinking coffee.

"Kid's doing good, huh?" Butchie said.

"They're going to wire you," Gus said.

"Phone tap?" Butchie said. "Or a bug?"

"Both," Gus said.

Butchie nodded. He tipped his pizza slice so that he could bite off a corner. He bit, chewed for a while, and swallowed.

"So"—Butchie shrugged his shoulders—"I'm careful."

"That's the way to be," Gus said.

"Course, you never know," Butchie said. "You could be wearing a wire."

"Sure could," Gus said.

"Maybe I should give you a pat," Butchie said.

"Nobody puts his hands on me," Gus said.

"Gus," Butchie said, almost gently, "I want to put my hands on you, I got enough people to hold you while I do it."

"You think I need a wire to hang you, Butchie?"

Butchie tipped his head to concede the point. "It ain't your style, Gus. But I'll ask it straight. You wearing a wire?"

"No."

Butchie nodded. Outside it was raining, dimpling the dark water of the canal, distorting the light that came through the wet windows.

"Just me?" Butchie said.

"No," Gus said. "Patrick too. It's about the war. They want the war over."

270

"I ain't thrilled about them bringing your kid in on this thing. Makes me worry about you."

Gus shrugged.

"This is between me and Patrick," Butchie said. "Got nothing to do with some Harvard guy who's read a lot of books."

Gus drank his coffee without comment.

"Can you control the kid, Gus?"

"No."

"If you could, would you?"

"No."

"You got to pick sides, Gus, you gonna be with the kid?"

"Yes."

"Family is family," Butchie said. "But it don't help our deal none, you know?"

"Am I here," Gus said, "talking to you?"

"So far," Butchie said.

"Settle for that."

Butchie looked out the window at the rain on the canal. He nodded slowly.

"You want some more coffee?" Butchie said. "Some pizza? Pizza's pretty good, for selling it by the slice, huh?"

Gus shook his head. He finished his coffee and put the empty cup down on the table and stood up.

"I got to take sides, Butchie, I'll let you know. I won't blind-side you."

"You're a thief, Gus," Butchie said. "But your word's good. We'll do what we got to."

Gus nodded and walked away.

Gus

Mary Alice sat astride him naked on the bed, her hips moving, her head thrown back, moaning softly to herself. Gus had his hands clasped behind his head on the pillow. He looked up at her, at her breasts tightened by the passionate arch of her back. He wondered if that made her choose this position. Probably not. Probably had to do with her ability to control her sensations. He smiled silently. Might have something to do with the fact that he weighed 240.

She was intense and noisy for a brief time, her hands pressed flat against the tops of her thighs, and then she relaxed and leaned forward and lay on top of him. She pressed her face against his chest, and then she rolled off of him and lay beside him with her head on his shoulder.

"You didn't come," she murmured.

"True," Gus said.

"You mind?"

"No."

"You don't come a lot," she said.

"Un-huh."

"You don't mind?"

"No."

"Maybe it's because you're never all there."

"I'm there," Gus said. "Whose dick you think you were just sitting on?"

"Not what I mean. I mean no matter what we're doing, you never let go completely. It's like there's always something else you're thinking about too."

"And you were thinking about me, while you were up there squirming and squealing?" Gus said.

"Thanks for saying it so sweetly," Mary Alice said. "I'm into

272

the experience, Gus—you and me. What it feels like. You're checking what my tits look like, or watching the way the light falls on the ceiling, or thinking about who else you've fucked."

Gus was silent.

"You got anything to say about that?" Mary Alice said.

"You're probably right," Gus said.

Mary Alice waited. Gus didn't say anything else.

"That's it?" Mary Alice said.

"Yes."

"And that's the way it is?"

"I'm sixty-one years old, Mary Alice. I am what I am."

"You won't be sixty-one until fall," Mary Alice said. "Stop talking like you're old. Is it me?"

"I don't understand the question," Gus said.

"Is it me? Do I fail to excite you? Am I boring? Why are you only partly there always?"

"I don't know, Mary Alice. You get everything available."

She put her left hand up and patted his chest for a moment.

"I know," she said. "That's the hell of it, isn't it?"

They were quiet for a time. The rain, driven by wind against the window, made a soft rattle.

"You're quiet about too much, Gus," Mary Alice said. "You keep too much in."

"Like what?" Gus felt tired.

"Like your work. Like your marriage."

Gus rolled out of the bed.

"Drink?" he said.

Mary Alice said no. He mixed a tall Scotch and soda and brought it back with him to the bedroom, and stood at the foot of the bed, looking at Mary Alice.

"Talk some more about you and Peggy," Mary Alice said. "Did you ever love her? Why did you marry her?"

Gus closed his eyes and took a long pull on the drink.

"My mother wanted me to be a priest," he said.

Mary Alice liked to leave a light on when she made love and the hundred-watt bulb in the ceiling fixture glared down on him.

The big window behind him was black and wet with rain. His clothes were folded neatly over a chair by the bedroom door. Mary Alice's were in a pile on the floor. His gun, in its holster, was on the bureau. Mary Alice had propped the pillows behind her and sat half upright watching him.

"It wasn't the religious part," he said. "It was the celibacy."

Mary Alice smiled. Gus walked to the window with his drink and looked out.

"Never saw a person hated sex so much," Gus said.

"Except Peggy," Mary Alice said.

"Yeah. Except her."

"What a coincidence," Mary Alice said.

He drank more of his Scotch, looked at the glass, drank the rest, and went to the kitchen for a refill.

"You can bring me some wine," Mary Alice called after him.

He came back with the two glasses and gave one to her and went back to the window.

"Aren't you afraid someone will look up and see your dinky?" Mary Alice said.

"Not from that distance," Gus said. "I'm Irish."

Mary Alice laughed. Cars went past on Storrow Drive, below him. Their headlights made the wet road gleam. Beyond that was the wide darkness of the river.

"Her and the goddamned priests," Gus said. "Both of them telling me how women were a deadly danger."

"That's why they became priests," Mary Alice said.

"Yeah? I thought it was so they could diddle altar boys in the sacristy," Gus said. "Anyway, my mother didn't like me to date. And I never had much luck with women."

"Might be a connection, huh?"

Gus turned from the window and smiled at her. His drink was empty and he went for a refill. She still had most of her wine.

"So I'm a young guy, on the cops, and I'm single and not getting much," Gus said when he came back. "And I get fixed up with this peppy little broad, who went to school with the nuns, and won't wear patent leather shoes. She talks all the time so I don't have to, she likes to drink, and she only lets me kiss her with her mouth closed."

"That's it?"

"That's it, no French kisses, no feeling the boobs through the sweater, no hanky panky under the skirt. Just some hugging and some cute kisses."

"Perfect," Mary Alice said.

"We were married in six months," Gus said. He drank most of the rest of his drink. "And the rest is fucking history."

"Or no fucking history," Mary Alice said.

Gus laughed. It was a harsh sound, and Mary Alice knew it had nothing to do with amusement.

"So here I am, Mary Alice, an old fat guy walking around bare assed getting drunk with his mistress and whining about his wife."

"You're not fat, Gus. You still got a back like a stonemason."

"Need it to support my stomach," Gus said.

"And I asked you about your wife, and I like being your mistress."

"Think I'll go to hell, Mary Alice?" Gus said.

Mary Alice felt her eyes fill.

"You probably have, Gus," she said. "Already."

"I hadn't married her, I wouldn't have the kid," Gus said.

Tommy

He went to the couch, and sat down. She came immediately and sat on his lap.

"She glad to see Tommy?" he said.

She nodded, her eyes wide as she looked obliquely up at him.

"Tommy's glad to see her too," he said. "It's been very hard out there for Tommy."

"You want some Pepsi?" she said.

He shook his head. She giggled.

"I bet I know what you want," she said.

He put his hand under her dress.

"She thinks she knows what Tommy wants?" he said. "What does she think he wants?"

She squirmed a little as he touched her under her dress, and she giggled again.

"You want to fuck me," she said.

"Tell Tommy what that means."

She told him carefully, and explicitly, reciting it as he'd taught her, anatomically, saying all the dirty words carefully and clearly. She knew he liked to hear them. While she talked he continued to touch her.

"Will you do that to me?" she said when she was through.

"What do we say?"

"Please?"

"Please what?"

"Please fuck me?"

He smiled then, and picked her up in his arms and carried her into the next room to the huge canopied bed. It too was cluttered with stuffed animals and clothing, food wrappers, magazines, and tissues. He shook his head with annoyance and put her on the bed on her back. She lay limply as he'd placed her, with a dreamy little smile on her face, and let him undress her, and lay quite still while he had sex with her. He had sex with her for a long time, trying to ejaculate, until finally he got tired and rolled off of her. They lay together quietly, on their backs, beside each other, looking up at the paislied canopy above them.

"You didn't come," she said.

"Tommy's got a lot on his mind," he said.

He felt frustrated, unfinished.

"Are you mad at me?" she said.

"No."

There was a pair of white cotton underpants on the coverlet near him. He brushed them angrily to the floor.

"She doesn't keep Tommy's house too nice for him," he said.

"I hate always picking up," she said. "Why can't I ever have a maid?"

"I've told you before, this is our secret place. Nobody else can come here."

She nodded silently.

Chris

Chris's office was down two corridors from Flaherty's, and looked out onto the big vacant brick plaza that had seemed so good an idea on the drawing board. *You could have war games on it*, Chris thought, *and no one would notice*. Behind him the door opened. He turned. It was Flaherty, with his jacket off and his shirtsleeves rolled. He had a newspaper in his hand.

"You seen this fucking Cityside column today in the *Globe*?"

"Just the headline," Chris said. "I didn't read the piece."

"Didn't read it?" Flaherty said. "Fucking guy eviscerates us and you didn't even read it?"

"Why would I want to read about my own evisceration?" Chris said.

Flaherty stared at him. Then he began to read aloud.

" 'The good Dr. Sheridan from Hahvad appears to be just another bit of window dressing in the five-and-dime store that Hizzoner runs out of our City Hall. Appointed two months ago with great fanfare and a lot of photo ops, Dr. Sheridan has kept unblemished the city's record of ineptitude. The son of Boston Homicide Commander Gus Sheridan, he has stayed dead even with his father. Neither has made any progress whatsoever in ending the Townie Gang Wars.' You want more?"

Chris shook his head. "Where would columnists be without moral outrage?" he said.

"Don't give me a lot of intellectual Cambridge bullshit," Flaherty said. "What kind of progress have you made?"

"We got phone taps on both Butchie and Pat," Chris said. "We've got a bug in Butchie O'Brien's liquor store. We haven't heard anything useful. We've interviewed everybody connected to either the O'Briens or the Malloys and no one has said any-

278

thing useful. Sergeant Cassidy and I have reinterviewed every-body who can be called a witness. And we got, in the words of the poet, Katz-an-goo."

"Well do something else."

"Like what? You think I'm Philo Vance? Run around with a magnifying glass, discover some heretofore unseen pecker tracks?"

"I didn't appoint you to tell me you couldn't do it," Flaherty said.

"There's this problem with evidence," Chris said.

"Don't evidence me," Flaherty said. "Find some. Manufacture some. I don't give a shit. You may as well be working for your fucking brother-in-law."

"He's not my brother-in-law," Chris said.

"Girlfriend-in-law. Whatever," Flaherty said. "Don't get distracted—November's coming."

"I didn't know I was working on your campaign," Chris said.

"Well, you do now," Flaherty said. "Everybody's working on my campaign. That's the current business of this administration, ya unnerstand, working on my fucking campaign."

"What about the part where you tell me you'll take care of me after you're elected?"

"Yeah, sure. That's how it works. I take care of everybody. You know that. What the fuck do you think we do this for? Christ, you sound more like your old man every time I talk with you. I never saw two guys said less and mean more."

"It's probably better than the other way around," Chris said.

"Not in politics," Flaherty said. "I can't fire you right now, make me look like an asshole. But I want something to happen, and it better happen quick. I go down on this issue, I'm going to take you with me."

"I guess that's a commitment of sorts," Chris said. "These days I'll take it where I can get it."

"Read the fucking column," Flaherty said, and dropped the newspaper on Chris's desk and walked out.

Chris picked up the newspaper, rolled it carefully, and put it in the wastebasket.

"Fuck you," he said out loud, and heard himself and laughed briefly.

Gus

Still in workout clothes, Gus stood with his son on the Larz Anderson Bridge in the late afternoon, with the sun warm on his back, leaning his forearms on the low brick wall, looking at the Charles River curving below them, watching the racing shells tended by motorboats beating upstream against the languid current.

"Grace and I are separated," Chris said.

Gus felt the sadness flicker in his stomach.

"You happy about that?" Gus said.

"No."

"Her idea?"

"Yes."

"Somebody else?"

"She says no."

Gus nodded, staring down at the slow water.

"You have your doubts?" Chris said.

"People like backup," Gus said.

"Yeah."

"Just happen?" Gus said.

"No. Happened a while ago, before Flaherty offered me the job."

"You know where she is?"

"No. Not exactly. I know she is in Boston somewhere. She calls me regularly. We try to meet once a week and talk. She says she doesn't want to lose me."

"What do you say?"

"I say she won't."

"You want her back," Gus said.

"Yes."

"Then you need to not quit," Gus said. "You need to be tough enough not to quit."

"You're the tough guy," Chris said.

Gus shook his head.

"I quit," he said.

On the bridge, people passed them walking dogs, joggers, people riding bicycles, people on roller skates, people in cars. Below them the eight-man crews drove the long shells along rhythmically.

"You gotta break the chain," Gus said. "My father, me, now you."

"Unlucky in love?" Chris said.

"Luck's probably not involved," Gus said.

"We do badly at love," Chris said.

"Yeah. Very."

"Family tradition?" Chris said.

"Whatever," Gus said. "You got a chance to break the chain."

"Why me?"

"Because maybe you're the one hasn't fastened onto the wrong woman."

"I think I may have fastened onto her in the wrong way, though."

"You can change that," Gus said.

"And if I can't?"

"Life goes on," Gus said.

The light changed at Memorial Drive and the traffic moved forward across the bridge.

"I'm not sure I would want it to," Chris said.

"I know," Gus said softly. "I know."

Laura

Grace and Laura Winslow sat together at a white wicker table in the atrium off the kitchen. The sun coming in through the glass roof enriched the polished flagstone floor. They were drinking tea.

"Has he been faithful to you?"

"Chris?" Grace smiled slightly. "Oh, I'm pretty sure he has."

"That's no small thing," Laura said softly.

Grace stared at her mother, and started to speak. "You—" Grace said, and stopped. "It isn't about anything like that."

"Sex?"

"We have enough sex," Grace said.

"That's no small thing either," Laura said.

"It isn't perfect, but it's frequent and it distracts us from our problems."

Laura gazed at her daughter for a long moment, and smiled—more to herself than at Grace.

"It's nice to have a distraction, I imagine."

Grace shrugged. Laura waited, her whole self focused on her daughter, this second self, grown up before her.

"But," she said, "it's imperfect."

"Chris is so fierce," Grace said. "Our relationship seems so all-important, there's no fun to it. He loves me so . . . grimly. I like sex"—she smiled at Laura—"if a daughter may say so to her mother."

"Her mother is very interested," Laura said.

"But Chris puts so much weight on it. On everything. Everything is hugely important. Nothing is frivolous."

"If someone never had experienced that," Laura said, "one might think it desirable."

Again Grace looked at her mother and paused. They sipped

some tea. Outside the atrium, the garden, still wet from the night, glistened in the sunshine.

"Are you talking about you and Daddy?"

Laura smiled.

"Probably," she said. "And we should be talking about you."

"Christ, I don't even know him," Grace said. "With me he's always stayed a hundred miles away."

Grace waited a moment as if Laura would comment. Laura didn't speak.

"It's very tiring," Grace said, "being the basis of someone's life."

"Yes," Laura said. "I'm sure it is. Is it out of fashion to ask if you love Chris?"

"No, it's the right question," Grace said.

"And?"

"And I think I do," Grace said. "And I think I'm not going to give up on him, and I'm not going to let him boil his life away like his father did."

The sun brought out the red tones in her daughter's auburn hair. *Not a little girl anymore.*

"But you can't marry him."

"No. He can't marry me."

"But he needs to be with you?"

"Yes."

"And there's a difference."

"Apparently."

"Do you want to marry him?"

"I might if he wanted me as me, and if there wasn't always this love-hate thing under the surface that I don't understand."

"You want unconditional love."

"Absolutely," Grace said. "I am, and deserve to be, a God-damned love object. Not some kind of functional necessity."

"I never quite thought of it that way," Laura said, smiling.

Grace grinned back at her.

"Well, it's time you started. You're still a good-looking woman."

"I could have done without the 'still,' " Laura said.

"Sorry, but you are. And you deserve some affection. Daddy appears to have no interest in you."

"Perhaps I too am some sort of functional necessity."

"Do you love him?" Grace said.

Laura was quiet, thinking about the question. She knew the answer, she was speculating on what to say to a child about her father.

"No," Laura said. "I don't. I guess I never did."

"Well, the hell with him," Grace said. "Find someone to love. You deserve to have someone to love you."

Laura nodded slowly.

"What will you do?" she said.

"I have done it already. I left."

"Though you love him," Laura said.

"Though I think I love him. It scares me. I'm so worried about him that I feel like I can't breathe. But something has to break the logjam. We can't be happy if something doesn't; and I can't think of anything else to do."

"That seems very brave to me," Laura said.

"I know what I want and I know it is okay to want it, and I will get it. If not with Chris, then with someone else. That's up to Chris. I can live without Chris. He has to be able to live without me. Then maybe we can live with each other."

There was a light wind outside, and it tossed the budding flowers in the garden and riffled the leaves of the low shrubs. Two sparrows splashed in the birdbath.

"What about Daddy?" Grace said.

"He'll barely notice."

"How do you think Cabot will feel?" Grace said. "The election and all."

"Cabot wants to please his father," Laura said. "For himself, he would be happy to play tennis, drink martinis, and fuck every woman who walks erect."

"Mother!"

"It's true, Grace. Your brother is a lovely boy, but his interests are simple."

"I don't think I've ever heard you swear before."

"I always tried not to in front of you."

"Cabot's just doing it for Daddy?"

Laura nodded.

"So why doesn't Daddy run himself, if he is so hung up on the Senate?"

"He feels that there are things in his past," Laura said.

"What things?"

Laura shook her head.

"You don't know?" Grace said.

Laura shook her head again.

"I never asked," she said.

"Why not?"

"It seemed to me that a good wife shouldn't ask," Laura said. "Though I know that is not the current correct definition of a good wife."

Grace held her teacup in two hands and took a small sip. She kept the cup there at her lips and stared at her mother over the rim.

"Maybe not," Grace said. "But you've been a hell of a mother."

"I have wanted to be. It has been what mattered."

"Only that?"

Laura was quiet as she thought about the question. Then she nodded.

"Only that," she said.

"Oh, Mother," Grace said, and put her hand across the table. Laura took it and held it in both of hers.

"We'll be all right," Laura said. "We'll be fine."

Gus

Gus met Laura Winslow for a drink in the bar at the Ritz-Carlton. They sat in the window that looked out onto Arlington Street, with the Public Garden beyond. She ordered a glass of merlot. Gus had Scotch and soda.

"I love this room," Laura said.

Gus nodded.

"But I don't get here often," Laura said.

"Me either," Gus said.

The waiter brought them a small bowl of nuts. Gus pushed the bowl closer to Laura.

"Oh, God," Laura said. "Save me from myself."

Gus smiled and took some nuts. Laura glanced around the bar.

"Are you wearing a gun?" Laura said.

Gus smiled again. "Always," he said, "except with my jammies."

"Probably not many other people in here wearing one," Laura said.

"No," Gus said.

There was a pause. Outside the window was a steady coming and going of taxicabs.

"We don't know each other very well," Laura said.

Gus nodded.

"But our families are so intertwined," Laura said. "And I've always—I've always thought we liked each other, even though we didn't know each other very well."

Laura's face was smooth and well made up. Her blue eyes were unusually large, and wide apart. There were small pleasant crow's-feet at the corners. Her mouth was wide, and carefully done, framed with faint parenthetical smile lines. She was trim and looked healthy, like someone who exercised a lot out of doors. Gus had always thought that her lower lip was sensuous.

"I like you, Laura," he said.

"And I like you."

"Perfect," Gus said. "Let's elope."

Laura smiled.

"What about the kids, Gus?"

"Let them elope on their own," Gus said.

He felt lighter with Laura Winslow than he ever felt. He always thought of bubble bath when he thought of her, and silk lingerie and high-priced perfume. The joke about eloping teased him.

"That doesn't seem to be their plan," Laura said.

"Not at the moment," Gus said.

"It's why I wanted us to talk."

Gus nodded. His drink was gone. So was hers. He signaled the waiter.

"Tommy can't talk about such things," Laura said, "And I don't seem really to know Peggy."

How kindly put, Gus thought. The waiter brought their drinks.

"So I thought maybe you and I should talk."

Gus nodded. He sipped some of the Scotch. Outside the window, across Arlington Street, tourists with children were trailing through the Public Garden toward the swan boats. He leaned back a little in his chair. The Ritz bar. The elegant face across from him. The perfect Scotch and soda. The unhurried late afternoon still waiting. He felt the tight coil of himself loosen.

"About my son and your daughter," Gus said.

"Yes."

"What's to say?"

"Does Chris love her?"

Gus was quiet, thinking about it. This beautiful woman was talking to him about the one thing that mattered to him.

"I think he does, but I don't think I know enough about love, Laura, to make much of a judgment."

"That's too bad, Gus."

Gus shrugged. He wondered exactly how much Laura knew about love. He wondered how much she knew about Tommy. *How could she love a creep like Tommy?*

"So, what do you think, does she love him?" Gus said.

"She says she loves him." Laura spoke softly. "But people don't always understand themselves. I'm afraid I have some of the same limitations you do."

Laura's face was full of intelligence, and decency. Gus felt excited. It was not a feeling he was used to. And he wasn't sure why he was feeling it now.

"Lot of people have that limitation."

"Love is hard," Laura said.

Gus took another drink. He felt as if he needed it, and a deep breath before he spoke again.

"It would help to have firsthand knowledge," he said.

Laura picked up her glass of red wine and studied it before she drank some. A trace of it remained on her upper lip, nearly the color of her lipstick. She blotted it with the corner of a napkin.

"And it's necessary," she said.

"For what?"

"For happiness."

"Yeah," Gus said. "It probably is."

They were quiet. Gus drank his drink and ordered another. Laura still had half a glass left and shook her head at the waiter.

"We talking about the kids?" Gus said.

Laura smiled at him.

"I don't know," she said. "I don't know exactly where we end and they begin."

The room had begun to fill up now, with men in name brand suits and women in designer dresses. The noise was subdued. A lot of martinis went by on small trays, crystalline in their little decanters. Outside the afternoon had darkened to a blue tone, and taxicabs had turned on their lights. Gus picked up his fresh drink. It was clear amber in the muted light, full of ice, in a tall glass. He made a small *salud* gesture toward Laura with the glass, and drank. It tasted right. It was surprising how many bartenders didn't get it right. If there was too much Scotch it tasted harsh. If there was too much soda it tasted thin.

"So," he said. "You got a plan?"

"No," she said.

"I'd like to see them together," Gus said.

"Yes."

"I don't know what to do about it."

"I don't either, Gus. But we can try to stay in touch, talk, share a viewpoint. Be there for them. Maybe we can help."

"Or maybe it's none of our Goddamned business," Gus said softly, "and we should butt out."

Laura smiled. "Maybe," she said.

She kept her eyes on him while she twirled her wineglass by the stem slowly on the table.

He smiled. "I think we should talk," he said. "Even if it doesn't do them any good. I like it."

"Yes," Laura said.

"Want to make a date?" Gus said.

"This time Tuesdays is good for me," Laura said. "I'm in town anyway for a New England Rep board meeting."

"Okay," Gus said. "You need a ride anywhere?"

"No, thank you, the doorman has my car."

Gus motioned for the check.

"So," Laura said as they waited. "If we were going to elope, where would we go?"

Gus grinned at her.

"I know the houseman here, I could get us a room upstairs."

Laura laughed aloud. The waiter smiled as he brought them the check. A good-looking older couple, enjoying themselves. Nice to see.

Gus

Chris stood near the subway kiosk on the edge of the vast brick plaza in front of City Hall. Around him was a hubbub of microphones, television cameras, sound equipment, reporters, still photographers, newspaper reporters, tape recorders, and notebooks.

"Obviously,"—Chris was reading a prepared statement—"this is a criminal gesture of open defiance. It will not divert us from our course. The investigation of this brutal war will proceed the way criminal investigations must—with diligence, with care, and with patience."

Gus stood past him near the front entrance to City Hall, among the cluster of squad cars and the unmarked cruisers where the tarpaulin-covered body lay. Gus was proud of Chris. The statement was a little ornate, but it was less full of shit than most things said at City Hall.

"We cannot," Chris was saying, "conduct an investigation in the press. We cannot be guided by the wishes of the media. We must be guided by the rules of evidence, and the facts of each crime. We are as eager as anyone in the Commonwealth to halt the killing and bring the killers to justice. . . . Questions?"

Many of the questions were about the effect of these murders on Flaherty's candidacy. Chris answered everything calmly and well, Gus thought, considering that he knew who was responsible for the murders, couldn't prove it, and knew in fact that the gang war was ruining Flaherty's campaign, and couldn't do much about it. *Kid's a politician.* Gus smiled. *Where did I go wrong?*

This killing worried him. They had dumped this body in front of City Hall, scornful of the new special prosecutor, scornful of Flaherty. It was a statement and Gus didn't think it was aimed at the mayor. *They don't care about Flaherty*, Gus thought. *This is for me.* He didn't even know who had done it yet. They hadn't ID'd the body. It was Butchie's turn, but that didn't always hold. *Whichever it was, I'm in their pocket*, Gus thought. *And they're reminding me.* What bothered him most was that suddenly what he was and how he lived would spill over on his son.

Billy Callahan stood with Gus, watching Chris talk to the press.

"This is a real fuck-you to the mayor, Captain," he said.

Gus nodded, watching Chris.

"Hear the question that guy from Channel Three asked him?" Callahan said. "Did he have ballistic match on the murder weapon. Fucking stiff still here. He figure we're going to dig the fucking bullets out with a fucking jackknife?"

"He heard it on *Perry Mason*," Gus said. "He doesn't know what it means."

"Chris's doing good," Callahan said.

"Yes."

"He's a smart boy, Captain."

"He's a smart man, Billy."

"Yeah, sure, no offense, I just meant how he's your kid, you know, and after a while everyone seems like a kid, you know?"

"I know."

Chris ended the questioning and walked over toward Gus. The reporter who'd asked about ballistics trailed along with a camera crew.

"Isn't it well known that this is a war between the O'Briens and the Malloys?"

Chris shook his head as he stood beside his father.

"No more questions," he said.

The reporter pushed in closer with his microphone, the camera crew following.

"Do you have anyone under surveillance?"

Again Chris shook his head.

"Enough," he said.

The reporter pushed between Gus and Billy Callahan.

"Dr. Sheridan—"

Billy Callahan was very quick for a man his size. He turned sharply into the reporter, caught the reporter in the middle of the chest with his right elbow, and sent him sprawling.

"Oh," Billy said, "I beg your pardon."

He bent over the reporter.

"You startled me, are you all right?"

The reporter said, "Jesus Christ."

Gus walked with his son toward the car.

"Billy has his moments, doesn't he?" Chris said.

Gus smiled.

"He does, in fact," he said.

Gus

They were standing on the fish pier, watching the fishing boats unload. After their third meeting at the Ritz bar, Laura suggested they try meeting in parts of the city she didn't usually get to.

"I've never been here," she said.

The harbor water was black and around the pier it floated a lot of debris. Gulls swooped frantically around the fishing boats, landing on the pier and strutting in perilous proximity to the people. The press of the sun was heavy. The smell of fish was strong. There was a wind off the water, that moved Laura's hair.

"Lot of people in the suburbs don't get into the city," Gus said.

Laura laughed. She had on big sunglasses like Jackie Onassis. And a white summer dress and white high heels.

"I don't get to anywhere, Gus. I'm fifty-six years old and about all I've done is have children, and play tennis."

"Nothing wrong with having children," Gus said.

Laura laughed.

"Gives you a lifelong rooting interest at least," she said.

"Yeah."

"That's not a bad thing," Laura said, staring across the harbor at the airport, "particularly if there isn't too much else to root for."

Gus nodded. He was leaning with his forearms resting on a piling. Laura stood next to him, her white purse over her shoulder. Her hands thrust into the side pockets of her dress.

"At least you have your work too," she said.

Gus laughed briefly.

"Or not," Laura said.

He smiled at her. "Mostly I root for the kid."

One of the harbor cruise boats went by, full of people. It would go to the mouth of the outer harbor and come back in a wide circle.

"Nothing else?" Laura said.

Gus watched the tour boat for a while before he answered.

"I sort of look forward to these meetings," he said.

Laura nodded slowly.

"Yes," she said. "I do too."

Peggy

"I told him straight out," Peggy said to Father Boyd, "I'm very disappointed. You had a chance to make me proud, I said, to marry into a fine family."

Father Boyd took a chocolate chip cookie from a white plate. The plate had a picture of a blue puppy painted on it. The cookie was the kind you bought in a bag at the supermarket. He ate half of it.

Awful, he thought.

"Being a mother is a heavy burden, Peggy."

"You'll never know how heavy, Father. It would have been a fine marriage, good family, money. And I told him so."

Father Boyd ate the other half of the cookie.

As awful as the first half.

He swallowed the cookie and drank some of the instant coffee from a small teacup that matched the cookie plate.

"I told him they both should have talked with me first, I could have set them straight. She was sort of highfaluting and full of ideas but she had money of her own and she wouldn't be after his, I told him. I said, Chris, you listen to me, any woman you go out with is looking to take you for all you're worth."

"I know, Peggy. I know. The things I hear in the confessional these days, Peggy, it would curl your hair. And from good Catholic girls too."

"Course, she wasn't Catholic," Peggy said. "But I'd have seen to it that the children were. He wasted nine years on that girl. Living together."

Peggy shook her head and popped a cookie into her mouth.

"It's the way nowadays," Father Boyd said. He sipped a little more of the coffee. She had made it too strong, and it wasn't hot enough. "It's sinful, yes, but God is merciful."

"I call a spade a spade," Peggy said.

And a spick a spick, probably.

"If he'd married her, and I told him, if he'd married her while he had the chance, she wouldn't have gotten away. He'd be safe."

"What's the captain say?"

"Nothing. That's what the captain says. That's what he always says. Mister Say Nothing." Peggy ate another cookie.

"Never know these were store bought," Peggy said. "Taste just as good as if I'd baked them."

Probably.

"They're delicious, Peggy."

"Chips Ahoy," Peggy said. "That's what they're called, Chips Ahoy."

That's why she bought them. They taste like a sawdust gumdrop, but the name is cute.

"He was always that way," Peggy said. "Never listen."

Unlike myself.

"Talk till I was blue in the face and he'd go right ahead and do what he wanted to."

"It's why God gave the job to women, Peggy. Motherhood's too hard for men."

"Damned right," Peggy said. "Pardon my French. And a mother goes through all of that, the pain of it—my womb is still tipped, you know, Father, ever since Chris—and they grow up and don't pay a damn bit of attention to you."

"It's the way of it, Peggy."

"Neither of them," Peggy said. "Father or son. They don't pay a damn bit of attention to me. My husband and my son. I talk and talk and they sit there like two bumps and when I'm through they go right off and do whatever they were going to do."

Father Boyd nodded sadly.

"Your prayers guide them, Peggy, I'm sure."

"I don't matter to them," Peggy said.

Robert B. Parker

For a moment there was silence. Father Boyd cleared his throat.

"They need you, Peggy," he said. "I know they do."

"And maybe one of these days they'll need me and I won't be here, by God. Then maybe I'll matter."

Father Boyd took her hand.

"Let us pray together," he said, "to Our Heavenly Father."

Peggy took his hand in both of hers and clenched her features and closed her eyes.

"Our Father," she began, and Father Boyd joined her. "Who art in heaven . . ."

Some pastoral visits are tougher than others.

Gus

Butchie O'Brien was alone, when Gus arrived. He was leaning on the rail of the Gilmour Bridge, looking at the train tracks. Butchie was usually alone. You went to talk with Pat Malloy and there were sometimes eight, ten guys around. And if you did business with the Italians there were cousins and brothers everywhere. But Butchie was different. There was something priestly in his aloofness. He seemed sometimes to Gus to be a sort of ascetic, alone with his meditations and plans.

"Payday?" Butchie said when Gus walked onto the bridge from the Cambridge side.

"You dumped Frankie Carey in front of City Hall," Gus said.

Butchie rested his chin on his folded hands.

"Yeah?"

"It was for me, wasn't it?" Gus said.

Butchie smiled and shrugged.

"It made my kid look bad," Gus said.

"Yeah?"

"You got a message for me, give it to me direct. Don't involve my kid."

"Your kid is involved, Gus. He's got a fucking bug in my office. He's got a tap on my phone."

"I warned you about that," Gus said.

"Sure you did, that's what you're paid to do. But it's still Goddamned inconvenient. I want to talk with someone, I got to come out here to do it."

"And I told you don't fuck with my kid," Gus said.

Butchie took an envelope out of his inside pocket, and held it up.

"You don't tell me, Gus. I tell you. The late Frankie's appearance in front of City Hall was just to remind you. I don't want this investigation to get too serious. This is between me and Patrick."

He held the envelope out to Gus. Gus took it and without a glance tossed it over the railing. It planed briefly, then heli-coptered down toward the tracks. Butchie glanced over the rail and smiled and shrugged.

"It's your money," he said.

"Not anymore," Gus said.

Butchie shrugged again.

"You're smart enough to know that it's not just revenge, Gus. When it's over this part of the city will belong to me or to Pat." He smiled his meaningless smile again. "Think of it as a corpo-rate takeover."

"No," Gus said. "It's finished. You and Pat work out a settle-ment."

"Gus," Butchie said, "get real."

"Or I'll settle it."

"How you going to do that, Gus?"

Butchie's voice was perfectly flat.

"You think all these years I haven't paid attention?" Gus said. "I could package you and Patrick tomorrow."

"You'd go too, Gus."

"So what?"

"I go, Gus. Everybody goes."

Gus took his gun from under his coat. It was a Glock 9-mm. He pressed the muzzle up under Butchie's chin. Butchie's ex-pression didn't change, though he raised his head slightly under the pressure of the gun.

"You could go right here," Gus said.

"Could," Butchie said.

"You and Pat don't settle this between you I'm going to blow both of you right out of the water. You embarrass my kid again and I'll kill you."

"You said you'd let me know when you changed sides," Butchie said. "This it? You back to being a cop?"

Cars went by steadily on the Gilmour Bridge. Their passage made a steady wishing sound behind Gus. No one stopped.

"This is it," Gus said, and lowered the gun and turned his wide back toward Butchie and walked away down the length of the bridge without looking back, or bothering to holster his gun.

Chris

"I want you to pick them both up and bring them in," Chris said. He was at his desk with coffee in a paper cup. John Cassidy sat across the desk with his coffee and Billy Callahan was leaning on the wall near the door.

"Butchie and Pat?" John Cassidy said. "Together?"

"Pick them up one at a time," Chris said. "Quietly. I want to talk with them together."

"Here?"

"I guess not here," Chris said. "Press would spot them for sure."

"I can take them to Area D. I know a guy."

"Warren Ave?"

"Yeah."

"Okay. Do it."

Cassidy finished his coffee. He came around Chris's desk and carefully threw the cup in the wastebasket.

"I'll give you a call," he said.

Chris nodded, and Cassidy went.

"You think you ought to talk to your father?" Billy Callahan said. He was eating a chocolate-frosted doughnut with a cream filling. There was a little spillage. Billy caught it with his forefinger and tucked it into his mouth.

"No."

"He might not think this was a good idea."

"I think it's a good idea," Chris said.

"Yes, sir," Billy said.

"And don't call me fucking *sir*. For Crissake, I've known you since I was like ten. You used to teach me to box."

"And you got to be pretty good too, Chris."

"Bullshit. I was awful. I never liked it," Chris said.

"Your mother used to hate it when we boxed."

"I know."

Billy went over to the open box of doughnuts on the table and took another one with the chocolate glaze on it.

"These Boston cream's are excellent," Billy said. "You want one?"

"No, thanks."

Billy went to the extra chair and sat down with his doughnut. However much he ate, he didn't seem to change. *He works out so much*, Chris thought, *that he can eat what he wants. One of those single Irish guys with nothing else to do.* Chris felt the bottomless down spiral in his stomach. *Like me.*

Laura

Laura Winslow gazed at her daughter's face across the table. In the bright sunlight, she could see the faint lines beginning to show around her eyes.

"His name is Jerry Davis," Grace said. "I met him at work. He's a partner in another law firm and he's married."

"And you like him," Laura said.

"Yes, of course, he's very nice."

"Have you known him long?"

They were outside under an umbrella on Newbury Street, drinking cappuccino in the late morning.

"Oh, sure, a bunch of years, since I started work. We got to be sort of pals, but nothing more than that until lately."

"And you slept with him?" Laura said.

"Of course. You disapprove?"

Laura smiled and shook her head.

"No," she said, "I don't. I probably ought to, I'm your mother and all that. But I find it—I don't know what exactly—charming seems too cute a way to say it. I guess I envy you."

"You do?"

"Yes, I think so. I envy the freedom to do it, and the impetuosity, and the"—Laura made a circular motion with her right hand while she searched for language—"the sense of ease that it implies," she said.

Grace put her hand out and held on to her mother's forearm.

"Ease is fun," she said.

Laura patted the hand that rested on her forearm.

"I imagine so," Laura said.

"It was like I'd come out of a cocoon," Grace said. "Like I'd been in traction. Mother, we—in New York—we did everything. We tried everything we'd ever heard of."

Laura smiled.

"That's nice, dear."

Grace laughed. "I know I shouldn't be talking like this to my *mother.*"

"Who better?" Laura said. "Besides, I'm fascinated."

"Always with Chris," Grace said, "it was like, about something. It was about who loved who, and who was willing to do what for who, and who controlled who, and it was always somber and heavy, you know?"

"I know something," Laura said.

"With Jerry, it's fun. We're doing this stuff because we like it. You know? No other issues. No unspoken tests. No passing and failing. Just a balls-out good time."

"Perhaps an unfortunate choice of metaphor," Laura said. And they both laughed. "And you've told Chris?"

"Yes."

"Must be hard for him."

"I can't help that."

"You didn't have to tell him."

"He has a right to know."

"Or you have a need to tell him."

"Or both," Grace said. "He knows there were men before him, he should know there can be men after him. It doesn't do either of us any good if he thinks I'm home sorting things in my hope chest."

"Perhaps you're right."

"And even if I'm not," Grace said, and she grinned at her mother, "what I need now is tea and sympathy. And as my mother you're obligated to provide it."

"At last," Laura said, "a job description emerges. How *are* you feeling about Chris?"

"God, that's hard. Relief is one feeling. He hasn't got hold of me anymore. All that grimness."

"But?"

"But we are so connected. I mean I've known him since I was

a child. Our families have known each other since, what? Grammy Hadley knew his grandfather, or something?"

"Yes."

"And I learned a lot of things from him. I mean, he's from a whole other place and in some ways he helped bring me up. And . . . I do love him."

"I think he's a good man," Laura said.

"Well, we'll find that out, won't we?" Grace said. "He has potential, but he's got to get some perspective on his family."

"I'm sure everyone ought to," Laura said. "His father seems like a good man too."

"Yes," Grace said. "I like Gus, but why doesn't he stuff a sock down that woman's throat."

"Peggy?" Laura said.

"Yes."

"I gather she's difficult."

"Difficult? She's hideous."

"Must have been hard having her for a mother."

"Probably was," Grace said. "But, at least for the moment, that's his problem. I hope he solves it."

1994
Voice-Over

"And the rage," Grace said. "What have you done with the rage?"

"Well, first I thought about killing that guy you went to New York with."

Grace nodded.

"And me?" she said.

"No. I never thought about killing you."

She looked at me for a while in silence, holding the big mug of tea at a level with her mouth. Only her eyes showed above the rim of it, resting on me. Then she nodded as if to herself. Outside the window the thunder and lightning came almost at the same moment, the fluorescent flash underscored immediately by the looming rumble.

"I believe that," she said.

"If you didn't," I said, "you took a hell of a chance having me come here tonight."

"I had to know," she said.

"Yeah," I said. "And now you do."

"So, what did you do with the rage?"

"I took Flaherty's job," I said.

"And now?"

"Now I know that I can do things without triggering the rage."

"That's a good thing to know," Grace said. "What about me?"

"Or perhaps, what about us," I said.

"I need to know how you feel about me. You have to be angry."

"Yeah, probably, but I know also that you did what you had to do. If you hadn't left, we'd have stayed in the strangled disaster we were in."

"You know that intellectually," Grace said.

"Last year I didn't know it at all," I said.

"So it's a start," Grace said.

"Get 'em by the head; the soul will follow."

"I hope so," Grace said.

"Consider," I said. "Last year I couldn't marry you and couldn't leave you."

"And this year?"

"I can do either," I said.

Chris

Butchie O'Brien and Pat Malloy were sitting quietly on straight chairs in a small room off the side entrance in the Area D station on Warren Avenue, when Chris walked in with Billy Callahan. John Cassidy, neat clothes, hair slicked back, round glasses, sat behind a yellowed maple table. His hands were folded on the table.

Chris went behind the table beside Cassidy and remained standing. Billy Callahan leaned widely against the door.

"I wish to call my attorney," Butchie said.

"Of course," Chris said.

"Me too," Pat Malloy said.

"Certainly," Chris said. "Anyone facing arrest has the right to an attorney."

Nobody moved. Nobody said anything. Pat Malloy glanced at the closed door against which Billy Callahan was leaning. Billy's arms were folded and his upper arms seemed to stretch the weave of his coat. Chris smiled at both of them. He looked at Cassidy.

"Did you place these men under arrest, Sergeant Cassidy?"

Cassidy shook his head.

"So we're free to go," Butchie said.

"Sure."

Billy Callahan continued to lean on the door. Everybody looked at him. He smiled.

"Cut the bullshit," Pat Malloy said. "Whaddya want?"

"I want the killing stopped," Chris said. "I know you two are in charge. I know if you say stop, it stops."

"You got any proof?" Pat said.

"Not a bit," Chris said. "That's why we need to talk."

Butchie and Pat looked at each other. Butchie smiled softly.

"So talk," Pat said.

"We are all over you," Chris said. "And I know it is hard to do business when the cops are all over you. Sooner or later we will get something and then one or both of you will be down at Cedar Junction looking out."

"I do land development," Butchie said.

"Yeah, sure," Chris said. "And Pat does import-export. And I'm a fucking movie star. What I'm saying is that we can end this now, before more of your people get killed. You're about even up with each other in the body count. Each of you give me one guy to take the jump, and we call it a wash."

"You want me to designate an employee to go to jail?" Butchie said with a small smile.

"Somebody's gotta go in for all the homicides," Chris said. "Can't be helped."

"You're as bad as your old man," Pat said. "He's fucking crazy. You're fucking crazy."

Butchie's eyes drifted aimlessly around the room. Chris saw it.

"It's not bugged," he said.

Butchie smiled at him and shrugged.

"But you don't know that, so you won't admit to anything," Chris said. "But consider the deal. The shooting stops. We get out of your face. Your business prospers. Neither of you gets bagged. Life goes on."

No one said anything.

"Think about it," Chris said. "You want to talk about this, I'll meet you anywhere you feel comfortable. You don't want to talk about this, we up the stakes. If you think we've been in your way before . . ." Chris shook his head, speechless in wonderment at the level of harassment to come.

"You don't have a fucking thing," Butchie O'Brien said. "And the press is on your ass and the fucking mayor is on your ass and this is all you could think of."

Chris took two business cards from his shirt pocket and handed them one each.

"Call me anytime," he said.

Pat crumpled his without looking at it, and dropped it on the floor. Butchie read his, and carefully tore it in half, and put the two halves neatly on the table in front of him. Everyone sat quietly again. Then Chris looked at Billy Callahan and moved his head. Billy stepped away from the door. Pat Malloy got up, walked to the door, opened it, and went out, leaving it open behind him. Butchie remained seated for a moment.

"Do I get a ride home?" he said.

Chris shook his head. Butchie smiled slightly.

"Take care," he said. And stood and went out.

Chris watched Butchie leave, and then went to the mesh-covered front window, and watched him enter one of two cars waiting at the curb. The cars pulled away and Chris stared after them until the red taillights disappeared. Then he turned back to the room. He hunched his shoulders and spread his hands and turned his palms up in a gesture of resignation.

"Was that a threat?" he said.

" 'Take care'?" Cassidy said.

"Yeah."

"Maybe."

"Chris," Billy Callahan said, "I think you oughta talk to the captain."

Chris didn't answer.

"It might not be a bad idea," Cassidy said.

"Why?" Chris said.

"Captain knows a lot," Cassidy said.

"Let's get out of here," Chris said.

Laura

Laura sipped from her third cup of cappuccino. The sun had shifted westward enough so that they were in the shadow now, and the memory of March still lingered in the June shade.

"When you say you 'tried everything,' and perhaps this is too intimate, what do you mean?"

Grace laughed. "Positions mostly—like him on top, me on top, in a chair . . . you know?"

"No, actually, I'm embarrassed to admit, I don't know. It's why I'm asking."

"Honest to God? You and Daddy . . . ?" Grace shook her head. "I don't mind, ask what you want to know."

"We seem to have reversed roles here," Laura said. "But your father and I come from a more constrained time. We have been, ah, quite . . . calm in our marital relations."

"The old missionary position," Grace said, smiling. Her face felt warm. She knew she was blushing. But so was her mother.

"At most," Laura said. "How does one do this in a chair?"

"There's a couple ways," Grace said. Her voice sounded hoarse and she cleared it before she went on to describe the options. Her mother bent slightly toward her, watching her face, nodding frequently.

"Really," Laura said. "And what about oral sex?"

"Mother!"

"Well, I'm sorry. I've heard about it but I've never known anyone I could ask."

"Not even Daddy?"

"It's not something your father would discuss," Laura said.

"Well," Grace said, "what about it?"

"Have you done it?"

"Sure."

Laura was very intent now as she leaned toward her daughter.

"Both"—she made a reciprocating gesture with her hands—
"I mean, you and him?"

"Sure."

Laura continued to lean forward, staring at her daughter.

"Oh, my," she said.

Both of them drank some coffee. Around them people at
other tables were conversing reasonably about restaurants and
fashion and sports and prices.

"Mother, I don't mean this to be critical, I just don't know
how else to say it. What kind of a marriage have you had?"

Laura took another sip from her cup. She looked at the coffee
and shook her head.

"I'll never sleep, tonight," she said.

Grace waited.

"We've had an uneventful marriage. Your father is orderly and
very remote. He has never been unkind to me. He is committed
to the business, and the family name. He is a good provider. He
wants there to be a Senator Winslow. He is not interested in
sex."

"My God, Mother. What about you?"

"I was brought up in a time, and by a family, which believed
that sex was something women provided in return for home,
family, financial security. Women did not initiate sex, they lay
still and accepted it, as was their responsibility."

"But, I mean you haven't been in a vacuum. You know there's
another way to think about it."

"Passionate sexual response frightens your father."

They sat still, looking at each other's face. The ambient buzz
of conversation seemed at a great distance. Laura's eyes were
wet. The waiter came and asked if they needed anything else.
Grace shook her head. The waiter put the check down on the
table between them and went away.

"Oh," Grace said.

"Exactly," Laura said. "Oh."

"Does it frighten you?"

"I don't think so," Laura said.

"And you never thought of looking for it elsewhere?"

"No. It was not a condition of my upbringing. I had two children to think about. And truthfully, the opportunity has not, so far, presented itself."

"If it did," Grace said, looking directly at her mother, "would you take it?"

"I think so," Laura said.

Tom

Tom Winslow sat at a small table in the middle of the food court at Cityplace in the Transportation Center. A styrofoam cup of black coffee sat untouched in front of him. Across the table with two honey-dipped crullers, and a cup of his own, was Barry Levine.

Tom Winslow's face felt frozen. His body felt stiff and clumsy. Barry Levine picked a piece of lint off his lapel and flicked it away. Nothing else marred his appearance. He was slim, tanned, tailored. He wore a double-breasted blue pinstriped suit, and a blue shirt with a white pin collar. His black shoes were Italian. His tie was scarlet with a white geometric pattern, and his display handkerchief was white. He knew he was worth money. He was Butchie O'Brien's lawyer.

"I don't think I've ever been in here," Tom Winslow said.

"Yes, it's a bit scruffy, but then we don't want anyone listening in on our conversation, Tom."

"We've done business in my office for years. You think someone would listen in?"

Barry Levine smiled.

"It seems prudent, Tom."

"You think I'm under suspicion?"

"Oh, I'm sure not, Tom. Just a lawyer's natural caution is all."

Barry Levine took a bite of his cruller, leaning carefully forward to make sure no crumbs fell on his shirtfront.

"Boy, I'm a sucker for these things," Barry Levine said. "I try to eat right, exercise, stay fit. But I get near a Dunkin' Donuts stand and I lose all resolve."

Tom Winslow didn't say anything. He sat stiffly and waited. The public sound system in the atrium area was playing a Frank

Sinatra album over the buzz of mostly adolescent conversation and the sounds of fast food being sold.

"You sure you don't want anything, Tom?"

Tom Winslow shook his head.

"Well, you're a man of firmer resolve than I," Barry Levine said.

He finished his first cruller and drank some coffee and carefully patted his lips dry with a paper napkin.

"We've got to do something about Gus Sheridan," he said.

"Gus?"

"Gus. He's the loose cannon in this whole situation. He pulled a gun on Butchie, for God's sake."

Barry Levine broke off a small piece of cruller and ate it over the table.

"The special prosecutor's office can be annoying, but as long as we all remain steadfast, they can be frustrated. They can prove nothing."

He drank coffee carefully, savoring the swallow. He touched his lips again with the napkin.

"Gus, on the other hand, knows most of our intimate secrets. And he can probably prove them."

"Gus, my God, why would he? He'd have to incriminate himself."

"Butchie's theory is that Gus is crazy, and that he might do anything. He's very supportive of his son."

Barry Levine leaned back in his small chair and stretched, arching his back. He shook his head.

"You get older, you pay more and more for the time you put in at the health club," he said.

"You think he would confess," Tom Winslow said, "—implicate me, us?"

Barry Levine shrugged broadly.

"You prepare for what your enemy is able to do, not what you think he will do," he said.

"Well, I mean, Jesus, can't we do something to stop him?"

"Butchie was hoping you'd talk some sense to him."

"Me? What can I say to him?"

"Butchie thinks, and I must say I agree, that what you say and how you control him, is largely your problem. Butchie, and rightly, I think, simply wants him controlled."

"But I can't control Gus Sheridan. For God's sake, he controls me."

"Butchie feels that you have a long family relationship, including his son and your daughter."

"They're, ah, separated or whatever, right now," Tom Winslow said.

"Shame," Barry Levine said. "But they have been together. The point is Butchie figures that there may be some basis for you and Gus to reason together. And Butchie would like you to try."

Tom Winslow was shaking his head.

"I can't—"

"Tom," Barry Levine said, "get real. Butchie isn't making a suggestion, if you see what I mean. Butchie wants you to get Gus Sheridan under control."

"What if I can't?"

"Butchie is in business. If he were to control Gus in some more direct way, it would add to the difficulty of doing business in the current climate."

"Direct way?"

Barry Levine was impatient. It was like talking to a child.

"If Butchie kills him," Barry Levine said. "It would solve the problem, but create others."

"Kill him?"

"Yes, Tom. It's part of the way Butchie does business. If he must. And he would not, of course, hesitate to kill you if it made sense to him. But right now it makes sense to him for you to talk with Gus."

"Jesus."

"Now I'm aware, as is Butchie, that you also do some business with Patrick Malloy. It is Butchie's intention that Patrick will be out of business in a while, and all the business will be done with Butchie. Butchie is very businesslike."

Tom Winslow was rigid in his chair. There was no color in his face. And the corners of his mouth were pinched with anxiety as he watched Barry Levine finish his second cruller.

"Unfortunately," Barry Levine said, "Pat is somewhat less businesslike than Butchie. More given to impulse. Butchie suggests, and I concur, that you be careful of Pat."

As he spoke, Barry Levine unconsciously wiped the corners of his mouth with the thumb and forefinger of his right hand.

"He's impulsive," Barry Levine said, "but he's not stupid. It will occur to him that you and Gus know too much. And, being less businesslike . . ." Barry Levine spread his hands, and raised his eyebrows.

Tom Winslow sat like a stone. Barry Levine smiled at him and stood.

"Anyway," he said, "it is important to you, I think, to get this situation under control before anything bad happens."

"To me?" Tom Winslow's voice squeezed out thinly.

"To all of us, Tom. To all of us."

Barry Levine nodded pleasantly, and turned and walked away toward the door that led to Boylston Place where, already, upscale young people were gathering for fun at outdoor tables, under bright umbrellas.

Gus

The first big leisurely raindrop hit the hot sidewalk near the small bandstand on the Tremont Street end of the Common and faded. And then another came and another more quickly, and soon it was raining.

"This will not help the look I spent so much time putting on," Laura Winslow said.

"Bedraggled?" Gus said.

"Think drowned rat," Laura said.

Gus took off his suit jacket and Laura draped it over her head and shoulders. He nodded toward the bandstand.

"We could take cover," he said.

"Are we allowed up there?"

"I'm a cop," Gus said. "I'm the one does the allowing."

"Yes," Laura said. "I forget."

The rain was coming hard enough to have wet Gus's shirt by the time they reached the bandstand. They could smell the steamy scent of the rain hitting the still hot pavement of the walkways.

Laura handed Gus's coat to him.

"No," he said, and draped it around her shoulders. "It's getting cold."

"Your shirt is wet," she said. "Won't you be freezing?"

"You ever see a cold whale?" Gus said.

"You're not fat. You're a big man, and you are always pretending to be fat, but you're not."

"Fatter than I used to be," Gus said.

With his coat off, Laura could see the gun on Gus's hip. How strange to be Laura Winslow and to stand here sheltered from a downpour with a man who carried a gun. She shrugged the coat closer around her and held it in place with her folded arms. Gus was more than big, as she stood beside him. It wasn't that he was tall. Tom was taller, in fact, but Gus was so wide. The sheer bulk of him was compelling. He seemed to loom beside her, his shirt-sleeves tight over his upper arms. She shivered, as much from strangeness as from cold, and moved closer to him so that they touched at the shoulder.

The top of the bandstand was rounded and it caused the rain to come straight down off it all around like a translucent curtain. She had the feeling of being inside a waterfall. There was a soundless shimmer of lightning, as there so often was in summer storms, and several seconds later the distant thunder.

"Grace says that both she and Chris are seeing other people," Laura said.

"Un-huh."

"I guess that's good for them?"

"It would be bad for them not to," Gus said.

"Why?"

"This way they'll know," Gus said.

"An informed choice, so to speak," Laura said.

Gus nodded, watching the rain.

"Tom is the only man I ever have slept with," Laura said.

Gus turned his head to look at her.

"Not an informed choice," he said.

"No. Were you . . . had you any experience when you married Peggy?"

Gus smiled. The lightning came soundlessly again, and Gus listened for the subsequent thunder before he answered.

"In Tokyo, on R and R from Korea."

"Prostitutes."

Gus nodded.

"So Peggy was the first, ah . . ."

"American," Gus said.

"Amateur," Laura said simultaneously.

They laughed.

"She was that, all right," Gus said.

They were quiet. The rain was hard. The thunder when it

came was now hard on the heels of the lightning. Laura leaned her head against Gus's shoulder. He put his arm around her.

"Still is," Gus said.

Around them, through the rain, the trees on the Common glistened murkily. They were alone in a green-gray silence made more quiet by the downrush of the rain.

Gus

Tom Winslow was sitting stiffly on a bench on the Mall on Commonwealth Avenue, near Berkeley Street, when Gus strolled four blocks down from Headquarters and sat beside him. Gus had some roasted peanuts he had bought in a brown paper bag and almost at once there were half a dozen pigeons around them. Gus offered the bag to Tom. Tom shook his head. Gus took a peanut from the bag and cracked it open. He dropped the shells on the ground and popped the nuts into his mouth. The pigeons ignored the shells.

"Gus, I'm scared," Tom said.

"Things kind of closing in, Tom?"

"Yes. On you too. Aren't you scared?"

Gus ate another peanut. He paid no attention to the pigeons that strutted anxiously around his feet.

"I haven't thought about it, Tommy. I don't guess I am."

"Well, you're a cop, you're used to this kind of thing."

"That's not really it, Tommy," Gus said. "Cops get scared. It's just that I don't give a shit."

"They are talking about killing us," Tom said. "You don't give a shit about that?"

Gus shrugged. "Who's 'they'?" he said.

"Barry Levine, representing Butchie. He said I better control you."

"You can't control me, Tommy. You explain that to him?"

"Yes, but he said I had to. He said Pat Malloy might kill me, and he implied Butchie would too if he had to."

Gus nodded thoughtfully.

"Well, what do you have to say about that?"

"Yeah. They might kill you. Butchie will do it when he thinks

322

it will be better for business to kill you than to let you live. Patrick will kill you when he gets mad enough."

"Jesus, Gus. You got me into this. He said you threatened Butchie with a gun."

"Got his attention," Gus said.

"Even if they don't kill me. What if it all comes out? You put me in bed with these people, Gus. What if it breaks open and everything comes out? You go down too."

"I told you before, Tommy, I don't give a shit. And you are one of the things I don't give a shit about most."

Tom's face got red and he started to cry.

"Gus, Jesus. For God sakes, if you don't care about me. I got a wife. I got two kids. My daughter and your son are still close. I mean, I know they broke up. But they still see each other. They may get together again. Gus, I haven't done you any harm. I've done what you said. You've got to get me out of this. Gus, please."

Gus looked at Tommy with the same absent stare with which he had ignored the pigeons. He ate another peanut. Then he crumpled the bag, stood, walked to a trash container, and deposited the bag.

"Gus," Tommy said.

"You're on your own, Tommy."

The tears were wet on Tom's face.

"Gus," he said again.

"Might be a smart thing for you to go tell everything to Chris. Then everyone goes down, and nobody's got hold of your balls anymore."

"You too, Gus," Tom said. His voice was thick with crying. "You'd go down too."

Gus shrugged.

"So fucking what?"

Gus turned away and started back up Berkeley Street. "You're the Sheridan version of original sin, Tommy."

Behind him the pigeons, deprived of peanuts, flew up briefly and settled on undulating wings to forage near the trash barrel.

Tommy

This time as he came up the hidden path toward the secret house he felt as if he were swollen from the inside and the pressure would make him burst.

She wasn't at the door when he arrived and he let himself in. The house was a mess. Where was she? Christ, of all times for her not to be here. He felt the inner self pressing harder on him. It made the blood pound behind his eyes. He called to her. She didn't answer. He went to the bedroom and found her. She was naked, lying flat on the bed, smiling. Her small new breasts pointed straight up.

"She should have been waiting," he said.

"I thought I'd give Tommy a surprise," she said, and giggled. Waiting.

He stared at her nakedness. His throat felt closed, as if the air could barely force its way through the dwindling passage. She put her thumb in her mouth and turned it slowly, sucking it in imitation of something she had seen on television.

"Roll over onto your stomach," he said.

His voice rasped as if he were speaking through an imperfect mechanical device. In their time together she had learned to do what he told her. She lay perfectly still facedown on the bed, her arms by her sides. He often liked her to lie that way, so he could pretend to spank her. Sometimes the pretend was too hard, but she had learned to relax and accept it. He stood over her for a moment looking at her little girl's back, and then he took his father's old Walther P38 automatic pistol from a drawer in the bedside table, and thumbed back the hammer, and put the muzzle just behind her right ear without touching her and closed his eyes and pulled the trigger.

Gus

In the late summer the days were beginning to shorten, and Gus and Laura were staying later and later at their Tuesday meetings. The sun was already out of sight behind the huge Rowes Wharf Arch behind them, and the harbor had a slick, glassy look to it in the blue light of early evening. They were in the big glassed-in pagoda at water's edge that served as a waiting room for the Harbor Ferry service. No one else was in there, and the emptiness seemed to insulate them from the people up at the outdoor café, or the people seated by the window in the hotel dining room.

"Since that first time at the Ritz," Laura said, "how many meetings have we had to talk about our children?"

"Thirteen," Gus said.

"And how many of them have we devoted to talking about the children?"

"Total? Half of the first one, I think."

They were quiet, standing together looking out at the water in the empty vaulting space. The quiet seemed balmy to them.

"And the rest of the time we've talked about ourselves," Laura said.

"Yes."

"What do you want, Gus?"

"House on the river," Gus said. "Some dogs."

"What do you want from me?"

He turned and looked down at her. "I want whatever you will give me."

She put her hands into the pockets of the light raincoat she was wearing. She turned slowly, pivoting on one spike heel, and slowly surveyed the pagoda.

"This must be the most romantic spot in Boston," she said.

"Why I brought you," Gus said.

Laura completed her pivot and stood very close to Gus.

"Good," she said, and put her arms around him, and turned her face up toward him.

She heard him say, "Jesus," very softly, and then he put his arms around her and kissed her and she closed her eyes and held his kiss and kissed him back and they stayed that way, swaying only slightly, for a long time.

With her mouth still touching his, Laura said, "Do you remember the first time we had drinks at the Ritz and we joked about eloping and you said you could get a room?"

"Yes."

"Can you?"

"Would this place do?" Gus said, and nodded at the Boston Harbor Hotel that loomed above them.

"Yes."

"I already got a room," he said.

"How did you know?"

"I knew."

It was a short walk to the hotel and a short elevator ride to the room. On the way Gus felt trembling inside him. He looked at his hand. It was steady. But he felt volitionless, as if he might suddenly sink to the floor. He took the key out and opened the door.

"I need to fluff up a little," Laura said when they were in the room. "I hope you don't mind."

"I got no other plans," Gus said.

Laura went into the bathroom and closed the door. Gus undressed slowly. He hung his clothes in the closet. He put his gun on the closet shelf, and lay down on the bed with the pillows propped and his hands behind his head. Their room was high up in the hotel, and from the bed all Gus could see through the window was the nearly dark sky. He waited, shivering invisibly.

Laura came out of the bathroom with no clothes on and shut the door behind her. She stood self-consciously at the foot of the bed. Gus smiled at her.

"Oh, boy," he said.

"It's kind of an old body," she said, "to be showing all of it to someone."

"I like it," Gus said. It was difficult for him to speak.

Laura came to the bed and got on it with him and turned on her side and put her head on his chest.

"Grace told me when she went to New York with this man they went to a hotel room and did 'everything.' "

Gus rubbed his hand between her shoulder blades in a small circular motion.

"Um-hm."

"I didn't really know what she meant by everything," Laura said. "I had to ask." Her mouth was very close to Gus's face. "Do you know everything?"

"Probably," Gus said.

"I've never done everything," Laura said. "I've never done anything except, once in a great while, lie still in the dark with Tom on top of me until he was through."

They lay quietly together, their faces close, looking at each other. Gus put his arms around her. They kissed. His hands moved over her body. She arched a little to make herself more available.

"Everything," she murmured with her mouth against his.

"Sure," Gus said.

Gus

Gus was carrying coffee in a paper cup as he walked across the hot top parking lot along the Charles River on Soldiers Field Road, with a homicide detective named Rafferty. He held it carefully so as not to spill it, and when he got to the body he stopped and took a sip.

"We wanted you to see this one, Captain," Rafferty said. "MDC guy found her this morning, just like this."

Rafferty gestured with his chin toward the uniformed MDC policeman standing with two homicide detectives. It was still early, barely eight o'clock, and overcast. Gus sipped more coffee. Behind him the sound of commuter traffic was steady, and out on the river a woman in a racing shell had stopped rowing, and was drifting, with the oars flat on the water, staring at the police activity on the shore. The form on the ground was covered with a pink blanket.

"The blanket there when he found her?" Gus said.

"Yes, sir. We checked her out—make sure it's not a Malloy or an O'Brien—then put the blanket back like it was." Gus lifted the blanket from the body. It was a young girl. Her head was on a small pillow. Her face was covered with dried blood. She was wearing a nightgown decorated with Winnie the Pooh characters. The nightgown was up around her waist. Tucked in her left arm was a teddy bear.

"I think she was shot in the back of the head," Rafferty said. "And the bullet exited through her left cheek. She was probably shot someplace else and brought here. There's no blood on the pillow or the blanket. But what's funny is there's none on the pajamas. Means someone dressed her long enough afterwards so that she'd stopped bleeding."

Gus stared down at the girl.

"Another thing," Rafferty said. "There's, ah, abrasions on her ass, like somebody bit her."

Gus felt as if everything in him had snapped shut.

"How old you think she is, Captain? Twelve, thirteen?"

Gus nodded. Very slowly took in air until he could breathe in no more. Then he let it out as slowly as he had inhaled.

"Soon as you get the ME's report, you let me know."

"Sure thing, Captain."

Gus didn't drive back to headquarters. He drove instead to a bank in Milton, just off the expressway, went into the safe deposit room, and got a large manila envelope out of his drawer. He got back in the car and drove back up the expressway to Morrissey Boulevard, past B.C. High School to Day Boulevard and along Day to Carson Beach, where he parked. He sat in the parked car for a time with the envelope unopened in his lap, staring across the empty beach at the lead-toned ocean rolling slowly in. Far out the gray sky merged invisibly with the gray ocean so that there seemed no horizon.

Gus drummed lightly with the fingers of his right hand on the top curve of the steering wheel. The waves on the beach were lethargic. They didn't crest. There was no white showing; only the slow oily swell and decline as they trudged into shore and slid back out. The sky was low and getting darker. *Soon it's gonna rain, I can feel it. Soon it's gonna rain, I can tell. Soon it's gonna rain, and what are we gonna do?*

He bent open the little butterfly closer on the envelope and took out a somewhat faded eight-by-ten glossy photograph in glassine envelope. He took the picture from the glassine envelope and stared at it. It was a picture of a young girl with blood on her face and a teddy bear in her arm. She too had been bitten. He put the picture back in its glassine envelope and back in the big manila envelope, and took some documents out. He read the medical examiner's report, the investigating officer's report. He read the confession. He put everything back in the manila envelope and reclosed the metal fastener. He put the envelope on the car seat beside him as the first fat raindrop splatted onto the windshield, then another one the size of a quarter, and then nothing, and then more, until it was raining hard. Gus sat drumming lightly on the steering wheel, staring straight ahead, as the rain sprawling across the windshield fused the outside world, and diminished reality to the interior of the car.

Mary Alice

Parnell Flaherty and Mary Alice Burke lay naked in the early evening on the big couch in Flaherty's office at City Hall. The door was locked and the building was quiet around them.

"Me," Flaherty said, "Gus Sheridan. You got a buzz for married men, Mary Alice?"

"Except the one I was married to," Mary Alice said.

"You balling anybody else?"

"Me to know," Mary Alice said. "You to find out."

Flaherty eased off the couch and stood and began to dress. Mary Alice continued to lie naked on the couch, watching him.

"I may have to fire Chris Sheridan," Flaherty said.

Mary Alice shook her head.

"Make you look even worse," Mary Alice said. "Remember McGovern in '72, a thousand percent behind Tom Eagleton and then replaced him on the ticket?"

"The papers are kicking the shit out of me," Flaherty said. He was wearing red silk shorts. He put his white shirt on and began to button it. "We got to do something."

"What? Appoint somebody else? You know it won't make any difference. Gus says it requires patience."

"Gus isn't running for the Senate," Flaherty said. He put on his red tie with the tiny white dots, and stood in front of the dark window to knot it.

"Gus says nothing will happen until they catch somebody in the act, and turn him," Mary Alice said, "make him testify, and that will cause other people to turn and then it'll unravel."

Flaherty finished his tie and sat down on the edge of the couch next to Mary Alice. He picked up his socks and put one on and paused and rubbed her thigh.

"You still fucking Gus?" Flaherty said.

331

"Yes," Mary Alice said.

"So how come you decided to fuck me too?"

"You're irresistible?"

"I been irresistible for a long time."

Mary Alice shrugged and patted his hand on her thigh.

"Gus's attention is beginning to flag."

"So you decided to develop bench strength?" Flaherty said.

Mary Alice smiled. "I suppose you could say it that way."

Flaherty laughed out loud. He bent over and put on his other sock and stood and got into his trousers. He was still laughing as he shrugged his shoulders into his bright suspenders.

"I'm in fucking reserve," he said.

"In more ways than one," Mary Alice said. "No offense."

Still standing, Flaherty slid his feet into his shoes, and put one foot up on the coffee table to tie the laces.

"Hell, no," Flaherty said. "I admire a practical person." He shifted feet. "But why me?"

"You're irresistible?"

"You don't do things because you can't resist," Flaherty said as he straightened up.

"I like strong men," she said.

"Ahh."

Flaherty slipped into his suit jacket. It was dark blue, a good suit, all his clothes were good, and he was built to wear clothes well. He checked himself in the dark window. "They talk about star fuckers. You're a power fucker. You fuck a cop, it's the homicide commander. You fuck a politician, it's the mayor. Your father a power guy?"

Mary Alice shrugged. "I don't know my father," she said.

"But you're always looking," Flaherty said.

"Sure, Daddy."

Flaherty looked down at Mary Alice lying calm and naked on the couch.

"Well, you got the build for the work," Flaherty said, "I'll give you that."

He went to the bar and made himself a drink.

"You want a little white wine or something, Mary Alice?"

"White wine would be nice," Mary Alice said.

He poured her some and brought it to her.

"You probably ought to get dressed," he said.

"Wham bam, thank you, ma'am?" Mary Alice said.

"Hell, no. Didn't I give you wine? Aren't we having a drink together afterwards? It's just that this is the Goddamned mayor's office of the City of Boston, and there's no good reason for you to be lying around in it buck naked, if you follow my thinking."

"I thought maybe you could have the City Council in, give those boys a treat."

"Get dressed, Mary Alice," Flaherty said. There was no banter in his voice. Mary Alice swung her legs off the couch and sat up, and began to sort her clothes out of the tangle on the floor.

"I'd hate to think macho man can't get it up anymore," Flaherty said. "Or is Gus just stepping out on you?" He rested his hips on the edge of his desk and sipped his Scotch on the rocks and watched her dress.

"Gus has never had a problem with up," Mary Alice said.

"Another woman?"

Mary Alice shrugged.

"Well," Flaherty said. "My gain."

"This shouldn't mean more than it means," Mary Alice said.

"Long as it means we'll do it again," Flaherty said.

"It probably means that," Mary Alice said.

"I wouldn't want Gus to find this out," Flaherty said.

"I don't think he'd care. Gus doesn't care about much."

"Well, he's trouble. I think sometimes that Gus is crazy."

Mary Alice was silent. Flaherty looked at her, his arms folded, his drink in his right hand.

"You think he's crazy?" Flaherty said.

"I don't know," Mary Alice said. "Gus doesn't say much."

"Even to you?"

Mary Alice shrugged. She was fully dressed now, and had

begun to work on her face, holding her compact mirror carefully to catch the light.

"Hiring his kid was your idea," Flaherty said.

"Um-hmm."

"You're an interesting woman, Mary Alice."

"Thank you, Your Honor."

Gus

"Your son said you needed to consult," Dr. Kramer said. "I'm happy to do Chris a favor. But of course, as your son's friend, I could not be your therapist."

"I'm not looking for a therapist," Gus said.

"If you were, or if in the future you are, I would be happy to refer you."

"Sure," Gus said.

Kramer smiled and sat back in his chair. He didn't look like a shrink. He was a big man, nearly as big as Gus. He had sandy hair, and thick hands, and a sort of healthy outdoor look to him. Maybe that's what shrinks looked like.

"You probably know I'm a cop," Gus said.

Kramer nodded so slightly that Gus wasn't sure if he nodded at all.

"I'm looking for information on serial homicide."

Again the barely perceptible nod.

"Say, as a young man, a guy commits a murder, and then he doesn't do it anymore for years, might he do it again? The same way?"

Kramer had his elbows on the arms of his swivel chair, his hands clasped resting on his chest, his chin lowered. Gus felt the completeness of Kramer's attention.

"Couple of things," Kramer said. "First we have a hell of a lot better track record in explaining why people did what they did, than in predicting what they will do."

Gus nodded.

"Second, why ask me? Certainly you have forensic psychiatrists available to you."

Gus nodded again.

"Cops don't have a hell of a lot of luck predicting either,"

Gus said. "But I want to talk with you because Chris admires you."

Kramer said, "And?"

Gus smiled. "And I want this to be informal, unofficial, and private."

"Confidentiality is not limitless, Captain Sheridan. It would depend on what you told me," Kramer said.

"I'll keep it in mind," Gus said.

"Yes," Kramer said, and nodded for Gus to proceed.

"Mr. X has a thing for young girls," Gus said. "Mr. X isn't all that old himself, maybe eighteen, twenty. He's rich, good family, nice looking, seems to get along okay in the world. But he has a series of, ah, incidents with little girls, ten, twelve years old. Family breaks them up, hushes it up; but he keeps at it, and one day he kills one."

Kramer was motionless as he listened. He had no reaction to what he heard, that Gus could see, but Gus knew that he heard everything.

"Homicide guy on the case solves it, gets a confession. But for his own reasons, he deep-sixes the confession, and lets the kid go free. Mr. X stays straight, at least he doesn't kill anybody, for like forty years. And then one day, out of nowhere, he seems to have done it again."

"This past Monday," Kramer said.

"I don't know," Gus said. "That's what I'm trying to figure out. Murder looks just like the one he got away with forty years ago."

"In what ways?" Kramer said.

"About the same age, this kid the other day was thirteen. Shot in the same way. Bite marks on her buttocks. Teddy bear."

"Did he have sex with these children?"

"Apparently. This recent victim was not a virgin."

"And the previous victim?"

"He confessed to having sex with her."

"Was there some pressure from the detective who let him go, to stay on the straight and narrow, so to speak?" Kramer said.

"Yeah. He kept the confession, used it as a hold on the family."

Kramer nodded slowly. He leaned back farther, letting his chair tilt against the spring. He rested one foot against the bottom drawer of his desk.

"In his current life, were there any startling changes, any sudden and unusual pressures that preceded this killing?"

"Yeah."

"Can you describe them?"

"Things were closing in on him," Gus said.

"The past murder?"

"Not exactly," Gus said. "He probably felt as if he were in financial, or legal, or physical danger, or some combination of all three. He probably also feared public disgrace."

Kramer smiled a little.

"Then," he said, "I guess it would be fair to say that things were closing in on him."

Gus nodded.

"Was there any hope of safety?" Kramer said.

"Yeah."

"Were the mechanisms of safety in his control?"

"No."

They were both quiet while Kramer thought about what he'd heard.

"Ritualized behavior," he said, "which is what you have described, devolves from an attempt to control circumstances which would otherwise overwhelm you. When confronted with something fearful, for instance, and beyond control, a child will create a fantasy which grants him at least the illusion of control."

Kramer paused and looked at Gus. Gus knew he was wording this carefully so that the uninitiated cop could follow it.

Gus nodded.

"The fantasy becomes life sustaining, so that in instances when the fantasy is threatened by reality, it must be defended.

And when one is enacting a fantasy the danger is great, because reality will almost certainly clash with fantasy."

Kramer paused again to let Gus digest the information.

"Fear is the mother of ritual," Gus said.

Kramer made a faint nod that hinted of approval.

"Yes," he said.

"So if Mr. X is, say, fantasizing about little girls," Gus said, "and then finds himself actually having sex with little girls, the actuality may scare him."

"Most fantasies, enacted, are less rewarding than they were as fantasies," Kramer said.

"So X might have been having sex with a kid forty years ago and some aspect of it scared him. And then he either didn't have sex with kids again, or he did but nothing scared him."

"Possible," Kramer said. "Though you have to understand that he has never not been scared. That's why he has the fantasy. It's when the fantasy is threatened."

"Would there have been other kids?"

"I know too little," Kramer said. "The human condition is too various."

"I know that," Gus said. "Give me a guess."

Kramer shrugged. "The fear that drew him to little girls might have continued to draw him. He may have been violent only under special circumstances."

"Something the girls did?"

"Not necessarily. People who defend themselves with ritual resort to it when there is external pressure. It doesn't have to be something about the little girls."

Gus nodded again, slowly.

"Except that it happens to them, it may have nothing to do with the girls," Gus said.

"Yes. The pressure of his situation could have driven him to seek a little girl again and, when he did whatever made him kill the first one, may have made him kill this one. Do you know why he killed the first girl?"

"No."

Kramer looked quietly at Gus for a while.

"Your son holds you in high regard," he said. "And he is not a fool. But I cannot conspire with you to conceal several murders. In due course I will need to know that you've acted."

Gus nodded. He sat for another long moment, and then he stood and put his hand out.

"Thanks for your help."

Kramer stood and returned the handshake.

"May I ask you a question?" he said.

"Sure."

"I asked you if Mr. X had the means to control his safety and you said no."

Gus nodded.

"Do you know who controls those means?" Kramer said.

"Me," Gus said.

Gus

They were in one of the chintz-and-maple bedrooms at the Red Lion Inn in Stockbridge. Gus lay on the bed, his head propped on the pillows. In the bathroom the shower was running. Then it shut off. In another five minutes Laura came out of the bathroom naked except for a pair of high heeled shoes. She stood at the foot of the bed with her legs apart like a fashion model, her head cocked and her hands on her hips. She was wearing lipstick, he noticed, and her hair was carefully brushed.

"So what do you think?" she said.

Gus looked carefully at her, running his eyes the full length of her, and smiled and silently applauded. She turned slowly so he could see all sides. There was an adjustable mirror attached to the dresser, and she tilted it so that she could examine herself full length in it, as she turned.

"All that tennis may have paid off," she said. She completed her turn and faced Gus again.

"You don't mind me posing, do you?"

"I like it," Gus said.

"Tom and I . . ." She shook her head and shrugged.

"Tom didn't like to see you naked?" Gus said.

"No."

"That's sort of unusual, isn't it?"

"I don't know what's usual, Gus," Laura said. "I've only known Tom and now you. Are you usual?"

"I think so," Gus said. "What was Tom's objection?"

She shook her head quickly, as if she didn't like the conversation.

"I don't know, really," she said. She paused, and reddened slightly.

"What?" Gus said.

"We didn't come here to talk about Tom, did we?"

"Tell me what you were remembering."

"My wedding night," Laura said. "Tom and I were never intimate before we were married. A few kisses. And our wedding night was very awkward."

"He didn't know what to do?"

"Neither of us was too sure, but that wasn't it so much. When he saw me for the first time"—she glanced down at her naked self—"he was frightened. . . . He didn't . . . we didn't . . . consummate the marriage until weeks later . . . in the dark."

"How old were you?"

"Eighteen."

"How'd you meet him?"

"My mother," Laura said. "My mother and his mother were friends. They sort of put us together."

"His mother was Hadley Winslow?"

"Yes. She was very eager that he marry."

"I'll bet," Gus said. "You love him?"

Laura thought about it, and after a moment shook her head.

"No," she said. "He was an appropriate mate: Ivy League, Episcopalian, wealthy. I was a good girl. I did what I was bidden."

"And you didn't learn to love him?"

"No. Everyone told me I would. But I didn't. Does anyone?"

Gus shook his head.

"I guess he matters to me. But he's very remote. We've gotten used to each other. I've lived with him most of my life. We've had children. He was not unkind. He never withheld money. We had barely enough sex to conceive the children"—she smiled sadly—"under cover of darkness. And beyond that, we were partners at dinner parties and doubles matches. We had twin beds and separate dressing rooms, and Tom was out more than he was in . . . in all senses. I don't really know him very well. He loves Cabot, I think. He seemed very far away from Grace. . . . He's remote."

Gus was quiet.

"What are you thinking?" Laura said.

Gus remained quiet another moment, then he smiled at her. "Enough with the love talk," he said. "Into the bed."

Gus

The house was right where his father's report said it was, the forty-year-old typescript looking somehow antique in the age of word processors. They weren't even his father's words really, just the cumbersome locutions of policeman speak. Only the signature, C. B. Sheridan, with the big flourished *S*, made him think of the man who wrote it. Conn was a long time dead.

"A fine mess you left for me, Pa," Gus said aloud as he tried the gate and found it fastened with a chain.

He went back to his car and got out a bolt cutter and returned to the gate and cut the chain. He opened the gate, put the bolt cutter back in his trunk, got back in his car, and drove up the dirt driveway under the overhanging foliage, across the little bridge, and parked in front of the house.

The sun filtered through the thick green overlay of untrimmed shrubs. The damp smell of the slow brook mixed with the smell of weeds and late summer heat. A trumpet vine as thick as a python coiled up the front porch pillars and hung oppressively over the front door. The door was locked. Gus knocked. There was no response. Gus went back down to his car and got a flat prybar from the trunk. He went slowly back up the steps onto the front porch, inserted one end between the door and the jamb, level with the dead bolt, and jimmied the door open.

The living room was messy, with soft-drink cans and movie magazines and stuffed animals scattered about. On the living room floor, near a door in the left-hand wall, was a long-dark smear. He went and squatted on his heels and looked at it. He didn't touch it. Then he stood and walked through the door in the left wall. It was a bedroom. There was another dark smear on the floor. The bed was unmade and a wide dark brown stain

343

blotched the sheets and one of the pillows. The stain had leeched a little way into the other pillow. Gus picked up the badly stained pillow and looked at it carefully. Then he put it aside and looked at the mattress where the stain had soaked through. He felt around on the surface of the mattress and found a hole. He hoisted the mattress and felt underneath it. There was no exit hole. He dropped the mattress and took a Buck knife out of the small case on the back of his belt and cut into the mattress. When he had cut a big enough opening, he put his hand in, and felt around, and came out with a distorted lead fragment that no longer looked like a bullet, having been misshaped by its passage. He took a small plastic sandwich bag out of his pocket and dropped the slug into it and sealed the bag by pressing the blue line into the yellow line until it looked green.

Gus went slowly though the rest of the house, looking at the children's clothes: the baby doll pajamas, and little girl's underwear; romance magazines, and comic books, and stuffed animals. He went back into the bedroom and stared down at the stained bed.

"Tommy, you are a weird son of a bitch," he said aloud. "And I let you walk around loose."

Then he turned and went out of the little house and got back in his car. At the foot of the driveway, he closed the gate and readjusted the chain so that the cut link didn't show.

Then he drove back to Boston.

Mary Alice

The sun poured into the mayor's office through the windows that overlooked Quincy Market. Mary Alice sat quietly on the other side of his desk while Flaherty talked on the phone.

"Lose it," Flaherty said into the phone. "I don't give a fuck what you do, get this office and my campaign separated from the fucking thing."

He hung up the phone and turned toward her.

"Autopsy report says that young girl they found last week in Brighton—she'd had sexual intercourse. Probably with an adult. And probably had been having intercourse for some time."

Mary Alice winced.

"How old?"

"Coroner's guessing thirteen."

"God."

"Even the fucking pederasts are trying to screw up my election," Flaherty said.

"Everything happens to me," Mary Alice said.

"What?"

"Just the punch line to an old joke," Mary Alice said.

"Yeah, well, your fucking boyfriend has no leads, he says. He ain't solving shit. And neither is his fucking kid."

"Parnell, Chris's not even on the case. He's your special prosecutor for the gang killings."

"Yeah, and has he solved one?"

Mary Alice sighed and didn't answer.

"He was your idea, don't forget," Flaherty said.

"How could I forget? You keep reminding me."

Flaherty got up and took his stance in front of the window, looking down on Quincy Market with his hands clasped behind his back.

"You're a smart broad, Mary Alice. And you give excellent head . . ."

"Everybody tells me that," Mary Alice said.

". . . but sometimes I can't figure you out. Why did you get me involved with your boyfriend's son."

He turned slowly from the window, his hands still behind his back, and stared at her, his thought half completed.

"And having done that, and still, as far as I know fucking his father, why are you now fucking me?"

"Girl's got to look out for herself," Mary Alice said.

He gave her his riveting gaze, the one he used on his campaign posters.

"No bullshit, Mary Alice. I want to know."

"Because you want to know, Parnell," Mary Alice said, "it does not necessarily follow that I have to tell you."

Flaherty held his look for another moment and then laughed.

"Hey," he said, "Mary Alice, I'm the fucking mayor. You're supposed to do what I say."

"Professionally," Mary Alice said.

"I'm not sure you do anything, except professionally."

"Meaning?"

"Meaning you are a career oriented broad," Flaherty said. "And you consider the career implications of everything you do, dressed or undressed."

"I'm a single woman," Mary Alice said. "I've been a single woman a long time, long enough to know that nobody's going to gallop up on a white horse and rescue me."

"You were married."

"Yeah, to the back end of the horse."

Flaherty grinned.

"And you latched onto Gus," he said.

"Not right away. Gus does not have a happy marriage. I was divorced. We latched onto each other."

"He pays your rent," Flaherty said.

"How would you know that?"

"I like to keep up with things."

"He's gotten as much out of the deal as I have."

"You love him?"

Mary Alice shrugged.

"I like him, at least," she said.

"He straight?" Flaherty said.

Again Mary Alice shrugged.

"I don't know," she said. "He seems to have a lot of money for a policeman, but . . . he doesn't say much."

"That's for goddamned sure," Flaherty said.

"He loves his son," Mary Alice said.

"Most people love their children," Flaherty said.

"I know, but for Gus, the kid is like all there is. Like if he does well it's some sort of redemption for Gus."

"Lot of weight for the kid to carry," Flaherty said.

Mary Alice smiled.

"Why, Parnell, that's damned near sensitive."

"Sure. Why'd you hang me with him?"

"I didn't hang you with him. You decided to follow my suggestion."

"Whatever. What's your deal?"

"I thought he might actually help. I thought it might get Gus energized. I thought it might help Gus and Chris get free of each other."

"And?"

Mary Alice smiled again at Flaherty.

"We're more alike than one would think," she said.

Flaherty waited.

"And I just figured if things happened that other things might happen. Gus might make some changes."

"Like dumping the old lady?"

"You never know," Mary Alice said, "once things start happening, there's a momentum. . . ."

"But he hasn't," Flaherty said.

"Not yet."

"And you're still fucking him in case he might?"

"And because I like to," Mary Alice said.

"And you're fucking me because you know that the whole idea may go sour and you want an edge when I start handing out blame," Flaherty said.

"And because I like to," Mary Alice said.

Flaherty put his hands in his hip pockets and stared at her for a moment, then he turned and went back and gazed out his window at Quincy Market again. He laughed.

"You are a liberated broad, Mary Alice. I'll give you that."

Below him in the Marketplace the last summer tourists milled slowly about in the Market, eating at the food stalls, buying Boston T-shirts and dark blue plastic-mesh Red Sox hats. There were jugglers there and strolling musicians, and people who sold little plastic balls with a winter scene inside. There was fried dough, and oysters, and kielbasa, and pizza, sweet and sour pork with pineapples in it, and spinach pies, and beer and doughnuts, and lobster rolls and apple pie and cheap wine and baked beans and bagels. There were also surely pickpockets and mountebanks and men who liked to grope women in a crowd.

He loved all of it.

"I'm going to put Chris on the murder of that girl," Flaherty said to Mary Alice, with his back to her, still staring down at the Market. "Before I blame him for the crime wave, and fire him."

"That's the smart move," Mary Alice said.

Tommy

At six-fifteen in the morning the Greyhound Bus terminal, hunched among the taller buildings off Park Square, was nearly empty. Tommy, who was there wearing sunglasses, a light tan raincoat with the collar up, and a Snowy River slouch hat that he'd bought at Bean's, went to the Burger King in the terminal and bought a cup of black coffee. He sipped it as he stood near the entrance, glancing occasionally at his watch, as if he were waiting for a bus. He let his eyes drift around the terminal, as he had yesterday. As he would tomorrow . . . until he found her.

A fat, middle-aged black woman in a too-small flowered blouse and too-tight stone-washed jeans pushed a broom past him. She paid him no attention, moving past him silently on a pair of Reebok running shoes with a cutaway area on her right shoe giving ease to a sore toe. One ticket window was open, but there was no one behind it. The smell of the terminal always reminded him a little of the smell of the monkey house at the Forest Park Zoo in Springfield, where once he had gone with his aunt.

He went to a newspaper rack, put in a quarter, and bought a copy of the *Boston Herald*. He took the tabloid to a bench, and sat in the corner of it nearest the door. He put his coffee down on the bench beside him and began to leaf through the paper. The contents didn't register. It was merely something to do, while he waited. He felt the bottomless feeling in his stomach. His throat was tight. His face felt hot and there was a trembling feeling along the backs of his arms down to his hands.

A panhandler in a filthy maroon parka came by and asked for change. The fur trim on the parka hood was matted into a nearly colorless fringe. Tommy shook his head, and the panhandler muttered, "Have a nice day," and moved away.

A bus arrived from somewhere and three people got off and came through the terminal carrying their cheap luggage. None of them was She. He waited, turning the meaningless pages slowly, conscious of his breathing, of how shallow it was; hearing his breath go flatly in and out.

Through the door from the St. James Avenue side of the terminal came a young girl wearing black lipstick and a lot of eye shadow. She had on a shiny crimson baseball jacket, a short denim skirt, and cowboy boots. Her hair was tinted maroon. She appeared to be around eleven years old. She was carrying no luggage, not even a purse, and she looked around the terminal as if she were frightened.

Tommy felt as if his skin were stretched to its limit, as if it might give way, and his self would scatter.

He stood slowly, and walked toward the girl.

"Hi," he said.

She looked at him, her eyes small, and fearful, and appraising.

"Are you alone?" he said.

"Yeah," she said.

"Could I buy you some breakfast?"

The girl smiled. Familiar ground.

"Sure," she said. "Why not?

Gus

They gathered again on the day after Labor Day, with a gray rain falling on Quincy Market outside the mayor's window. Gus stood in back of the couch; his raincoat was unbuttoned, his hands in his hip pockets. Sullivan, the police commissioner, was there, and Robinson, the DA, wearing a polka-dot bow tie. Fiora Gardello, Robinson's chief prosecutor, stood by the window, looking at the rain. Chris sat on the couch beside Mary Alice.

Flaherty stood behind his desk with his coat off. He wore a white shirt with French cuffs, and red suspenders. His pinstriped suit jacket hung on the back of his chair. There were copies of the *Globe* and the *Herald* on his desk, as well as neatly typed transcripts of television news programs and radio talk shows. The *Globe* headline read, FEAR GRIPS HUB. The *Herald* said, MORE MURDER.

Without preamble, Flaherty picked up one of the transcripts and began to read:

" 'Death played a doubleheader yesterday in the Athens of America.' "

Kendall Robinson said, "Parnell, we've all heard this."

"Shut up," Flaherty said. " 'The slaying, gangland style, of thirty-eight-year-old Marty Kiley in City Square, and the apparently serial murder of an as yet unidentified girl whose body was discovered near Jamaica Pond . . . blah, blah, blah . . . the failure of the police, and of the mayor's Ivy League special prosecutor to stem the blood-dimmed tide underscores the unraveling of our civic fabric . . . blah blah.' "

Flaherty looked slowly around the room, still holding the transcript.

"That," he said, "is from a Channel Three editorial that ran yesterday at six and eleven. It's restrained. The *Herald* guy says the special prosecutor was imported from the Planet Cambridge and promised a lifetime supply of Brie. The Johnny Rollins show this morning invites callers to discuss the fact that three children have been shot this summer."

"Three white children," Gus said.

"Don't get starry eyed on me, Gus," Flaherty said. "The electorate doesn't give a fuck if the coons shoot each other." He looked around the room. "Anybody got anything more than what's in the media?"

"Girl's name is Trudy Boudreau," Gus said. "Eleven years old, a chronic runaway from Lewiston, Maine. She took a bus to Boston and apparently got out at the Greyhound station in Park Square. Lewiston cops say she ran away a lot because her old man probably molested her."

"Swell," Flaherty said. "How 'bout you, Chris, you got anything?"

"Nope."

"Anything on the other girl?"

"Probably killed by the same guy."

Flaherty slammed the flat of his hand down on his desk.

"Don't tell me 'probably,' Goddamnit. How about the gang war?"

Chris shrugged. Flaherty circled the room with his gaze. No one spoke.

"Okay," Flaherty said, "it's head-rolling time."

Chris looked at Gus, and ran his forefinger across his Adam's apple. Gus nodded.

"You got that right, Chris," Flaherty said. "Nothing personal, and I know it's not your fault. But it's got to be somebody's fault and you're not running for the Senate. I'm going to wait until next Monday, so it won't look like I'm knee-jerking to the media, and then I'm going to fire you."

Chris said, "It's not going to change anything. What are you going to do when the killing doesn't go away?"

"I got two months till the election," Flaherty said. "If we get some kind of break in the crime wave, good. If we don't it's time for smoke and mirrors." Flaherty looked at the police commissioner. "Can you get Gus off this case, Sully?"

"Be easiest," Sullivan said, looking straight ahead at Flaherty, "if Gus was to resign."

"How about it, Gus," Flaherty said. "Ready to step aside?"

"Fuck you," Gus said.

"I'll take that to mean no," Flaherty said. "Can you reassign him, Sully?"

"I guess I got the legal right, Parnell," Sullivan said.

"Then do it."

"Gus could kick up a lot of dust."

"Do it anyway," Flaherty said. "You want to get in a pissing contest with me, Gus?"

Gus didn't speak but their eyes locked and Flaherty felt a jolt of fear. It startled him. He knew people were afraid of Gus, but he wasn't, or he hadn't thought he was. He hadn't thought he was afraid of anyone. He raised his voice a little.

"If you do you'll regret it, because I got the machinery, the troops, you understand, to blow you and the kid right out of the water. If I have to I can make the public think you two are personally responsible for everything since Sacco-Vanzetti. You think I can't?"

"Don't get shrill," Gus said.

He put his hand on Chris's shoulder. Then turned and walked out of the room. Chris stood and looked at Flaherty for a moment, and then went out after his father.

Gus

When Mary Alice came into her condo, Gus was there looking out Mary Alice's window at East Cambridge across the river. A Nike gym bag stood, zipped and uncompromising, on the hassock in front of the leather chair in the living room.

Mary Alice looked at the gym bag and at Gus.

"Clean out your part of the closet?" she said.

"Yeah."

"Were you planning to leave a note, or just let me figure it out when I came home and found your clothes gone?"

"I waited for you," Gus said.

"What a guy!"

Gus turned from the window.

"We don't love each other, Mary Alice."

"You're so sure?"

"We like to fuck, and we're friends. But . . ." Gus shrugged.

"Say it's true. This is a news flash? You just discovered it?"

"No."

"Then why now?" Mary Alice said. "Why today did you decide you had to move out because we don't love each other?"

"You ever been in love?" Gus said.

"Who knows, Gus? Who the fuck knows?"

"You got a right to it, you know."

Mary Alice stared at him.

"I got a right to it," Gus said. "You and me, maybe we gave up on it too easy."

"Or maybe you did," Mary Alice said.

Gus shook his head.

"No, you're not it, Mary Alice. You're a nice woman, but . . . you're not the one."

They stood across the room from each other in silence. Mary

Alice was standing very straight. She walked slowly to the dining alcove and put her purse on the table. Then she went to the kitchen and got out some single malt Scotch and poured a shot into a short, thick glass. She carried the glass back into the living room and leaned on the wall by the front door and folded her arms and took a small sip of the Scotch.

"So," she said. "Who's the one?"

Gus shook his head.

"Sure as hell isn't Peggy," Mary Alice said.

Gus shook his head again.

"Got anything to do with Flaherty firing Chris?"

Gus shrugged.

"I can't prevent it," Mary Alice said.

"I know," Gus said. "I'm not blaming you. It's just . . ."

Mary Alice sipped some more Scotch.

"It's just what?" she said.

"I need a drink," Gus said.

Mary Alice jerked her head toward the kitchen.

"You know where," she said.

He went and mixed a strong Scotch and soda with a lot of ice in a tall glass. Even under duress he'd never liked it straight. He brought the drink back to the living room. Mary Alice hadn't moved. He went back to the window and stared out at East Cambridge again.

"It's just what?" Mary Alice said.

"It's over," Gus said.

"You and me?"

"Everything," Gus said.

Mary Alice waited. He might talk or he might not. But she knew pressing him was useless.

The days had shortened. To Gus's left, upriver, the sun was setting out of sight beyond his field of vision. Its low-slanted peach-colored light showed faintly on the river before he lost sight of it as it flowed under the Longfellow Bridge. There were a few white sailboats scattered on the wide, dark water where it backed up behind the dam.

"My life's caught up with me," Gus said. He made a sound which could have been a laugh. "And my old man's life before that. Time to put it away."

Mary Alice waited some more, but Gus didn't say anything else. Finally Mary Alice spoke.

"Is there somebody else, Gus?"

"Maybe," he said. "But there won't be next week."

"Gus," Mary Alice said, "what are you talking about?"

Gus finished his drink in a long swallow and went to the kitchen and rinsed the glass and put it back in the cabinet over the sink. Then he came back in the living room, picked up the gym bag, and walked to the door.

"Good-bye, Mary Alice," he said.

She stared at him for a moment and then turned her head away. He opened the door.

"I hope it works for you, Mary Alice. You're a nice woman."

Mary Alice didn't speak or turn her head back. Gus went out and closed the door. Mary Alice stood silently with her arms crossed beside the door staring at nothing. Then she walked slowly into the kitchen and poured another shot of Scotch. She raised her full glass as if to give a toast.

"Well, Parnell," she said aloud, "it looks like you and me."

Then she drank some of the Scotch and walked slowly back to the living room, hugging herself.

Gus

They were heading west on the Mass Pike in Newton.

"Where are we going, Gus?" Tom Winslow said.

Gus didn't answer. It was the start of the evening rush hour and the pike was thick with traffic heading for the western suburbs.

"I mean, Jesus, Gus. You got no right to just come along and tell me to get in the car. I've got banks to run. Laura and I have guests at home this evening. Sometimes you get carried away, you know, with being a policeman."

Gus took the Route 30 exit.

"Why are we going here?" Tom said. "What on earth reason would you have to take me out here?"

Gus drove through Weston's minimal downtown and turned right. They drove in silence for several minutes. Gus stopped the car in front of the inconspicuous gate in the tall bushes and took his car keys and got out. He opened the gate and got back in the car and drove in the narrow driveway and over the little bridge and parked in front of the cottage.

"What is this place?" Tom said. "Why are we here?"

Gus again took his keys and got out. He jerked his head at Tom.

"Gus, I don't like this," Tom said. "I don't want to go in here."

Gus waited and after a moment, Tom got out and stood beside him.

"Why do we have to go here?" he said. "What's here? I don't want to be here."

Gus took hold of Tom's arm, just above the elbow, and steered him to the front door. Holding Tom's arm with his left hand, Gus opened the door with his right and they went in. It had been cleaned up since Gus was last there. Everything was neatly put away. They went silently to the bedroom. The bed was made. The sheets were clean.

Gus let go of Tom's arm and stood against the wall with his arms folded. Tom looked around, and then looked at Gus.

"What is this place, Gus? What the hell is going on?"

There were no lights on in the cottage, and the fall afternoon had darkened, so that the room was dim, full of the coldness and the silence of a place unlived in.

Gus walked to the bedside table and opened the drawer. In the drawer was the old Walther P38. Gus picked it up, and ejected the clip. The clip was full. He put the clip back in, jacked a round into the chamber, and put the gun back and closed the drawer.

"Gus."

"Everything's over, Tommy," Gus said.

"Gus."

"I'm going to arrest you. I know you killed those two girls."

Faintly, from out front, came the sound of the small brook.

"You killed at least one of them here, probably both of them."

Tom's mouth was open as if he would speak. But no speech came.

"You been a fucking pervert all your life, and I helped you sit on it," Gus said. "And for forty years, as far as I know, you didn't kill anybody."

"I didn't, Gus. Honest to God I didn't."

"Just banged a few little girls," Gus said. "And sent them on their way when they got older. Until this year when it all fell in on you. And you couldn't sit on it anymore and you had to do it again."

"Gus, I couldn't help it," Tom said. "I couldn't help it the first time, I couldn't help it now. You understand that, Gus. You know. I been good all this time. But everything . . ." He gestured wordlessly.

"I know, Tommy, and it's my fault too. But we're going to clean it up."

"Gus, you can't tell. If you tell they'll get you too. You'll go to jail too. I can give you tons of money, Gus."

"You've given me tons of money," Gus said. "That's what this has been about."

"I've got more. I'll give it to you. And I'll never do it again, Gus. I promise I'll never touch another girl."

"This is going to be lousy for your wife and kids," Gus said. "I want you to think about it a little. I'll be outside. You can come with me, or"—Gus nodded at the drawer where the Walther was—"you can try to shoot your way past me. . . . Or whatever. You don't have many choices. Take some time. Think about them."

"Gus," Tom Winslow said. His voice was strangled, barely louder than the faint hush of the brook. Gus went out of the bedroom and closed the door behind him. He walked across the living room and stood by the fireplace, facing the bedroom door. He took out his service pistol and cocked it, and waited.

Tommy

Again, Tommy thought.

Dimly Tommy could hear the sound of the brook out front. Where Gus was. All this time from Conn to Gus. All this time and Tommy was back trapped in a little room by a cop named Sheridan. All this time. *And Mommy can't help Tommy now.* It made Tommy feel hot to think that Mommy knew. She never talked about it, but she had to know. The other cop had told on Tommy. Tommy could kill him for that, the mean bastard. Tommy could kill Gus too, why couldn't they leave poor Tommy alone? All this time, all the money, the deals with gangsters, all the time scared. Sick with being scared. Now Cabot would know, and Grace and Laura. Unless Tommy killed Gus. *He's right out there.* Tommy could walk through that door and kill the spoil-everything-sonova-bitchen-bastard. And no one would know anything. No one knew they were there. Tommy looked at the door. He cocked the gun. Then Tommy's legs got suddenly weak, too weak, too weak even to hold him up, and Tommy sat suddenly on the bed. The gun that had belonged to his father was heavy. Too heavy. Tommy had to hold it in both hands. Gus was too big. He had no kindness. Tommy thought of him standing outside the door like a rock. A bad hard fearful rock . . . Tommy can't kill Gus. . . . I wish my mother were here. . . . He put the muzzle of the gun in his mouth and bit down hard on the barrel and pulled the trigger.

Gus

There were four of them in Gus's car, plus six uniforms in squad cars, with body armor and shotguns. They parked in the little turnaround in front of the liquor store with the blue lights turning on the squad cars. Gus got out with Chris and John Cassidy. Billy Callahan waited behind the wheel. Cassidy leaned on the car.

"It might make sense," Cassidy said, "if we knew what we were busting these people for."

"Chris and I know why," Gus said.

Cassidy nodded.

"Maybe, when I'm older," he said.

"I'll go in with Chris," Gus said. "If we don't bring him out in five minutes, John, you and Billy know how it works."

Billy Callahan said, "You should wear a vest, Captain."

Gus shook his head.

"Chris?" he said.

"Like father like son," Chris said.

Gus started to say something and stopped. He tucked his badge in its leather holder into his breast pocket, so it showed, and started for the liquor store. Chris walked beside him. Butchie was out front when they came in. The pale clerk was expressionless behind the counter.

"This is my son Chris," Gus said.

Butchie nodded at Chris and then looked back at Gus.

"Two carloads, Gus?"

"I know we don't need them," Gus said. "But we're going to collar Patrick too."

"What for?" Butchie said.

"Same as you."

"What for?"

"Money laundering."

Butchie stared at Gus.

"You have the right to remain silent," Gus recited.

"I know my rights," Butchie said.

Gus ignored him and recited the rest of it rote. Butchie waited.

When Gus finished, Butchie said, "I think maybe you have gone over the fucking edge, Gus."

"We come in here straight up," Gus said. "No body armor, no guns showing. We walk out together, ride downtown pleasant."

"Gus, this is dangerous."

"We need to be going, Butchie," Gus said.

Butchie looked straight at Chris for a moment. "You know how dangerous this is?"

"I guess I'll find out," Chris said. He felt surprisingly steady. Part of it, he knew, was being with his father. But part of it . . . Have to think about that.

"We need to be going," Gus said.

"Gus, you're jumping off a fucking bridge here," Butchie said. "You don't think I'm going alone?"

"Don't matter none to me," Gus said.

Butchie looked first at Gus then at Chris, then back at Gus. Then he shrugged.

"Gus, we know each other a long time."

Gus nodded.

"I tell you something you can take it to the bank."

Gus nodded again.

"I don't like riding downtown in no squad car. Don't look good in the neighborhood."

"True," Gus said.

"I'll come in with Barry, today, before five."

"Sure," Gus said.

He turned and left the store. Chris paused for a moment. He looked at Butchie.

"You'll be there," he said. "Won't you?"

"Honor," Butchie said, "among thieves."

Gus

Gus took off his jacket outside the three-story frame house. He slid into the fiberglass vest and tightened the strap. Everyone was out of the cars. Three of the uniforms carried shotguns. Two of the uniforms went around to the back of the house.

"Chris, wait in the car," Gus said. "This one won't go smooth."

"No," Chris said. "I'm the special investigator. In theory I'm in charge."

Gus started to speak, stopped, looked at his son.

"That's right," he said. "Billy, get him a vest."

Billy Callahan got a vest from the trunk and helped Chris put it on.

"You know what to do," Gus said.

Billy nodded.

Two uniforms took up positions in front, and two, one with a shotgun, followed Gus and Chris and the two detectives up onto the front porch of the house. They spread out on either side of the front door. Callahan stood between Chris and the door. He and Cassidy both had their guns out, at their sides. Gus rang the bell. No sound. He rang it again. Some women walking baby carriages on the narrow street stopped. One of the uniforms spoke to them and they moved down the street and lingered near the corner watching. Nearby someone was cooking onions. Gus tried the knob. It didn't turn. He turned and nodded to Billy Callahan. Billy stepped forward and drove his foot against the door near the knob. The wooden jamb gave way, and the door burst inward. Gus and John Cassidy went in. Billy came behind them in the cabbage-smelling hallway, still in front of Chris, and the three of them headed toward the back door, open at the far end. They paused at the back door. There was movement in the yard, and someone shouted. Gus and Cassidy went through the door and down the back stairs with the two uniforms. The uniforms fanned out to either side of Gus; the one with the shotgun had it at his shoulder. The yard was shallow, mostly dirt with some unsuccessful grass scattered in occasional patches. Two weedy sumacs shadowed most of the yard, and some unhealthy-looking shrubs marked the boundaries. The two uniforms who had been guarding the rear stood one on either side of the back stairs to the next three-decker, weapons aimed.

Pat Malloy stood near one of the sumacs. He was red faced and breathing hard. There was sweat on his forehead. He held a big pistol in his hand, by his side, pointed at the ground. Chris thought it looked like the Colt .45's that the army used to issue. Pat's brother, Kevin, was beside him, with no weapon showing, and a third man whom Gus didn't know.

"I ain't going in, Gus," Pat said. His voice was raspy.

"You got to, Patrick," Gus said.

"No."

"Don't be an asshole," Gus said. "Look around."

"Fuck you," Patrick said, and brought the gun up. Chris was trying to see, blocked as he was by Billy Callahan's bulk. He knew that wasn't accidental. It was what Gus had meant by *You know what to do.* Everyone fired, the sound of the police-issue 9-mm's sharper than the heavy boom of two shotguns. Kevin Malloy, and the man Gus didn't know, fell flat, facedown. Pat Malloy was turned half around by the gunfire, the front of his shirt was suddenly rich with blood, and he fell all at once, landing on his left side with his legs twisted under him and the big .45 still in his hand.

The silence after the gunfire was ringing. Gus thought for a moment how it was always like that, as if all life had been suspended and there was only silence and the smell of the gunfire. He looked at Chris. He seemed steady. Facedown on the ground Kevin Malloy kept repeating, "No trouble, no trouble." He and the other man had their hands clasped behind their heads.

"Heard about Butchie," Cassidy said with no emotion in his voice.

"Yeah," Gus said.

He looked at Kevin and the other man.

"I got no interest in you, beat it."

Kevin stayed flat on the ground.

"You ain't going to shoot us and say we were trying to escape?"

"No. We need you we'll come get you."

Both men got up carefully, and moved very slowly toward the back stairs. They went up the stairs and into the hallway.

"Wrap this up," Gus said to Chris. "I'm going."

Chris nodded.

"Captain," Cassidy said, "you can't—"

"Chris will handle it," Gus said.

"For Crissake, Captain, I don't even know why we came to get him."

"Go ahead," Chris said to his father.

They looked at each other for a moment, and Gus smiled suddenly.

Then he walked through the house and out the front door to his car.

Behind him he heard Cassidy saying, "What do I tell the shooting team?"

"I'll take care of it," Chris said.

Gus

Each with a drink, Gus sat across the kitchen table from Peggy. The table was white enamel, with folding leaves at either end. When he used to come home for supper, he had sat on this side and she had sat on that side, and Chris had sat at the end, with one of the leaves folded out to make room for him. Peggy had always cooked simple things adequately—with the emphasis on hamburgers, and Kraft dinner, frozen peas, and meat loaf. She was proud of her meat loaf, which she made with packaged stuffing mix.

It hadn't been so bad once. The child was there, and it gave their lives a center, and their purpose a commonality. When he was with them they talked with him. When they were alone, they talked about him. Even at night, lying in their twin beds, they would talk sometimes about Chris.

Then he grew up and went away, and there was nothing to talk about, and the distance between their beds became unbridgeable.

And now it was about to end.

"So how was work?" Peggy said. It was her first drink and she wasn't slurring her words yet.

Gus gave a small laugh.

"Kind of a big day," Gus said.

Peggy's face was tight. She was scared. She had been scared since Gus said, "Let's have a drink."

"Will you get a raise or a promotion or anything?" Peggy said.

Again Gus did that laugh.

"No," he said. "I don't think so."

"Too bad," Peggy said. "I saw a nice dining room set I was thinking about getting. I was shopping with Rose Mary and, you know I'm a shopper. I know where the bargains are. And we went into the discount place on Morrissey Boulevard, I know quality, you know that. Well, there was a solid mahogany table, four chairs, and a sideboard. . . ."

Gus leaned back and closed his eyes.

He said, "I'm in bad trouble, Peggy."

She felt the scaredness sharpen and thrill along her nervous system.

"What have you done?"

He took a long pull on his drink, and swallowed and took in a long breath and let it out and told her. While he told her she sat staring at him with an uneasy, half-embarrassed expression. He spoke slowly. He knew she had trouble tracking ideas, and when she was scared, which he knew to be often, she was unable to grasp even the most ordinary of remarks. It was a catatonic terror that hid behind her half-embarrassed, slightly quizzical expression.

When he finished, she was silent for a moment and then she said, "What?"

"I been on the take," Gus said. "I covered up three murders. I'm going to turn state's evidence."

Peggy's face got paler than it had been and the lines around her mouth and nose became deeper.

"What's going to happen to me?" she said.

"You're going to be all right," Gus said. He took out a bank book and handed it to her. "There's money. It's in your name," he said. "Chris'll help you manage it."

She took the bank book and stared at it, without any sign that she knew what it was.

"What did you say Chris would do?"

"He'll help you manage your money," he said.

She poured herself some more bourbon.

"I don't know anything about money," she said.

"I know."

"You think I'm stupid, don't you? Well, let me tell you right now, that if you would have listened to me you wouldn't be in trouble. When Ellie Gavin's husband retired they had a nice home in Scituate, only two blocks from the water."

Gus smiled. Some things change, some things don't.

"I'm not retiring, Peggy. I'm going to jail."

"And what am I supposed to tell people?" Peggy said. Her face wasn't pale anymore. It was flushed with anger, and bourbon. "That my husband's a crook?"

"That's about right," Gus said.

"Well, all I can say to you, Mr. Big Shot, is that I am dreadfully disappointed."

"Yeah," Gus said. "Me too."

"And not just in you. Chris can't even hold on to a girlfriend and now he's going out with God knows who, and you mark my words, they'll take him for all they can get."

"I don't think he's giving them money, Peg. I think they're fucking him free."

"And don't you bring that policeman gutter talk into my kitchen."

Gus stood.

"We've known each other forty years, Peg. And it's been a long time since we liked each other."

"What are you talking about? We're married."

"I'm leaving," Gus said. "You keep the house. You got enough money if you don't let somebody take you for all they can get."

"What do you mean you're leaving? Leaving to where?"

"I'm leaving you, Peg."

"You're leaving me? You mean for good?"

"Yeah."

"You mean you're going to divorce me?"

"Yeah."

Peggy drank more bourbon.

"You let some whore get her claws into you. You think I didn't know, all those nights you were out, you pig. You think I didn't know you were with some prostitute?"

Peggy had had enough bourbon to have trouble with the word *prostitute*.

"Doesn't matter, Peggy," Gus said.

He turned and walked from the kitchen.

"You think you can get away with this," Peggy shouted, "you've got another think coming. I'll take you for everything you've got."

Gus opened the front door and started out.

"You already have," Gus said.

Gus

Gus was sitting on the steps of Chris's half-house condo in Cambridge, when Chris came home.

"Jesus, Dad. You look like a homeless waif sitting there," Chris said.

"I was thinking about dogs," Gus said. "What kind of dogs you'd have if you owned property on the Concord River, and you had it fenced, and they could run around."

"You been talking about that as long as I can remember," Chris said as he unlocked the door to his side of the house. "You want a drink?"

"Yeah."

Gus followed Chris into the kitchen and sat at the kitchen table, which had natural-stained pine legs, and a green top painted to look like marble. The house was all Crate and Barrel, Grace had told him once, when she used to live here too. Gus had never been in Crate and Barrel. Chris made Gus a Scotch and soda and got a bottle of Saratoga beer from the refrigerator. *Chris drank every new local beer that appeared. Fresh is best. Would you go to Germany for bread?* He put Gus's drink in front of him and sat across from his father at the table. His black knit tie was open. His white button-down shirt was loosened at the collar. His gray tweed jacket fitted him easily. Gus always envied that. His own cloths never fit. Always his jackets were tight at the arms, and pulled across the chest. Chris's face was clean shaven. His features were regular, his big eyes were full of intelligence. Sometimes Gus saw Peggy in Chris's face, sometimes himself, but mostly, almost furtively, the look of Gus's father. Gus reached across the table and patted his son's forearm. Chris smiled. Gus stood and made himself another drink and took in a third of it at a single swallow.

"We going to get drunk?" Chris said.

"We might," Gus said. "We're Irish."

"We got a genetic right," Chris said. He drank some beer.

"You ever have a dog?" Chris said.

Gus shook his head.

"My mother wouldn't have an animal in the house. Said it was filthy and uncivilized. Your mother felt the same way."

"I was thinking I might get one," Chris said. He grinned. "Being a single guy, soon to be unemployed, I can do whatever the hell I want."

Gus nodded and swallowed most of his drink.

He made another one and leaned his hips against the counter, and sampled it. Chris's beer bottle was half empty. Gus reached in the refrigerator and got another one and opened it and set it down beside Chris.

"Getting fired bother you?" Gus said.

Chris shrugged.

"Yeah. I mean I'd like to say no, fuck 'em. But, yeah, it bothers me. It was my chance to do something. It bothers me that I failed."

"You didn't fail. You got sold out."

"By who?"

Gus took another drink.

"Butchie and Patrick had a cop in their pocket. They knew everything before it happened."

Chris had his bottle half raised to drink from it. He held it there without drinking and looked past it at his father.

"Cassidy?"

"Me," his father said.

Chris held the bottle rigid for a moment, then slowly put it down, centering it carefully in the wet ring it had left on the tabletop.

"Oh, shit," he said.

He leaned back in his chair, his head lowered a little so that his chin rested on his chest. He didn't say anything else. But Gus could see that his breath was deep, just the way he used to breathe when he was six, in first grade, watching *Captain Kangaroo* on television before the school bus came. Then he straightened and took a drink from the beer bottle.

"Well," Chris said, "you'll tell me about it. Before you do you need to keep one thing in mind. You're my father. I love you. And whatever you tell me, when you're through I'll still love you."

Gus's throat was nearly closed. He took a long pull on his drink to relax it. His breath was short and rapid. He could feel the layered containment of a lifetime begin to crack. He felt as if he would cry. He drank again. It was going to break. What would be left, he wondered, after it was over?

"When my father was a young man in Ireland," Gus said, "he was in the war with England." His voice sounded remote to him, as if someone else were speaking. "During that time he had an affair with a woman named Hadley Winslow."

"Grace's grandmother?" Chris said.

"Yeah. She was a married woman, and when he wanted her to leave her husband she refused, and later, betrayed him to the British."

Chris smiled at his father's old-fashioned locution. Gus saw the smile.

"I don't know how else to say it," Gus said.

Chris nodded. His father's voice was devoid of inflection.

"She returned to Boston with her husband, and my old man dodged the British and came here too. He claimed he was just running from the Brits, and I believe him. But I always figured he ran to Boston, because she was here. He got on the cops, and did okay and married my mother and had nothing to do with Hadley Winslow until one day her son, Tom, got in trouble with the law."

"Grace's father?"

"Yeah."

Gus finished his drink and made another one. He walked down the narrow length of the rehabbed kitchen and looked out the back window at the narrow half yard surrounded by a high board fence.

"Not much room for dogs," he said.

"No," Chris said.

Gus turned and leaned against the wall beside the back window. The kitchen had exposed beams. There were dried herbs hanging from them, and copper pans that showed no sign of use.

"My old man fixed it, so that nobody knew—about the kid."

"What was the crime?" Chris said.

Gus shook his head.

"I gotta tell it in order," he said.

Chris nodded. The automatic ice maker in the refrigerator cycled on and rattled some ice crescents into the storage container. Gus glanced toward the sound and then looked back at his son.

"The kid, Tommy, went on to grow up and marry and have kids and be a big deal in the family bank. But my old man kept the evidence in a safe deposit vault in a bank on the South Shore, and he blackmailed Hadley for the rest of their lives. When he died he left me the story and the safe deposit key."

Outside the kitchen, the late afternoon had darkened. Chris got up and turned on the overhead light. It thickened the outside darkness, and the room seemed smaller around them. Chris sat down again. He finished his second bottle of beer. Gus swirled the ice around in his glass.

"And?" Chris said.

"And I been using it to blackmail Tommy," Gus said.

Chris pushed his beer bottle away from him and folded his arms on the table and leaned forward as if to rest his chin on his folded forearms. Then he paused and sat back up straight and looked as if he didn't know what to do with his hands. Finally he folded them and rested them on the edge of the table. He took in a long, slow breath and let it out.

"So what's this got to do with the Malloys and the O'Briens?" Chris said.

"I been taking money from both of them since I worked out

of the old City Square station, thirty years ago. Not so much, pocket money, routine street graft. And as I got promoted where I could do them more good I'd get like a raise." Gus smiled. "Get a raise from the cops and a raise from the robbers.

"Mostly they were doing loan sharking, numbers, truck hijackings," Gus said. "They hustled a little pot, some heroin, but mostly they stuck to strong-arm stuff, until around 1983–84 when crack came along. Coke was upscale, but crack was for everybody. Butchie and Patrick saw the mass-market potential a long time before the Guineas did. Between them, they got control of all of it, north of Columbus Avenue and east of Mass Ave."

"White Boston," Chris said.

"More or less. And the Jamaicans got the ghetto."

"I'm surprised the Italians would give it up."

"They didn't have much choice," Gus said. "When they don't fight with each other, Patrick and Butchie are pretty much of a load. And Butchie knows how to deal. Patrick was always a loose cannon. But Butchie . . . Butchie says to the Guineas, 'We'll do it whether you like or not, because you can't stop us. But as a sign of respect, we'll pay you a royalty of such and such.' And the Guineas say, 'Butchie knows how to treat a man,' and they take the royalty and everybody's happy."

"So where do you come in? And Tom?"

Gus took a drink. If it affected him he didn't show it.

"So now Butchie and Patrick got all this cash they got to do something with. I mean it's coming in a million, million and a half a week. Five, six million a month. Cash. They gotta launder it. They try smurfing it for a while, but there's too much. They need a bank and they consult me, because I'm an upstanding motherfucker and probably know a lot of bankers."

Gus drank.

"And you did," Chris said.

"Tommy Winslow."

"And, even better," Chris said, "you had something on him."

"Bingo," Gus said.

Chris blew his breath out.

"Jesus, Dad. Drug money."

"Yeah," Gus said. "Anyway, I talked with Tommy, and he was scared as shit of getting into bed with a couple of bone breakers, but"—Gus shrugged—"he arranged for both Butchie and Patrick to buy numbered CDs at the bank, and the bank would then lend them the amount of the CDs back. That way anybody looking at the bank records could see that the loan was collateralized by CDs. And Butchie and Patrick would buy apartment houses, and Laundromats, and self-storage lockers, which would generate clean money. And anyone looking at Butchie's finances, or Pat's, could see that the money came from a legitimate loan. And, because it was a loan, they didn't have to pay taxes on it."

"And only Tommy knew the identities of the people with the numbered CDs," Chris said.

Gus nodded.

"And, let me guess," Chris said. "The bank filed CTRs, and kept a copy on file. But they didn't send the original to the IRS."

"Probably," Gus said. "Or they exempted Butchie and Pat. I don't know. I never cared much about the details, long as it worked out. And it worked out dandy until some asshole scragged Corky O'Brien for looking at his girlfriend, and everything unraveled."

"What did you get out of it?"

"Besides the pleasure of doing good? I got two points on everything they laundered."

Chris thought about it for a moment and then whistled soundlessly.

"That's high," he said.

Gus nodded.

"They didn't have to give any to Tommy," he said.

Gus got up and poured himself another shot and got another bottle of beer.

"So what was Tommy's crime?"

"Forty years ago my father covered up the fact that Tom

Winslow molested a thirteen-year-old girl. He bit her on the ass and raped her. Then he shot her and dumped her in the basement of a church in Charlestown with a teddy bear in her arms."

Chris stared at his father. They were both quiet while Chris thought about what Gus had said.

Then Chris said softly, "Jesus Christ!"

Neither of them spoke for a time. Chris got up and mixed Gus another drink, and opened himself another beer.

"So why are you telling me all this stuff now?" Chris said.

"Because I'm turning myself in to you, Special Prosecutor. I'm blowing the fucking whistle on the whole fucking deal."

"You could have done that anytime," Chris said.

Gus shrugged.

"You're doing it now because Flaherty's going to fire me."

"Well," Gus said, "Patrick's dead. Butchie goes up for money laundering. The gang wars are over. The special prosecutor did a hell of a job. Flaherty can't fire you."

"I can't let you go to jail," Chris said.

Gus grinned briefly. "I can cop a plea with the special prosecutor."

Chris shook his head.

"Walk away from it," Chris said. "You must have money. Get the fuck out of here. Go to Seattle. I'll do something about Tom Winslow. I can't let you just blow yourself up for me."

He was pacing slowly back and forth in his narrow kitchen, his jacket off, his hands in his back pockets. Gus nodded. Chris paused at the counter and gestured at the bottle of Scotch. Gus shook his head.

Chris said, "Me either," and went back to pacing.

"What about Ma?" he said.

"She sees this as something I've done to her. I knew she would."

"You've talked to her."

Gus nodded.

"She can't"—Chris tossed his hands—"she can't deal with this."

"I've left her," Gus said.

Chris paused in his pacing again. He looked at his own reflection in the dark window over the sink. He shook his head.

"Well, I gotta give you credit," Chris said. "You decide to revise things, you go full fucking bore."

"There's another woman," Gus said.

"Your friend," Chris said.

"No . . . Laura Winslow."

Chris turned slowly from the window. He took his hands from his back pockets and folded them across his chest as he gazed at his father.

"Laura Winslow," he said.

"Un-huh."

"Grace's mother."

"Yeah."

"The wife of the serial killer."

"Yeah."

Chris stared at him and then began slowly to smile. The smile got wider and became a soft laugh and grew. Chris laughed harder. He bent over with laughter. Tears rolled down his cheeks. He was having trouble catching his breath. Gus heard the edge of hysteria in it. He sat and waited. Slowly Chris got control. He wiped his eyes and then turned to the sink and splashed cold water on his face. He dried his hands and face on a paper towel and threw the towel in the wastebasket under the sink.

"Sorry," he said.

He shook his head.

"This family . . ." he said.

"Yeah," Gus said. "And that family. Three generations now."

"And what happens between you and Laura?" Chris said.

"Nothing good," Gus said.

"Be hard on Grace too," Chris said.

"Should pretty well sew up Flaherty's election, though," Gus said.

"My opponent's father is a serial killer? Yeah, that'll play,"

Chris said. "Maybe we could just do him on the money laundering thing, and not mention the pedophilia. It would get him out of circulation."

Gus shook his head.

"It would be in his own best interest to cover that part up," Chris said. "And you don't have to tell the world you covered up a murder."

"And let two more happen."

Chris began to pace again, hands in his back pockets, looking at the wide boards of the yellow pine flooring.

"We could rig this," he said. "You turn state's evidence. Robinson'll plea-bargain. Flaherty will love this. He'll climb all over Robinson to do it."

"No," Gus said. "You're starting to trim. You can't trim."

"Why the fuck not?" Chris said. "You trimmed. Christ, you slashed."

"That's why," Gus said. "You're all that's left."

"Left of what?"

"Left that matters," Gus said.

Chris stared again at his father for a silent moment. Then he began slowly to nod.

"What about Tom Winslow?" Chris said.

"Tom's dead," Gus said.

Chris walked around the table and stood behind his father. He bent over and put his arm around his father's shoulder and rested his cheek on the top of Gus's head.

"What a fucking mess," he said.

Flaherty

Mary Alice was leaning on the wall near the window, with her arms folded, and one ankle crossed over the other. Flaherty was behind his desk, his swivel chair turned sideways and tilted, one foot on the lower drawer. He was wearing a dark blue double breasted suit that went elegantly with his high color and his silver hair. He glanced at himself reflected in the long mirror opposite. Senator Flaherty, he thought. Chris Sheridan was there looking young and athletic, and Kendall Robinson, the DA, looking very Harvard, and Fiora Gardello, looking determinedly equal to anybody.

"Okay," Chris said. "Your gang war is over, and your serial child-killing is finished, and you're going to be the junior senator from Massachusetts."

"Are you aware that Cabot Winslow withdrew this morning?" Flaherty said. His voice was neutral.

Chris ignored him.

"What I'm after," Chris said, talking to Kendall Robinson, "is a deal for my old man."

"No deals," Flaherty said. "He goes down too."

Chris continued to ignore Flaherty, talking to Robinson.

"He handed us this thing," Chris said. "Wasn't for him we'd be floundering around on this until the twelfth of never."

"He's a crooked cop," Flaherty said. "With all due regard, Chris, he's guilty as sin."

Chris turned his gaze on Flaherty. It was almost like Gus's, Flaherty noticed. Not as crazy, but still uncomfortable.

"And he got you the election," Chris said.

"He didn't do that for me. He wanted you to be a hero."

"And I'll be one," Chris said. " 'Incorruptible son arrests own father.' And I'll be a media darling and I'll be on all the talk shows, and every chance I get, I will try to stick it into you and break it off."

"You think you can scare me?" Flaherty said.

"I can appeal to your pragmatic sense," Chris said.

Mary Alice left the wall and walked to the coffee table. She took a small notepad out of her purse, and wrote something, and tore the sheet from the pad, and folded it in two.

"He gave it all to us," Fiora Gardello said to Flaherty. "And he'll testify."

"Unless, of course, his testimony is self-incriminating," Chris said. "In which case, of course, I can't let him do it."

"This is a conflict of interest," Flaherty said. "You can't be my prosecutor and his lawyer."

"Quitting this job will be easier than anything I've ever done before," Chris said.

"He has a point, Parnell," Robinson said. "If we're to get convictions we need Gus's testimony, and we'll have to deal with the self-incrimination problem."

Mary Alice walked to Flaherty's desk, and handed him the slip of paper, and winked at him and walked back to her post by the window. No one paid attention. She knew they wouldn't. They were used to her, the trusted gal Friday, barely visible.

Holding the unopened note, Flaherty said, "The sonova bitch sat right there and drank my Scotch and lied his fucking brains out."

He opened the note and read it. The note said: *Take the deal or the press gets a detailed description of your cunnilingus skills on the office couch.*

"You want his testimony, you work with me," Chris said. He knew he was bluffing. His father would testify anyway. But nobody here was capable of understanding that. It was a workable bluff.

Flaherty finished reading the note and looked up at Mary Alice standing by the window. His face had no expression on it. Mary Alice smiled at him. He folded the note back in half and slipped it into his inside jacket pocket.

"What do you think about this, Mary Alice?"

"You're an old hand, Parnell, whatever you think is the best course."

Flaherty looked at Chris.

"I don't like disloyalty," Flaherty said. "And I don't like threats. But I am paid to do what's best for the people of this city."

Chris was quiet. He could feel the direction changing. Flaherty turned to Kendall Robinson.

"You want the deal?" Flaherty said.

"Fiora," Robinson said. "You'll prosecute. It's your call."

"Sure," she said. "Immunity."

Chris nodded.

"Your word?" he said to Flaherty.

"I'll abide by the recommendation of my district attorney and my prosecutor," Flaherty said.

"Your word," Chris said.

Their eyes locked for a moment. Then Flaherty smiled.

"Hell, yes, Chris-boy. You've got my word."

Chris said, "Thank you," and stood.

No one else spoke.

"My father and I will be in touch," Chris said. He looked at Mary Alice and smiled and turned and walked out of the office.

In the elevator, riding down, Chris thought, *What was in the note?*

1994
Voice-Over

"Gus gets immunity for testifying," I said. "Your brother withdraws. I'm a great hero of the people for fifteen minutes. And Flaherty gets elected."

"And my father is dead and my family is disgraced."

"That too," I said.

"And you ran."

"I like to think of it as getting some distance," I said. "But *ran* will do. I called you once, you didn't return the call. I was almost relieved. I couldn't think what I could say about all of it, anyway. So I went to Dublin."

"There wouldn't be much you could say, would there?"

"No," I said. "And I see that I'm not the only one with some rage to work on."

Grace nodded. "Yes, I know. I've been working on that. I also know that the calamity was not in fact of your doing, or mine."

"Do you also feel it?" I said.

"Get 'em by the head," Grace said. "The soul will follow."

I smiled at her. The storm was beginning to settle, the snow kept coming, but the thunder was maybe more distant now, and the time between the light and the sound was increasing.

"You know, a little sort of sidebar. Flaherty was always so certain that your brother, being what Flaherty called a Goo Goo, if elected would destroy Flaherty's city. And when Flaherty gets elected to the Senate he leaves the deputy mayor to fill out his term."

"Piper?"

"Yes," I said. "Look up *Goo Goo* in a dictionary and there's a picture of Winston Piper."

"So we got the city after all," Grace said.

"I guess you did."

We were quiet, like survivors looking over the field where the battle had been fought. I could hear Grace's breath as she took in some air and let it out slowly. It was late. We were tired, but neither of us seemed to have arrived at anyplace where we could stop.

"After the shootout?" Grace said. "With, ah, what's his name?"

"Patrick Malloy," I said.

"After that, why did Gus leave you? What did he do?"

"He never said," I answered, "but he had to get clear with my mother. It's like once the purge started it had to be complete before he could sit and talk."

"So he went and made his peace with Peggy."

"Yeah," I said. "His peace, not hers—she'll never forgive him."

"Even though he did it for you?"

"Ma doesn't work that way. Everything is about her."

Grace reached toward me and patted my hand.

"My father was a child molester," she said. "And I had a better deal than you did."

"Ma'd be pleased to hear that," I said. "There was another thing, I think, unless I'm just thinking pretty."

"What?"

"He wanted me to have the chance to be in charge. He did whatever he did with my mother, she won't talk about it, and then he just went over to my house and sat on the steps and waited for me."

"And did you know what it was you were in charge of?"

"I knew we were arresting them for money laundering. I knew my father had evidence. I didn't know what."

"You didn't know about my father yet."

"No."

"It's so odd, to think of my father like that, as a—a monster. I didn't really know him. He was so remote. He stayed so far away from me."

"Probably why," I said. "He knew he was a pedophile. He didn't dare come near his daughter."

"Isn't that crazy. That's what I resented. He seemed to give all his attention to Cabot. I was so jealous of Cabot, so angry at my father. And he did the best thing for me he could have done."

"It's why you weren't destroyed, I guess."

"Yes, and my mother cared about me. She made me feel that I mattered."

"Maybe he stayed away from you because you mattered," Chris said.

"I know. Maybe he was being as good a parent as he could be, given what he was."

"The poor bastard."

"What a dreadful world," Grace said. Her face was angry. "Where you have to give up what you love to save it."

"And you're only able to get what you need by not needing it," I said.

"Makes one believe in a grand design, doesn't it?" Grace said.

"If design governs in a thing so small," I said.

Mary Alice

Winston Piper didn't look right to her in what she thought of as Flaherty's office. When he stood at the window and looked down at Quincy Market, his pants legs reached to the ankle-bone.

They may know how to conserve money, Mary Alice thought, *but they sure don't know how to dress.* She sat on the couch. Piper turned from the window and went to the desk. *They all look as if their wives cut their hair.*

"So, my little chickadee," Piper said. W. C. Fields was his favorite, and he was sure he did a convincing impression of him. "You're not in Washington with Parnell."

Mary Alice shrugged and smiled.

"Well," Piper said, "Parnell's loss is certainly my gain."

"It certainly is," Mary Alice said.

"I know you had Parnell's confidence, and I want you to know that you have mine."

"Thank you, Your Honor," Mary Alice said. *I wonder if he's hinting for a blowjob.*

She smiled. Piper smiled back.

"My friends call me Win," he said. "No need for formality."

"Sure, Win." *He's hinting.*

Piper sat down. He was wearing a gray suit with narrow lapels. The suit jacket seemed pinched around the shoulders. His tie was narrow and was narrowly patterned with blue and gray stripes. Behind the desk he sat straight up, both feet on the floor, his back not touching the chair. He drank a sip of coffee—black, no sugar, decaffeinated.

"What do you think of the way I'm portrayed in the press, Mary Alice?"

"The press is full of overeducated Paddies," Mary Alice said, "that still want to be Irish homeboys. And one way to stay loyal to your roots is to make fun of affluent Protestants."

"Like me."

"Exactly like you."

Piper looked into his coffee cup for a while as he thought about what Mary Alice had said.

"I like this job. I'm going to run for a full term this fall," Piper said. "I even have a campaign slogan. Win with Win!"

"Great slogan," Mary Alice said. "Now what you need to do is something that will get the anti-Wasps on your side without alienating the Wasps."

"I'll be guided by your recommendation. I know Parnell counted you among his most trusted advisors."

"Most trusted," Mary Alice said.

Piper stood and walked across the room and sat beside her on the couch. His face was bright red. There was a hint of sweat on his forehead. He put his hand on her thigh.

Mary Alice grinned at him.

"Perks of office, Winston?"

"I"—Piper cleared his throat—"I admire you very much, Mary Alice. I'd like it a lot if you were to be my trusted advisor too," he said.

Mary Alice nodded, still grinning.

"Shall I just lie back here on the couch and we can advise and consent for a bit?"

The sweat was clearly visible on Piper's high forehead.

"I don't want you to misjudge me, Mary Alice."

"No problem, Winston," she said. "I'm a modern gal. Just a collegial toss on the couch. We may do it again. But fun is all that's at stake."

"I love my wife," Piper said. His voice was raspy.

"Sure you do, except she wears Birkenstocks and no makeup and thinks head is the opposite of foot."

Piper blushed. Mary Alice smiled.

"So we'll get to know each other and when it's over maybe I'll have a recommendation you'll want to implement."

"Yes," Piper said. His voice was very hoarse. "Anything. Please."

Without his clothes Winston Piper was as narrow and pale as his wardrobe. His shoulders were narrow. His legs were pale. Mary Alice showed him things to do. When they were through he got up immediately and began to dress. Mary Alice lay back comfortably on the couch. She made no effort to rearrange it. As he dressed, Piper stared at her nakedness.

She smiled at him.

"Win," she said, "I recommend you name Chris Sheridan police commissioner."

Laura

She met Gus for a drink at the Ritz bar, where they had met first to talk of their children. People looked covertly at Gus. His picture had been everywhere.

"Been a while," Gus said.

"Yes," Laura said.

She glanced around the bar. "People recognize you."

Gus nodded.

"How are you?" he said.

Laura nodded.

"I'm all right," she said. "You?"

Gus smiled.

"Divorced, out of work, publicly disgraced," he said.

Laura nodded again slowly.

"And our children are still estranged," she said.

"Yeah."

It was late afternoon, the bar was beginning to fill with people having a drink after work. The waiter came and took drink orders. Gus asked for beer. Laura, white wine.

"I'm sorry about everything," Gus said.

"I know."

"Is there anything you don't know, anything you'd like to ask?"

Laura shook her head.

"I know too much already," she said.

The waiter brought drinks. He put them carefully in front of Gus and Laura, each neatly on its little paper doily. He poured beer into Gus's pilsner glass until it was half full.

When he left Laura said, "Did you know you were going to drag the whole department into it?"

Gus shook his head.

"That was Butchie, he plea-bargained a sentence reduction." Gus picked up his beer bottle and carefully filled the glass, measuring the foam. "And, he took a lot of people with him. Evened it up, so to speak."

"But you got off," Laura said.

"I had a good lawyer," Gus said.

"Chris."

"Yeah."

"And you plea-bargained."

"Yeah."

"And my husband is dead."

Gus's voice was soft. "Yeah."

"It would have been worse, had he lived and stood trial," Laura said. "For him, for us."

Gus was quiet. Outside the window the bright yellow taxis came and went, bringing well-dressed people and taking them away.

"I sometimes think you might have had something to do with it."

Gus shrugged.

"You were there."

Gus nodded.

Laura waited.

Gus didn't speak.

Laura shrugged.

"It has hit Cabot hard," she said.

"I'm sorry."

"I don't know what it means to Grace . . . and Chris."

"If they're going to have a chance it had to happen," he said.

"You truly think so?"

"Chris will be the first Sheridan I know anything about got a chance to live a genuine life. I hope that includes Grace. But if it doesn't, it doesn't." Gus sipped his beer. "Still a genuine life."

"And you've never lived a 'genuine life'?"

"Not till now."

"Not even when you were with me?"

Gus folded his thick hands together, and rested his chin on them. He looked at her and she could feel the weight of his gaze, as she always had, tired and cynical, yet full of power and passion and seriousness. It seemed to fill her up as it always did. It made her feel as if there were more of her.

"Probably the only happiness I've ever had has been the time with you," he said. "In terms of men and women, it's the only love I ever had."

"What other terms would there be?" she said.

"I love my son."

"Yes," Laura said. "Of course."

She twirled the stem of her wineglass slowly without lifting it from the table. She hadn't drunk any.

"I guess that's almost exactly true for me," she said. "In fact for me it was genuine."

"Yes," Gus said.

"But it couldn't be for you, could it," Laura said. "You knew what my husband was. You knew, at least toward the end, what was coming."

"It was like a train bearing down," Gus said.

Laura smiled. "And we were doing it on the tracks."

Gus's beer glass was still half full. There was a wisp of foam along the inside of the rim. Laura twirled her wineglass some more.

"So where are we?" Gus said.

Laura stared into her slowly turning wineglass.

"I think what you did was right, Gus."

She turned the glass slowly.

"But I don't think I can get past it."

Gus nodded.

"I didn't love Tom, and, God, what I've learned makes me glad that I didn't. But he was what I settled for and he was my husband and the father of my children."

"Lot of history," Gus said.

"Yes."

"Be kind of hard to move right over from him to the guy who may have caused his death."

"And who, even if he didn't, exploited his life."

Gus nodded slowly.

"Too hard," he said.

The tears began to form in Laura's eyes.

"I have loved you, Gus. And I know you have loved me."

"Still do," Gus said.

"Yes." She patted her eyes with her napkin, but they filled again. "I'll ruin my makeup," she said.

"We can go," Gus said.

"I want to go alone," she said.

"You going to be all right?"

She paused for a moment and seemed to think about the question.

"Yes," she said finally. "I think the time with you may have made me all right."

Gus nodded. Laura stood and bent over and kissed him on the mouth and turned and left the bar. From where he sat by the window, Gus could see her as she went out the Arlington Street door of the hotel and spoke to the doorman. He watched as the doorman got her a yellow cab and held the door, and took her tip, folding it smoothly into his pocket as he closed the door behind her. The cab pulled away down Arlington Street and turned left onto Boylston Street, and went along that side of the Public Garden, past the Four Seasons Hotel, mingling with the rest of the late afternoon traffic, and out of sight behind the still thick foliage of the early fall trees.

Gus

The house was in Concord, a three-hundred-year-old farm-house on twelve acres of land that sloped gently down toward the Assabet River. He was ripping out lath and plaster in the kitchen when Chris arrived. The back door was open and the radio was on. A music-of-your-life station was playing loudly. Gus wore tan shorts and work boots and a gray sweatshirt with the sleeves cut off. He put down the pry bar and slid the hammer into a holster on his belt. He went to the refrigerator and got out two cans of Budweiser Dry and opened them and handed one to Chris.

"What's that song?" Chris said. He drank some beer.

"Tommy Dorsey," his father said, " 'Song of India.' " He pointed out the back kitchen window.

"Look," Gus said.

Through the window Chris saw three pointer puppies scrambling up the slope from the water toward the house. They were so young they didn't run well and bumped into each other and fell down often. The shape and movement clear against the yellow-green, nearly April meadow.

"Jesus Christ," Chris said.

"Coming to meet brother," Gus said.

"Pointers?" Chris said.

"Yeah. German shorthairs."

The dogs moiled into the house through the open back door and banged into Chris's legs and rolled around on his feet and between his legs and licked his face as he squatted to pat them, and nipped with their pointed puppy teeth at his fingers and wrists.

"Guy I know in Canton raises them," Gus said. "I bought all the females from his litter."

393

"No males?"

"Males are trouble," Gus said.

Chris smiled. "So are females."

"I'm talking about dogs," Gus said.

"They got names?"

"Patty, Maxine, and LaVerne."

Chris straightened and looked around at the house. One of the puppies began to chew on his shoelace.

"Ill-gotten gain?" Chris said.

"All those years on the pad," Gus said, "I managed to put a little something aside."

"Needs some work," Chris said. The puppy had his shoelace loose and was tugging on it. He reached down and picked her up. She lapped frantically at anything she could reach.

"I'm going to peel it back to the studs first, see what I've got. Then I'll start the rehab."

Chris nodded.

"Want some help?"

"Sure."

The puppy began to chew on Chris's wrist.

"What's this one's name?" he said.

"The brown one's Patty," Gus said. "The other two I can't tell apart yet."

They took their beer and went out and sat on a couple of folding chairs in the yard and watched the dogs dash around. The land was overgrown with wild grass and evergreens; only a small area around the house was mowed. The generational additions on the house made it ramble idiosyncratically. The foundation plantings needed pruning. At one corner some desolate roses clung tiredly to a sagging trellis.

"Lot of work," Chris said.

"Yeah."

"Be nice when it's done," he said.

"Nice to do," Gus said. "Even if I don't finish."

"I was thinking that," Chris said.

There was a little wind. It brought the smell of the river up to them. Gus got up and went to the kitchen, stepping over the lath and plaster that littered the floor. He got two more beers and brought them back and handed one to Chris. The puppies were out of sight in the tall grass, which moved as they rummaged through it.

"Whole place is fenced," Gus said. "So I don't have to worry about them."

The road that curved by Gus's house was empty of traffic. Where they sat they could see no other houses, only the over-grown fields, and the ragged evergreens, and the narrow gleam of the river at the foot of the hill.

"I can help you with this on weekends if you'd like," Chris said.

Gus nodded. Across the sloping meadow, beyond the river, the sky was dark.

"That'd be good," Gus said.

"I won't have as much time as I used to," Chris said. "I'm going to be police commissioner."

Gus stopped with the beer can nearly to his lips.

"Boston?"

"Boston."

"Jesus Christ," Gus said.

Far to the east, lightning flickered against the sullen sky, so far away that they couldn't hear the thunder. Where they sat the pale spring sunshine was still on them. Light, but not much warmth. Gus put his left hand out and took Chris's right hand and held it for a moment. It wasn't a handshake. Then he let go and leaned back in his chair.

"That's the balls," Gus said.

Chris grinned at him. "A touch of the poet," he said, "in every word you speak."

Gus smiled and drank some more beer.

"Well, it may be inelegant, but it is, in fact, the fucking balls," Gus said.

The lightning flickered again and one of the puppies picked it up, or picked up the sound of thunder still inaudible to Chris and Gus. She scuttled under Gus's chair. The other two ignored her and continued to snuffle through the grass, bumping frequently into each other. Two were ticked chocolate-white, one was nearly all chocolate.

"Piper wants to be mayor on his own."

"So he hires Flaherty's heroic prosecutor," Gus said.

"Yeah. He figures I appeal to the Micks, being Irish, and to the Goo Goos, being Harvard."

"Piper's too stupid to of thought that up."

"I think Mary Alice put it together."

"Probably," Gus said.

"She's a hell of a woman," Chris said.

"I know."

"I gave her your address."

"Yeah. She's been out here."

Chris waited. Gus said nothing more. Chris didn't press.

"I'm seeing Grace tonight," Chris said.

"I hope it's all right," Gus said.

"Either way, I'll be all right," Chris said.

"Good," Gus said. He stood and walked with Chris to the car.

"I'll be over this weekend, if you want, to help."

Gus nodded.

"Good luck tonight," he said.

"Thanks," Chris said.

The lightning flickered again, and now for the first time they could hear, faintly and long after the flash, the sound of the thunder. All the puppies heard it and scrambled trying to get under Gus's feet.

He bent and scooped them up in his arms, and held them, squirming and scared.

"We'll be fine," Gus said.

"Yes, we will," Chris said.

He and his father stood silently for a moment, then his father put a free arm around Chris's shoulder and hugged him. Chris hugged him back for a moment and pressed his cheek against his father's face, feeling the day-old stubble of his father's beard. Then he got in the car and drove away.

After he was gone Gus took the puppies inside and fed them and, when they had eaten, followed them outside. The thunder had stopped for the moment, and so, no longer hearing thunder, they forgot that there had been thunder. He stood on the porch watching them as they made their final run of the day across the meadow. It was evening and he could no longer see the river. All he could see were the three dogs, against the now darkening grass, running, sniffing the ground, tracking, jostling one another, occasionally stopping to roll in the grass, and jumping up again to run free across his land, where his house stood that he was building with his son. There were a few wide slow flakes of snow beginning to spiral down. The thunder sounded louder, and the dogs turned and started back, away from the river, like horses for the barn, picking up speed as they came, running full out their still uncoordinated, ambling puppy run, only white showing now, in the grass-scented darkness, running toward home, toward him. He could see them so brightly and then they blurred and he realized he was crying. . . . And though he tried as hard as he was able, he couldn't remember when he'd done it last.

1994
Voice-Over

The snow had stopped and there was a faint milky hint of dawn outside Grace's window.

"Two sleepy people," I said. "By dawn's early light . . ."

"I'm not sleepy," Grace said.

"I was sort of implying the next lines of the song."

"I know," Grace said.

I stood and went to the window and looked out. The cars in the parking lot were shapeless with snow. We'd have to dig to get out of here. A big plow came slowly down Grace's street, the thick, wet snow peeling off the canted blade. There was no thunder anymore, no lightning. The mercury streetlights were still on, looking yellow in the encroaching morning. I turned back toward Grace.

"I'm done," I said. "I don't have anything else to say."

"How do you feel about this police-commissioner thing?" Grace said.

"Scared."

"Of?"

"Of the responsibility. Of facing the men, when I've never even been a cop. Scared I'm not tough enough."

"Why'd you take the job?" Grace said.

"All the reasons I took the special prosecutor job."

"And?"

I took my hands from my pockets and locked them behind my head and pressed my neck back against them.

"There's more?" I said.

"I think so."

"Yeah. There is."

"Gus," Grace said.

"Yeah. When I saw him this afternoon, actually I guess it's yesterday afternoon, now. I . . . there was a point where he picked up all three of the puppies—they were scared of the thunder—and held them in one arm. And they sort of squirmed in against him. It haunts me. That image of him . . . he has an arm like a tree limb, you know? and these three little brown heads peering out. It's my father. I wanted to sit in his lap."

"You did it for Gus?"

"No, not quite. I did it because of Gus. Because of who he is and was and what he is and did, and because Gus never got it straight with his father, and who the hell knows what my grandfather had going with his father. And because . . . I don't know. Just because."

"This is my beloved son," Grace said, "in whom I am well pleased."

Grace's face was tired. It was almost shocking to see. She never got tired. She never looked tired. The strain of the night had been for her one of restraint, of listening, of containing herself while I ran free.

"And what about us?" Grace said.

"Ah," I said, "the overwhelming question."

"The other man is gone," Grace said.

I held on. Don't spill it now.

"That's a start," I said.

I could hear the clatter of the plow, softened by snow, as it forced its way along Grace's street.

"You're alone now."

"Yes."

"I would like to marry you," I said.

Grace was quiet.

"Or I want to say good-bye."

Grace stayed quiet. I was quiet with her.

"You can do that?" Grace said.

"Yes. I told you when I came in. I'll miss you for a while. I'll be sad for a while. And I'll find someone else in a while and be happy with her."

"There's Gus," Grace said.

"Gus?"

"In your eyes, in your voice," Grace said. "I don't know the word for it. A benign craziness, maybe. 'Here I come and the hell with you.'"

"Remember the puppies," I said.

"Yes."

There was no sun, the clouds were still too thick. But the faint luminosity of the morning became a little pinkish as the sun came up behind them.

"When you said you would like to marry me," Grace said, "what were the conditions?"

"Monogamy," I said.

"No others?"

"None."

"Seems a reasonable condition."

I waited. The morning was entirely quiet. The street outside Grace's place was cleared and the plow had moved on.

"When you said you wanted to marry me," Grace said, "was that a formal proposal?"

"You may consider it such," I said.

"Then I accept," Grace said.

The morning was slowly warming and the wet snow that had piled up during the night had already begun to melt. I could hear in the silence the slow, wet sound of its melting as it dripped from the window ledge and the eaves.

"Are you too tired to make love?" Grace said.

"No," I said, and the opening in my throat seemed very narrow.

"Then I think we should each shower," Grace said, "and brush our teeth, and go upstairs, and lie down, and start over."

"Yes," I said. And we did.